GREEN VALLEY SHIFTERS

COLLECTION 2: BOOKS 4-6

ELVA BIRCH
ZOE CHANT

A QUICK GUIDE TO GREEN VALLEY

Green Valley Shifters is a series of gentle, funny, found-family standalone short shifter novels with single dads, spinsters, and sweet second chances, plus hilarious children and pets. This collection includes *Bearly Together*, *Broken Lynx*, and *A Green Valley Christmoose*. Each book can be read independently, but you may enjoy them most in order, as you'll see the following characters:

Patricia runs the local preschool. Lee is a bear shifter and his daughter is Clara. Find their story in Dancing Bearfoot (Book 1).

Andrea is Patricia's assistant at the preschool, and a hawk shifter. Shaun Powell is a tiger shifter, Trevor is his precocious lion shifter son. They meet in The Tiger Next Door (Book 2).

Tawny is a local spinster who meets big city lion shifter Damien, the father of Shaun and Shelley, in Dandelion Season (Book 3)

Shelley, a lion shifter herself, comes to Green Valley in Bearly Together (Book 4) and finds single dad Dean, a bear shifter, and his son Aaron (with two As!).

Local prankster Jamie returns from firefighting in Alaska to run into new resident Devon, a lynx shifter raising his kid sister, Abby, in Broken Lynx (Book 5)

Fire chief Turner, a moose shifter, meets his destiny when he rescues Linda Powell, Shelley's mother, from a stray dog in A Green Valley Christmoose Disaster.

BEARLY TOGETHER

1

*S*omeone had handed Shelley a baby.

Shelley was too surprised to thrust it back before the golden-haired woman who gave it to her was hurrying off after another small shrieking person, and then she was stuck with it.

The squishy little thing stared at her with big blue eyes and made a bubble with its tiny alien mouth.

It was almost hairless, and it smelled weird.

Shelley tried to give it to the woman that her father had just married, but Tawny only laughed. "Patricia will be back in a few moments," the white-haired woman said cheerfully. "Look, she likes you." Then she hurried off to supervise something concerning food.

Shelley looked at the thing in her arms with horror as it squirmed and flailed chubby fists.

"You're my aunt, Shelley," a suspicious voice said from her waist, and Shelley looked down to find a little dark-haired boy staring up at her.

"You're my nephew, Trevor," Shelley agreed crossly. Was she supposed to be supporting the thing's head? It was a little uncomfortable where it was lying in the crook of her elbow staring at her;

did she dare adjust it? What if she dropped it? She'd rather let her arms cramp up in place than risk it.

Trevor squinted up at her. "Are you Grandpa Powell's favorite?"

Shelley looked down at the boy in consternation. "Who would tell you that?"

"Oh, Trevor, no…" Shaun, her brother, looked mortified as he came into the sunny little room filled with plants where Shelly had been waylaid with the infant. "I swear I didn't mean him to hear that… kids, they absorb everything…" he sputtered.

Shelley tried to carefully extricate the baby from her arms. "Take this thing and I will pretend it never happened. Besides," she told Trevor, "*you* are now Grandpa Powell's favorite and you are welcome to it."

Trevor grinned at her. "I thought so. It's cuz…" The boy clapped a hand over his mouth as if he had been about to reveal state secrets. "I CAN'T TELL YOU!" he shouted, and to Shelley's relief, he fled the room.

One down, one to get rid of.

"We're trying not make a big deal out favorites and the whole… shifting thing…." Shaun said, in that disapproving, big brother *I know better* tone he'd always been perfect at.

"Sorry," Shelley said without apology. "I don't really… do kids. About the best you're going to get out of me is that I'll try not to swear around him or let him play with sharp things. Much. Will you please take this thing before I break it?"

To her relief, Shaun willingly put out his hands for the infant. "This is Victoria, Patricia's new daughter."

But Victoria had a drooly fistful of Shelley's hair and a grip on her shirt now, and she was bizarrely bendy and uncooperative for something so small and made out of butter. "Oh good God, she's thrown up on my Chanel," Shelley realized in horror as she tried to peel the minuscule fingers from the silk blouse without damaging the fabric. "Ow! How can something that small have a grip like that?!" The baby was tugging on her hair now, delighting in Shelley's grimaces of pain.

Shaun actually laughed, not offering to help.

The mother who'd left the baby with her in the first place returned to find Shelley trying to pry the infant off of her, pleading, "Get it off me! There is *vomit* on my blouse!"

She was embarrassed and frankly terrified; she didn't want to accidentally harm the uncooperative baby, and everyone was smirking and giggling at her rising panic.

"Here, I'll take her," Patricia said with a smile that Shelley was too humiliated to find kind. "Thank you for holding her."

The baby finally let go and went willingly to Patricia, bouncing easily in her arms and burbling happily.

"Sorry," Shelley said tightly, knowing she'd done a terrible job at a simple task. "I'm not a baby person." She wanted to sink into a hole and die.

She focused on the blouse, because outrage seemed better than a panic attack over the way that everyone was looking at her. "I need to soak this stain before the shirt is ruined," she said stiffly. "Excuse me."

She heard Shaun make excuses for her as she stalked out. "Sorry, that's my sister. She's got a thing about her clothes."

It's not clothes, she wanted to stop and protest, but what else would they assume? That she was afraid of kids?

2

____

$\mathcal{D}$ean looked up from his paperwork at the jingle of the store door and bit back a groan. Possibly the only thing worse than quarterly tax estimates had just walked in.

"Good morning, Gillian," he said with all the patience he could dredge up.

"Good morning, Dean!" she trilled in return. "Isn't it a beautiful morning?"

"Sure is," Dean said briefly. He hoped that bending back over his papers with his calculator would be enough to dissuade her, but he wasn't particularly surprised when she didn't take the hint, coming to lean on the counter conversationally.

"How's your darling little Aaron doing?" she pried.

"He's doing great," Dean said politely. "He likes first grade. How are your kids? And *Brad?*" Being married didn't seem to keep Gillian from being very obvious about her predatory ways. She was ten years older than Dean, at least, and not unattractive, but Dean was not the slightest bit interested and the woman would not take a hint.

"They're great," Gillian said airily. "Really busy at school. Brad's *away* a lot."

Dean nodded. "Mm-hmm." What kind of expense was a ream of paper? And if he took a roll of duct tape from inventory and used it to tape Gillian's mouth shut, how did he account for that? Did it become an office supply?

"I hear there's snow in the forecast for next week," she said, playing with the display of carpenter pencils on the counter.

"Early, but not unheard of," Dean sighed. "Can I help you with something?"

"I've got a slow drain in the kitchen," Gillian said, giving him a look from under her eyelashes. "I'm just not sure what *parts* I might need."

"Have you tried Draino?" Dean suggested.

"That stuff is so toxic," Gillian said. "I just hate to use it."

"Can you remove the trap and check for a clog there?"

"Oh, that sounds so complicated," Gillian said, managing to lean over so that her cleavage was trying to make a jiggly escape from her shirt. "I'm sure I couldn't do that *myself*. Oh, but *you're* good at that stuff," she said, as if it had just occurred to her. "Could you come by and take a look? I just know you could figure it out."

Dean wondered if he had the word 'sucker' tattooed on his forehead and ran his hand through his hair. He needed a haircut.

"I don't mind paying," Gillian said coaxingly. "I know things are tight for you and Aaron."

The jingle of the store door was the sweetest sound that Dean had ever heard. "Sorry," he said, hoping he sounded a little more sorry than he felt. "Have a lot to take care of here."

"Hey Dean," Turner called. "You got a five-eighth ratchet head? I don't need a whole set."

Dean showed him personally where the clearance bin of broken sets was. "Don't know if we've got that size, but there's a chance."

Gillian, pouting, purchased a half gallon of Draino and gave him a lingering gaze as she left.

"Find what you needed?" Dean asked Turner. "The common sizes usually get snapped up fast."

"Didn't need one," Turner said with a chuckle. "Came in for a snow shovel, but those are right up front. Figured I'd look like an idiot asking you to point those out to me."

Dean smiled gratefully at Turner. "Thanks, Chief." Turner was in charge of the three-man local fire department.

"She's shameless," Turner said, shaking his graying head. "And you're not great at saying no."

"Give me some credit," Dean protested. "I have standards!"

"She doesn't," Turner scoffed.

"Hold on, now…" Dean laughed. "I think I've been insulted."

Turner picked out a snow shovel and Dean rang him up.

The third jingle from the store door might have been a record number of customers in an hour, but this one was only Henry, shuffling in looking—if possible—more disheveled than ever.

"Got any work?" Henry asked. He always looked a bit like he expected someone to kick him.

Dean looked down at his taxes. "Yeah, could you just watch things for a little bit? I've got to get this postmarked today." It was just an estimate; he could probably call what he'd already figured up good enough.

Henry's eyes brightened. "Sure," he said, standing taller.

Dean swiftly wrote out a check for entirely too much money and found a twenty-year-old envelope to stuff it into. The seal tasted bad and didn't seem to want to stick, so he ended up closing the envelope with a strip of duct tape.

"I'll be back in a bit," he said.

Outside, Green Valley was in full autumn color.

Trees along the lanes sported gold and orange and red, and merry breezes sent swirling leaves along the sidewalks. People were out raking their lawns, or mowing them one last time before the overnight frosts sent them into their long brown hibernation.

The mention of hibernation made his bear make a sleepy murmur of longing. It had been a long time since Dean had taken an opportunity to get out and stretch on four paws. He was overdue for slipping out into the woods around Green Valley for a little time in his other form.

Dean mailed his letter at the little post office and gathered the business mail from his box. Bills. Lots of bills.

He looked through them wistfully. He wasn't sure how his life had gotten where it was, and he couldn't imagine it any differently, but he couldn't help thinking that something was missing.

3

In a fresh shirt, with her hair brushed and her make-up touched up, Shelley felt considerably better.

"I know you were planning to head out tomorrow, but you are welcome to stay a few days," Tawny told her when she ventured back down to the kitchen. "The house came with several spare bedrooms, and if I have guests in them, I can't accidentally fill them up with books."

Shelley laughed because it was expected of her. Everyone else was thankfully gone; evening was falling, and probably they were all putting their sticky children into bed.

"Thank you, Tawny," she said genuinely; she did honestly like the woman her dad had just married. "I plan to leave tomorrow, but I was hoping to have someone look at my car before I left. It's making a terrible rattling noise every time I go over bumps and I don't want to get stranded halfway back to Minneapolis. Is there a good shop in town?"

Tawny handed her a piece of carrot from the cutting board she was working on before Shelley could tell her that she didn't like carrots.

She put it down at the edge of the cutting board when Tawny turned back to the sink to wash her hands.

"There's only one shop in town," Tawny said cheerfully. "And it's great. Dean owns Ted's Hardware, and his shop is right next door. You can't miss it."

As advertised, it was impossible to miss the auto shop next to the hardware store. The town wasn't big enough that you could miss anything even if you wanted to.

Shelley pulled up in front of the single garage door and walked carefully around to the side door with its crooked 'OPEN' sign in the window. The sidewalk was cracked, and the last thing she needed to do was snap off a heel.

Open seemed to be a slight exaggeration.

There was a tall, greasy-looking counter in the tiny room with an old-fashioned register as well as a modern credit card machine (to Shelley's relief). There was a pile of take-out menus that also gave her a moment of hope... until she noticed that they were all from Madison. It was too much to believe that there could be decent food in Green Valley to eat while they did the diagnosis of her car.

Two chairs with cracked vinyl seats flanked a water dispenser with a leaning stack of tiny paper cups. The entertainment selection —and for that matter the decor—seemed to be limited to car magazines and farm economic journals. An open door behind the counter led out to the shop, to one side was a closed door that said 'Ted's Hardware,' and a smaller door open in the corner suggested a restroom that no amount of money in the world could have convinced Shelley to use.

"Hello?" she called hesitantly.

"Yeah?"

The man who suddenly sat up from behind the counter had clearly been sleeping. Shelley had a moment of wondering if a homeless man had wandered in.

"I... have a problem with my car," Shelley said cautiously, looking around. She was beginning to think it was worth the risk just to drive to the city.

"I'm Henry; I'll check you in. Dean'll be back in a few. He had to walk to the post office."

A pad of carbon copy paper was put on the counter and a drawer was rummaged for a pen. "Make and model?"

"Lincoln Continental," Shelley said.

The scruffy man whistled. "Nice. We don't get so many of those, you know. Lotta tractors. Subarus. Pickups."

She gave him the rest of her details and very reluctantly passed him her key. "Is there a Starbucks nearby?" she asked plaintively. "Or some place with coffee? Maybe WiFi?" She knew there was decent coffee at her brother Shaun's bakery, but this was the one day a week he was closed.

"Best coffee in town is Gran's Grits," Henry said helpfully. "Two blocks over past the Presbyterian church across from the liquor store. I dunno about WiFi, but there's a television in the kitchen."

"Thank you," Shelley said primly. "Do you know how long it will take?"

"Oh, I dunno. Maybe an hour?" Henry guessed. "Course, if we gotta order parts, it might be longer."

Shelley could imagine no torture worse than being trapped in Green Valley several extra days. Maybe her insurance would cover a rental. It was probably worth paying for a rental out of pocket if the alternative was being stuck here.

"I'll be back in an hour," she said firmly.

"You do that," Henry said cheerfully.

4

Dean furrowed his brow at the unexpected car in his garage. A Lincoln Continental was not the type of vehicle that any locals drove.

Well, not any of the *real* locals. There had been an influx of big city billionaires over the past few years; first Lee Montgomery who owned a bunch of big construction companies came in and married his daughter's preschool teacher. Then there had been Shaun Powell, some kind of financial investor, who'd followed the trend by marrying *his* son's preschool teacher. And just this summer, Shaun's big shot engineer father, Damien, had surprised the whole town by sweeping spinster Tawny Summers off her feet.

This wasn't a car any of those men drove, which meant someone new, and Dean sourly wondered if there were any other preschool teachers in town to romance.

Then he had a moment of hope; maybe they would run off with Gillian, and save the whole town a lot of trouble.

"Got a car to look at," Henry told him helpfully as he came into the office, waving a ticket at him. "Some fancy lady with clicky shoes and red lips."

Dean was disappointed for a moment, then hoped briefly that

maybe Gillian's man-eating ways really hid a closeted interest in women. *That* would certainly keep the town talking for a while. He squinted at the paper Henry gave him. "What's the problem, exactly?" he asked. Henry's handwriting was awful, and the problem probably wasn't a rattlesnake.

"Rattles going over bumps, she said," he explained. "Worried about getting back to the city if it was something major."

Dean looked at the name on the key fob. Shelley Powell. She must be related to Shaun and Damien, he thought.

"I'll take a look," Dean said. "Thanks for watching the counter." He gave the man a certificate to Gran's Grits. Cash in Henry's hands would be spent at all the wrong places, but he didn't want the man to starve, so he gave him what work he could do (and remembered to show up for) and paid under the counter in gift certificates to local stores.

Henry took the certificate with a grin. "Much appreciated," he said sincerely, giving a courtly bow. "I'll be back tomorrow."

He probably wouldn't be.

He sauntered out as if Dean had just given him a golden ticket, whistling his way off-key down the street.

Dean turned on the shop radio and put the bell back up on the counter; Henry had put it on the floor for some reason.

Ten minutes and a test drive later, it sang out demandingly and Dean pushed himself out from beneath the car with a disparaging snort.

Rich city people, he thought derisively. This one probably couldn't even pump her own gas.

He was wiping his hand off with a rag, trying to come up with a diplomatic way to break the news without laughing in the face of Henry's fancy lady with clicky shoes.

But everything he'd planned to say vanished at the sight of the young woman standing in the office, frowning at a metal print of a tractor.

Shelley Powell.

She was absolutely beautiful: tall and elegant, with touchable, tousled blond hair, and she was dressed to impress, with a perfectly smooth straight knee-length skirt and a slinky, low-cut shirt under an open jacket that left very little of the curves of her generous breasts to imagination.

She turned back to the counter, already starting to say, "I'm here about the Lincoln—"

Silver eyes met his and if Dean had thought she was beautiful a moment before, now he was utterly enraptured.

His bear woke within him a start. *She's ours*, he demanded. *Ours forever.*

I wish this for you, Deirdre had told him when she left. *With all my soul, I want you to feel this, to know what it's like.*

At the time, still nurturing the heart she'd broken, Dean had vehemently denied that it was anything he wanted.

Now, he couldn't imagine anything he wanted *more*.

This woman was his *mate*.

She was gazing at him from the most beautiful, wide eyes he'd ever seen, her brilliant red lips perfectly parted in shock.

She knows, Dean realized.

It wasn't just a look of interest, it was a look of recognition, of instant understanding.

It was interest, too, Dean thought breathlessly, and it was decidedly mutual.

Her father was a lion shifter, and her nephew was, too; shifting wasn't something that always bred true, but it wouldn't be too crazy to assume she was one also.

"The… car…"

Dean had to grin, he couldn't help himself. "There's nothing wrong with it," he said apologetically. "It was just a loose license plate."

5

*S*helley had never spent much time thinking about weddings and true love and making babies like other girls. Wedding *dresses*, because she'd always loved fashion, but the whole idea of waiting around for the perfect guy only made her roll her eyes.

She hadn't even believed in mates until her father introduced her to his, and later casually mentioned that Shaun had married his as well. It was too ridiculous to bear.

But here they were, and her lioness was growling with avid recognition, leaving no doubt in Shelley's mind that *this* was her destiny, *this* was her mate.

If she had ever bothered to imagine meeting her mate, it would not have been like this.

She was sweaty and disheveled from having to walk to the diner, and she'd gotten unexpectedly caught in the arc of a sprinkler on her way back, so her jacket had water spots and her hair was limp.

And the most gorgeous man she'd ever laid eyes on had just looked straight into her soul and was explaining to her that she was the biggest idiot in the entire sad state.

"The… license plate?" she repeated. "The noise from my car was just a *loose license plate?*"

"That's all it was, ma'am," he said, gazing back at her in a way that would have been creepy if it had been anyone else... or if she had not been staring back at him with equal avarice. "The bolts were loose and that's the rattle you were hearing when you went over bumps. I... tightened them for you."

"Not ma'am," Shelley squeaked. She didn't want to be 'ma'am' to this man. "Shelley." It sounded like a kid's name to her ears. "Michelle." Ugh, no, too formal. "Shelley. Shelley Powell." She realized that he probably already knew her name, since she'd left it with her car key.

She was not doing much to redeem her image of intelligence.

"I'm Dean," he answered, and he offered her a hand. "Dean James, not to be mistaken for James Dean."

Shelley laughed breathlessly. Dean could certainly have been a movie star, with his broad shoulders and strong jaw. She very slowly took his hand to shake and was instantly lost.

If his gaze had left her knees feeling boneless, his handshake did things to parts not much higher, and her chest was suddenly too small for her lungs. She was dizzy, and excited, and... she was ready for this. This was coming home. Her lion was rumbling in delight.

"So, you're..." she started, just as he blushed beautifully and said, "I guess..."

"You first," she said swiftly, and by virtue of her speed, he was forced to continue.

"Are you... a... ah... lion shifter like your nephew and your father?" he said with understandable hesitation. Being wrong about an assumption like that in a world where shifters were secret would have been a stunning mistake to bring up aloud.

But *this* wasn't a mistake. He was clearly feeling the same thing, the same crazy, perfect, stomach-dropping realization she was tumbling through. He was drinking in her gaze just as she was his, and they hadn't let go of each other after the handshake. Their clasped hands hung just above the countertop. If the counter had not been between them, Shelley was not sure what they would be doing now, but she would bet that it would start with a kiss from those amazing lips, and once the thought occurred to her, she couldn't shake it.

"I am," she finally remembered to confirm, because it seemed impossible that there was anything he didn't know about her. "And… you?"

"Bear," Dean said faintly, like he was imagining the same kiss. "I'm… a bear. Grizzly."

It was the stupidest conversation, dragged out a stupid amount of time, because Shelley couldn't keep a thought in her head that wasn't kissing this man. "I'm a lawyer," she said impulsively, then thought it sounded like she was bragging and blushed. "I mean… I just don't want you to think I'm an idiot. Because of the… license plate."

"Happens all the time," Dean lied kindly.

"You're just being nice," Shelley told him suspiciously.

"Yeah," Dean agreed with a smile.

"Do I owe you anything?"

"No, no charge for tightening your… license plate."

They were still clasping hands over the greasy counter.

"I'm never going to live this down, am I?" Shelley guessed sheepishly.

"It'll be one of those inside jokes that we have."

"You mean, it will actually be funny someday, instead of just horribly humiliating?"

"I promise," Dean breathed.

There was a moment of silence, then they both tried to say, "So, you're…"

This time Dean was fastest. "You first."

"You're my mate," Shelley said boldly. It was thrilling to her own ears. This beautiful man, with his strong hands and his piercing eyes: he was *hers*.

His grin was like a bolt of lightning. "That's what I was going to say," he said.

"It's… it's nice to meet you," Shelley said. Nice was so insufficient! "I… would you like to get dinner or something?" Dinner was the last thing she wanted to do with this man; she wanted to wrap herself around him and see if he tasted the way she was imagining.

She let go of his hand, but only because he was coming around the counter, and she would finally be able to...

"Daddy! Daddy!"

Shelley stumbled backwards instead of taking the step forward that she had intended.

A curly-haired boy about the same age as Trevor bolted into the room like a whirlwind, smelling like leaves and mud puddles. He just missed crashing into Shelley's legs, careening around her and wrapping himself around Dean possessively as the man bent and intercepted his hug.

Shelley stared in horror.

"You... have a kid?" she said hesitantly.

"This is my son, Aaron."

Everything about the mood had changed. Dean was bristling protectively, his arms around the little boy, his gaze challenging.

Shelley felt like someone had just hit her in the face, and she probably looked like it, too.

Her mate... had a kid.

Every brief, delirious fantasy she'd had about a life with Dean suddenly had a four-foot-high *nope* in the middle of it.

6

____

*D*ean's heart was somewhere near the pit of his stomach.

He hadn't missed the whiplash-fast change in Shelley —in his mate. Aaron's entrance had turned what had been a moment of discovery and delight into something so stiff and awkward that Dean wondered that he was looking at the same woman.

Shelley's look of horror had faded behind a mask of distant disdain, and she was smoothing her jacket as if Aaron had somehow mussed it with his breakneck entrance.

Dean could actually *feel* the dismay radiating from her.

"How was your day at school?" he asked.

"It was only a half-day," Aaron scoffed. "Like Kindergarten for babies. It was stupid but I liked the games and we learned about *mold* and Trevor said a bad word and Clara fell down and skinned her knee and I'm *starving*."

It was, as usual, a moment before Dean could get a word in edgewise. "I brought granola bars," he said.

"The healthy kind?" Aaron asked skeptically, letting go of him at last. "I like the kind that Trevor gets with the chocolate chips."

"You get what you get—" Dean reminded him, standing up again.

"—And you don't throw a fit," Aaron sighed. But he also muttered defiantly, "I still like Trevor's better."

Dean was keenly aware of Shelley, watching them. She had backed up another step, as if she was afraid that Aaron had something contagious, and was playing with the buttons on her jacket nervously.

He didn't want her any less than he had before Aaron had interrupted them—his bear was still growling inappropriate suggestions in his ear—but the rest of him was in a whirlwind of protective instinct.

It didn't matter what his bear or his body said, she clearly considered Aaron a deal-breaker, and the only thing that Dean could do with that was watch her walk away before they got more invested.

"Your car is ready to go," he said, as coldly as he could manage.

"Thank you for fixing my... er... license plate," she replied, in exactly the same chilly, polite tone.

"Any time."

There was a moment of stiff silence broken only by Aaron rummaging behind the counter for the promised granola bar.

"My key," Shelley finally said, just as Dean said, "Sorry, you'll need your key." It was sitting on the far side of the counter.

He went behind the counter, stepping over Aaron, who was trying to put *all* the granola bars in his pockets, and handed it over to Shelley.

She had to take a step closer, and she held her hand below it so that Dean could drop it into her palm with risking any brush of skin.

Dean's bear protested, but Dean let the key go, just as Aaron suddenly stood up, his mouth full of granola bar. "You're Trevor's niece!" he exclaimed, spewing crumbs onto the counter.

"Aunt," Shelley corrected, stepping back quickly with her key clutched in her hand. "He's my *nephew*."

Aaron started to slurp his spewed crumbs off the counter and Dean was still watching Shelley's face as she realized he was going to eat off the dirty surface.

"Let's toss those, kiddo," he suggested swiftly.

Aaron made a face, but let Dean sweep them off the counter into his hand and drop them into the trash can.

When Dean looked up again, Shelley was still standing there, face unreadable, keys held so tightly in her hand that they must be biting into her palm.

It suddenly struck him that it wasn't *only* dismay that he was feeling from her. There was dismay, yes, and regret, and surprise, all in a knot of chaotic emotion. And underneath it all… fear.

She was afraid of… Aaron?

This was confirmed when Aaron went out from around the counter, staring at her, and she took an involuntary step back and shot Dean a quick, panicked look.

"Trevor and I are in a SECRET club," Aaron told her. "It's SECRET. I can't tell you about it."

"Didn't you *just* tell me about it?" Shelley said scathingly.

Aaron considered this.

Dean was torn between wanting to throw her out of his shop and out of his life and wanting to laugh hysterically. "Hey Aaron, can you go hang out in the store for just a second? I need to talk to Trevor's aunt."

"Okay!" Aaron said cheerfully. "Bye, Trevor's aunt!"

He tripped away through the door, holding all the extra granola bars in his over-laden pockets.

"I'm sorry," Shelley said hastily. "I'm… not… good with kids. It's not… I mean, I don't hate babies or anything. I just…"

"You're afraid of kids," Dean finished when she couldn't.

He felt unexpectedly sorry for her, with her perfect outfit and her perfect hair, and the way she was fighting to keep her expression calm when he could feel how much fear she was hiding underneath her smooth demeanor.

"They terrify me," Shelley admitted. "Someone gave me a baby yesterday and I nearly cried. I'd be a terrible mom. Or step-mom. Not that I'm suggesting marriage, that's crazy. Oh my god, are you married?"

Dean couldn't keep the wince from his own face and he knew that Shelley would assume the worst, so he hastened to explain, "No, not any more. Divorced. Five years."

Five godawful years, pretending he was heart-whole because he couldn't bear to hurt the woman who'd destroyed his happiness.

"Good," Shelley said crisply. "I mean, not good that you… I mean… this is complicated enough already."

Dean got the impression that she wasn't used to this kind of complication.

"Dinner," he reminded her. "Do you want to try dinner?"

Shelley looked at him and a grateful smile cracked the ivory of the mask she was still trying to settle over her features. "Yes," she said quietly.

"Me and Aaron," Dean said firmly. "We're a package deal."

The smile froze in place, but she nodded anyway. "Is there a good place in town we can go?"

"Neutral ground?" Dean said, unable to keep from teasing.

The smile twitched back into life. "Neutral ground," she agreed.

"Gran's Grits is really the only place in town," Dean said. "It's over past the post office at the corner across from the Presbyterian church."

"It's not hard to find things in this town," Shelley observed. "Tonight?"

"Six okay? I like to get Aaron in bed by eight."

Shelley nodded. Was she blushing? "Six," she said faintly, and then she nodded and smiled and Dean was positive she was blushing and it was absolutely adorable.

"Six," he echoed. "See you then."

"See you then," she said softly, and for one beautiful moment Dean thought he might get the kiss he'd been imagining since they met.

Then she cast a nervous look at the door to the shop and her face went abruptly careful and polite. She gave a crisp nod. Then her feet were clicking away over the floor and the door to the office was shutting behind her and Dean felt like the whole world had suddenly lost a lightbulb.

7

"Bad news about the car?" Tawny asked, opening the door for Shelley. "And you're our guest, you don't have to knock."

"Except on the bedroom door!" Shelley's father, Damien, called from the living room.

Tawny gave a smirk completely at odds with her 'sweet old lady' image. "Yes," she agreed. "That's probably a good idea."

"Oh, gross," Shelley said, following Tawny into the house. "I assure you, I have no desire to barge into your bedroom."

"What's wrong with the car, Shelley?" Damien asked.

"Nothing," Shelley said shortly. "It was just…" the most humiliating introduction to her mate that she could ever have imagined. "Would it be okay if I stayed a few more days?"

"Of course," Tawny said immediately.

"Why?" Damien demanded.

Shelley gave him a much more successful stoneface than she had managed with Dean. "I just need to figure some things out," she said vaguely.

Her father wasn't fooled, but his return frown was a poor shadow of what a scowl would have been from him before Tawny had taken the reins of his heart. "Are you in some kind of trouble?" he asked at once. "Is it money? Does the car need repairs?"

"It's not money and the car is fine," Shelley snarled back at him, stung. "I'm not a *kid*, Dad."

She stalked away to the kitchen, hoping that filling her empty stomach would make some dent in the hunger that Dean had awakened in her.

The kitchen had nothing to tempt her, and Shelley found herself caught in familiar patterns of thought.

She wasn't the staggering billionaire that her father was, or even the successful millionaire that her brother Shaun was, but she'd done fine for herself; she was a successful contract negotiator for a major engineering firm and there were contractors and lawyers that trembled at the sound of her name. In some circles she was known as Shelley the Shark. She was on track for a comfortable early retirement, and had a luxurious standard of living. She was doing *great*.

On the outside.

The bottle of pills in her purse said otherwise.

What would those lawyers think if they knew that Shelley the Shark was toothless? She had them all fooled into thinking she was powerful and fearless, when the truth was the exact opposite.

She was broken inside, constantly fighting thoughts of doubt and self-hatred. Her logical mind, so good at unraveling legal issues and finding weaknesses in contract language, seemed to relish pointing out to herself all the ways she'd failed, all her blunders, every stupid statement. She only got where she was by playing on her looks, only succeeded because other people let her, only frightened people because they didn't know how fearful she actually was.

Her mate knew, she thought, feeling her chest tighten warningly. Her mate had seen her make a complete idiot out of herself, watched her flinch from a child. *His* child.

How could he possibly still want her?

Tawny found her standing in front of the open refrigerator staring sightlessly at the shelves.

"Here, sit down," Tawny told her with a tone of amused tolerance. "I'll whip you up a little snack and you can tell me why you suddenly want to spend extra time in a town that smells like cows."

Shelley sat at the little kitchen table obediently. "Tawny... when you met my Dad...?" She didn't know how to finish the sentence she'd started.

Tawny gave her a knowing look. "Did you meet someone?" she asked.

"Dean," Shelley breathed, without meaning to. It was his grin that she remembered most, white teeth in that tanned face.

Tawny laughed. "Green Valley's most eligible divorcee," she said approvingly. "You wouldn't be the first to fall for that handsome face and broken heart."

Such a handsome face. "Wait, broken heart?"

Tawny put a plate down in front of her: sliced cheese, fresh bread, and a tidy pile of vegetable fingers, including carrots. Plain fare, but it seemed like just the right thing. Shelley took a nibble of cheese as Tawny sat opposite from her.

"Dean James married his high school sweetheart, Deirdre, not long after they both graduated. They... were young. I won't say the marriage was perfect, but they cared for each other, and they had a darling little boy about five years later."

"Aaron," Shelley said, surprised to find that she had finished the slice of cheese. "We met."

"When Aaron was about two, Deirdre left Dean for another man."

Shelley promptly hated Deirdre and took a savage bite of the bread.

"Dean put a really good face on it; the divorce was completely amicable, and they share custody. He never lets anyone say a word against her, or the man she left him for, and to all appearances, they're all friends. But the light... sort of went out of him when it happened."

Shelley blinked at her, trying to resolve Dean as someone the light had gone out of. He was *all* light, with that amazing smile and those hazel eyes.

"Every eligible woman in Green Valley and a whole lot of

women who aren't even slightly eligible have offered to be Aaron's new mom, believe me," Tawny said.

And there was the rub.

"I would *not* be a good mom."

Tawny blinked at her. "You're thinking that seriously about him?" Understanding dawned in her eyes. "Oh, honey, is he your mate?"

Shelley's lioness gave a yearning rumble and Shelley didn't answer Tawny, only looked down at her plate of food without appetite for it.

"I don't want kids," Shelley said miserably, rolling a cherry tomato around on her plate. "I never did. You saw me with Patricia's baby, I'm hopeless! How can someone so right for me be so completely wrong?"

"Well, kids aren't babies," Tawny pointed out. "Aaron's a little past bottles or needing diapers changed."

"He's still a kid," Shelley pointed out. "In his formative years, and all. I don't want to screw that up. I have tons of terrible habits and I don't know the first thing about small people or what to do with them." Shelley thought longingly of the pills in her purse. She could feel the tightness in her chest, and the way that breaths didn't feel quite deep enough, her mind already in familiar spirals.

"No parent ever does," Tawny assured her. "Everyone who's ever had a baby has been dumped feet-first into I-have-no-idea-what-I'm-doing soup. All you can do is muddle through and love them."

"What if I *can't* love him?" Shelley asked desperately. "What if I never even like him? What if *he* hates *me*? Dean won't want to have anything to do with me if I can't do that... nurturing mom crap, and I don't know if I have that in me. Maybe I was just born without it. Maybe I'm... broken."

Tawny was laughing, and it was a warm, non-judgmental laugh. "You're not broken," she assured Shelley. She reached over and stole a carrot from the edge of Shelley's plate. "I never particularly wanted children, either. There was a period I went through where I sort of mourned *not* having them, but I wasn't really sure if I was just regretting that I hadn't followed the usual patterns of love and marriage and kids. And now I've got you and Shaun, and your father, and I have never been more sure that my life unfolded exactly as it was supposed to."

"I'm twenty-seven," Shelley pointed out. "That's a far cry from suddenly having a kid who is *seven*."

"All the same rules apply," Tawny pointed out. "You listen when they talk to you and you learn to love them, because they came from something that you already love."

Her smile across the table was direct and Shelley felt an involuntary swell of affection that seemed to loosen the band around her chest. She squirmed, as uncomfortable with topics of emotion as she was with children. "I... I don't know if I love him," she said hastily. "I just met him. And oh... he must think I'm a complete idiot."

"I don't think first impressions are everything," Tawny advised her. "Your father dumped a potluck plate down my shirt when we met and then made a little kid cry."

"Remember the sound I took the car in for?" Shelley asked. "The sound I thought was the shocks or something? It was a loose license plate. Dean had to look me in the eyes and tell me that he tightened the *license plate* bolts for me."

Tawny stared at her for a moment, then burst out laughing. "A... loose license plate?"

"He must think I'm a complete moron," Shelley said in despair. "And then I acted like his son was... a plague bearer or something."

"Fortunately, being seven is not contagious," Tawny said drolly. "What are you going to do next?"

"Dinner," Shelley said, eating the last of the tomatoes from her plate. All that remained now were the detested carrots. "I have to go to that dreadful little diner with the plastic bench seats and try to redeem myself over gravy-laden, greasy spoon food."

"Gran's Grits may not have the oversized square plates with the fancy drizzles," Tawny said, rather severely. "But they serve good hearty food that will fill your belly at a decent price, and you'll sleep well knowing that you've helped support one of the pillars of our community."

It was as close to a scold as Tawny had ever given her, and Shelley was instantly abashed. "You're right," she said as graciously as she could. "I will keep that in mind."

Tawny softened. "Just keep your heart open," she suggested, rising and taking Shelley's plate with the disdained carrots to the counter.

Shelley rose, too. She needed a long, hot shower. And a different wardrobe. And to be a different person. She paused at the doorway. "Thanks, Tawny," she said sincerely.

Tawny's smile was brilliant. "Trust your instincts," she said gently.

But Shelley couldn't tell what was instinct and what was terror.

8

It was everything that Dean could do to keep from fidgeting, playing with the menu that he already had memorized, the glasses of ice water, the napkins.

"Why are we having dinner with Trevor's niece?" Aaron wanted to know.

"Trevor's aunt," Dean corrected. "Shelley's brother is Trevor's dad."

"Oh," Aaron said, but he was undeterred. "Why are we having dinner with her?"

"Because I like her," Dean said, not at all sure how to explain something he wasn't at all sure about.

"Does she like you?" Aaron asked avidly.

"I think so," Dean said. But he knew that *he* wasn't the problem, and he certainly wasn't going to explain to his son that Shelley was dubious about the baggage that he came with. He would never let Aaron think he was baggage.

"Is this a date?" Aaron asked, disgust on his face. He had something on his chin and Dean dipped a napkin into his water glass and tried to scrub it off. "Are you going to kiss?" Aaron asked skeptically, trying to squirm away.

"It's just dinner," Dean said, triumphant over the... whatever it had been on his son's face.

But the thought of kissing Shelley was deeply disturbing, and he was still helplessly thinking about it when the door to the diner gave a tinkle.

Andrea was bringing him a new napkin, and she looked over to the entrance.

"Hey Shelley," Andrea called loudly. "Dean's over here!"

"Thanks, Andrea," Dean hissed at her.

"Any time, Sausage." Andrea grinned at him knowingly, entirely too amused by the entire situation.

Dean didn't think that she guessed Shelley was his mate, she was just enjoying the novelty of seeing him out with someone, and was entertained by the idea that Shaun's prim sister would date a rough-edged mechanic like him.

Then he edged out of the booth to greet Shelley and got lost in her silver eyes.

She was tall to start with and with her heels on—who wore heels to a diner like Gran's?—she looked directly into his face. Everything about her said that she didn't belong here: her glamorous make-up, her designer blouse, her seductively short skirt, her perfectly high-lighted hair.

And everything inside of him said that she did belong here, with him, in his arms.

"Hi," she said, as breathlessly as if she was somehow as enam-ored with him as he was with her. Dean realized that he'd been staring at her for several moments and wasn't sure how he was supposed to proceed.

Aaron climbed into the bench seat behind him. "Are you going to kiss my Dad?" he asked point-blank.

Dean winced. "Aaron…"

But Shelley gave a crooked smile that looked like she didn't prac-tice it as much as her frown or her serene mask. "It's a valid ques-tion." She looked past Dean to where Aaron was kneeling on the bench seat. "Do you want me to?"

"Oh, gross, no, ew!" Aaron keeled over on the bench,

pretending to throw up and spasm in disgust. Laughter from the few other tables that were occupied only encouraged his antics. "Yuck, yuck, YUCK."

"Okay, that's enough," Dean said, embarrassed. He sat down next to Aaron and pushed him over on the bench. "Restaurant manners," he reminded the boy.

Shelley sat gracefully across from them. The crooked smile had been replaced by a perfect company smile, but her eyes on Aaron were deeply skeptical.

Aaron gave one last seizure of disapproval and to Dean's relief, chose to sit up in his seat rather than test his audience. They'd had a long talk about manners before they left the house, but Dean wasn't sure how seriously he was taking this.

Andrea brought a glass of ice water and a straw for Shelley. "Thank you," Shelley said gravely, and she fastidiously tore off the end of the wrapper and pulled out the straw, leaving a perfect paper tunnel behind.

Is that what she would do to him? Dean wondered poetically. Would she decide that a mate with a child wasn't what she was looking for and walk away with his heart?

And when had he given her his heart?

Dammit.

"Can I get you started with some drinks?" Andrea asked, all innocence.

"Diet cola," Shelley said.

"Can I have a pop?" Aaron asked, voice treacherously close to a whine.

"Too close to bedtime, sorry. Do you want a glass of milk?"

"I want a pop," Aaron said stubbornly.

Keenly aware of Shelley's neutral expression from across the table and Andrea's amused observation, Dean asked, "Do you want milk, or just water?"

"Milk," Aaron sulked, to his relief.

"Just water for me," Dean told Andrea.

"Coming up, Sausage!"

"Sausage?" Shelley asked, once Andrea had left. "What's that about?" Her glance flickered nervously to Aaron, as if she was afraid she'd asked a question that she shouldn't have in front of him.

"It's… a stupid name thing," Dean said, embarrassed. "Andrea and I went to high school together when we were kids. Dean James, James Dean, Jimmy Dean… the brand of sausage. That was the one that had to stick."

Shelley looked amused.

"We're not supposed to use the word stupid," Aaron reminded him, still pouting about the pop.

"You're right," Dean told him. "Sorry about that."

Shelley played nervously with her water while Dean dredged for a topic that would work for the three of them.

"Did you have fun at school today?" Shelley asked Aaron before Dean could come up with anything.

"Yeah," Aaron said with a shrug.

"What's your favorite topic?" she asked into the unhelpful silence he left her. She was trying so hard.

Aaron shrugged again. "Recess, I guess."

"You like math," Dean prodded him.

"Yeah."

It would have been an awkward silence if it weren't for Andrea's arrival with their drinks. Shelley looked at her gratefully. "Thank you."

Aaron muttered his thanks after Dean reminded him, and proceeded to make a paper rocket ship from his straw wrapper.

"Have you decided what to order?" Andrea asked. "Or do you need a little more time?"

"I'll take the special," Shelley said demurely.

Dean glanced at the sticky note on the menu. Shelley didn't seem like the chicken fried steak type, but maybe she would surprise him.

"Corn dogs!" Aaron chorused, holding up his half-colored paper menu. "Fries! Lots of ketchup!"

"I'll take the special, too," Dean decided.

Andrea took their laminated menus. "Be about ten minutes," she said cheerfully.

9

This whole thing was a terrible mistake, Shelley decided.

The date, the diner, the clothes she'd picked out, the fact that her mate had a kid...

But most of all, the chicken fried steak.

After closer to fifteen minutes of awkward conversation dominated by Aaron's nearly-indecipherable but very enthusiastic explanations about something called Minecraft (Shelley guessed it was a cartoon she wasn't familiar with), Andrea brought her a steaming plate... of gravy.

A cautious poke revealed a sublayer of some kind of deep-fried meat, and there was a side of hashbrowns completely submerged in the lumpy cream-colored goo.

Keenly aware of the scrutiny she was under from what felt like the entire diner, Shelley sawed off a tiny piece of the mystery meat and prepared for the worst, already practicing her best smile and pretend enjoyment. She was *not* going to be the snobbish *prima donna* she knew that everyone must think she was; she was going to choke down the greasy food like it was ambrosia from heaven for politeness sake.

Dean was busy trying to keep Aaron from upsetting his milk

onto his plate as the little boy poured half a bottle of ketchup over his fries.

Shelley put the bite into her mouth… and was pleasantly relieved to find that it was nowhere near the flavor or texture she was expecting. The lumps in the smooth gravy were little pieces of sausage, popping with flavor, and the meat had been tenderized into something far more chewable than she had feared. The breading was a neutral layer that perfectly complemented the rest.

A tentative taste showed that the hashbrowns were just as good; fried crispy but not soaked in oil.

Shelley looked up and accidentally met Dean's eyes.

"Like it?" he asked, a smile twitching at his mouth.

"Yeah," Shelley said honestly. Did she sound too surprised? "It's really good."

"Old George is the best short order cook in a hundred miles," Dean said with satisfaction. "Gran's Grits may not have the fanciest menu, but what they serve is always great."

He reminded Aaron not to talk with his mouth full of food and took a generous bite from his own plate.

As good as the food had turned out to be, Shelley was suddenly hungry for something else altogether.

He was so handsome, and every move he made was graceful and strong. Shelley had never considered eating particularly sexy until she was watching him draw a fork from between his lips, and she had to blink carefully and make herself eat several mechanical bites before she could look up and meet his eyes.

Those hazel eyes were dancing again and Shelley realized with chagrin that he knew exactly what he'd done to her. His next bite was deliberately slow and he actually licked his lips afterwards.

Shelley knew a challenge when she saw one, and two could play that game. Her next bite was just as slow as his, and she closed her eyes and gave a little shiver of pleasure.

"Glad to see you're enjoying your meal," Andrea said, and Shelley's eyes flew open as her cheeks turned scarlet.

"My… uh… compliments to your chef," Shelley said in a squeak.

"Can I get you guys anything?" Andrea asked drolly. "Like, a room?"

"More milk!" Aaron said enthusiastically, thankfully oblivious to anything else happening at the table. Somehow his plate was already mostly empty.

"How do you ask?" Dean reminded him, still grinning at Shelley.

"MayIpleasehavemoremilk?" Aaron asked.

"I'm good," Shelley said faintly.

"I'll be right back with another milk," Andrea said cheerfully.

Shelley continued to eat her food trying not to meet Dean's eyes because every time she did, they both broke into laughter... much to the mystification of Aaron.

"What's funny?" he finally asked, around a mouthful of fries. "I don't get it."

"You will someday," Dean told him.

To her own surprise, Shelley finished her entire plate, wiping up the delicious gravy with her toast. She usually tried to eat light, and often found heavy food like this too much to finish.

"Dessert?" Andrea offered.

"I couldn't..." Shelley said just as Aaron stuffed his final bit of corndog in his mouth and declared, "I ate all my food canI-haveabrownie?"

"Chew and swallow, kiddo," Dean told him.

Aaron did so, obediently, then politely asked, "Could I can I may I have a brownie?"

"Please," Dean whispered sideways.

"PLEASE."

"One brownie?" Andrea confirmed.

"Make it two," Dean said magnanimously.

Andrea took their plates and the half-dozen crumpled napkins that Aaron had managed to generate.

"Thanks for coming out with us," Dean said, almost shyly. How could someone look so heart-bendingly adorable and so undeniably masculine at the same time?

"Thanks for inviting me," Shelley said, feeling just as shy. "I've had a really good time."

She had, she realized.

Aaron had been disruptive and there were several times she had wondered exactly how he could pack that much food into such a small mouth and still try talking. But he... was kind of cute, she supposed, and he at least made an attempt at manners; it was hard to dislike something that was so *happy* and trying so hard. And the food was much better than she had expected; her stomach felt comfortably full and warm.

The brownies that Andrea brought were served warm, with ice cream, and Aaron dove into his with enthusiasm, nearly unseating his ice cream scoop in his attempt to cut the brownie with his fork.

"Want to try a bite?" Dean offered Shelley, holding out a square of warm chocolate draped in melting ice cream at the end of a fork.

Shelley couldn't figure out how to say no, and she didn't really want to, so she leaned forward and opened her mouth.

Feeding someone else was supposed to be something seductive and sexy, and this might have been the kind of moment a younger Shelley might have written about in her journal, dripping with purple prose.

Instead, Aaron dropped his current bite of brownie directly into his lap with a loud yelp of surprise, startling Dean into veering off from Shelley's mouth and he stabbed the brownie he was offering directly into her cheek instead. The soft brownie disintegrated and the ice cream coated crumbs dropped straight down Shelley's cleavage.

10

---

*S*helley gave a squeak of dismay as Dean tried to rise to offer a napkin and bumped the table, nearly toppling Aaron's milk. "I got it, I got it," she protested, trying to fish the pieces out of her shirt.

Aaron howled in laughter, and Dean chuckled and tried to clean up his son's lap while trying very hard not to stare as Shelley, embarrassed and laughing helplessly, mined into her shirt.

"This is going to take a bathroom visit," she finally admitted sheepishly. She gathered up her purse and clicked off in her heels like a runway model and Dean watched her go helplessly.

"Why are her shoes like that?" Aaron asked, his laughter finally fading. They were the last people eating in the diner and the sound of her steps was very loud in the quiet little room.

"They're just fancy," Dean said. Everything about Shelley was fancy. "Do you... like her?"

Aaron considered the question as he put his last bite of brownie into his mouth. "She's okay," he decided.

Dean's bear wanted to protest that she was much more than okay. She was beautiful and elegant and she was trying so hard to look like she wasn't completely out of her element. She listened to

Aaron's monologues patiently, even if she looked utterly confused by them, and she was polite and gracious.

And when she laughed…

When she laughed, Dean could see straight through into her joyous heart, and he loved what he saw there unreservedly.

"She's kind of… funny," Aaron declared.

Andrea brought the check and Dean opened his wallet and gave her a credit card. "How'd the date go, Sausage?"

"It wasn't a date," Aaron said with authority. "It was just dinner."

Dean cast a glance at the bathroom, but there was no sign of Shelley yet. "It went fine," he said briefly. "Thanks."

"Are you going to kiss her?" Aaron asked again, fortunately waiting until Andrea had gone to run the credit card.

Dean looked thoughtfully back at him. "Would you mind if I did?" he asked.

Aaron dragged his fork through the melted ice cream on his plate, considering. Finally, he shrugged. "It would be okay."

Shelley's heels gave ample warning across the linoleum floor, and by the time she had returned to the table, Dean had gotten Aaron into his jacket and pulled his own on.

Taking the cue, Shelley put down her purse and put her own jacket on. Dean tried not to gaze foolishly at her. Had she put new makeup on in the bathroom? She looked like she was straight out of a magazine, almost distractingly perfect.

"Don't forget your credit card!" Andrea called.

Dean signed the receipt, left a tip in cash, and the three of them walked out into the darkness.

"I, ah, drove," Shelley pointed out. Hers was the only car in front of the diner.

"We walked," Aaron volunteered. "We live right over there."

"This is goodbye, then," Shelley said nervously. "Ah… thanks again for tightening my license plate. Next time I should get dinner. If there… is…"

"I'd like to see you again," Dean said swiftly.

They were standing very close on the narrow sidewalk. Aaron

had walked a few steps away and was kicking a rustling drift of leaves. Dean closed the distance between them before he could lose his nerve, putting a hand on Shelley's face and bending forward to kiss her with his bear leaning on him avidly.

She hesitated, drawing away. "What about Aaron," she whispered. "He didn't…"

"He said it would be okay," Dean assured her, grateful that she cared.

Then she was meeting his mouth with hers and she was in his arms at last… and it was all much more than just *okay*.

He tried to keep it a chaste kiss, a polite first kiss that you'd have in public, knowing that Aaron's weren't the only prying eyes around. Shelley trembled in his embrace, like she was fighting her own instincts, and opened her mouth with a whimper of need.

It wasn't very chaste after that.

Shelley's arms slipped up around his neck, and Dean claimed her mouth with a crushing, probing kiss, cradling her face with one hand, holding her close at the waist with the other. Her whole body pressed up tight to him, in all its gorgeous, curvy perfection, and it still wasn't close enough. He needed her, craved her like a starving man.

"Can we go now?"

Aaron's unimpressed voice dragged him back and Dean reluctantly let go of Shelley and stepped away. She was panting, eyes wide and her cheeks flushed. She licked her lips and swallowed.

"Deirdre's going to be picking up Aaron tomorrow after school. Do you want to come over and have dinner… maybe watch a movie?"

"I want to watch a movie," Aaron said enthusiastically.

Dean definitely didn't, and he watched Shelley realize what he was suggesting. Her silver eyes widened and her breath caught in her throat. "I'd like that," she said softly.

"Can we watch *Iron Man*?" Aaron suggested. "Trevor got to see it already."

"You're going to your mom's," Dean reminded him.

"Will she let me watch *Iron Man*?"

"That's up to her," Dean said. He was still gazing at Shelley, who had turned several interesting colors and was back to flushed. "At six?"

"Six sounds great," she said, and she gave that shy half-smile that Dean was sure she had never practiced, because it was so tentative and real.

Then Aaron took him by the hand and drug him away as Shelley got into her car.

11

"*Y*ou never used to go out with us," Shelley said skeptically as Damien's car pulled into the parking area at the end of the short drive. "Are you sure this place is safe?"

"Roar!" Trevor said enthusiastically from the back seat. "I'm going to be a lion!"

"Wait!" Damien said severely, ignoring Shelley. "I don't want clawmarks on my seats."

"Yes, Grandpa," Trevor said meekly.

Shelley filed Damien's tone for a time she might need it with Aaron. A few days before, she would have considered an afternoon out with Trevor some kind of torture, but now anything that could help her understand Aaron seemed like a misery worth enduring.

And it had been a *long* while since she'd let her lion out to stretch.

"This is private property," Damien explained. "There shouldn't be anyone else around."

"We're here already?" Trevor said. "Can I get out? Can I change? Can I can I can I?"

"It's so close to town," Shelley said, opening her own door and frowning at the dirty leaves littering the ground. "Aren't you worried someone will wander here by mistake?"

Damien gave her an impatient look. "Do you want to get out, or not?"

Shelley sighed and slipped off her heels. While Damien got Trevor out of the other side of the car, she undressed swiftly and put her clothing neatly in her seat. Then she shifted, and closed the car door with her heavy feline head.

"Now, you think about what it feels like to be a lion," Damien was saying to the little boy. "How it feels to be covered in fur, and walking around on four paws. What your tail feels like, how clear your hearing is."

"Springy!" Trevor said. "It feels springy!"

Quick as a blink, he was flinging himself at the ground and cavorting away as a lion cub.

"Good job!" Damien said warmly. Shelley turned away while he undressed himself and after a moment, there were three lions wandering into the autumn forest.

Her lioness was nearly as tall at the shoulder as her father's thick-maned, silver-touched lion. Trevor, half-grown and tripping over his big paws, still had adolescent spots and barely came to their bellies. He pranced as tall as he could behind them, scampering to chase leaves and bat at low branches.

One of his adventures brought him tumbling into Shelley's legs, and she had to rein back her lioness' instinct to send him rolling away with a cuff from her paw.

We wouldn't hurt him, her lioness insisted. *But you have to keep him in line. Play rough, because the world is hard.*

Even her animal knew more about parenting than she did, Shelley thought bitterly. All she knew was that she was sorely unqualified, and she was terrified of doing it all wrong.

There is no wrong way to do it, her lioness said reassuringly.

Then it's me, Shelley protested. ***I'm** wrong. I'm not supposed to be a mom.*

*Our mate has a cub, so you **are** supposed to be.*

Shelley wished she could be as confident as her lioness. She wanted to be with Dean, but she couldn't help wondering if fate had just… messed up on this one. Gotten everything wrong, somehow.

She sat, tail swishing, and watched Damien teach Trevor about stalking and how to step quietly. Shelley was amused to note that Damien had no hesitation about sending him crashing into the brush with one of his big paws when he was getting over-enthusiastic. Trevor simply rolled and bounced back up to attention.

When had Damien picked up parenting? He had always been the absent one when Shelley and Shaun were growing up, as safely distant from the child duties as he could manage to be. He showed up for the requisite concerts and recitals, but it was always with a suffering air, like he couldn't wait to be back to *real* work.

And yet here he was, with Trevor, looking completely comfortable in the role of guide and teacher, and acting surprisingly patient.

A bird caught her attention and Shelley stilled her tail, watching it from the corner of her eye.

She crouched, gauging the distance between them, and the bird flitted a little further away. Shelley froze, and it hopped along its new branch. She was aware of Damien, nudging Trevor to watch, and she moved a step forward in careful slow motion, staying low and gathered.

She sprang without pausing, using her powerful hind legs to drive her into a leap—not at the bird, but at the space above the bird. It rose in terror, and she trapped it between her front paws and landed on her side, rolling onto her back as she fell.

Then she opened her paws, and let the petrified bird, unharmed, fly free.

It scolded her from the safety of a nearby tree.

"Wow!" Trevor exclaimed, standing again as a little boy. "That was amazing! Did you see that Grandpa? It was so cool! I want to do that! Aunt Shelley is incredible!"

Shelley licked her paw casually and Damien gave a cough of humor, staying in lion form.

Trevor looked between them, and fell on all fours… but was still a little boy. He looked down at himself curiously. "I'm not a lion," he pouted.

Shelley twisted back up onto her feet and shook the leaves off of herself while Trevor tried various tricks to get back into lion form. "It's not working!" he complained. "Why isn't it working?"

An idea occurred to Shelley and she walked to where Trevor was standing—and bowled him over with her head.

He bounded to his feet a lion again, making happy loud noises that weren't really roars. Shelley wondered how close they were to Green Valley, and winced when Damien put his head in the air and gave a true lion roar. Doubtlessly someone had heard *that*.

Shelley turned back the way they'd come and heard the others follow: Damien's paws heavy but quiet, Trevor like a small whirlwind through the dry leaves.

Once they had shifted back and dressed, they piled back into the car and returned to Damien's house.

Trevor, full of energy, went with Tawny for a piano lesson.

"Might have been a mistake to wind him up first," Damien admitted as he and Shelley watched them go down the hall to the music room, Trevor making his best—and loudest—lion sounds while Tawny tried to quiz him about his practice time that week.

Shelley shut down her snarky instinct to say *you think?* and just shrugged.

"Shelley…"

Shelley looked at her father and immediately knew that Tawny had already told him about Dean. She braced herself for doubt and anxiety and was surprised and relieved that she didn't feel either.

"Thanks for inviting me out," she said swiftly as she hung up her jacket. "It's been a long time since I was out on four paws and it was nice to stretch."

"Might snow next week," Damien said mildly. "Thought it would be good to get out before we would be leaving too many tracks."

Shelley made a neutral noise of agreement.

"Do you want an apology?" Damien growled unexpectedly.

Shelley returned his scowl. "For what?"

Her father looked desperately uncomfortable behind his

customary frown. "I haven't been the greatest role model of parenting."

"I never asked you to be," Shelley said shortly. This wasn't about Dean, this was about *Aaron*.

"But maybe you deserved… better," Damien said stiffly. "I could have been… more involved with your life."

"You mean, like not shipping us off to boarding schools when we got difficult?" Maybe it wasn't about Aaron, either.

"I'm not going to excuse the mistakes I made," Damien said firmly. "I wasn't very present for you and Shaun. I thought someone else could do a better job with you than I could, and I was wrong."

Shelley looked at Damien warily, not sure what to do with an admission of fault from the man who never admitted weakness.

"You kids scared the spit out of me," Damien said honestly.

Shelley knew she was staring openly now, with no control over her face whatsoever, or the tears that were pricking at her eyes.

"I wanted the absolute best for you, and it never occurred to me that what you really needed was just for me to be there for you."

"Dad…"

"I love you, Shelley-bean. And I'm proud of you. And you can do a better job at this than I did."

"You… didn't do a bad job," Shelley choked.

"Of course I didn't," Damien scoffed with a hint of his usual arrogant self. "Look at you! But I could have done a lot of things better and you don't have to go and make the same mistakes." He folded his arms and looked at her severely. "I am *assuming* you aren't going to turn tail and run away from a little problem like this," he challenged.

A little four-foot problem with a snotty nose and the power to strike utter terror into Shelley's heart.

She drew herself up. "Whatever else you did, you didn't raise a coward, Dad," she said fiercely.

"That's my girl."

Impulsively, Shelley stepped forward, and they shared a swift hug. "Thanks, Dad," she murmured into his shoulder, softly enough that he might not hear her. "I love you, too."

Then she straightened and backed away and they exchanged frowns.

"I might not be back tonight," she said frankly.

"I wouldn't expect you to be," Damien agreed. Then he unexpectedly grinned. "If you do come back, you'd better knock. It'll be the first time Tawny and I have the house to ourselves since we got married."

Shelley made a gagging noise. "Oh my god, Dad. No. Too much information. Let's go back to being cold and distant now, please."

He walked away laughing, and Shelley went bemusedly back to her room to change.

This weekend, at least, she could have Dean to herself, the way everything inside of her yearned to have him, and next week she could jump feet-first into I-don't-know-what-I'm-doing soup.

12

*D*ean paced.

"I'm boooored," Aaron moaned, laying upside down with his feet over the back of the couch. "Can't I watch TV?"

"Your mom should be here at any moment," Dean said, looking at his watch for at least the seventeenth time. "I want you to be ready to go."

"I'll turn it right off," Aaron wheedled. "My bag is already packed, and I've got my shoes on already."

They were indeed on, pointing straight up into the air with shoelaces untied and tongues crooked.

But Dean knew better than to think that Aaron would be able to shut off the television himself without a physical intervention. "She'll be here soon," he growled. He pulled out his phone and looked despairingly at the unread status of the text he'd sent.

It didn't really mean much; Deirdre was constantly letting her phone run out of charge. And it wasn't even that unusual that she was running late. Still, an hour late was into the territory where he was allowed to be a little put-out, wasn't it?

"I'm so boooooored," Aaron repeated. Then he sat up. "I'm hungry! Can I have a snack?"

"Get your shoes off the couch," Dean reminded him. "Yeah, how about…" what was easiest? "A cheese-stick?"

Aaron managed to drag his shoes across nearly the entire couch getting them down to the ground. "Can I have crackers with it?" he begged.

Dean grimaced, dreading the time it would take but unable to come up with a good argument against it. "Let's make you a bag to go," he suggested. "But don't get crumbs in your mom's car."

Aaron danced off to the kitchen merrily and Dean's heart rose up in his chest as he heard a car pull up outside. It was a few minutes before six… Shelley might be early. He ran a hand through his hair and tugged the wrinkles out of his shirt.

"Sorry I'm late!" Deirdre called, walking in as she knocked. "I was a little delayed and then there was construction just outside of Madison."

"Aaron, your mom is here, let's go!"

Dean thrust the bag at Deirdre. "His allergy medicine is in the outside pocket, he's got a page of math homework, and he says he left his favorite hat at your place so he doesn't need one." His words tumbled out over each other; Dean didn't realize how fast he was talking until he heard himself. "Come on, Aaron!"

Deirdre gave him a puzzled look. "I think I saw his hat at home," she said with a slow nod. "Hi sweetie!"

Aaron had apparently tried to fit the entire box of crackers into a bag, and was now struggling to close it. Bingo trailed behind him hoping for overflow. "Hi Mom! Can you close this for me?"

Deirdre gave him a hug and a kiss on the head, then deftly ate a handful of crackers from the bag so she could close it. "Have a good week, honey?"

"He was great," Dean answered for Aaron. He didn't want to actually shoo them out, and it took all of his self-control to keep from flapping his hands anxiously at them.

Aaron, predictably, started a lengthy, rambling story about something that Trevor had done at school.

"You can tell her in the car, kiddo," Dean said desperately. "Get your hug!"

Aaron took a breath and started part two of his story, tolerating Dean's hug distantly.

"I'll miss you," Dean reminded him.

"Yeah, Dad," Aaron said, returning the hug more sincerely.

"Thanks," Deirdre said cheerfully. "See you on Sunday night," she said as they started down the sidewalk to the curb.

Part three of the tale was unwinding and Dean was ready to close the door when Aaron suddenly turned around. "I don't have my Batman pajamas!"

Dean groaned. "You have your green pajamas," he said hopefully. "Won't those do?"

Aaron stared in horror. "No, I need my Batman pajamas! Otherwise, I might get scared."

"There's nothing scary in your room," Deirdre reminded him with an amused smile.

"I neeeeeeeeed them!" Aaron insisted.

"I think they're in the hamper," Dean said despairingly.

"We can wash them tomorrow morning," Deirdre said with a shrug to Dean.

"Go get them," Dean said to Aaron, defeated.

Aaron scampered past, shoes flapping. "Wait, wait," Dean insisted. "You can't run upstairs with your shoes untied."

He knelt to tie up the shoes and Aaron fidgeted, making the task even harder. "Okay, go," he said at last, and Aaron was off like a shot.

When he stood up, Deirdre was looking at him suspiciously.

"What?" he asked.

"You picked up the house," she observed.

"I do that, from time to time," Dean said defensively.

"You also got a haircut," she pointed out.

"I do that periodically, too," Dean said, resisting his urge to run his fingers through it again.

"I'm sorry I was late," she said, eyes narrow. "It's not usually a big deal."

"It's fine," Dean growled. "Aaron, did you *find* them?" he called.

"You're trying pretty hard to get rid of us," Deirdre pointed out.

"Trevor's niece is coming over!" Aaron hollered, appearing at the top of the stairs. "They're going to watch a movie, can I watch *Iron Man*?"

"Trevor's…?"

"Aunt," Dean groaned. "Trevor's *aunt*. Shaun's sister."

Comprehension dawned in Deirdre's face. "Oh my God, Dean, you have a *date*, that's *great*!"

"Aaron, are you ready to go?" Dean begged.

Bingo, hearing the word *go*, barked in excitement.

And that's when Shelley pulled up.

13

It wasn't like Shelley dated a lot, but she wasn't a nun, either. She knew what to expect from a second date, especially on the heels of a first date and a kiss like Dean's.

But when she pulled up to Dean's house, nothing was the way she had expected it to be.

Shelley had to sit in the car a moment and screw up her courage to get out when she realized that Aaron was still there… and worse yet, a woman who must be Deirdre, standing in the open door.

She put her chin high as she stepped out, and tugged her skirt down into place. This was undoubtedly going to be ugly. Deirdre, Tawny had said, had broken Dean's heart. That wasn't the kind of thing that left emotions unruffled. And she was the new woman in Dean's life, she reminded herself. Maybe. Hopefully?

Two steps up the sidewalk, a dog came barking to greet her: a large, slobbering, brown and white mutt with floppy ears that immediately tried to jump up and lick her face.

"Nice doggy!" Shelley squeaked, trying to push it down and keep her purse out of its reach and not fall over, all at once. Why wasn't it afraid of her lion?

"Bingo! Bingo down! Bingo leave it!" Dean came running to her rescue, pulling the dog down and ruffling its ears affectionately as it wiggled in joy.

"You have a *dog*," Shelley observed brilliantly, further cementing the impression of intelligence that she'd started with.

"His name is Bingo," Dean said, looking sheepish. "Aaron named him. Like the kid's song, you know. B-I-N-G-O."

Was it a dig on the fact that she knew nothing about kids? "I remember that song," she said tightly.

"He's a goon, sorry."

"It's fine," Shelley said faintly as they closed the distance to his porch. Clearly, her mate starter-kit came with everything: an old farmhouse, a dog, a kid... and a gorgeous ex-wife who'd broken his heart.

Deirdre was effortlessly beautiful, in a sunny, country way, with curly brown hair highlighted golden and big blue eyes.

She even had adorable freckles, scattered all over her cheeks and nose.

She beamed at Shelley rather alarmingly, and immediately offered her a hand to shake. "I'm Deirdre," she greeted. "Aaron's mom."

"It's nice to meet you," Shelley said, hoping she didn't sound as chilly to Deirdre as she did to her own ears. She reminded herself to smile.

The handshake was swift and utilitarian and Shelley wondered if the glance that Deirdre gave Dean wasn't a little skeptical.

They had the mannerisms of people who were used to talking to each other without words, who knew each other so well that they were having an entire conversation with eyebrows and angles of the shoulder while Shelley stood there feeling left out and out-classed, even in her custom-altered designer clothes, with her name-brand purse and $300 shoes.

Even the dog, Bingo, had decided that she was no longer new enough to hold his interest, and went to investigate bushes around the yard.

Aaron came thundering down the porch stairs in a way that made Shelley flinch, expecting him to fall at any moment. "Bye,

Shelley!" he called. "Bye, Dad!" He paused to give Dean a hug, and Shelley stepped back out of his way before she realized he was planning to do the same for her.

"Er…" she knelt uncomfortably and gave Aaron a cautious embrace. It probably looked as weird as it felt, and Shelley was hyper-aware of Deirdre's eyes on her. He smelled like cheese and dirt.

"Do you have my crackers?" he asked, bounding away to put his hand in his mother's. "Bye, Bingo!"

"Right here," Deirdre assured him. "See you on Sunday! Nice to meet you, Shelley!"

It seemed weird to go inside while they were still there, so Shelley stood with Dean and forced herself not to fidget as Aaron buckled himself into a booster seat and Deirdre gave him his crackers, and they finally—finally!—drove away. Aaron waved out the window as Shelley half-heartedly waved after him.

"Well, that was awkward," Dean said cheerfully.

14

*A*wkward was an understatement, but Dean tried to smile.

Shelley gave him her boardroom smile—the corners of her mouth turned up just exactly the right amount and her face otherwise completely blank. He could feel the roil of confused emotion underlying it, and couldn't blame her.

"So, that was your ex." Her voice was as bland as her face was. "She seems nice."

Bingo, having finished his farewell circle of the lawn, returned to sit next to Shelley and try to lean on her knees adoringly.

Shelley edged back and Bingo leaned further. Shelley took a full step away, and the dog was forced to sit under his own power, choosing instead to lean into space until he flopped over on his side.

"You look beautiful," Dean said, the way he'd originally planned to greet her. And she did look beautiful, like she'd just stepped out of the pages of a fashion magazine. Her legs were long and smooth and her tight skirt barely reached her knees. She was wearing a beige designer jacket against the autumn chill, and a fluttering red scarf that looked too thin to be warm.

Her eyes flickered to his and the smile looked a little more genuine. "Thank you. You look… really great."

Dean might have tried kissing her then, no matter how awkward things seemed, but Bingo was lying between them, and he knew that the moment he stepped over, the dog would stand up, and the opportunity for a kiss would be ruined.

He didn't want her any less than he had in the office of the shop, or when he'd kissed her in front of Gran's Grits. But he wasn't sure how to get from where they were to where they both really wanted to be.

"I made dinner," he said desperately, and the timer had the good grace to go off then.

She followed him into the house, and even if Dean hadn't been able to hear her heels clicking along the floor, he would have known exactly where she was behind him. It wasn't just her smell—how was it possible for someone to *smell* so put-together?—it was the sense of her: a sweet, desperate yearning for her wherever she was.

"I hope you don't mind casserole," he said apologetically. It wasn't city fare, but Dean's sole criteria for the meal was something that could stay in the oven a little longer than intended, or reheat well, in case they got… distracted on the way to the meal.

That hope had been dashed by the chaos that Shelley had come into, and the stiff wall of doubt and discomfort that she'd put up when faced with an unexpected dog and an un-planned-for ex-wife.

"Casserole sounds fine," Shelley said, utterly politely. "Can I help somehow?" She sounded dubious.

"Nothing left to do," Dean assured her. "The table's all set."

"Oh," she said with a smile. "Candles."

They were emergency candles, because that's what Dean could find, but he didn't think they looked too inelegant in the antique holders.

"There's a lighter by the fireplace," he said as he bent to take the casserole from the oven. Damn, he meant to make a fire before she came, something cozy and warm to curl up in front of.

Too late now.

"Get back, Bingo. This isn't for you. Out of the kitchen!"

He heard and felt Shelley go to the fireplace and find the lighter on the mantle.

"This is a cute house," she said quietly, lighting the candles. It was just starting to get dark outside.

"Thanks! I grew up here. Bought it from my parents when they moved to Arizona. Mom couldn't handle the winters, with her asthma." It wasn't as bad as still *living* with his parents, but Dean wondered if it was far off.

"It's a really good use of space," she observed.

Was it code for *this place is tiny and poor*? She did come from a family of millionaires.

He put the casserole on the potholder on the table, and Shelley replaced the lighter on the mantle, nearly tripping over Bingo when she turned around. Bingo wagged his tail and tried to get her to pet him, but Shelley skirted around him carefully.

They sat opposite from each other at the little table and Dean was decidedly weirded out to be looking at his mate—his graceful, gorgeous mate!—in the seat where his son usually sat.

He poured her a glass of wine and they made careful conversation.

She told him that she did contract negotiations for one of the largest engineering firms in the Midwest and they shared a forced laugh over Shelley's nickname, Shelley the Shark. "I'm not a lawyer like you see in television in court," she explained shyly. "I'm the lawyer that keeps everyone out of court. My specialty is contract law. I help write the contracts and make people sign them, and then use them to make people do what they promised to do."

Dean, feeling rather out-classed, explained that he worked as a mechanic and owned both the shop and the tiny hardware store next door as well.

"Well, the bank owns it, technically, of course. Ted wanted to retire and… well, really no one else wanted it," he said sheepishly. "I scraped the down payment together and it does alright for itself."

"All that and a single dad," Shelley observed. "It probably keeps you really busy."

Dean decided not to add anything about the volunteer work he also did. He'd wanted to fill his life to the seams when Deirdre left him.

"Yeah," he said sheepishly.

"Can I help clear up?" Shelley asked when they were done. "It was delicious."

Dean hadn't made plans for dessert, he realized, standing and letting her help gather her dishes. He should have picked up something from Shaun's bakery.

He'd had high hopes for something else happening after dinner.

Instead, everything was…

"This is weird, isn't it," Shelley said, standing next to him in the kitchen with her plate in one hand and her glass in the other.

"I didn't want it to be weird," he confessed to her. She was so beautiful, and he wanted her so badly that it made it hard to think.

She gave a wry smile that wasn't part of her practiced repertoire and a shy, downcast look. "I thought a mate would be… simple. Straight-forward. Instead…"

"Weird," Dean finished for her.

"Weird," she agreed, putting the dishes on the counter.

"Shelley…"

Dean finally accepted his bear's relentless suggestions and stepped forward to kiss her, and then it wasn't weird at all.

15

His mouth was home, Shelley thought, when he kissed her at last.

Home like she'd never thought a home could be. She longed to be there whenever she wasn't, and it made everything better and safer and sweeter.

He tasted like wine and tater tots, which had never featured in any of the romance books Shelley devoured, but nothing else could have been so perfect.

She kissed him back with all of her heart, winding her arms up around his strong shoulders. As complicated as they had managed to be, this was simple and straightforward. She knew exactly what to do, pulling him as close as they could get while still wearing clothing, passionately kissing him and regretting nothing.

Her lioness growled in her ear, and she knew that his bear was doing the same from the frantic way he was trying to find an enclosure on her shirt and the way he was dragging his teeth along her skin.

She tugged at his shirt, trying to get it off him, trying to pull him… wasn't there a couch in the living room?

Then she gave a shriek as one of her heels hit the threshold for the kitchen and Bingo managed to be directly behind her again. She ungracefully fell over backwards, dragging Dean with her.

"Bingo, out of the kitchen!" Dean said, but it was too late even for shifter reflexes; between her heels and their entanglement, they both went over and Bingo gave a yip of dismay, fled two steps, and then returned to lick everything he could reach.

"Ack, ew, oh my god!" Shelley couldn't help saying, but she was laughing, how could she *not*? There was dog tongue all over her swollen mouth, and in her ear, and across her forehead, and her arms were pinned by Dean's weight so she couldn't squirm very far away. "I'm pretty sure my mascara isn't lick-proof!" she giggled.

Dean was laughing, too, one arm still around her as he shoved the dog with the other. "Bingo, back!" he ordered ineffectively.

They finally regained their feet, chortling and clinging to each other, and Shelley kicked off her heels.

Bingo sat at their feet and looked up, panting hopefully. Clearly he thought he had done something worthy of praise.

"I'm washing my face before I kiss you again," Shelley declared. "My own face," she told Bingo.

As she did, she heard Dean washing his hands in the kitchen sink, scolding Bingo good-naturedly.

She returned from the bathroom in her bare feet.

"You're short," Dean said breathlessly.

"I am not," Shelley protested. He was even more handsome-looking flushed from their exertion, and he was smiling more naturally than he had all night. "You just hadn't seen me without heels." She had to look up at him.

"It's hot," Dean said, his grin spreading. How could *teeth* make her knees weak? "Now, where were we?"

"I think we were finding a safer place to continue this," Shelley purred.

"I have a suggestion," Dean said, and he took her by the hand and led her past the disappointed dog and up the stairs, to the bedroom that Shelley had been desperately hoping he was taking her to.

She shed her shirt before he had a chance to kick the door shut behind them, and was gratified by the way he stopped and stared without breathing at the sight of her blue lace bra.

"Your turn," she told him, pulling up his shirt.

He tore it off so quickly that Shelley heard stitches snap, and then she had her own moment of breathless awe at the vision of his beautiful, broad chest.

She could not have later described how the rest of their clothing came off. She only knew that his fingers were like fire on her skin, and his kisses took her places she'd never imagined. Want and need warred with something deeper, something more real.

Shelley wanted this man differently than she'd ever wanted anyone… or anything… in her entire life.

She wanted to wrap herself around him, protect him, bare herself to him, tell him every secret and learn every one of his. With every piece of clothing, she felt like some part of her shell was peeled away, like he was seeing the real Shelley, not the Shelley she had to show everyone else.

It was only when they were both completely naked that he laid her back on the bed, one hand at her waist, the other catching their fall. His weight on her, his hard cock pressed against her thigh… it was almost too much.

She spread her legs and begged, "Please…"

She was so wet that he slid straight in with just the slightest change in angle and pressure, and she clawed the bed and rose to meet him.

He paused, buried in her, and Shelley could hear his teeth grind in concentration; he was as tightly wound as she was.

She whimpered and tried to move, craving the friction, and he withdrew a tantalizing inch and drove back in.

A cry escaped her… pleasure and desire… and he thrust again, and again, until they were coupling desperately and Shelley was falling from heights she'd never known.

They lay together a long while afterwards, hands trailing lazily over each other's limbs. He had the most fascinating ripples of muscles, and such long, clever, calloused fingers. Shelley thought she could lie there forever, her whole body utterly content.

Suddenly Dean stiffened in alarm and sat up. "Did anyone blow out the candles?"

"I… I don't think so," Shelley said.

They both scrambled out of bed and raced downstairs naked.

Bingo, who had been sleeping at the foot of the stairs, sprang to his feet in surprise and began barking in random directions, clearly not sure what was happening, but determined to be a part of it.

One of the candles had guttered out entirely and the other was giving its last dying flickers. Hot wax had pooled under the holders.

Dean blew out the remaining flame and Shelley clung to him as they laughed in relief. "I'm sure it would have made a very poor impression to burn down my house on our second date," Dean said sheepishly.

Shelley kissed him. "After what we just did, I would have forgiven you even having to stand out naked in the cold waiting for the fire department."

To her surprise, Dean blushed. "Considering I'm a third of our fire department, that would be pretty humiliating."

"You're a firefighter?" Shelley exclaimed in surprise.

"Volunteer," Dean said dismissively. "I should have warned you, I'm pretty much always on call. Chances of a call are really slim, our district is just Green Valley and we don't get called out further unless both Farshoot and Dashum are already on multiple jobs; they've got real stations. We're not even NFPA qualified. It's basically some guys with cellphones, ugly suits, and an old surplus Forestry Service truck that I've kept running with duct tape. Most of our callouts are cats in trees and Stanley wanting us to get a tractor out of mud like some kind of free tow service. Why are you staring at me?"

"Because I did not realize that you could get even sexier," Shelley purred, sidling up to him. They were still naked and it seemed like the perfect excuse to touch him.

He leaned over and kissed her, drawing him into her arms where she belonged.

It was like puzzle pieces, or Pringles: everything of her seemed to fit everything of him absolutely perfectly.

"Wait," he murmured. "The curtains are open…"

"Maybe you should close them," Shelley suggested. "For the rest of the weekend…"

"That is a *great* plan," Dean agreed.

16

---

*D*ean knew that the closed curtains would have the neighbors talking... but what happened behind them would have caused even more gossip.

They made love on every surface in the house: the kitchen table, the kitchen counter, the washing machine, the couch—which had to be abandoned because Bingo kept sticking cold wet dog nose where it was wildly unwelcome—the stairs, the shower, the sunroom, Dean's desk, the bedroom floor...

Every time that Dean thought they might have finally satisfied their animals' wild needs, Shelley would cast a playful sideways look at him, or he'd accidentally brush up against her, which obviously meant he had to kiss her, and they were off again.

He didn't leave the house except to take Bingo out at odd hours, and they returned swiftly.

He and Shelley didn't really talk in depth until Sunday afternoon, when Deirdre's looming return made them shower in earnest and straighten the house.

"Should I... go?" Shelley asked tentatively, folding the afghan over the back of the couch. Her face was back in what Dean was calling boardroom mode, perfectly serene if you didn't know her a little.

He knew her more than a little now, didn't he?

Dean stopped scraping wax off the kitchen table and came around to her. "Shelley… I want you to be a part of my life. Of *our* lives. Please stay."

To her credit, she didn't flinch.

"Package deal," she murmured, nodding slowly. "I know."

"But we don't have to do it all at once," Dean reassured her, taking her hands in his own. "We can figure this out as we go. I don't… want it to be awkward."

There was the real smile, the crooked, amused little glimpse of the Shelley beneath the mask.

"We've got a lot of details to resolve," she agreed like the lawyer she was. "Living arrangements, financial decisions… I'd like to read your custody contract."

"My what?"

"Your custody contract. What we do could impact child support or custody schedules."

"I don't even know where the divorce papers are," Dean told her, baffled. "That was five years ago. Deirdre and I just work things out on a week-by-week basis. It changes all the time."

Shelley looked at him skeptically. "You don't have a settlement that says who pays for what or divides your custody time?"

"If Aaron needs something, one of us gets it for him," Dean explained, trying to understand Shelley's surprise. "He's at my house for school because his best friends are here and we try to work out all the weekends and holidays with Deirdre's schedule that we can manage."

Shelley was silent.

Finally, she looked down at her hands where Dean still held them. "I guess I just assumed it was like my parents' divorce, where every hour and dollar was held accountable."

"Deirdre and I don't do that," Dean said gently.

"You still love her."

Dean knew he was quiet too long, but Shelley didn't pull away. "Not like that," he was finally able to say. "Not like *this*."

He looked at the clock. The others wouldn't be there for another half an hour, at least.

"C'mon," he said, pulling her to the couch. "Let me tell you what happened. It's… important that you know." If he didn't tell her, someone else was going to tell her something worse.

Sitting on the couch was an inevitable invitation to Bingo, who immediately jumped up to get cuddles. He could sense the somber mood and didn't attempt to lick anyone or crawl into Shelley's lap. He did sit beside her and lean into her shoulder until she pushed him away and then he lay down and put his head into her lap. After a moment, she stroked his ears and he closed his eyes with a groan of bliss.

Dean wanted to think that her acceptance of Bingo was a good sign of further domestic compatibility, but he knew better than to read too much into it.

"Why isn't Bingo afraid of my lion?" Shelley asked thoughtfully. "Or your bear, for that matter?"

"He's too stupid to fear things," Dean said. "I watched him try to get a big, angry bull to play with him, and you can play fetch with nothing for about an hour before he figures out there never was a ball to start with."

They weren't sitting as comfortably with each other as they had all weekend, draped casually together, but when he put an arm around her, she leaned into him with a sigh.

"Deirdre and I went to high school together. First real love and all, and we thought it would be forever. Forever and a family." Dean paused, waiting for it to be hard to say, and was surprised by how distant it all felt.

"Deirdre's a deer shifter, and we never kept secrets from each other. So… when she met Juan… she came straight to me and she told me."

I'm so sorry, Deirdre had said, weeping. *I didn't ask for this. I never wanted to do this to you.*

"She cheated on you," Shelley said ferociously. Bingo opened his eyes warily. "Maybe I *shouldn't* be here when she gets back."

"No!" Dean said promptly. "I mean, I know that's what people think. It's the obvious answer. But... Juan was her mate. Nothing *happened* until I let her go."

"Oh," Shelley said breathlessly. "*Oh.*"

She returned to petting Bingo and he closed his eyes again, tail thumping on the arm of the couch.

"She offered to stay. For Aaron, and because she'd promised. But I couldn't do that to her. I couldn't keep her, knowing she'd never be happy, just because I wanted her for myself."

Shelley tucked herself closer to Dean's side and he wondered if he only imagined the wave of her love and sympathy.

"I mean, don't think that our marriage was perfect, or that we didn't drive each other crazy on a regular basis. We were two clueless parents in an impossible situation. But Juan loves Aaron as much as Deirdre and I do, and I loved her too much to keep them apart. We had enough reasons to put in the work. Even when it was hard."

He shifted Shelley in his arms and lifted her chin so he could drown in her eyes. "I didn't understand what Deirdre felt then, I had to trust what she told me. But I understand now, I know how badly that must have torn her up inside, how strong and deep and amazing meeting your mate can be. And I know you don't want all the things I come with, but I know that it's worth it, even if it's hard, and I will do whatever it takes to make *this* work."

17

Shelley had spent the weekend thinking there was no possible way to fall harder in love with Dean.

But every time she turned around, there was some new revelation about him: he was a firefighter, he periodically hired a local homeless guy under the table with diner gift certificates, he'd rescued Bingo after he'd been hit by a truck and nursed the tragically dumb mutt back to health. Shelley was beginning to think she must be living in some kind of dream; he was so good, so selfless.

And then he told her how much he loved another woman and managed to make even *that* about how much he loved *her*.

"Shelley..." he said, in that deep, honey voice. "Shelley, you're crying..."

"I never thought it could be like this," she whispered back. "I never guessed."

Then he was kissing her and Bingo was panting and trying to get in on the action with his tongue, tail wagging against the back of the couch as he squirmed into their laps.

"This... is a lot... harder... with your help..." Dean told the dog between kisses.

Then there was an unexpected beep of a horn from the curb

outside and they were drawing away from each other in alarm. Bingo leapt from the couch, barking and running for the door.

Shelley tried to pull herself together, wiping away her tears and straightening her blouse as Dean rose to open the door.

A quick check in her powder mirror showed Shelley that the damage wasn't too bad; she really needed a full round of make-up to feel ready for what was coming, but Dean had convinced her that she shouldn't wear any over the weekend. (It tastes bad! he had complained, and Shelley wasn't willing to risk fewer kisses for flawless matte skin.)

"Why did you honk, Mom?" Aaron was asking as he burst into the house. "You told me that you were only supposed to honk if there was going to be an accident. Was there almost an accident? I didn't see one, was there another car?"

"Never mind, Aaron," Deirdre said cheerfully. "Down, Bingo. Hi, Dean! Hi, Shelley!"

Shelley replied with a tiny *hi* that was completely lost in the chaos that swirled into the house.

Bingo was still barking happily, cavorting around everyone's feet and trying desperately to get someone's attention.

Aaron made a beeline for Dean and was swept up into a tight hug. "Hi Dad!"

Shelley braced herself for another uncomfortable hug, but Aaron, once released, dropped his bag and hat and raced for the kitchen. "I'm starving!"

"Don't believe him if he tells you I didn't feed him this weekend," Deirdre said, handing Dean what looked like a laundry bag. "He ate two and half hot dogs for lunch and a three-egg omelet this morning for breakfast."

"Growing boy," Dean observed. "Pretty sure I was the same way."

"He's decided he doesn't like bell peppers any more."

"Weren't they his favorite vegetable last week?"

"That was last week. Aaron! I have to go, come give me a hug!"

Aaron trailed out of the kitchen holding an apple with two giant bites out of it.

"Bye, Mom!" he said around the missing part of the apple. He gave her a distracted hug and finally seemed to notice that Shelley was there. "You look less fancy."

Shelley had no idea what to say to that.

"Juan and I want to go out with you two soon—you three," Deirdre corrected herself, ruffling Aaron's hair. "Shelley, we're dying to get to know you, I'm sorry I can't stay, if you're ever in Madison, we've got to have lunch. Dean can give you my number. Dean, give her my number. Bye, sugar! See you next weekend!"

"I thought you had plans next weekend and I had him," Dean said, looking not nearly as bemused as Shelley felt.

"I've rearranged. I'm sure you'll need next weekend off. I'll be on time, promise."

Deirdre winked at Shelley and Shelley felt her cheeks turn scarlet.

There was a flurry of additional 'byes' and hugs and then Deirdre was gone, and it wasn't much quieter without her.

Bingo was still trotting between everyone in the room, tail wagging so enthusiastically it sounded like a drum whenever he passed a wall, and Aaron was talking non-stop about his weekend away. "Mom asked a lot of questions about you," he told Shelley. "We had stuffed peppers for dinner but I didn't eat the pepper part but the middle was really good. It had sausage and cheese."

"Oh," Shelley managed before he was going on.

"Mom didn't let me watch *Iron Man*, can we watch *Iron Man*? Trevor's seen *Iron Man* and I really really really really really want to see it."

"We were just talking about what we were going to do tonight," Dean said peaceably. "What were you thinking about, Shelley?"

Shelley looked gravely down at Aaron. He had hazel eyes just like Dean, but she could see some of Deirdre's face shape beneath his childish cheeks, and he had her curly hair. "I thought I would stay for dinner and sleep here tonight and... tomorrow I might go to Minneapolis and spend a day or two getting a few of my things to bring over and extending my leave of absence at work. I'd stay here for a while, if that's okay."

"Can we watch a movie?" Aaron asked, clearly not caring about the rest of the plan.

Dean was not looking at Aaron, he was looking at Shelley and his eyes were like suns. "Sure, kiddo. Anything you want."

"Can we watch *Deadpool?*" Aaron tested.

"Goodness, no!" Shelley surprised herself by saying at the same time as Dean said, "No!" Even she knew *that* much.

Aaron shrugged and grinned.

"I'll go start dinner," Dean said. Shelley wondered if she'd been wrong about seeing Deirdre in the little boy's face, because their grins were exactly the same. "Who wants grilled cheese on the couch while we watch *Iron Man?*"

"Meeeeeeee!" Aaron hollered.

"Yes, please!" Shelley said with a smile. "I'll get the movie set up."

Aaron, still chewing on his apple, directed her, showing her which remote was which. Shelley reminded herself that his sticky fingers wouldn't do any lasting damage.

As they settled onto the couch with plates of grilled cheese and carrot sticks, Shelley found herself wondering if being there *really* was all that she needed to do.

Because she was sure there wasn't anywhere else she would rather be.

She fed Bingo her carrots.

18

Dean hadn't known that he could miss someone after knowing them such a short, precious time.

The days without Shelley felt endless.

They talked together every night on the phone like teenagers, about every subject under the sun except the ones that mattered, and neither of them wanted to be the first to hang up.

He texted her a photo of Aaron's first lost tooth before he thought to text it to Deirdre, then wondered if he should done it as a group text, then despaired at the complexities of the situation.

Shelley texted him back a photo of her Inbox, piled high with contracts, and despaired of ever making it back. "Thursday, I hope."

Sexting turned out as awkward as their second date, without the kiss to take it from weird to wonderful.

He did a brake pad replacement on Mrs. Fredrickson's beater… and gapped the spark plugs and topped off the oil while he had it in, neither telling her, nor charging her. He sold a new outdoor spigot to Old George, and a basket of plumbing parts to a rather frigid Gillian. Stanley spent an hour in his store telling him about all the ways that things used to be constructed better, then bought one thirty-three cent carpenter's pencil with exact change.

Dean got a call-out halfway through the week and got into full turnout gear for the report of a fire.

When he and Turner arrived, it turned out to be a backyard brush pile fire being carefully watched by a man who could produce a county burn license and had a garden hose coiled nearby.

The neighbor who had called it in was not remorseful. "Could have burned down the whole town!" she said with a sniff. "And it took you long enough to get here. Your new girlfriend keeping you too busy to be a hero anymore?"

News of his weekend with Shelley had spread like the fire the neighbor predicted.

When Dean walked into Gran's Grits that night, the waitress smirked at him.

"Over here!"

Andrea was sitting with Shaun and Trevor at the big curved booth in the corner. Aaron bolted to sit next to Trevor and argue over the best crayons.

Their most recent feud seemed to be over, at least.

Aaron had been telling all his friends at school, rather prematurely perhaps, that Trevor's aunt was going to come live with them and that made them basically cousins. They then made Clara cry by pointing out that she didn't have any cousins, felt bad about her tears, and got in a fight with each other.

Andrea had orchestrated this dinner with the pretense of making sure the boys mended fences.

But she was clearly not there for a long-forgotten argument and her smile was predatory.

"Sorry," Shaun said with a shrug as Dean took his seat beside Aaron. "She's been grilling me all week and I told her that if she wanted to know anything else, she'd have to ask you."

"Thanks," Dean said wryly. He gave a resigned sigh. "What do you want to know, Andrea?"

Andrea, apparently, wanted to know everything. When was Shelley returning? Were they going to be living together? Looking for a new house? Getting married? Had she met Deirdre? Did she get along with Bingo?

Dean only realized halfway through that he was grinning helplessly during her entire interrogation.

Shaun seemed mostly mystified by the new development, if grudgingly accepting.

"I dunno," he said skeptically. "I'm suspecting body-snatchers, because nothing you have said even resembles my sister. My sister does not like dogs. My sister does not like kids. My sister likes clothes and make-up and making grown men cry over clauses and terms. Do you know they call her Shelley the Shark in some circles?"

Trevor found that hilarious and repeated 'Aunt Shelley the Shark!' several times until Andrea shook her head at him disapprovingly.

Aaron looked suspiciously at Shaun and didn't say anything.

Walking home together after dinner, Aaron was unexpectedly clingy, and wanted to hold Dean's hand. It seemed tiny and fragile in his.

Aaron didn't say much during the usual slow progression through the chores of going to bed, but after Dean had tucked him in, read a chapter of their current book, and turned off the light, a small voice called him back.

"Dad?"

Dean paused in the hallway and looked back through the doorway. "Yeah?"

"Does Shelley like me?"

Dean froze, then quickly lied, "Yeah, of course." *Was* it a lie? Was Aaron something she had to endure on his behalf, or was she actually warming up to him?

"Trevor's dad said she doesn't like kids."

"She's just... not used to kids. That doesn't mean she doesn't like you."

Aaron digested that in silence.

"Will I have to go away and live with Mom and Juan all the time?" he asked plaintively.

Dean was back in the room in a flash, kneeling by the bed. "Never," he promised. "I would never do that."

Aaron sat up, face serious in the light of multicolored night-lights. "But if she doesn't like me…"

"Do you remember when we got Bingo?" Dean asked.

"Yeaaaahhhh?" Aaron said in tones that didn't indicate he actually did.

"You were afraid that because I had Bingo to love that I wouldn't love you anymore."

"Yeeeeaaaaaahhhh."

"Did that happen?"

"Nooooooo."

"No matter who else there is, no matter what else happens, you and me, we're a team. That doesn't mean that you and I won't be in other teams, like your mom and Juan are a team, and you and Trevor are a team, and maybe me and Shelley will be a team. But you and me… you and me will always be a team, too."

That seemed to satisfy Aaron. He snuggled back into his pile of blankets and seventy stuffed animals and Dean tucked a few more around him. By morning they would be scattered on the floor and Aaron would be sleeping soundly, sideways in the bed.

The second call-out that week was the next day: an old farmer who'd taken a fall and undoubtedly broken his ankle. It was faster to send Turner with the fire truck to take him to the first care in the next town over for x-rays and a brace than it was to wait for an ambulance, so Dean walked back to the shop in half his turnout gear.

Someone had made a purchase and left cash on the counter. He had no idea what had been bought or who had bought it. Hopefully it would come out even at inventory time.

It was the third call-out that upended his life.

19

Shelley half-heartedly scrolled through her Instagram feed as she waited for the elevator, liking occasional random posts, then went through the messages she'd been ignoring.

"*What are you wearing, girlfriend? Missing your photos on IG! <3*"

"*Let's do lunch and snark about the Sallies fashion show!*"

"*Shell! I need you to alter a dress for a date TONIGHT. Drinks on me!*" (*It was from nearly a week ago*)

"*Check out my new boots! OMG! They cost $500 but my feet deserve it!*"

Had she never recognized how shallow and insubstantial her life really was? In trying to pack, she realized she had a wardrobe of clothing she'd only worn once, and nothing was practical. It was a sea of silk and fine Egyptian cotton and the best Shetland wool, the finest vegan leather, all name brands or hand-crafted.

But she had nothing the slightest bit suitable to wear for walking a dog in the woods, or playing ball with a seven-year-old.

Did moms even play ball? Was that just a dad thing? Were gender roles still in place like that?

Pinterest assured her that moms and their sons did precious crafts together with old buttons and lace scraps, and baked healthy cookies, while wearing cute pastel plaid shirts and jeans.

"Are you really quitting? Didn't we just lose your father?"

Shelley looked up to find that Jack, co-owner of the company, had joined her in the wait for the elevator.

She hadn't intended to quit, only to extend her leave of absence for a week or two, go back and make sure this thing with Dean was really a thing... and then convince him to come live with her here.

But this wasn't a life for him, and it certainly wasn't a life for Aaron. She'd never noticed how distant people here were, compared to Green Valley. She knew the names of the pets at her condo, but not their human owners. She locked and dead bolted her condo door and remembered that Dean never even locked his shop.

And she knew beyond the shadow of a doubt that she didn't belong here without him.

"I'm trying to get the Connor contract finished before I go," she promised. "And you can always call me if you have questions."

"This isn't two weeks' notice," Jack said, frowning.

"I'm spending two weeks' vacation time," Shelley said icily. "Would you like to argue about the details of my employment contract?"

Jack laughed. "I wouldn't dare," he said peacefully. "I'm sorry to hear you're going, and I hope you will be available for consulting work in the future."

Shelley nodded. "You have my contact information; I'm very amenable to helping you in the future. As my schedule allows."

Jack looked at her with curiosity that he was doing a poor job of hiding. "What is it you're going to be doing in Green Valley...?"

Shelley stared back at him.

She was going to be a *mom*.

Because her mate was a package deal, and she already couldn't imagine her life without him.

It was ridiculous, and she'd known this guy a few days, and kids terrified her, and here she was, quitting her job and weeding through her impractical shoes and wondering where she could buy hiking boots that didn't make her look like an elephant.

Shelley realized she was still staring at Jack without answering, with her very best blank expression plastered over her face, and he was starting to squirm like he was being interrogated. "Sorry to pry," he said sheepishly as the elevator reached their floor.

Shelley blinked. "No, no, it's fine. It's… just… an unexpected life change."

"Not a bad one, I hope," Jack said sincerely. "You and your dad are okay?"

Shelley walked into the elevator next to him and smiled at her own reflection as Jack pressed the lobby button. "Yeah," she said in wonder. "More than okay. It's really good." *I got this.*

We got this, her lioness reminded her.

She left Jack utterly mystified behind her as she walked swiftly to the parking garage, her heels clicking across the concrete.

20

---

*D*ean was just biting into a sandwich at his dining room table when the call came. He put it down reluctantly and shoved his phone in his pocket.

His house was only a block and a half from the station, so he planned to simply jog there, but what he saw when he got to the sidewalk and had a view down the street froze his feet to the ground.

Oily black smoke was pouring from his shop down the street, dark and ominous against the sunny day.

Dean made his feet move at last, bolting down the block.

A small, alarmed crowd was starting to gather, pointing and talking.

Black, acrid smoke pouring from around the garage door, turning the familiar lines of his shop and the store next door into wavery alien shapes. It was eerie, and so quiet that Dean could hear the crackle of flames from within, even though he couldn't see any yet.

Dean had to make the split-second decision: sprint two buildings down to the station and get into turnout gear, or battle the blaze *now* in the clothes he was wearing.

Seconds mattered in structure fires. Dean did a conscious check for loose clothing, tucked his pants awkwardly into his boots (he was, at least, wearing fireboots), pulled a handkerchief from a pocket to tie around his face, and waded in to assess.

The office door handle wasn't hot, but the office was thick with dark smoke that burned at Dean's throat. This wasn't friendly campfire smoke, to make eyes water and send people scrambling for new seats when the wind shifted; this was its demon cousin, sending harsh fingers of pain instantly to protesting lungs.

There was no fire here, yet, but the smoke was coming in all around the door to the shop. Dean ducked impulsively into the bathroom, turned on the tap, and then broke off the faucet so that the water was squirting directly into the air, soaking the entire bathroom. He didn't have a sprinkler system, but he could improvise, and the bathroom was nestled between the shop and the store. If he couldn't save one, maybe he could save the other. He wet his handkerchief, and for good measure, got as much of himself wet as he could.

The fuse box was between the bathroom and the door to the store, and Dean wrenched the door to it open and shut off every fuse in succession. Something sparked, there was a crash from the garage, and the dim light on the coffee maker went out. It would be better to kill the main breaker, but that was around back, and at least another few minutes of detour. This would at least keep outlets from being active and prevent live wires.

There was an industrial-sized fire extinguisher behind the counter, and Dean could only find it by feel, grasping around and coughing. It was a comfortable heft in his hands, and he drew in a breath that hurt to the bottom of his stomach, knowing it would be the best breath he would have until this was over.

Then he kicked in the door to the shop, not even bothering to try the handle, and the heat and smoke doubled in intensity.

He couldn't see flames—the oily smoke was too thick—but he could see dirty flickering light, and hear the roar of the fire. It must be towards the back of the shop, to his right, against the wall to the bathroom. There was another extinguisher inside the door, so Dean wasn't frugal with the one he was holding, knocking off the safety and spraying everything in the direction of worst heat.

He held a map of the shop in his head, trying to figure out what was on fire, what hazards he wouldn't be able to see; it would be deadly to trip over the lift, or knock over an oil can. The welding setup was fortunately on the other side of the garage near the overhead door; the oxy-acetylene tanks were as far from the inferno as possible.

His eyes watered uncontrollably; even if the shop had not been filled with impenetrable smoke, he would have been blind.

I can smell, his bear told him helpfully. *The fire is* there.

Dean forged forward, hopeful he wasn't letting any fire get behind him, and he could hear when he managed to hit open flame by the angry hiss of dying fire. He unloaded the extinguisher in that area, completely blind by now, choking for air, and trusting his bear's direction.

It grew gradually lighter in his hands, and Dean finally threw away the empty cylinder. Another extinguisher. He had another. It was back by the door to the office, an agonizing distance behind him, now. Somewhere, glass shattered.

Dean turned, and had no idea which direction to go.

He could hear the fire, which had begun to gutter under his assault, gain new strength.

Behind him.

Never let the fire get behind you.

Dean was down on his knees now, pressing the handkerchief to his mouth and dragging air through it. Should he shift? Would it do any good, or just confuse a coroner later?

Then he heard the wail of a siren, an uncommon sound in the sleepy little town of Green Valley, and there was a sudden rush of fresh air to his lungs as the overhead door was wrenched open with a grinding squeal.

"Dean, you moron!"

"Get the water on!"

"Do you see him?"

"Don't hit him with the spray!"

Then Dean heard the grumbling motor of the water cannon pump, and the roar of water.

"Let's go, you idiot." Someone in turnout gear, voice muffled by their SBCA, had an arm under him, helping him back up. Carter, Dean realized.

Turner must be on the water cannon, which was blasting into the garage to one side of him, creating waves of thick steam that mixed with the smoke, hot and thick.

Dean tried to get his feet under him, failed, and when he tried to breathe there was only fire and darkness.

21

$\mathcal{S}$helley didn't realize exactly how many people lived in Green Valley until she drove in that afternoon and found the entire population gathered downtown. For a moment, she thought there was some kind of celebration going on—then she recognized the flashing lights as a police car, and an ambulance—and they were right in front of Dean's shop.

But it wasn't Dean's shop, it was a ruin of Dean's shop, blackened and burnt, and the side of the store was coated in soot.

There were too many people for Shelley to pull directly up to the action, so she parked the car at the nearest curb and jumped out.

"Dean, Dean?"

Shelley pushed her way carelessly through the crowd and found him at last, sitting on the sidewalk with his head in his hands. He was almost black with soot, and his shoulders were slumped in exhaustion and defeat. He was flapping a hand at an EMT who was trying to put a blood pressure cuff on him.

Seeing him did a whole host of things to Shelley's insides. She was terrified and joyful and relieved and she wanted him even though he was as dirty as she'd ever seen anyone in her life. She hardly even noticed the people who were staring and whispering and standing around gossiping about the fire.

"Dean," Shelley said in soft sympathy as she sat down beside him. "Dean, your shop, I'm so sorry. Are you okay?"

He gave her a desperate look, longing and hungry, then his expression shuttered in a way that Shelley practiced in the mirror.

"No one was hurt," he said roughly. "That's the important part. No one got hurt."

The grief in his voice belied his optimistic words.

Shelley had seen the damage to the building; she knew that the shop was a total loss, and it was something of a miracle that the attached hardware store wasn't also.

She tried to put an arm around him, but Dean stopped her. "You'll ruin your jacket."

"I don't care," Shelley said honestly. "It's just a jacket." But she settled for taking Dean's ash-blackened hand. He held onto her hand like he was drowning and Shelley's world reduced to his touch. This was not the reunion she had imagined. The kisses she'd fantasized seemed impossible in these circumstances.

She was keenly aware of her out-of-place businesswear and the eyes of the grandmas and gawkers. A few people were taking pictures on their phones.

"You're an idiot, Dean."

Shelley looked up with a flash of anger, to see a firefighter nearly as dirty as Dean standing behind them.

"I'm glad you got there when you did, Turner," Dean said simply, without looking back.

"What the hell were you thinking, Dean? You don't go into structure fires without gear."

"Saved the shop," Dean said grimly. "Maybe more."

"It wasn't worth the risk!" Turner said sharply. He was older than Dean, with a head of silvered brown hair. His glance at Shelley was unfriendly.

Shelley's hand tightened in Dean's. She wasn't sure which one of them was squeezing.

"I thought it was," Dean protested, standing and turning stiffly to face him, dropping Shelley's hand as he did. Shelley got to her feet and barely kept herself from trying to get between them to protect Dean. She had to fight to rein in her lioness' instincts. This wasn't her battle, even if it was her mate.

"I disagree," Turner growled. "You're reckless and irresponsible, and this isn't the first time you've made a stupid choice."

Dean's hands went into fists at his side. "No one got hurt."

"You'd be dead if I hadn't gotten here when I did," Turner reminded him.

Dean didn't deny it.

"Look, Dean, I'm not going to watch you break your kid's heart. You're off the squad."

"You can't do that," Dean said in disbelief. The catch of his breath made him cough alarmingly and Shelley swayed in place keeping herself from reaching out to him.

"I just did," Turner said gruffly.

"There are only three of us," Dean reminded him hoarsely.

"Now there's two."

Shelley wanted to step in, wanted to do… anything. But she knew that she was an outsider here, an unknown stranger, so she hovered anxiously to one side and steamed.

"Look," Turner said more gently. "You've got a big mess here to deal with, and a kid, and—" he glanced at Shelley skeptically but didn't finish the sentence. "Maybe you just need a little time off. I'm not saying this is permanent, I'm just saying you need a break. Because stupid—"

"It wasn't stupid," Dean growled.

"*Stupid* decisions are going to do more harm than good."

"You're making a mistake," Dean told him, shaking his head.

"It's mine to make," Turner said firmly.

Someone called from within the burnt-out garage, "Hey, Turner!" and he left Dean with a final scowl and one sour glance at Shelley.

"Dean…" she said achingly.

He shrugged, angry and distant. Shelley could feel the prickles of humiliation and despair from him.

"Can I help?" she asked desperately. "If you need money to rebuild…"

"I don't want your money!"

Shelley had never heard Dean angry. She knew that he was hurting, and feeling uncertain; it was like a wave of emotions that wasn't hers, and she knew just as clearly that his anger wasn't intended for her, but for himself.

"It doesn't have to be money," she said gently. "If there's something else I can do…"

He gave a great, tired sigh. "Aaron gets off from school in an hour. I've… got a lot of paperwork and cleanup to do. Could you see that he does his homework, and get him dinner? I… might be home really late."

Babysit.

He wanted her to babysit.

Without a single hesitation, Shelley said, "Yes. I can do that."

Even as she wondered if she really *could*.

22

Dean knew what kind of courage it took Shelley to accept his request to watch Aaron; even through his anger and frustration he could feel her fear and resolve.

"Thanks," he growled. "The house is unlocked. You can ask at the neighbors if you need anything."

"We'll manage fine," Shelley said serenely from behind her smile.

He considered kissing her, because it had been four whole days since he'd last tasted her lips, but the murmurs of the gawkers and the prying eyes of the gathered neighbors made him hesitate.

She was the one who stepped forward and gave him a perfectly chaste kiss on his sooty cheek, then walked away down the sidewalk with her heels clicking.

Dean felt like his world was walking away and wished he could call her back. He wanted her arms around him, he wanted the smell of her to chase away the reek of smoke in his nose.

He wanted his chest to stop hurting.

I can help you, his bear promised. *We'll find a quiet place and I can help heal you.*

Dean reached for the phone that had been in his pocket, but it refused to turn on. He wasn't sure if it had gotten too hot, if he'd fallen on it, or if smoke had somehow damaged it. Maybe the battery was just dead.

He felt made of smoke, like it had crept into all his pores and transformed him into something dark and oily.

And Turner... maybe Turner wasn't wrong.

"Are you Dean James?"

Dean looked up from his contemplation of his dead phone to find a paunchy, frowning man regarding him.

"I'm Dean," he offered cautiously. It was unusual to see strangers in Green Valley.

"Fred Averly," the man said, offering a hand. "I'm the adjuster with Midwest Insurance."

Dean shook Fred's hand. He'd bought the policy on-line when he first bought the shop and attached store. He held up his phone. "I haven't even had a chance to call them yet."

Fred's smile looked forced. "I've already talked to the police and requested a copy of the incident report, but I understand that you were the first one on the scene." His look was nothing short of suspicious.

"Yes," Dean said, as mildly as he could. Was he going to be accused of insurance fraud? His bear growled a warning from his chest. "I'm... I *was* part of the volunteer fire department." Did that seem too pat?

Fred looked him up and down even more skeptically, then started handing Dean paperwork. "It's best if you get these things filled out as quickly as possible so we can expedite your claim. Do you mind if I start taking photographs?"

Dean took the forms, leaving dirty fingerprints on every page as he flipped through them. "Go ahead. The cops already have some."

The shop had stopped smoldering, and Fred fastidiously went into what was left of it, careful not to brush up against anything in his cheap suit as he started snapping shots.

Dean watched him a little while, then took the forms and walked to the fire station for a shower; he had a set of spare clothes there, and what he was wearing couldn't be salvaged. Maybe Carter could help him figure out the forms when he'd gotten the worst of the black off.

But it wasn't Carter who was sitting at the crew table when Dean staggered out of the shower, it was Turner.

The station was little more than a glorified garage, with a basic bathroom in the back, a work bench and a table with three chairs that was comfortable to sit at only if the fire truck—a battered surplus wildfire truck—wasn't parked there occupying most of the space.

Dean had left the paperwork sitting on the table, and Turner was flipping through it thoughtfully.

"Pretty ridiculous how much crap they think people keep track of," he said dismissively. "Who the hell knows when the last time the trees were cleared back from the edge of the building."

"Probably when the place was built in sixty-three," Dean suggested warily. He still sounded like a lifetime smoker, his voice rough. If he breathed too deep, he coughed.

There was coffee in the pot and Dean took a cup, black, and sat down across from Turner, mostly because his legs didn't want to hold him up anymore. His bear was anxious to get somewhere to shift, but Dean wasn't even sure if he could get somewhere private without collapsing. The hot shower had taken more out of him than he expected.

"I wasn't kidding," Turner said, putting the paperwork down.

"Maybe they figure the claim period will expire before I can get everything filled out," Dean said with a crooked grin. The coffee was old, but still hot.

"I'm not talking about the insurance crap," Turner said grimly.

"I'm not sorry," Dean grumbled. "It turned out fine."

"I'm not even really talking about this fire," Turner said, taking off his hat and rubbing his short hair. "Dean, you've been… really hard on yourself since… since Deirdre left you."

Dean blinked at him. He hadn't thought about Deirdre once that day. He wondered if anyone had called and told her about the fire yet. The town had pretty well turned against her during their divorce, despite his best efforts, but gossip was gossip and it would be hard for some of the town hens to resist sharing the news.

"You've been taking a lot of unnecessary risks," Turner pointed out. "Not just on call-outs, either. You've pretty well bankrupted yourself on that shop, haven't you? Is that why you went in to try to save it?"

Dean scowled across the table, the coffee cup clenched in his hands. He didn't answer.

"Look, Dean, you've got friends, people who care about you…"

"If you remind me about Aaron and give me a guilt trip about taking risks when I've got a kid at home…"

Turner frowned. "That's not where I'm going with this. You've been burning your candle at both ends, Dean. That's not good for you, and no, that's not good for Aaron, and it's not good for your judgment. What I'm saying is that you should just step back a little, take a break. Regroup. That girl…"

Shelley. His mate. "What about her?" He sounded as defensive as he felt.

"You serious about her?" Turner's look across the table was suspicious.

Serious didn't begin to cover what he felt for Shelley. He was more serious than he'd ever been in his life, more determined, more focused. "Yeah. Yeah, I am."

"I wouldn't have guessed she was your type, but she's a fine-looking woman, and you look happy with her. So go do that, for you."

"What do you mean…?"

"You've been doing what's right for everyone else, Dean. Ever since you got out of high school, you were working for other people, arranging your life trying to be everything to everyone. You can't be the best business owner and the best mechanic and the best dad and the best fire fighter all at once. Take a step back, try to be the best for you for once."

"Is that why you pulled me off the squad?" Dean protested. "Because you're trying to play psychiatrist? Green Valley needs…"

Turner stopped him. "Jamie's coming back from her summer

job in Alaska next week, we'll put her on the squad for the winter. We can re-evaluate your participation in the spring. See where the store is, what the shop is doing… where you are with your new girl. Green Valley Fire can weather a season without you."

Dean knew when he was beaten, and to be honest, felt a little relieved.

If he had to admit it, he was tired. Not just the bone-deep tired from inhaling too much smoke and standing in the hot shower too long. It was the tired of working two jobs on top of being a small town firefighter and trying to be an on-point single dad. It was the exhausted tired of keeping a brave face to the world, pretending he didn't feel completely alone.

And now there was Shelley, and he didn't have to be alone. Suddenly, the heart-whole face he tried to show to the world was the unexpected truth, and everything else felt like empty busyness.

Turner, watching him, must have guessed at the turmoil in Dean's chest. "If you need a reference, I'll vouch for you." He put a hand across the table and Dean thoughtfully shook it.

2 3

Shelley stood in the middle of the house and stared around. Bingo sat down and leaned against her while she absently scratched his ears. His tail beat a steady swishing thump on the floor.

She wasn't ready for this, for Aaron without Dean to act as a buffer. There was no way she could handle an active seven-year-old boy by *herself*.

There weren't enough mom blogs in the world to prepare her.

Shelley could feel the panic rising in her throat. She'd kept it under control with Dean, because Dean needed her, and because she was an expert at keeping everything stuffed down around other people.

Except that Dean *didn't* need her.

He didn't want her money, he knew she was hopeless at... at basically everything useful. She didn't know what to do with dogs or kids, she couldn't cook, and she was barely capable of cleaning. She had brought her car to the shop with a *loose license plate*.

Dean hadn't asked her to quit her job; he probably knew that this whole thing was doomed. She'd just been impulsive and stupid and overly-optimistic and she'd felt like maybe a mate could fix her, and here she was on the brink of a panic attack because she was pretty sure she couldn't do the *one thing* he'd asked of her...

Her hand was wet.

Bingo was licking her hand enthusiastically, because she'd stopped scratching his ears.

Shelley crouched tentatively. "You're a good dog," she said, because that seemed to be what you were supposed to say to a dog.

Bingo obviously thought this was the best thing anyone had *ever* said to him, and went into a spasm of wiggling and wagging his tail and butting his head against Shelley's neck and licking the air noisily. Only shifter strength kept Shelley from keeling over backwards at his loving assault.

"Okay, that's good, that's enough, down or back, or whatever," Shelley said, but she laughed as she said it, and scratched his ears.

Suddenly Bingo's ears pricked and he gave a happy bark and bounded for the door, just as Aaron threw it open. "Dad?"

Bingo gave him a joyous lick and bounced around him, sniffing his backpack hopefully.

"Hi Aaron," Shelley said, standing up again.

Aaron's face understandably fell. "Oh, hi." He dropped his backpack in a heap by the door and Bingo investigated it with a wagging tail.

"Your dad is really busy tonight getting everything sorted at the auto shop," Shelley explained nervously. "He asked me to come over and keep an eye on you."

Aaron shrugged. "Okay," he said morosely. He wandered towards the kitchen and Shelley followed him helplessly.

He must be worried about his dad, about his dad's shop. Shelley resisted the urge to use her smart phone to look up 'cheering up 7-yr-old.'

"Do you, ah... want a snack?" Hadn't he been all about eating the last few times she'd seen him?

"Maybe."

Bingo gave up on his search of the backpack to trot into the kitchen hopefully and Aaron hugged him around the neck and ruffled his ears.

"Do you want something to drink?" Shelley tried desperately. What else did kids *do*?

"Nah," Aaron repeated.

Shelley had already opened the fridge and was frowning into it. There was some kind of meat, thawing in a shallow dish, a few dubious leftovers in tupperware that Shelley couldn't identify, as well as vegetables, milk, eggs, cheese. Not food, just ingredients. "Carrots?" Shelley offered helplessly.

Aaron flopped down on the floor with Bingo and they started roughhousing, Bingo licking and wagging his tail so vigorously that his entire backend was in motion. They hit the little table in the corner and it danced in place.

Shelley shut the fridge door and stared at them in consternation. Was this the kind of activity she should discourage? Or would that just make her a big meanie? She thought longingly of the pills in her purse, but they left her feeling wrung out and slightly dazed. She needed all of her wits for this large challenge in a small package.

She was saved having to make any decisions by a knock on the door.

Bingo went into a flurry of happy barks, bounding for the front of the house. Shelley kneed him out of the way and opened the door to a woman with gray braids that she recognized from her father's wedding; one of Tawny's friends. She was holding a casserole dish and Shelley hoped they hadn't been introduced before because she had no idea what her name was.

She looked at Shelley without smiling. "Brought a casserole for Dean," she said.

"Oh," Shelley said, equally surprised. That was a thing people actually did? "Thank you…" she was trying to keep Bingo back, hampered by Aaron trying to squeeze around her other side to see what was happening.

"Who is it?"

"Shame about his shop," the woman said. "Very tragic."

"Yes," Shelley agreed. "Very trag… oh, Bingo!"

The dog escaped and trotted straight to the woman, who was

not very tall. She put the casserole up in the air, which Bingo took as a challenge, bouncing to investigate.

"Bingo, no! Sit! Don't!" Shelley cried, as Aaron came around her other side saying, "Hi Mrs. Fredrickson!"

Shelley took Bingo by the scruff of the neck and held him firmly back, only wondering afterwards if it was a demonstration of more strength than she ought to show. "I'm so sorry," she said, trying to make it look as if she was struggling. "Sit!"

Bingo panted happily and sat, tail swishing on the porch. Shelley tentatively let go of him and he flopped over on his side, pretending he'd never had any interest in the casserole whatsoever.

"I'm Marta," the woman introduced herself. "Marta Fredrickson. I live in the brick house on Parker."

"Shelley," she said, feeling shy. "Shelley Powell."

Marta gave her a narrow-eyed look. "You're Shaun's sister, then. Damien's daughter."

"I… yes."

"Lot of you Powells around these days with your money and your shiny cars," Marta said with a sniff. She handed the casserole to Shelley. "Heat it up for 30 minutes at 350." She said it dubiously, as if Shelley might not be capable of such a task.

"Thank you," Shelley said, blinking at her. "It's very… er… kind of you."

Marta made a harrumph, and Shelley couldn't decide what she meant by it. "Dean's a good young man," the woman said, and her skeptical look at Shelley's impractical heels said plenty.

Aaron had disappeared, and Shelley wished she could do the same. Bingo had sat up to lick himself noisily, one leg in the air as he investigated his genitals with his tongue.

Trying not to laugh at the absurdity, Shelley politely agreed, "Dean *is* a good man. He will appreciate the casserole very much and I will tell him that you stopped by. Thank you."

Marta seemed pleased by her response and nodded crisply. "You'll do," she said cryptically, with a glance at Bingo, who was still very busily grooming himself. "Good luck."

Shelley closed the door behind her, mystified, and brought the casserole dish in to the kitchen.

"I don't want to eat that," Aaron declared.

Shelley supposed she should be glad that he had waited until Marta had left to voice his opinion.

She didn't particularly want to eat it, either, but knew she should say something to set a good example. "It was very kind of Mrs. Fredrickson to bring it by." She sounded unbelievably uptight.

The casserole looked singularly unappealing, with its hard brown noodles and green peas. Canned peas, Shelley suspected. It definitely didn't look anywhere near the caliber of the casserole Dean had made her. "Maybe it tastes better than it looks?"

It didn't.

Shelley sat across from Aaron at the table and they both pushed it around on their plates and took skeptical bites that weren't rewarded.

"Oh, screw it," Shelley finally said, causing Aaron's head to jerk up and his eyes to go wide. Shelley put down her fork and stood up. "Get your jacket, Aaron. We're going shopping." She put on her jacket and sunglasses and swung her purse over a shoulder.

Aaron obediently grabbed his jacket and stuffed his arms into it, never once taking his eyes off of her. "What are we shopping for?" he asked.

"Junk food."

Aaron nearly fell over Bingo, who had gotten excited by people putting on coats and was trying to make sure no one forgot him.

"Junk food?" Aaron shoved Bingo back from the door as Shelley opened it.

"Junk food," Shelley said firmly. "There are some days that require it, and this is obviously one of them."

Bingo whined as they shut the door and shortly appeared in the window, looking wistfully after them.

It took a little effort to figure out how to walk with the little boy; Shelley was used to a long, confident stride, but he had to scamper to keep up, and then when she tried to take shorter steps, he was pulling her faster.

The grocery store had no name out front, but Shelley was sure it must be named Shirley's or Mary's or Mom's. Shelley took a basket at the door. Aaron, his hand still in hers, led her directly to an aisle of treasures.

"What do you want to get?" Shelley asked, snagging a personal bag of ridged potato chips for herself.

Aaron start to agonize between cheese puffs and seasoned corn chips. Shelley waited for a few moments as he hemmed and hawed, then tipped both of them into her basket. "We're going to need chocolate," she declared.

Sweets were on the next aisle over, beside a display of rakes and cow-patterned garden gloves. Hot tamales went into the basket, and a bag of peanut M&Ms. "They have nuts in them, so they're sort of healthy," Shelley told Aaron. "Next we'll need root beer."

Aaron looked at her like she'd just announced that down was up and led her to the tiny soda display, where Shelley grabbed a liter of root beer. "Ice cream," she directed Aaron, whose eyes got very big indeed.

There were two upright freezer displays and one small chest freezer, absolutely jam-packed with local meat, frozen vegetables, and an eclectic selection of expired ice cream. Shelley selected a pint of vanilla almost unreadable with frost.

"They have corn dogs," Aaron said wistfully, and Shelley remembered how avidly he'd eaten them at Gran's Grits.

Shelley picked up the box of frozen corn dogs and threw them into her heaping basket as well. "Where do we check out?"

The vacant cashier's desk was cluttered with stands selling candy, and obviously home-printed pamphlets for local churches. There was a t-shirt rack sporting cheap Halloween costumes in all sizes.

"Have you thought about what you want to be for Halloween?" Shelley asked as they waited for someone to show up.

"I want to be the Flash!" Aaron said enthusiastically, flipping through the offerings. There were seven sizes of ice queen costumes, an Iron Man, a few Batmen, a scarecrow, two pirates, and several sexy nurses and police officers in adult sizes.

Shelley fingered the cheap material and the terrible seams and frowned. "Do you want me to make you a costume?" Halloween was a few weeks out; it shouldn't be too hard to whip up a pair of pajamas in the right color and appliqué a logo.

Aaron was staring at her. "You can *do* that?"

Was it a dig on her ability to do anything?

"Sure, I sew all kinds of things," Shelley said. It would be a first for a kid's costume, but Shelley wasn't going to mention that. She altered her own clothing all the time, and she'd made a lot of doll clothing as a child, this would just be halfway in between. She eyed the cluttered store. "Do they sell fabric here?"

The fabric section was next to some dusty greeting cards. It was one shelf about three feet wide, and nearly half of the selection was plaid, but there was a half bolt of red polar fleece and some yellowish bric-a-brac. Shelley looked up Flash on her phone and made Aaron point out the best costume. "We could probably make this work," she said, giving the fleece an experimental stretch. "I bet Tawny has a sewing machine."

Aaron was ecstatic, and hugged the bolt of material to his chest, bouncing around. "I'm going to be the Flash!" He demonstrated by running as fast as he could down one of the aisles, and crashed into a display of seed packets. The fabric fell to the floor and unrolled off its cardboard core, while little paper packets of seeds scattered in all directions.

I just quit my job for this, Shelley thought in sudden panic. *What was I thinking?* She clenched her purse in her hands desperately.

"I got it!" Aaron hollered, righting the display. He picked up the seed packets and jammed them back into the wire pockets at random. He stepped on the fabric several times.

"You can't— I just— Let me—" Shelley winced at every creased seed packet and every dirty foot on the fleece and fought her terror back, aware of her lioness' anxious presence. She wasn't going to freak out *now*. She'd been doing so well this week!

She marched down the aisle and began putting the seed packets back in the appropriate pockets. "You can't just jam them in anywhere," she scolded.

Aaron, subdued, handed her the seeds as she worked, and she sorted swiftly. She chose alphabetical because she had no idea what the original organization had been, each variety in its own space, bent corners smoothed. A few of the seed packages were ripped, so Shelley threw them on top of the basket.

"Sorry, Shelley," Aaron said sheepishly, hugging the loose fleece to himself.

"It's okay," Shelley assured him, and herself. "It's all picked up now. We got this."

The merry mood was bruised, and their ice cream and corn dogs were sweating in the warm air as they went back to the cashier.

There *was* a cashier now, at least, a dark-haired, no-nonsense Asian woman who was talking with… the woman who had delivered the casserole. Marta? Was that her name? And here were Shelley and Aaron with a basket full of corn dogs and sugar like a slap in the face.

You're on a roll, Shelley, she told herself sarcastically. *Let's just insult Dean's friends and family and let his kid run wild in the store. Great adulting.*

She briefly considered saying that Bingo had eaten the hapless casserole and then raised her chin defiantly. If Marta didn't mention it, neither would she. She worked well under pressure, Shelley reminded herself firmly. This felt like more pressure than a whole room full of lawyers circling bloody waters as both women turned their eyes to the basket she put defiantly down on the counter.

"You must be Shelley," the cashier said neutrally, picking up the seed packets. It earned her a second look, and Shelley realized she'd managed to get six packets of frilled red cabbage. "I'm Julia."

"A little late for planting," the grey-haired woman said, not commenting on the other contents of Shelley's basket.

"Oh, I don't garden," Shelley said, only hearing how snobby she sounded when the words were out of her mouth. "I knocked over the display and these got damaged."

Aaron stared up at her. Did he really think she would throw him under the bus? It was only an accident.

"You don't *have* to pay for them," Julia said dubiously.

"I insist," Shelley said firmly.

The cashier rang them up at seventy-two cents apiece, then started in on the contents of the basket.

"Shame about Dean's shop," Julia said, shaking her head. "He's worked so hard to keep it running since..."

Both women looked at Shelley and the gray-haired woman asked point blank, "So, did you two meet on the Internet? One of those dating app things?"

"Oh, ah, no," Shelley said. "We met just, last week. I was here for my Dad's wedding and I needed some... work done on my car." A loose license plate. Shelley made a mental facepalm at the memory.

"Dean's a good mechanic," Julia observed blandly. "Good dad, too."

Shelley was keenly aware of Aaron at her side. She made a generic noise of agreement and wondered if it was a dig on her clear inadequacies.

She kept her chin high. She could do this.

24

Dean opened the door wearily, and was surprised when Bingo failed to come greet him. It was quiet and the light from the TV was flickering in the dim room.

Shelley was sitting at the couch watching the muted TV, and she craned her head around to look at him awkwardly. Dean realized as he walked in that she was pinned down, Bingo on one side of her with his head in her lap, Aaron on the other, asleep against her.

"Help," she mouthed.

"Bingo, down," Dean said quietly.

Bingo kept his head in Shelley's lap and his tail thumped happily.

"Bingo…"

Bingo gave a suffering sigh and oozed off of the couch onto the floor, where he promptly fell over on his side.

Half free, Shelley tried to squirm out from Aaron, freezing when he mumbled and held on.

"I don't want to wake him up," she whispered plaintively.

Dean came around the couch and scooped the un-protesting boy into his arms. "It's amazing what they can sleep through," he whispered back.

Aaron did come awake, though, halfway up the stairs, and mumbled, "You smell bad," into his shoulder. Dean had showered thoroughly at the station, twice, but he knew from experience that the smoky odor and the black pores would remain for a day or more.

His lungs at least felt better, after he'd shifted a few times privately out in the woods.

Aaron fell immediately back to sleep when Dean tucked him into bed, in exactly the position he lay down in.

Dean watched him sleep for a few moments, then trudged back downstairs.

Shelley was picking up the living room; the blankets they'd been wrapped in were folded over the back of the couch and she was putting dirty dishes in the kitchen.

"How did it go?" he asked.

Shelley looked stricken. "Oh, Dean. I did everything wrong. I fed him nothing but junk food, I burnt the corndogs, we watched a movie that was way too scary and stayed up long past his bedtime, and I swore in front of him at least six times. I forgot about homework. He ran into a display at the store and I had to buy six packets of frilled red cabbage seeds."

Dean stared. "Frilled red cabbage?"

"I'm a disaster," Shelley said. "I don't know why I thought I could do this. I'm so sorry."

He could feel the tension in her, fear and anxiousness in a tight band around her chest, and he forgot his own problems. "You did great," he said sincerely, pulling her into his arms.

She came willingly, sighing onto his shoulder. "You should be able to rely on me," she said mournfully. "I wanted to do this right."

"Did he get hurt?"

"No."

"Did he spend the whole night worrying about me?"

"Er, no… We actually had a pretty fun time."

"Have you ever babysat before?"

"Not once."

"And were you great at your first law contract?"

Shelley gave a hiccup of a laugh. "It came back bleeding with markups."

Dean put her at arm's length and looked into her distractingly magical silver eyes. "You did great," he repeated firmly.

She smiled at him and gave a little sniff, blinking fast. "Oh good grief," she said. "Here I am whining about my motherly inadequacies and you just lost your shop. Dean, I'm so sorry. What can I do?"

Dean had managed to forget for a moment, and it all came crashing back at once. Bingo's snore was loud in the quiet room.

"I... don't know," he said, remembering the sour-faced insurance inspector and the way he had pounced on the fact that the fire station wasn't accredited anymore. He remembered Turner, cutting him off the squad in front of the whole town... and Shelley.

"Did they figure out what caused it?" Shelley asked quietly.

Dean shrugged. "It's not official, but there was a power surge reported by the power company shortly before smoke was spotted. Old wiring, a pile of greasy rags or something flammable... they're calling it an accident."

"How bad was the store?"

"Some pretty good smoke damage," Dean said, trying not to feel pained. "I'll have a fire sale in the fullest meaning of the term."

She gave him a narrow-eyed look that suggested she was picking up on what he was really feeling. "Oh, Dean," she said tenderly. "I hope the insurance doesn't take too long to get it all replaced."

Dean stuffed his doubts down as far as they would go. "I'm sure it will be fine," he lied.

It would have worked with Deirdre, he thought, but Shelley wasn't fooled. She stepped close to him and put her hands gently on his face. "Whatever you need from me, let me know," she said firmly. "I will stuff your kid with junk food and watch inappropriate movies with him anytime you want. Though I may have to buy some earplugs because oh my god, there were times I was afraid he was *never* going to stop talking."

Dean had to laugh. "That's definitely a thing," he agreed. "You get used to it..." Standing so close to her, her hands soft on his cheeks, he was reminded that it had been a whole week since he'd kissed her and it was suddenly very urgent that he make up for that lost time.

"Aaron?" Shelley asked, with a nervous look at the stairs.

"He once slept through a tornado siren," Dean assured her.

She met him with her mouth open, and her arms slid up around his neck. All of her fears and all of his despair melted away in the wave of need and desire that welled up from the pit of his stomach... and places lower.

"I *missed* you," Shelley murmured, when he moved his mouth to her elegant neck.

"I love you," Dean whispered in return.

Bingo was still asleep, so the couch was a safe place to lay her down and peel all of her clothing off.

He kissed every inch of skin as he uncovered it, lingering at her hot, neatly-trimmed pussy as he pushed her tailored pants down over her curvy hips.

"Dean," she cried softly. "Dean!"

He kissed down her long, long legs, even tickling her feet with his tongue as he slipped her socks off.

She giggled, and Bingo gave a groan in his sleep that made them both freeze for a moment.

Then he was stripping off his own pants and coming to cover her... awkwardly, because dog or no dog, the couch proved not to be a particularly comfortable place, and not quite wide enough to accommodate them both. She was hot and wet enough that it didn't matter for the first several thrusts, and she bit back cries of pleasure and scratched his back as she arched to meet him desperately.

They moved briefly to the floor, then scrambled up the stairs as quietly as possible, creeping past Aaron's room like nude thieves.

Then, finally, he was laying her down on the bed and slipping inside her again, where nothing mattered but his bear's demands and her soft cries.

They curled together afterwards, and Dean drew more comfort

from her long limbs in his arms than he would have guessed possible. He'd missed her so badly, needed her so deeply…

They dozed for a while, and when he went to get another blanket against the chill of the autumn night, she woke up and touched him. One touch led to another, and another, and the rest of the night was spent in an exhausted blur of making love.

25

The alarm woke them both entirely too early.

Shelley fumbled at the bedside table with her face still buried in her pillow until Dean finally reached over her and turned off the alarm.

"Didn't your shop burn down yesterday?" she groaned. "Doesn't that at least mean you don't have to get up today?" Then she rolled over, mortified. "Is it too soon to joke?"

"School day," Dean said grimly. "You can sleep. I have to get the slowest kid in the world ready to go."

"I'll get up, too," Shelley said, sitting. She yawned. "We probably should have spent more of last night sleeping."

Dean looked over at her and smiled. His hair was sleep-rumpled and his eyes were tired. "It was worth it," he said, leaning over to kiss her.

"It was worth it," she echoed, when he finally released her.

"I'm going to take a shower," he said with a parting kiss on the forehead.

She lay back on the bed as he left. "I'll be up," she mumbled unconvincingly.

She half-expected to fall back to sleep, but her brain woke up then, and dragged her into a spiral of all the things she'd done wrong. She'd quit her job, she reminded herself, burned her safety net, moved to a town where no one liked her... except Dean and maybe Aaron. But Aaron deserved a better mom, Dean deserved a better mate...

I love you, he'd said, the night before, but did he *really*? Was it just his bear? Was it just the sex? Who could love her?

Too late, Shelley recognized the trap her own mind was leading her into, and a wave of disappointment washed over her. She'd done so well, this entire week, kept herself so together. Having a mate had... *fixed* her, she'd thought. And wasn't sex supposed to cause lots of happy endorphins in the brain? Tears pricked her eyes. Dean didn't know what he'd *really* gotten, and she should just leave now and spare him the heartache of finding out how broken she really was.

It was getting hard to breathe and Shelley could feel her heart pounding irregularly in her chest. She needed one of the pills from her purse, but her purse was downstairs, with her clothes, and it seemed like an impossible distance. Her lioness was looming in her head like a terrifying shadow, angry at her weakness.

Let me help you, she growled.

But Shelley didn't trust her animal's help. Given the choice between flight or fight, she would always run.

"Shelley? Shelley?!"

Dean found her later, half-dressed, sweaty and shaking, sitting on the floor next to the couch with her arms around Bingo, who was utterly delighted to be the center of her attention but less wiggly than usual.

"Are you okay?"

Shelley raised tearful eyes to him. "Not really," she admitted. He was barefoot, hair damp and sticking up in all directions. He was so *beautiful*.

Guilt swamped her. She was supposed to be the one being strong. Dean had just lost his business, his volunteer position. She should be comforting *him*.

Dean settled to a seat beside her and Bingo's little brain nearly exploded with the joy having two of his people so close, abandoning Shelley as she sat up and wiped her tears away. He head-butted Dean, tried to lick him, and when Dean went to gather Shelley into his arms, licked her, and tried to insert himself between them.

Dean shoved him away gently, pulling Shelley into his lap and wrapping his arms around her. "Tell me," he ordered.

"Anxiety," Shelley said into his chest. "Panic attacks. Things shifters aren't supposed to have." She gave a little hiccup of a laugh. "It was fun finding a therapist qualified to diagnose my special case, let me tell you."

"Pretty bad?" Dean prodded. He was making gentle circles with his hands on her back and Shelley could feel the last of her shakes ebb away into the dull, distant aftermath.

She felt numb, like she was wrapped in bubble wrap. Her lioness was a faraway growl and she could feel her body like it wasn't her own. Bingo had his head wedged into the half of her lap he could reach, panting happily.

"Sometimes," she admitted. "I usually get through things and have an attack later, when I'm safe. I have... pills, for when it's really bad. It's kind of a cocktail of prescriptions, because of course I burn things off faster than a human would."

"Of course," Dean agreed.

"I hate them. And... I... thought I was better. I hadn't had an attack since we met, and the anxiety... has been understandable and pretty low key. I thought... maybe I wouldn't do this again. I'd hoped." She'd hoped that finding her mate would magically fix her, she thought with chagrin. Like true love's kiss from a fairy tale.

"You've had a lot of changes, the last week or so," Dean observed.

Shelley was starting to think logically again. "Not as many as you have... but yeah." She gave a humorless chuckle. "I quit my job."

Dean's arms around her tightened in surprise and he was quiet. Doubtful? Angry? Was it too much pressure?

"I could probably get my job back, if things don't work out with us," she promised, glad for the buffer of the drugs. She knew it hurt to think that it might *not* work out, but she didn't *care* that it hurt right now. "You don't have to feel guilty or… obligated or anything. I didn't mean it as a… trap. I just thought that if this was something that was going to happen, it was going to happen all-in. I didn't want this to be just a fling, just a vacation."

"Even with… everything I come with?" Dean's voice was gentle, and Shelley couldn't get a read on his emotions through the muffling effects of the drug.

"Earplugs are cheap and I clearly have my own… baggage. Not that Aaron is baggage," Shelley added swiftly. "He's your son, and I will do my best to love him because you do. I will even try not to swear too much around him or let him watch scary movies. I just… wish I wasn't such a mess. You deserve better. You've got everything figured out, and I drop into your life like a new complication you don't need."

"You are every complication that I need," Dean murmured near her ear. "And if you think I've got everything figured out, you're sadly mistaken."

"You're a hero," Shelley reminded him.

"I'm an idiot," Dean corrected her. "My businesses are all failing, I'm mortgaged to my ears, I've barely been keeping my own life going. I've spent the last five years trying to be everything for everyone else because I didn't know how to say no to anything… because I had a hole in my life that I didn't know how to fill."

Shelley looked at him, feeling stupid. "You have Aaron."

"And I love Aaron," Dean agreed. "But there are only so many conversations I can have about Legos and farts before I go insane." He paused, and Shelley knew she was supposed to be figuring out what he was trying to say. "You, Shelley. I need *you*. I need your advice, and I need your good sense, and I need your humor and your kisses and that skeptical look you give me when you think I'm making fun of you."

His hand was on her cheek, this thumb making gentle circles. "We don't have to be perfect people to be perfect for each other."

"We're going to make our own life," he said firmly. "Our own future. Together. You and me and your brain, and if you sometimes need to take a pill and sit in a quiet room, I will never love you less for it."

Shelley wasn't aware that she was crying until he wiped the tears away for her, kissing her cheeks tenderly. "I love you, Dean," she said hesitantly. Even through the haze of her pills, she was absolutely sure of it. "I love you, and I will do everything I can to show you that every day."

"Can you help me with insurance forms?" Dean asked, with a crooked smile. "I feel like the world's biggest moron trying to figure out what they are asking for. I'm terrified I'm going to implicate myself for fraud or something. The adjuster seemed really interested in the fact that the fire department wasn't accredited anymore."

"Oh, yes," Shelley agreed instantly. "I'm great with contracts. And you should hear me on the phone; I will make them tremble in fear. I will squeeze them for every penny they owe you and they will hand it over gratefully."

"Man, I am glad you are on my side," Dean said, dragging a dramatic hand across his brow and Shelley giggled.

She sat up suddenly. "Wait, doesn't Aaron need to get to school? You should be doing that, not dealing with my stupid brain chemistry, shouldn't you?"

"It doesn't matter if he's late," Dean said. "You needed me."

Just like that. As if it was simple. She needed him, and he was there for her.

Shelley was sure it would feel amazing to know that if she weren't being cradled in the comforting dullness that her pill had created. She managed a grateful smile. "I'm okay now. I got this."

"We got this," Dean reminded her, and Shelley felt a well of love and trust breach the wall around her as he kissed her. "I love you…"

Bingo sighed longingly when he was ejected from their laps and they stood up.

"What can I do to help?" Shelley asked.

"Can you make a peanut butter and jelly sandwich?"

"Three ingredients, I think I can manage."

She finished buttoning up her shirt, and went to the kitchen while Dean went upstairs to wake Aaron up.

26

After they got a very sleepy and grumbling Aaron off to school with his lunch, Shelley went with Dean to work on the shop inventory and forms.

"You aren't required to answer some of these questions," she told him gravely, flipping through the forms. "They like to throw in all this optional stuff to trip you up. I swear, insurance is one big intimidation game, it's like they're trying to scare you into just not filing."

They talked about the fire department accreditation, too.

"We don't have enough money to keep up with the testing," Dean explained. "We keep things in good shape, we just can't prove it."

Shelley took notes on her phone with a stylus. "I wonder if you'd be eligible for grants," she said thoughtfully. "I'll do some research."

She waded into the ashy shop without hesitating, neatly writing down items that Dean pulled from the burnt wreckage and identified, looking them up on her smartphone and jotting down a current market price.

By the afternoon, they were both sweaty and sooty and Dean thought she had never looked so beautiful.

Her hair was pulled back up into a handkerchief, blonde strands of it sticking to her damp face. If she had started the day with any makeup, it was long gone, and she had a thick black smudge across one cheek that Dean didn't want to tell her about.

Various neighbors wandered in and out while they were working, commenting on the general awful state of things, sympathizing with the workload and the loss, speculating on the damage that might have been done, and without fail, offering to help with the cleanup.

Shelley shook her head in warning. "Don't clean up until the claim is settled," she warned. "It's all evidence."

She got many curious, speculative looks. Even her black cheek smudge and dirty clothes couldn't make her look less out of place.

He caught her frowning down at her shoes when everyone was gone, sitting on the sidewalk. They were smudged and scuffed.

"They're probably never going to be clean again," he said apologetically, handing her a lukewarm diet cola from the hardware store vending machine. The structure didn't have any power yet.

"They're just shoes," Shelley said firmly, as if she was trying to convince herself. She took a drink of her soda, grimaced at the temperature, and followed it with a thirsty second sip.

"Thank you," Dean said sincerely, popping the top to a warm root beer. "You didn't have to do this."

Shelley bumped shoulders with him. "I'm good at filling out paperwork," she said with a crooked smile.

"We make a good team," Dean told her.

The black smudge on her cheek hitched up with her smile.

They called it a day shortly before Aaron was due to get off of school and Shelley took the first shower.

Dean was shaking ash off of his pants on the porch when Deirdre pulled up with an out of character shriek of her car brakes.

She stomped up from the curb and Dean caught her wiping angry tears off her face.

"Dammit Dean! They said you charged in without turnout

gear! That you could have been killed! What were you thinking, Dean? Did you think about what that could do to Aaron if you'd died?"

"I wasn't killed." Dean kept his voice calm and reasonable. "I'm fine."

Deirdre gave a little whimper, and Dean automatically opened his arms. She stepped close to hug him, and he could feel her sigh against him. "Oh, Dean, I was so worried."

"I'm fine," he assured her. "I'm *fine*."

"I'm so sorry about the shop," she mumbled into his shirt. "It's not fair."

He was just thinking that her embrace felt so much different than Shelley's did, and that the strangest part was that Deirdre's was the one that didn't feel normal anymore, when Deirdre froze and then backed away from him.

"Shelley," she said carefully.

Barefoot, Shelley's approach had been cat-silent, and she was standing just inside the screen door. The black smudge was gone from her cheek and her hair was still damp around her face.

"Deirdre," Shelley replied, just as carefully.

Deirdre scuffed one foot along the porch. "I... ah... actually came a little early because I wanted to see if you wanted to grab a coffee at the bakery before I took Aaron home." Her voice suggested that she didn't expect Shelley to accept.

Dean could feel the prickly anxiety from Shelley, but he wasn't surprised when she nodded solemnly. "I'd like that," she said evenly. "Let me get some shoes."

"Sorry," Deirdre said sheepishly, when Shelley disappeared. "I hope I didn't make things... awkward by giving you a hug."

Dean had to laugh. "Awkward is kind of a running theme. We'll manage."

Deirdre chewed on her lower lip. "Are you... happy?"

The approach of Shelley's clicking heels prevented Dean from answering. The screen door swung closed after her with a bang, and she only hesitated a moment before stepping close to give him a swift goodbye kiss. Dean caught her face in his hands to make it slightly more than a utilitarian peck and there was a soft, real smile at her lips when she stepped back.

Deirdre looked delighted. "Oh, I'm so glad we're doing this," she chattered. "I've got so many questions, I'll try not to pry, and I've got so many stories to tell you about Dean! Do you mind if we walk? It's just a couple of blocks and isn't it a gorgeous day? I just love autumn, with all the colors and it's not so hot anymore, and of course, it's nearly Halloween, which is my favorite holiday. What's your favorite holiday, Shelley?"

Dean knew Deirdre was covering her nervousness with her babble, and it struck him that she was very different from Shelley, who tended to retreat to distant silence and formality when faced with the same stresses. Then he realized that he was watching his ex-wife walk away with his new girlfriend with the sole purpose of getting to know each other better and he had a moment of sudden dread.

This was a *terrible* idea.

27

"Have you had the pastries here yet? They're really amazing. Better than Clausen's, even, if you've ever been there. Of course, Clausen's doesn't have coffee, or a place to sit. I'm sorry, I'm just non-stop, you've barely got a word in edge-wise, do you know what you want to order?"

Shelley had more sympathy for Deirdre than the other woman probably imagined. She was clearly very nervous, and just as deter-mined to be friendly.

There was no line, and Shaun was behind the counter wiping off the espresso machine.

"A cinnamon roll and a…"

"Latte," Shaun finished for her. "Are you two together?"

"Yes," Shelley said, just as Deirdre said, "No."

"I'll get this," Shelley insisted.

Deirdre blushed. "You have to let me get the next one," she said. "An Americano and one of the cherry-filled danishes. Messy," she said to Shelley, "but worth it."

"For here?" Shaun asked with a grin.

"Yes," Shelley and Deirdre said together. Deirdre and Shaun were eyeing each other curiously, clearly trying to decide who the other person was and Shelley finally gave a sigh as Shaun passed plates over with their pastries. "Shaun is my brother," she explained. "He moved to Green Valley a little over a year ago and married Andrea. Shaun, this is Deirdre. Dean's ex-wife."

"Oh," they each said knowingly. "Oh."

"You must be Trevor's dad! Aaron talks about him all the time. It's nice to meet you," Deirdre said brightly, and they exchanged a handshake over the counter.

"You, too," Shaun answered, bemused. "I'll bring your coffees out."

They were the only customers, and they took the seat furthest from the counter, looking out the window.

"This used to be a general store when I was a kid," Deirdre offered, using a fork to take a bite of her danish. "And see that big brick building on the corner? That used to be a bank. Marta lives there now, and the inside is amazing. It still has the teller cages and her closet is in the old vault. Giant, tall ceilings, and marble everywhere."

"Green Valley is a really sweet little town," Shelley offered. Shaun's baking was as good as she remembered; the cinnamon roll was light and fluffy, with sticky, delicious frosting. He had sprinkled nuts on top without asking, remembering that she liked them.

"Emphasis on little," Deirdre said with a wince. "I... don't know what Dean told you. Or what anyone else has told you..."

Shelley was too busy feeling sorry for Deirdre to be nervous herself. "He told me," she said sympathetically. She leaned forward. "He's..."

"Your coffees," Shaun said, setting steaming cups in front of them. Like the entire image of the shop, they were cute and quaintly mis-matched. "I'll be closing up, but it will take me a while to finish in back, so don't let me rush you."

"Thanks," Deirdre said, and as soon as he had gone in back, she leaned forward avidly. "Dean's what now?"

"My mate," Shelley said, and just hearing the words raised a wave of satisfaction and peace in her.

"I knew it!" Deirdre crowed. "He wouldn't come out and say it, but it's obvious you're a shifter, and there was just something about the way you looked at each other." She lifted her cup and toasted a bemused Shelley. "I am so happy for you both."

She seemed greatly relieved and far less nervous after that, and Shelley found herself letting her guard down as they chatted. Just as she'd promised, Deirdre did have embarrassing stories about Dean in childhood, and Shelley shyly asked questions about Aaron that opened absolute floodgates.

"He tried to explain a game to me yesterday and do you sometimes not understand him even though he's using perfectly clear English words?" Shelley asked. "Because he was telling me about it for probably thirty minutes and I knew less about it at the end than I did at the beginning."

Deirdre held her sides and laughed. "That is completely normal," she assured Shelley.

They talked about the food he liked (nearly everything), and the tricks that Deirdre employed to get him to do chores and go to bed.

"He's allergic to cats," Deirdre added, and Shelley was glad she'd already drunk most of her coffee, because she startled and the contents of her cup sloshed to the edge.

"Probably not big cats," Deirdre said with a grin. "Tiger?"

"Lion," Shelley confessed, finding herself smiling in return.

"I'm a deer," Deirdre said cheerfully. "Which is a little easier, if you ask me. I got caught in our backyard last year, and it's a lot easier to explain a deer than it is an exotic wild animal. I just pretended to eat some flowers and was glad it wasn't hunting season. My neighbor posted photos on Facebook and I tagged myself before I realized that was a bad idea."

"I don't get a lot of chances to shift in the city," Shelley said wistfully. "That's one advantage to Green Valley. Lots of forest around here to go running in."

"Madison isn't too bad. Plenty of parks."

They talked until Shelley was sure that Shaun was regretting his invitation not to feel rushed and the sun outside was starting to set.

"Oh gosh," Deirdre finally said. "I bet Aaron's been home for ages and the boys are wondering where on earth we are."

Shelley left a generous tip and they walked outside.

"Do you mind if we walk the long way around?" Deirdre asked. "I… wanted to go by and see the shop. What's left of it."

It wasn't quite as alarming with the garage door down as it had been with the charred interior exposed. Black smoke stains around every entrance and vent only hinted at the damage inside.

"He was working there when we were both in high school," Deirdre observed, subdued. "He talked about going to school for engineering. He could have gotten a sports scholarship, but he didn't think it was fair because he was a shifter. He's always thinking about everyone else, you know. And later, when we were thinking about it again, suddenly Aaron."

"He's… a great kid," Shelley said, guessing she ought to say something.

Deirdre flashed her a swift look. "The best," she agreed, and her mouth was firm and without a trace of regret.

"I… I don't know a lot about kids," Shelley said, as if it wasn't the most obvious thing in the world. "He'll… probably come home with new swear words and bad habits, so I'm sorry in advance for that."

Deirdre's eyes softened and she laughed. "You'll do fine," she promised. "Aaron already thinks you're 'okay, I guess,' which is more enthusiastic than he gets about most people."

"I'll take 'okay, I guess,'" Shelley chuckled.

"If you need anything, just let me know," Deirdre said warmly. "I didn't know a thing about kids, either, and honestly, you just make it up as you go. They're a lot more resilient than you might think."

"Thank you," Shelley said genuinely. "I really appreciate that."

They walked around the back side of the shop, where the damage was more apparent: the back wall had been eaten clean through by fire at the top, the roof noticeably missing in places. Charred bones of the structure held up a blue tarp that rustled in the autumn wind, bright against the soot darkening everything else.

"It could have been a lot worse," Deirdre said practically, as they came back around the front.

Shelley wondered if that was the Green Valley motto.

They walked quietly back to Dean's house and paused at the curb before going in.

"Oh," Shelley said, suddenly remembering. "I offered to make Aaron a Halloween costume. He wanted to be Flash, we've bought fabric. I don't know if you'd planned anything…"

"Oh, that's wonderful," Deirdre said, to Shelley's relief. "I would have picked something up last minute at the store. It wouldn't have lasted five minutes into trick-or-treating. If I could have even found a Flash costume. Seven hundred ice queen costumes, a billion Batmans…"

"Lots of options if he wanted to be a sexy nurse," Shelley said dryly. "Even here."

Deirdre laughed. "You should get one of those for yourself," she suggested with a wink. "Dean would love it."

Shelley felt her cheeks heat.

"I like you," Deirdre said frankly. "I'm so terribly glad that Dean met you and I'm so happy to have you as a… er… step-ex?"

"I'm really happy to have you as a… step-ex, too," Shelley confessed.

"Moooooom!" Aaron was a small blue streak, accompanied by Bingo, who had only just noticed them when Aaron did and was barking twice as much to make up for it. The screen door was still slamming shut when the two reached them.

Aaron flung his arms around Deirdre and Bingo tried to lick her, then moved to Shelley, who patted him sedately on the head. "Dad's shop burned down, Mom! Did you know? The kids at school say it was a trad-egy and that Dad's a hero even if he's not a *super*hero and Trevor says they're going to give him a parade and Clara said that was stupid and the teacher told her not to say stupid and I'm hungry and did you bring me a cookie from the bakery?"

28

Handoff was always a measure of chaos, and Dean could not figure out how Shelley, with all her outward serenity, seemed to make it louder and more crazy just by being there. It took a solid twenty minutes of packing snacks for the drive and remembering a favorite stuffy that had to be brought and there was laughter and Deirdre was teasing them both without remorse and Bingo was so excited by everything that Dean worried his little dog brain was going to explode.

Finally, they were waving Deirdre and Aaron away down the quiet street and Bingo, exhausted, herded them back into the house and lay down at the threshold like a doorstop.

"Did you have a good cup of coffee?"

"It was good," Shelley assured him. "What's with the boxes?"

Dean grinned. "I'll show you."

He took her hand and led her to the back of the house. "This was my mom's sewing room. I thought you should have it. I don't have a lot of closet space upstairs, but there's another closet down here, and you should have your own space."

He'd only gotten about half of the boxes moved out. "I've been using this to store stuff my folks didn't want when they moved, and I just never got around to getting rid of it."

It was a sunny little room, looking out over the backyard. Blackberries had grown up and were filling in the bottom of the windows.

Shelley was quiet.

"We could… look for another house if you'd rather," Dean said. It was a pretty small room, and a small closet. Shelley was probably used to spacious apartments with matching furniture and coordinating decor. "I mean, once the insurance is settled." Probably she had enough of her own money to outright buy a house. There was so much they hadn't talked about.

"I love it," she said in a very small voice. Her hands were trembling and Dean realized that some of the tension he was feeling was hers, bubbling up.

Dean swept her into his arms without pausing to think about it. "What can I do?" he asked. "Do you need a pill?"

She turned in his embrace and sighed into him. "No," she said. "This is perfect. This is absolutely perfect. Just hold me."

They stood that way for an unmeasured time and he could feel her settle. "I'm sorry you have to have to deal with my stupid brain," she said, muffled in his chest.

"We don't use the word stupid in this house," he scolded her, just as if she was Aaron. Then he kissed the top of her head and added, "Besides, it's no hardship to have an extra excuse to hold onto you. You tell your brain to do whatever it needs to."

She smiled up at him. "I don't know about my brain, but the rest of me is exactly where I want to be." Her hands slipped up around his neck.

Dean leaned over and kissed her, slowly and full of promise. "We can live anywhere you want," he said seriously, drawing back. "Maybe… maybe the fire at the garage was a good reminder. It's just stuff. And this is just a place. We can be a family anywhere we go, anywhere we choose to be, whatever we decide to do. This is our chance to redefine our lives, make a new start. Yours and mine. Together."

Shelley looked at him so warmly, her silvery eyes full of wonder, that Dean wanted to drown in them. "Together," she agreed. "*Here.*"

"It's a small house," Dean warned. "It's a small *town.*"

"Then you'll never be very far away from me," Shelley said softly.

Then his mouth was on hers, and her arms were around his neck and he was perfectly, absolutely home.

29

Sure enough, Tawny did have a sewing machine, and she was more than happy to set it up for Shelley.

"I haven't unpacked this since we moved," the gray-haired woman said, putting it out on the desk in the spare room. "I'll show you how to thread it… if I remember."

"I've got it," Shelley said, popping the bobbin out and looping the thread around the pick-up hook.

"You know your way around a sewing machine," Tawny said with surprise.

"Why is everyone shocked when I can do something domestic?" Shelley asked more sharply than she intended. "I like nice clothing. Sometimes I make my own."

"Ever thought about going into fashion design?" Tawny asked innocently.

"It's not practical," Shelley said dismissively.

"Not everything has to be practical," Tawny said and Shelley gave her a wry sideways look because Tawny was the absolute epitome of a practical, down-to-earth grandmother. Shelley doubted she had ever done anything impulsive in her life.

She wondered if Tawny had talked to Damien; Shelley had once dreamed about working in fashion. Did her father even *know* that?

They set up the machine and Shelley lay the fabric out with the pattern pinned on top. It all looked adorably small and she held it up several times as she worked, bemused that someone so short could be so full of life as Aaron was.

Tawny offered to help and Shelley graciously accepted. Tawny cut the top while Shelley sewed the bottoms.

"I was looking at kids costumes online," she said. "You can find some really nice handmade costumes, but they are expensive, and it seems like a lot of investment into a one-time costume for a kid that will grow out of in a few months."

"I think that's why those cheap, disposable costumes are so popular," Tawny observed, adding a sleeve to Shelley's pile.

"It seems like there ought to be some kind of middle ground," Shelley mused. "A well-made costume that doesn't cost the world. Maybe with hems you can let out as they grow?" She held up the pants, which she had deliberately made longer than Aaron's measurements. They could be tacked up for now, and let out as he got taller.

"That's a great idea," Tawny agreed.

"I didn't think to get elastic," Shelley said, when the bottoms were otherwise finished; she wouldn't hem them until she had a chance to try them on Aaron.

"I'm sure I have some," Tawny said. "Let's see…"

That led to dismantling an entire closet of boxes containing fabric. "I should make your father something out of this," Tawny laughed, holding up a folded square of bright yellow fabric with cartoon bees all over it.

"That… doesn't look like Dad," Shelley said skeptically, biting off an extra string from the pajama shirt she had just put together.

"It's an inside joke," Tawny explained. "Your father is allergic to bees."

Shelley stared. "I had no idea. I didn't realize shifters *could* be."

"He went into anaphylactic shock right in front of me," Tawny recounted. "Collapsed right in my living room. I've never been so frightened."

"What did you do?" Shelley asked curiously. 911 wasn't exactly an option for shifters.

"He shifted. He explained that shifting can cause muscles and bones to heal, so there was no reason that it shouldn't also help stop an over-active histamine response."

"And it worked?"

"He was right as rain, in just a few minutes. Faster than a shot of epinephrine."

Shelley knew the trick for healing faster after shifting, but she hadn't imagined that the process would apply to the more complex parts of the body. "Curious," she said, filing away the information. "Oh, that's perfect!"

Tawny was holding up a strip of white elastic, excavated from the bottom of a bin.

"I'll take this with me," Shelley said. "And I can put that in by hand and pin all the cuffs for sewing tomorrow once I've had a chance to try this on him."

She glanced at the clock. School didn't get out for another hour, but she wanted to be sure to be there when Aaron came home. Dean was working late at the store to get ready for the fire sale and Shelley was already feeling anxious about helping Aaron do his homework and keeping him fed and entertained.

"This is a good stopping place, can I come back tomorrow morning and finish these up?" Shelley folded up the pants and shirt with the loose elastic.

"That sounds like a great plan," Tawny agreed. "He's going to love them."

"I hope so," Shelley said fervently.

She got back to Dean's house in plenty of time—her house? Could she think of it as her own? As *theirs*? Certainly nowhere else Shelley had ever been had felt as much like *home*.

But Aaron didn't come home. Shelley paced the house until Bingo whined at her anxiously, and the clock ticked past the time she had expected him… and then ten minutes past that.

She checked her phone, even knowing that Dean's phone still wasn't working, and wondered when it was acceptable to open a search with the police.

Finally, when Aaron was officially fifteen minutes late, she called her brother Shaun's number.

"Welcome to the zoo," Andrea answered the phone merrily. "How can I direct your call?"

"Hi Andrea," Shelley said, feeling the tightness of worry in her chest and the panic that was starting to make her breathe funny. "I was just wondering if Aaron had come home with Trevor. I…" I've lost him, Shelley thought in horror. I've lost Dean's son and proved that I'm the worst mother ever. "He was supposed to come straight home, but he never showed up." She sounded as hysterical as she was starting to feel.

"I haven't seen him," Andrea said, sobering. "Hang on, let me go see if Trevor knows anything."

Shelley concentrated on breathing, running through all the meditation tricks in her mental bag. She wasn't going to freak out. She was going to think logically. She was going to find Aaron and strangle him (just a little) for making her worry so much and then they'd laugh and everything would be fine.

"Shelley?"

"I'm here, I'm here!" Shelley almost shouted into her phone. "Does he know where Aaron is?"

"He says they had a fight and Aaron went to the place where Trevor was practicing shifting. Do you know what that is?"

Shelley blinked, remembering their outing—had it really only been two weeks ago? "Yes, I know where that is."

"Do you need any help?"

I need *Dean*, Shelley thought. But she could do this. She scrawled a note to Dean and left it on the table. "No, I'll just drive up there and see if I can find him first. He can't have gotten very far yet."

It was a few blocks from school to the deserted property they'd gone running in. Aaron was fast, but he wasn't that fast. He couldn't have gotten very deep into the forest in such a short time. Could he?

"Call me when you find him," Andrea said firmly. "If I haven't heard from you in half an hour, I'll send out the cavalry."

"Thank you, Andrea!" Shelley was already at her car when she hung up, making a swift, squeaking-tire spin in the middle of the deserted street to point herself in the right direction.

It was cold, and the friendly, warm sun of the past few days was hidden in a gray bank of clouds that threatened snow. There were more leaves on the ground now than there were on the trees, and they swirled away from Shelley's car as she drove down the isolated drive.

As she pulled up at the trailhead, she had a moment of doubt. What if Aaron was just now arriving home, confused because no one was there? She reminded herself firmly that if he was, the house was warm and full of food. But if he was here, if he'd gotten lost, he would be cold and hungry.

She closed her car door and stood in the chilly air for a long moment, listening and scenting. Her senses were not as good when she wasn't a lion, but they were still better than a normal human's, by a long shot.

There was a strong scent on the breeze. *A bear*, her lion supplied.

Had Aaron successfully shifted, the way he'd always wanted to?

Shelley walked into the woods, confident in her ability to retrace her steps, and followed her nose and her ears. Several times, she questioned her choice to stay in human form—she'd be better at this as a lion. But she didn't want to terrify Aaron.

They'd had a talk, the three of them, about Shelley being a lion shifter like Trevor—another of those conversations that wasn't covered in any mommy blogs or child care manuals. But knowing she was a lion was a lot different than coming across one in the woods

She heard him snuffling at last, and was, for once, grateful for his non-stop running nose.

He was sitting in the center of a tiny clearing, not quite crying, but looking very close to it.

"Aaron!" Shelley cried in relief, running the last few steps to drop to her knees beside him. "Are you okay? I've been looking for you!"

"I wanted to be a bear," Aaron explained. "Or even a deer, like Mommy. Trevor gets to shift, and I want to. He showed me this is where he comes, and I thought maybe I could…"

"You shouldn't ever come by yourself," Shelley scolded as she checked him over. There were scratches on his face and his hands, and he looked cold and dirty, but he seemed unharmed. "You have to ask. Someone grown up should *always* come here with you."

Aaron's chin quivered and he stared at his filthy tennis shoes. "I didn't want to ask you," he said sheepishly. "Because…"

"Because you heard that I didn't like kids," Shelley guessed with a stab of guilt. Dean had told her about what Shaun had said and about the conversation he'd had with Aaron afterwards.

Aaron didn't say anything, continuing to stare down.

"Aaron," Shelley said, her voice breaking. "Aaron, I may not be great with other kids, but I… I like *you*. I want *you* to ask me for things. Like your Halloween costume, or whatever. I want… I want to be your mom. Not to replace your mom, of course, just… could you ever think of me as family? Because I'd really like that."

She wasn't prepared for him to look up at her, tears in his hazel eyes, and then throw his arms around her neck, and she almost fell backwards from the force of it before folding her arms around him.

He was so slight and fragile in her embrace. Shelley held him tight, burying her face in his curls and willed her heartbeat to slow. He was okay, he was safe, and everything was going to be *fine*.

"We can be a team," Aaron said near her ear. "Team Aaron and Shelley."

Then he gave a little squeak. "Dad!" he cried, squirming out of Shelley's arms, just as the hair on the back of her neck rose in alarm.

Shelley turned to find a bear snuffling its way out of the brush, nose in the air.

"Aaron, wait!" Shelley cried, as Aaron started to run towards it. "That's not your dad!"

Wild bears in the fall should be fat and sleepy, but this bear was skinny, with a ragged coat, and its eyes were anything but sleepy. This was a hungry bear, maybe sick, and it had a bead on Aaron, who had stopped in confusion halfway to it.

"Don't run!" Shelley yelped too late.

Aaron, realizing the danger he was in, turned on his heel and bolted back for Shelley.

The bear, its hunting instinct triggered by the small, soft prey fleeing it, charged forward with unexpected speed...

...and was met by a snarling lioness as Shelley shifted, shreds of her clothing scattering in a flurry of silk and linen.

Shelley's unsheathed claws slashed across the bear's face, before the greater bulk of the bear bowled her over. It roared at her, striking with heavy clawed paws and Shelley snapped her teeth, trying to get a grip on its sensitive nose. She had to stay between it and Aaron, she *had* to protect him.

Shelley was so focused on keeping Aaron safe, on driving the bear away from him, that she was incautious in her attacks, and the canny bear struck back, sinking teeth into her shoulder.

She roared in shock, then turned to bite back, able only to reach an ear from the angle of the hold the bear had on her. She twisted to claw at the bear's neck and belly and the bear bellowed in pain and released her.

Both of them scrambled to their feet and faced off, Shelley circling deliberately so that she was once again in front of Aaron. She was limping.

The bear snuffled and swung its head back and forth, clearly trying to decide if the temptation of the prey was worth fighting the lioness. He outweighed Shelley considerably, but wasn't as healthy or as fast. They were both bleeding, Shelley in sluggish lines from the place he'd locked his teeth, the bear from a dozen deep scratches and one torn ear. His injuries were largely cosmetic, but Shelley was clearly more invested in the outcome of the battle. She raised her head and roared a challenge, her tail lashing.

It was too much for the injured bear and he turned and shuffled back into the brush that he'd come from.

Shelley sat stiffly, and let her lioness twist to lick her injured shoulder while she decided what to do next.

"Sh-shelley?"

Shelley swung her head to see Aaron, eyes filled with frightened tears, arms clutched around himself. "Sh-shelley?" he repeated.

Shelley padded slowly up to him, and gave him a gentle head-butt. She was much larger as a lion than he was, but he fearlessly held his ground, and when Shelley leaned her big head against him, he wrapped his arms around her.

She licked him, and he giggled. "Ow," he protested. "Your tongue is scratchy!"

They stayed that way a moment, Aaron hugging into the thick fur of her neck, Shelley leaning into his embrace. It was starting to snow.

"Your clothes got all ruined," Aaron observed sorrowfully. "They were so fancy."

Shelly shrugged, then pulled away. They needed to get back to the parking lot and she needed to find something to wear before they both got hypothermia. When Aaron started to walk beside her, she stepped in front of him. He tried to go around her, but she cut him off again.

Figure it out, she willed at him.

His eyes got big. "Can I ride you?" he asked enthusiastically.

Shelley let her jaw go loose in a big cat grin and nodded her head.

Lions were not built as riding animals, but Aaron was barely a burden, and he quickly figured out how to sit and where to hold on so that Shelley could carry him swiftly back to the parking lot, following her path by scent back the way they'd come.

30

*D*ean pulled into the wide spot at the end of the drive, swearing and fighting down panic. It was starting to snow, very lightly, and he almost slipped stepping out of the truck. Shelley's car was already there.

"Aaron!" he hollered desperately. "Aaron!" Shelley's hasty note only said she was coming to look for Aaron here, no details about why Aaron would be here or why she had to look for him.

There were no signs of either of them. Not signs he could follow as a human.

He was unbuttoning his shirt and still struggling out of his work boots when he heard a distant, "Dad?"

Staying in human form, he ran towards the voice, and after a moment, met Aaron on a narrow trail, riding a limping lioness. "Dad!"

Dean's heart nearly stopped as he realized that they were both covered in blood.

Then the lioness was shaking Aaron gently off her back and shifting into Shelley, naked and shivering. "It's my blood, don't worry," she said, standing stiffly. "It's already healing."

Since his shirt was already half unbuttoned, he took it off the rest of the way and helped her, wincing, into it.

"Dad! She fought a bear! It was amazing! It was all rarrrrgh and whoosh and scary and Shelley roars way better than Trevor and it was really scary and can I go home now?"

"What were you doing out here?" Dean demanded, gathering the boy into his arms. Aaron was shivering, but seemed unharmed.

"I wanted to come practice trying shifting," Aaron whined. "I'm sorry. I should have asked… but you were busy and I was scared to ask Shelley."

Dean exchanged a look with Shelley.

She looked back at him and smiled, her silver eyes filled with relief. "We're good now."

"We're a team," Aaron agreed.

"Well, team," Dean said, almost shaky with relief. "What do you say we head home and have a snack and take hot showers?"

"Can I have a bath?" Aaron suggested.

"You boys go ahead," Shelley said. "I'm going to shift again and heal up the worst of these bite marks. I don't want to get rabies from some wild bear if I can help it."

"What's rabies?" Aaron wanted to know. "Is it like babies? Eeewwwwwww!"

Dean gave her a swift kiss and tried to buckle Aaron into his booster seat. "I can do it Dad, geez. I'm *seven*." Torn between wanting to scold him some more and wanting to crush him in a hug, Dean stopped fussing over Aaron and went around to the driver's seat. "See you soon," he said to Shelley.

He drew Aaron a bath as soon as they got home, reminded him about splashing on the floor, and piled toys into the water with him.

He got downstairs just as Shelley pulled up. She looked around furtively, then dashed to the door, still wearing nothing more than his shirt. She was holding her purse and a large bundle of red material in her arms. Dean could only imagine the stories that was going to spark.

He caught her in his arms just inside the door, and Bingo

bounced around them, barking and wagging his tail because all of his people were back where they belonged.

"Do you need something?" he asked. "A pill? You said the attacks usually happened after the stress, when you were safe again. Would a back rub help?"

"I'm fine," Shelley said, embracing him awkwardly with her arms full of fabric. "I'm… actually fine." She stepped back and looked at him with glowing eyes. "I'll show you." She put the things she'd been holding down on the table and unbuttoned his flannel shirt. The bite marks on her shoulder looked like old scabs now, or fresh scars. There was still dried blood on her skin.

"When I shift, it heals things up, right? Like, if you're defying physics and changing into a completely new body, it's going to make it the *right* new body, all healed up." She tapped her forehead. "This, this is a chemical imbalance. Tricky to treat, more complicated than just muscles and skin, but still, the body not quite working right. And when I shift, it *fixes* things. That's why I felt so great and in control after our first date—I'd gone running with my Dad and Trevor just the night before."

She laughed and shook her head. "My lioness kept telling me that she could help, but I was sure that her idea of *help* was to turn into a lion and eat someone. I didn't even consider that she could *actually* help me."

"You beautiful, clever, brave, wonderful woman," Dean said.

Her arms were free again, so Dean swept her up into a less encumbered hug, and added a probing kiss to it.

"I don't think this is a permanent fix," Shelley warned as they broke apart. "I mean, I really want it to be, but there will probably be times I don't recognize what is happening, or can't shift for some reason."

"I love you and all your quirks," Dean promised. "And even if this isn't a fix-all, I will still love you."

She sagged into him embrace, full of relief and gratitude.

"My water is cold!"

Aaron was standing at the bottom of the stairs wrapped in a towel.

"Let's get you dried off and dressed for bed!" Dean let go of Shelley and she buttoned his shirt back up over herself.

"Oh, wait! Before you get dressed, I want you to try on your costume!" She walked to the table and unfolded the fabric to reveal a hooded pajama set trimmed in gold bric-a-brac. "I've got the logo patches on expedited order for the front and for the lightning bolts above the ears. They should be here tomorrow for the finishing touches. I just want to get the cuff lengths right. We'll tuck up the extra so you can let it out when you get taller."

"That looks great," Dean said, impressed. He didn't know much about sewing or design, but the costume looked well made.

Aaron frowned, and reluctantly tried it on. It fit him perfectly, with just enough room in the armpits that he'd be able to run around easily, and Shelley pinned up the legs and arms. She tightened the elastic at the waist and safety pinned it, then sat back on her heels.

"Well?" she asked. "Do you like it?"

Aaron petted the soft material and traced some of the trim. "It's... nice."

Shelley looked confused and then her face shuttered to her boardroom mask. "Okay," she said patiently. "What would make it better?"

Aaron chewed on his lip and finally said. "I don't want to be The Flash. I want to be Iron Man!"

"You *said* you wanted to be The Flash," Shelley said in disbelief.

"Yeah, but I changed my mind because Iron Man can fly and blow things up."

"But... I made you a *Flash* costume," Shelley protested.

That was the point at which Dean could no longer hold his laughter in. "Aaron, why don't you get out of that now and go get into your sleeping PJs."

"But I'm huuuuunnnnnnggggggry," Aaron protested, wriggling out of the costume with Shelley's help.

"You can eat dinner in pajamas," Dean promised him, still chuckling. "Wait, take your wet towel and hang it on the rack in the bathroom."

He knew there was an even chance that the towel would be found on the bedroom floor.

Shelley had a mixed expression of betrayal and bemusement on her face once Aaron had skipped up the stairs.

"Welcome to parenting," Dean said, unable to keep from grinning at her. "Please don't kill him."

"I spent $23 for the expedited shipping," she said in frustration. "This is a bait and switch!"

Dean tucked a piece of stray hair behind her ear. "We'll have a bit of a talk before bed about being grateful and he'll probably draw you a few apology cards. But he's also seven, so it's... a work in progress."

Shelley pulled up her phone with a sigh and began googling photos of Iron Man. "I can probably order a new patch that looks like that glowy chest thing, and we can put on some gold mechanical looking bits on the sleeves and legs. Some red gloves, maybe? It will be hard to match that red."

"You're a good sport," Dean said sincerely.

Shelley looked up from her phone and gave him a crooked smile. "I have good reasons to put in the work," she said warmly. "Two of them, at least."

Bingo groaned to his feet from where he'd been laying and trotted to get in on whatever activity he might have slept through, tail wagging.

"Three reasons," Shelley amended, ruffling his ears.

She put her phone down as Dean gathered her into his arms again and kissed her. She was still wearing only his flannel shirt and her hair was still damp from the snow.

"So worth the work," she murmured in his ear as he kissed down her neck. "Can I eat dinner wearing my pajamas, too?"

"Pajamas for all!" Dean declared magnanimously.

Hand in hand, they went upstairs to change. Aaron met them at the top of the stairs, dressed in his favorite pajamas. "Are you going to kiss?" he demanded in disgust.

"Probably a lot," Dean said cheerfully.

"Ugh, ew! Gross!" Aaron mimed throwing up, or possibly choking; the particulars were uncertain, but the disgust was clear.

EPILOGUE

The shrieks of two happy children playing echoed across the spring lawn as they went hunting for Easter eggs. Bingo barked, romping with them. Trees were just starting to bud overhead, and early flowers were coming up in the beds.

"I think that your costumes are a success," Dean said to Shelley as she put their crockpot down on the table on Shaun's porch. "That is the sound of utter delight."

"I'm never going to get Trevor out of it again," Andrea lamented, bringing out a plate of cookies and a stack of napkins.

Aaron was wearing a blue costume, Trevor a red one. They were, at a glance, wearing simple, bright colored pajamas, but each garment was completely reversible. One side of the fabric was plain, the other printed with mechanical patterns. Cleverly placed Velcro, snaps, buttons, and zippers allowed the application of superhero logos, capes, and accessories so that each outfit could have dozens of costume variations.

Currently, Trevor was dressed as Superman on the top, with mechanical wrist braces, cyborg legs, and no cape. Aaron had the Iron Man gloves, but was otherwise dressed as the Flash, with a cape of his own waving behind him as he streaked across the lawn in search of the hidden Easter loot.

Shelley personally thought they'd have a lot more luck finding the eggs if they slowed down and actually looked for them, but they were having so much fun that it was hard to criticize their methods, even if their baskets were empty.

"Those turned out wonderfully," Tawny said. She was carrying a platter of vegetables and deviled eggs, and she put them on the potluck table on the porch. "Such clever touches! They'll be able to imagine up their own superhero combinations."

"We're getting the licensing finalized this week and the work-shop in Minneapolis should have them in production by the end of next month," Shelley said, feeling shyly pleased. "And did you see? The cuffs all unfold so you can get an extra three inches out of the arms and legs. It's good fabric, and quality stitching, plus all machine wash and dry."

"Nice work, Shelley-bean," her father said approvingly. He was carrying a platter of ham and Bingo was drooling and cavorting at his heels.

"They're talking about a line for girls, too," Shelley said, grinning, as Damien set his tray on the table with the other food. "A princess, fairy, witch line, as well as a superheroine set. It will have a little skirt, a cape that is just as long as the boys' capes, bracelets, a crown... I'm really excited to start on it."

"They're very practical," Tawny teased, handing her a carrot stick. Shelley took it automatically, then didn't know what to do with it.

"How's school going, Dean?" Damien asked.

"Fine," Dean said, sounding embarrassed. "Lots of math."

"He says *fine*," Shelley added with a snort. "He's top of all his correspondence classes, he's finished two of them early, and his mentor says he wishes his other students had half his work ethic. He's already saying that Dean can test out of some of the engi-neering intro classes." They had decided to close the shop rather than rebuild it, and the insurance settlement had been generous enough to cover several semesters of school.

Dean actually blushed, which Shelley found utterly adorable. She vowed to make him do so again as soon as possible. Without thinking, she put the carrot she was holding into her mouth, only realizing as she bit down that it *was* a carrot.

She didn't like carrots.

Flavor burst into her mouth and Shelley chewed in wonder. "This is good," she admitted when she caught Tawny watching her.

"It's from my garden," Tawny said, pleased. "They're better than what you get at the store."

"I didn't think I liked carrots," Shelley said, still surprised by the delicious crunch.

"Maybe you just didn't have the right carrots," Tawny suggested.

There was a pounding on the steps as two boys making far more noise than their size indicated stomped up to the porch.

"Can we eat now?" Aaron asked, eyeing the table… particularly the end of the table with the cookies and pie.

"I'm *so* hungry," Trevor agreed. "Can we start with dessert?"

"Did you find all the eggs?" Shaun asked. "No food until you've found them all."

They held up their battered baskets, which both appeared to have been involved in some kind of duel or possibly had been run over in the road. "We found nine of them."

"Eight," Aaron corrected.

"No, I have five," Trevor argued. "You have four. That's nine."

As they counted them over, Shelley asked Shaun in an aside, "What happens if they don't find them all?"

"We hope we don't find them with the lawnmower in a few weeks after they've ripened in the sun," Shaun replied with a knowing wince.

"That's probably enough eggs to earn some lunch," Tawny said peacefully, and no one waited for further invitation.

Settling into one of the Shaun's lawn chairs with a plate of food in the spring sunshine, Shelley thought that her whole life was like Tawny's carrots—something she'd thought she'd never like, and now something that she gleefully loaded onto her plate.

Aaron took a seat next to her, nearly upsetting his plate onto the lawn as he wiggled into his chair. "I like my new costume," he said around a mouthful of ham. "You're the best second mom ever!"

"That beats being second best," Shelley teased him. And, because she was a responsible adult, she added, "You're not supposed to talk with your mouth full." But she did it with her own mouth full, and winked at him.

"Oops," Aaron said, grinning so widely that a piece of ham fell out onto his lap.

"Your family puts out a great spread," Dean said, settling into the lawn chair on her other side while Shelley and Aaron giggled about his runaway ham.

Shelley's lion purred in contentment. This was, in every way, exactly where she belonged.

She had her mate, she had her *family*.

It didn't matter that her life wasn't the way she had planned, or that everything wasn't in neat, tidy boxes.

Kids were messy, and that was fine.

Life was messy, and that was fine, too.

They hadn't decided what to do when Dean had exhausted the parts of school that worked long-distance, and for some reason, it didn't bother Shelley not to have a plan. He might put the rest of the degree off until Aaron was out of elementary school. The hardware store was open again, but Dean hadn't reopened the shop.

She was a mess, sometimes, if less than before, and even that was fine.

She knew that whatever happened, wherever home ended up being, she'd found the people—and the dog—she would be there with.

"You good?" Dean asked with a sideways look.

Shelley smiled at him. "So good," she said sincerely. She leaned sideways in her lawn chair and Dean scooted to meet her with a kiss.

"Ewwww," said Aaron on her other side, but when Shelley sat back down into her chair, he impulsively put his plate down and threw his arms around her. She folded her arms around him and pressed her cheek to his.

"Am I good?" he asked cheerfully.

"So good," Shelley repeated.

Bingo, hearing the word *good*, came nosing into the action, all wiggling tail and hopeful ears.

"You're good, too," Shelley assured him.

And as far as he was concerned, that was all that mattered.

KEEPING SECRETS

lara Montgomery was seven. She was nearly eight, just a few weeks from her birthday, a fact that she managed to bring up in nearly every conversation that she had.

"I'm going to have a *Halloween* birthday party," she told everyone. "There will be spiders and pumpkin pie with candles. You have to wear a costume."

"I'm going to be Flash!" Aaron said enthusiastically, when she gave him his card. They were in his backyard on a sunny Saturday morning, while the grown-ups did something boring inside involving paperwork and Mr. James' burnt-down car shop. "Miss Shelley is making me a costume!"

Trevor was lying back in a pile of dry leaves, damp from overnight frost. It was the biggest pile of leaves the neighborhood had ever collected; Abby and Devon from next door had added all of their leaves, and Marta had brought by a big wheelbarrow that was filled with even more.

"I don't know what to be," Trevor confessed, then, confusingly, "I don't know what I *am.*" Aaron's dog, Bingo, was writhing on his back next to him, kicking leaves everywhere and growling.

"Well, you'd better figure it out," Clara scolded him as she put his invitation in his bike basket. "I won't let you come to my party if you aren't dressed up." She tucked the remaining invitations back into her fluffy pink unicorn purse. They were splendidly fancy cards, with gold lettering that said, "You are *cordially* invited to my birthday celebration." They didn't really match the Halloween theme, but those options had all been silly and cartoony, and they didn't mention her *birthday* at all.

"Abby, next door, says she's not going to dress up or go trick or treating," Aaron said, tearing open the perfectly-sealed envelope of his own invitation so carelessly that Clara wanted to pinch him. "She says it's for babies."

"I don't want to grow up if I can't trick or treat," Trevor declared.

"I want to grow up," Aaron declared. "I want to be able to change into a—" He got suddenly silent, and Trevor sat up with a warning look and they both looked incredibly guilty and suspicious and Clara wasn't sure if she was more irritated because they weren't talking about her birthday at all, or because it was clear that they were keeping some kind of secret from her. They'd been doing this for weeks now.

"I'm going to be a ballerina scientist president," she declared. "Or a teacher."

"You can't be all those things at once," Aaron scoffed.

"I could, too," Clara said stubbornly. Already, she was the best in her class at science, and she had all the Magic Test Tube books. Twice a week, Miss Patricia drove her to Madison for private ballet lessons, and her teacher said she was as graceful as a *swan*. She wasn't really sure what being a president entailed, but she was confident she could handle that, too.

"I'm going to be a firefighter," Trevor said thoughtfully. "And a doctor."

"You can't be a doctor and a firefighter," Aaron said skeptically. "The hours are incombat-incombable."

"I could do it," Trevor said, throwing a fistful of leaves at him. Bingo ran and jumped and tried to catch the falling leaves in his mouth, tongue lolling.

"You're going to be in a circus!" Aaron declared, bending to get his own handful of leaves. "I'm going to chase you around the ring with a chair!"

That precipitated a leaf fight that Clara desperately longed to join in with...but she was wearing her best white shoes and she didn't want to have to brush leaves out of her hair...

She turned away to pout, and then gave a sputter of surprise as the boys crept up behind her and dumped armloads of rustling leaves right over her.

After a good wail of protest, Clara turned on the toe of her best white shoe and tackled the closest one, Trevor, knocking him straight over into the pile. Bingo came bounding after, determined to be a part of the excitement as Aaron heaved another scoop of leaves over them and then dove in after.

It was exactly what autumn ought to be, Clara thought, as they wrestled in the huge pile of crunchy leaves and Bingo barked and everyone laughed and she didn't even care if her shoes got scuffed.

She wasn't sure exactly how it happened, later.

Someone's foot hit her shoulder, and she accidentally elbowed Trevor harder than she meant to and Bingo, who was so excited by now that he was throwing himself bodily into the fray, bit down on her foot and immediately let go. Clara knew the dog didn't mean to hurt her, but she was already trying to scream and struggle away and for a moment there were leaves over her face. She inhaled a big handful of them and had a terrible moment where she couldn't tell what was up and what was down in the endless mountain of leaves and she was absolutely terrified and couldn't breathe.

For a moment, she thought it was Bingo diving into the leaves after her, and she clung to his furry body like he was some kind of rescue dog saving her from a snowy avalanche.

But it wasn't Bingo, she realized as she coughed up her lungful of leaves and tried to open her eyes.

It was Trevor, he wasn't furry at all, and for some bizarre reason, his shirt was half ripped off.

"Are you okay, Clara?" he asked anxiously.

"Clara!" Aaron called, climbing over the hill from the other direction. "Are you hurt?"

For a moment, spitting out leaves, Clara continued to hold on to Trevor, trying to make sense out of the idea that he'd been covered with fur just a moment before.

Then she let go, shoving him away. "I'm fine," she sputtered. "What happened to your shirt?"

She was watching his face when she asked, and his eyes got wide with alarm.

"Nothing!" Aaron said, entirely too loudly. "Nothing happened!"

When Clara looked at him suspiciously, Aaron clapped his hand over his mouth like he'd said too much.

They both looked as guilty as Bingo, who was lying on the ground with his nose pressed into the grass, quite aware that he'd crossed a terrible line.

"Fine," Clara said angrily, feeling tears sting her eyes. "Keep your stupid secrets. I don't care!"

The grown-ups had come out of Aaron's house, her papa, Aaron's dad Dean, Shelley, Trevor's dad Shaun, and Miss Andrea. Miss Patricia was trailing behind, bouncing a fussy Victoria. Clara wasn't sure if they'd been summoned by her leaf-smothered scream, or if they were just done with whatever they were doing, but she stood up and wobbled over to meet her papa and throw her arms around him.

He obligingly swung her up into his arms. "What's wrong, cub?"

"Did you do this, Trevor?" Shaun asked in horror so stark that Clara had to look down. Trevor was clutching at his pants like they would fall down if he let go of them.

And her best white shoe had very obvious teeth marks in it.

"No," Clara said, puzzled. "Bingo bit me." Why would they think that Trevor could have done that to her shoe?

This led to a whole flurry of worried confusion. Dean yelled at the already sheepish Bingo, who fled the yard with his tail between his legs to wedge himself underneath the porch, and her shoe was carefully removed.

"No damage," Miss Andrea cheerfully reported. "That's the value of good shoes."

Trevor and Aaron vanished while Clara was being inspected, and she told herself she didn't care. "Can we go home now, Papa?" she asked plaintively. She had itchy leaves down the back of her shirt and up the legs of her pants, and her best white shoes were dirty and scuffed, on top of the teeth marks.

"Sure, cub, we can go."

Miss Patricia started gathering up all the things that the baby required, and Clara went to sit in the car by herself.

~

*S*he wasn't sure if Aaron and Trevor were even going to come to her birthday party, and Clara told herself that she didn't care. Not one bit. They ignored each other at school, as much as possible, and Clara played with the girls during recess.

There was plenty to be distracted by, especially her party.

It was going to be the prettiest, creepiest Halloween birthday party in the history of the world. Papa had turned an entire wing of their house into a haunted house, with spiderwebs and doors that actually creaked. Her pumpkin pie had three tiers, decorated with liquorice spiders and striped with white webbing. There were cupcakes for people who didn't like pumpkin pie: red velvet like blood, chocolate, and vanilla for the really boring people.

Clara spent three whole days putting together the party favors, decorating paper bags trimmed in white lace filled with toys and treats and labeled with her guests' names. She almost hadn't put together bags for Trevor and Aaron. If they wanted to keep secrets from her, they didn't need her party favors.

She finally did, though, stuffing Aaron's full of the most candy of all, and Trevor's with extra practical joke toys. They each got matching decoder rings so that the three of them could write in code. If they ever wanted to write in code with *her* again.

To her surprise, they arrived separately, and glared at each other across every game and event. Trevor came as a pirate, and Aaron was Iron Man. There was bobbing for apples (which Clara didn't want to do because she didn't want to get her dress dirty), and ring tosses, just like a real Halloween carnival, and the grown-ups made sure everyone won prizes, and she blew out all the candles on the cake, wishing with all her heart…

Then there were presents, but they all blurred together after a while: new dolls, jewelry, dance-themed movies and books, a pink tutu with glittery crystals on it that made every girl in the room sigh in envy, hair clips, stuffed animals, sweets, a real baking kit, and a microscope.

After that, everyone broke into little clusters, to marvel over their favor bags and nibble at their slices of pie and cupcakes while the grown-ups tried to coax them to eat the healthy snacks, too.

"Happy birthday," Aaron said, when he caught up with Clara at last. She had escaped the chaos to go out to the back and sit by herself on the porch swing. It was bitterly cold, despite the sunshine, and Clara wished she'd brought out her coat.

She considered snubbing him, but she had missed him at recess. "Thanks," she said shyly. She was wearing her best white shoes again. The scuffs had been rubbed out and the bite marks had been filled with one of Papa's special leather repair creams. They looked as good as new.

"Are you mad at Trevor?" she finally asked.

Aaron climbed onto the far end of the porch swing, causing it to sway lopsidedly. "I don't know," he admitted. "It's just...we don't *want* to keep secrets, Clara."

"Then don't," Clara said crossly.

"We're not allowed to tell!" Aaron wailed. "We'll get in trouble! They might take Trevor *away*."

"Away *where?*" Clara wanted to know. She wasn't sure she exactly believed Aaron, but he certainly was agitated about this.

"Clara, honey?"

Aaron scrambled off the swing and it swung crazily. Clara clung to her handle.

"Oh here you are!" Miss Patricia said. "The Hendersons are

leaving. I thought you'd want to say goodbye to Vanessa and the twins!"

Clara went to dutifully say her goodbyes, and ran headlong into Trevor when she returned to her party.

They stared at each other awkwardly.

"It's a nice party," Trevor finally said.

Clara considered snapping that it had been until *he* got there, but that was really too mean, and she wasn't actually mad at him anymore.

"Thanks," she said instead. "I'm glad you came."

When Trevor didn't volunteer anything else, Clara went on. "Did you have pie or cupcakes?"

"Vanilla cupcake," Trevor said, because he was apparently the most boring person in the world, except for the secrets. "I liked the party favors." He was toying with the decoder ring.

"I thought we could write in code, with the decoder rings," Clara said desperately. "Are you mad at Aaron?"

Trevor shrugged. "I guess not. It's just...kind of complicated."

Clara dragged the toe of her best white shoe along the floor. "I wouldn't want them to take you away," she said.

Trevor's eyes got very big and he frowned, like maybe Aaron shouldn't have told her that much.

"You know what...!" she started, feeling like she did when Miss Patricia called her over-wrought. She reined in her frustration with effort and heaved a sigh instead. "Never mind. It doesn't matter."

"I want to show you," Trevor blurted. "I will. Where can we go?"

"My room?" Clara said. She was feeling equal parts elated that she would finally know, and guilty that she might be making Trevor do something wrong. "You don't have to," she said reluctantly.

Trevor very suddenly grinned at her, a slow, rare smile. "I want to," he declared. "C'mon!"

He dragged her by the hand up the stairs to her room. "Turn around. Promise you won't look."

"What are you...?"

"Promise!" Trevor said.

"I promise!"

He went into the closet anyway, leaving the door cracked, and Clara wondered if he was secretly a superhero and he had to change his costume. But in that case, wouldn't he just have worn it to the party? She was really confused by this whole thing and wondered if Miss Patricia wasn't right about eating too much pumpkin pie without healthier food in her stomach.

Then the closet door gave a creak and Clara turned to look before she could remind herself that she'd promised not to look.

There was a cat walking out of her closet.

Not just a domestic cat like she'd been begging her papa for, but a big cat. Half-grown, she thought, with long legs and big paws and spots that looked like they were fading to a seamless tawny gold. A *lion.*

"You're a lion," she breathed, and she sat down very hard right where she was, her princess skirt poofing up all around her.

The lion—Trevor!—walked straight up to her, silent on his soft paws.

She was at eye-level with him and she stared into his golden eyes like she could see one of her best friends there.

"You're a lion," she repeated in wonder. Then she clapped her hand over her mouth because she wanted to shriek in delight and the people downstairs were probably already wondering where she'd gone. She whispered, "You're a lion!"

The lion's mouth lolled open in delight and Clara almost reached for him when there was a knock on the door.

Trevor swapped ends like only a cat can and scrambled back into the closet as Clara stood back up. "Who is it?"

"Who's in there with you?" her papa's voice demanded.

"Trevor!" she replied. She could hear Trevor hastily dressing in her closet, and when the door opened, he was standing beside her, adjusting his eye patch over one eye.

Papa was standing with a smiling Miss Patricia, and he gave them a very skeptical look indeed. "Your party guests are starting to leave and you should be saying thank you. What are you doing up here?"

While Clara was still trying to come up with a reason that wasn't "Trevor is a *lion!*" he cleared his throat and said, "I wanted to apologize to Clara for keeping secrets from her."

The two grown-ups blinked at him in surprise and exchanged a look that Clara couldn't read.

"That's very kind of you," Miss Patricia said sweetly. "But you don't want to keep your guests waiting."

"Okay!" Clara took Trevor's hand and pulled him out into the hallway.

Behind her, she heard her papa groan and quietly say, "I'm not ready for this."

Miss Patricia said something even quieter that had the words *perfectly innocent* in it.

They met Aaron at the bottom of the stairs and he looked anxiously between them, and then slowly smiled. He was wearing his decoder ring from the favor bag.

Clara fished hers out of her silver princess purse and put it on her finger.

Trevor dug into a pocket and found his.

None of them said anything, but they all shared a big, *secret* smile before Clara ran off to say goodbye to all her guests.

BROKEN LYNX

1

"There is no jam," Devon said in deep frustration, closing the side of the printer too hard. "Nothing is jammed. Why do you insist that there is a jam?"

He reminded himself that the printer could not hear him, and that destroying it with his bare hands wasn't going to give him more than a moment or two of satisfaction. Also, Gran would probably fire him, and he needed the job at her little cafe more than he wanted to admit.

The door chime sounded, and Devon yanked the power cable from the back of the printer. "Have you tried turning it off and back off again?" he mocked himself.

He heard a party enter the front of the cafe, just as Old George growled, "Customers."

"Be right out!" he called, plugging the cable back in after a swift count of ten.

Then he grabbed menus and went out to greet the new customers. Turner was sliding into a bench seat, opposite from someone Devon didn't recognize from the back. "Welcome to Gran's Grits," he said, dropping a menu in front of each of them. "I'm Devon, I'll be your waitress tonight," he joked.

Then he made the mistake of looking down at the young woman sitting across from Turner and everything he'd planned to say about drinks and dinner specials vanished from his head.

Blue eyes in a tanned face framed by a halo of short, mousy blond hair smiled up at him, sparkling and confident, crinkled in humor.

Yes! his lynx said in triumph. *We have amused her! Be more funny!*

But Devon was absolutely lost, drowning in those eyes, drinking in the beauty of her face, and the graceful lines of her neck, and the pale skin that the scoop of her shirt revealed.

"I'm…ah…it's…"

Her smile slipped slightly in the face of his utter inanity, and Devon realized he was staring. "Drinks!" he sputtered. "Start you with drinks! Dinner special!" For a moment his head was completely blank, like his code was missing an end-tag and his compiler had no idea what to do with the input. Then he remembered, "The special tonight is the fried chicken basket with coleslaw. It's good slow. *Slaw*. It's good *slaw*. Cole*slaw*."

Funny, his lynx said, vexed. *Not stupid.*

It helped if he looked at Turner instead of the stranger, but not by much.

Turner was looking at him quizzically, probably wondering if he'd just witnessed Devon having a stroke. "Just water for me," he said.

"You have Coke?" The young woman asked, and her velvety voice was every bit as unsettling as her eyes.

"P-P-Pepsi," Devon managed, making the mistake of looking back at her.

"Not equivalent," she said with a shake of her head. "Root beer?"

"On top," Devon said. Then, swiftly: "Tap. On *tap*."

Laughter danced at her mouth as she said, "Yes, please."

For a moment, Devon's brain really did seem to stroke out, wondering what it was that she had agreed to. Was he imagining the interest in her eyes? Was it just pity because it must seem like he had some kind of brain injury?

"This is Jamie," Turner said, clearly trying to save him. "She's just back in town from fighting wildfires this summer in Alaska. Going to take Dean's place on the volunteer squad."

"For a little while," Jamie cautioned him. "I'm not committing to anything long term. I hate this town, and I'm only here as a favor to you."

Devon felt like he was witnessing an old conflict, but neither Jamie nor Turner seemed to be taking it very seriously.

"Welcome to Green Valley," Devon cleared his throat and said. "Let me get you those drinks."

The printer was still complaining about an imaginary paper jam when he passed it.

The root beer tap spat foam and Devon groaned and went to hook up the fresh keg.

"Order up," Old George told him, and for a moment, Devon could only stare, because he honestly had not remembered that there was anyone in the cafe but *her*. His world had reduced to Jamie. Jamie from Alaska. Jamie the firefighter. Jamie, with her brilliant blue eyes and her expressive mouth.

Our mate.

Devon nearly dropped the keg he was carrying as he felt his lynx's words settle into his soul.

"I don't have time for that," he said ferociously, putting the keg down too hard. He almost broke the connections as he took the old one off the system, and made himself slow down and be careful.

He didn't have time, and he didn't have room in his life for a mate, he resolved. It didn't matter what his lynx thought. He had Abby to look out for. He had two jobs and a languishing freelance business to manage.

By the time he'd finished hooking up the new root beer keg and pouring Turner's water and serving food to the local gray-haired gossip, Marta, he had convinced himself that he had simply over-reacted, and that he had enough control over himself again that he would be able to face down the woman without making a fool out of himself again.

He was wrong.

Even just a glimpse of the edge of her face as he came out of the kitchen set his heart racing and his lynx cavorting in his head.

Don't try conversation, he told himself. Don't attempt jokes. Just take the order and *go*.

"Turner tells me you might be able to fix my phone," she greeted him, and Devon was so startled he nearly dropped the root beer in her lap.

Once it was safely down in front of her, Devon swallowed. "Maybe? What's it doing?"

"It just won't hold a charge," Jamie said, pulling out the phone and holding it out.

It was a standard model, one that had a reputation for chewing through batteries. "Oh, yeah, you probably just need a new battery," he said confidently. "Don't take it to the store, they'll charge you an arm and a leg for five minutes of work and a twenty dollar replacement part. I could do that for you. I might even have one at my house."

He was pretty pleased with the steady way he'd said it, then he made the mistake of taking the phone and her fingers brushed his.

If her eyes had been dangerous, her touch was much worse. It was like fire through his veins.

He was staring again, and he made himself speak. "If I don't have the battery, I'll have to go to Madison for it. Might take a day or two. Have you backed this up? I could take it now. If you wanted. I mean, it's your phone." *Obviously*.

"Everything's on the cloud," Jamie said, with a slight smile. "You can take it. I've got a loaner from the fire station while I get this one sorted. It's sort of important to be on call, and mine's too unreliable."

"Yeah," Devon said. "Okay."

There was something else he needed to do, but for the life of him, he couldn't remember what it was. "I'll call you when it's done," he said, and he started to walk away.

Then he was back, saying sheepishly, "And your order. I need to take your order. For food. To eat."

2

It was everything Jamie could do not to stare at Devon as he left with their order. He was the cutest thing she had seen, and nothing like she had expected.

When Turner told her that a guy named Devon who waited tables at Gran's could probably fix her phone, she had immediately assumed he'd be a geek. And sure, geeks could be cute, but Devon wasn't geek cute. He was bodybuilder cute. He was movie star gratuitously removing his t-shirt cute. His arms were ropy with muscle, and his shoulders strained the seams of his cafe logo shirt. His golden-green eyes weren't behind the thick-rimmed glasses that Jamie had imagined. They were under perfect arched brows and above cheekbones like a chiseled statue. His jaw would have made Clark Kent cry with jealousy.

If Jamie knew a thing about people, which occasionally she did, he was absolutely bowled over by her.

And that was even more unexpected than his appearance.

Unfortunately, Turner was no more unaware of Devon's stuttering awe than she was.

"No overnight visitors at the station," he said, archly.

Jamie was temporarily staying at the station itself, in the tiny efficiency above the garage. It was basically a bed in a tiny room; she used the utility shower downstairs, and a glorified coffee counter in the common area served as her kitchen.

She ignored Turner. "This place hasn't changed," she said casually. The decor was all dreadfully dated, but not cohesive enough to be a specific era. It was equal parts plastic bench seats and little tables with quaint white chairs. Gran's elderly-looking cat was sleeping in the front window on a pile of soft, folded fabric. There were a few other customers having quiet, casual conversations and Marta was reading by herself at the window. It was just like a million other times Jamie had come here since she was a kid.

"It's Green Valley," Turner pointed out. "It pretty much stays the same."

"I hear you're up a few new millionaires," Jamie said. "Haven't a rash of them swept in and snapped up some of our eligible singles?"

"I don't think that Tawny would have called herself eligible," Turner chuckled. "But yes, the Powells have done a good job of finding…partners in town." Jamie wondered if she imagined the pause before partners. Like he was using it as a substitute for another word. "They've also done a good job of not changing things with their money. Not in big ways that will unsettle the locals. Just small, subtle ways. Things are *better*, but not a lot *different*."

Devon returned with plates of food much faster than she had expected, and Jamie wondered if he didn't put hers down a little further from her than strictly necessary. Like he didn't want any chance of accidentally touching her again.

"Can I get you anything else?" he offered, looking only at Turner.

"I think we're good," Turner said, and Devon fled without meeting Jamie's eyes.

Jamie looked back to find Turner watching her again. He looked smug.

"What are you looking at?" she demanded.

"I've just…got a suspicion," Turner said with a shrug.

"Spit it out," Jamie said.

"Not mine to share," Turner said. "But I can tell you a little about Devon, if you want."

Jamie desperately wanted, but she didn't want to admit that. "Whatever. You got Tabasco over there?"

Turner passed her the Tabasco sauce, and she slathered her eggs.

"Devon's new in town," Turner told her, voice quiet. "Moved here in the spring with his kid sister from Twin Cities. He was renting out in the Jefferson neighborhood, but just moved into Tawny's old house next to the James place."

Jamie gave him a suspicious look as she put a mouthful of eggs. "Okay," she said, not wanting to encourage him, as much as she wanted to know more.

"Word is, their parents died when his little sister was just a kid. He was seventeen, and he got guardianship, so he's been raising her by himself. I guess she was having a hard time with school in the city, and he wanted to bring her someplace smaller, make a new start."

"Tough gig," Jamie said thoughtfully. Devon was refilling drinks across the room, and her gaze kept drifting towards him, no matter where he was, or how good her potatoes were.

"He's a good fit for Green Valley," Turner said, with a rare note of approval. "Works hard, doesn't complain, trying to do right for his family."

"Geez, Turner, you're half in love with him already," Jamie teased with easy camaraderie. "Are you sure you're trying to set *me* up with him?"

Turner gave a great guffaw of laughter. "Saw through that, did you?"

"You're about as subtle as your fire boots," Jamie said, rolling her eyes. She was keenly aware of Devon's reluctant approach with the water pitcher.

He splashed water into Turner's glass. "Refill your root beer?" he asked a spot on the table between them.

"I'd like that," Jamie said, trying and failing to catch his gaze.

He managed to snag the glass before she could hand it to him, and vanished back into the kitchen.

"He's kind of a rube," Jamie observed. A really *cute* rube.

"He's as naive as they come," Turner agreed. "So be nice to him."

"Have I ever been anything but nice?" Jamie protested.

"You locked Minnie Carter in a locker once," Turner reminded her. "I suspended you for a week." Turner was the vice principal at the Green Valley high school and taught history. She had been a senior the year he started and there were times that Jamie thought he was like the dad she'd never had.

"Yeah, about that…"

"No pranks at the station," Turner warned her, suddenly serious.

Jamie chased her last potato cube around her plate and sighed. "No pranks at the station," she agreed slyly. "I'll cancel my order for itching powder."

Devon returned with her root beer and the bill, hesitated as if he was going to say something, then fled.

Jamie watched him go thoughtfully as she sipped her root beer refill. She hadn't come back to Green Valley looking for a boyfriend, and the idea of something serious with this gorgeous, grave man gave her an unsettled feeling in the pit of her stomach. She couldn't deny that he appealed to her at an animal level, but she doubted he was the type for a quick fling and she wasn't sure she wanted to commit to anything more.

She wasn't sure she *could* commit to anything more. Most of her life had been footloose and free, and she wasn't sure she knew how to be anything else.

"I've got some paperwork for you at the office," Turner was saying, and Jamie wasn't sure how much of the conversation she'd missed.

She put cash down for her meal on the table and grabbed her coat. "Oh goodie. Paperwork is my favorite."

3

She was gone.

The table that his mate had shared with Turner was empty, and Devon's heart dropped to his toes. *What if I can't find her again?* he wondered in a cold panic, utterly forgetting his earlier resolution that he didn't have time for her anyway. He was tearing off his apron in a hot moment, scrambling out the door absolutely prepared to chase her down by scent and instinct if that's what it took—and he nearly plowed into Turner and Jamie still standing on the porch as they buttoned their coats against the cold wind.

"I'm sorry," he said, just catching himself before he managed to crash into them. "I just…" *didn't think through this.* "I don't have your number."

"That's because you have my phone," Jamie pointed out. "I'm at the fire station."

"Right. The fire station." Because she was a firefighter. Every time that Devon felt like he couldn't feel stupider, he managed to make more of an idiot out of himself. "I should have this fixed tomorrow if I have the battery in stock. A couple of days if I have to drive to Madison for it." He'd already told her all of that, he remembered.

"Oh, look at the time," Turner said, not even bothering to look at his wrist. "Really must be back at the office. See you later, Jamie. A lot later."

"See ya," Jamie replied, rolling her eyes after him. Then they were alone on the porch and she looked at Devon, almost shyly, and Devon suddenly remembered that he couldn't do this.

He couldn't do any of this. He was way out of his depth.

"So, do you want to grab a coffee?" Jamie asked, after he'd let the silence get weird between them.

"Coffee?"

"It's a drink brewed from roasted beans," Jamie explained. "They serve it here, actually."

"I like coffee," Devon said stupidly.

"I think you could use some," Jamie suggested kindly. "When do you get off?"

Now is good, his lynx hissed suggestively.

That is not what she meant, Devon protested. *Stop helping.* He looked at his wrist and realized he wasn't wearing a watch. "Three," he said. Then his brain caught up with him. "But I have to meet Abby after school. She's my sister. And then we make dinner. And…it's not a good night."

"When's your next day off?" Jamie asked patiently.

It took Devon a ridiculously long time to remember. "Tomorrow. I don't work tomorrow." He should be doing more of the heavy lifting here, he thought in despair, but he was still vacillating between certainty that his existence had no meaning without this woman and conviction that he'd never deserve or win her. She didn't want a place in what passed for his life.

His mouth hadn't caught up with his doubts. "Do you want to get coffee tomorrow morning at the bakery? About ten?"

"There you go," Jamie encouraged him with laughter in her eyes. "Ten o'clock tomorrow at the bakery sounds great. I'll see you then. Aren't you freezing?"

He should be, Devon thought, shrugging. But he was flushed with heat, filled with excitement and dread. Was this what falling in love was like? A confused, aching, terrible feeling of anticipation and hope and despair? He wanted to kiss her, and warn her away, and fall at her feet and pledge himself to her.

He couldn't do any of that, so he just gruffly said, "I'll see you tomorrow," and fell back in through the door of Gran's Grits as she strode away.

Old George was picking up the apron that Devon had shed; he'd managed to rip off one of the ties when he pulled it off.

True to character, Old George didn't say anything, but he did give Devon a long, inscrutable look.

Devon wasn't sure how he got through the rest of his shift, or how he got home; he just wandered through his day, his lynx purring in his head, his body a tangle of anticipation. He found himself standing in front of the sink staring out the kitchen window. He hadn't even bothered taking his coat off, and he had no idea how long he'd been there.

"I hate this town!" Abby stormed in, slamming the front door behind her and bringing Devon back into awareness at last.

"What's wrong?" he asked in dread.

"I hate this school. I hate everyone here!"

To Devon's horror, she looked tearful, and he desperately offered, "Do you want a snack?"

It was exactly the wrong thing to say.

"I'm not *five* anymore!"

Her backpack went flying, further than she clearly expected it to, and it smashed into the bookshelf. The books were too tightly packed to move, but a vase on the top shelf toppled and fell. It was, fortunately, both empty and metal, so it only bounced off the floor and rolled away, unharmed.

Abby burst into tears and fled for her room.

Devon helplessly collected the vase and her backpack, staring at her closed door. His chest ached for her. He'd hoped it would be easier in Green Valley, that she'd have more chances to make friends than in a big faceless school in the city.

His lynx had always wanted space to run, which was why he'd picked this town, after careful research, already certain that Abby was going to be a shifter, too, in a few years. He hoped, from the cryptic exotic animal sightings in the area, that there would be other shifters, though he had yet to find any confirmation. He had suspicions about Turner, given his size and strength, and he was pretty sure that Gran was her own elderly cat, but he hadn't figured out how to broach the subject without making himself look crazy if he was wrong.

It suddenly struck him that Jamie might be a shifter, too and he had a rush of hope. Had she recognized him as *her* mate? He'd never had much luck with girls—understanding them, attracting them, or talking to them. But she'd seemed...interested. Interested enough to put up with his desperate fumbling at trying to ask her out. Maybe she had an animal inside her, urging her on like he did.

He shook his head. He shouldn't be thinking about Jamie right now. He had to be there for *Abby*.

Had he failed his sister, with this move? Sometimes he felt like he'd done nothing *but* fail Abby, over and over. He'd been hopelessly unprepared to suddenly be an acting single dad, and all the webpages in the world couldn't advise him on how to help a five-year-old handle overwhelming grief, when all he really wanted to do was lie down with her and cry himself.

They had muddled through with counselors and therapists, fought with each other, and spent long nights talking as frankly as they could. They had clashed over rules and bonded over movies and video games, argued about clothing, agreed wholeheartedly about food. He was always completely transparent about money and feelings and reasons, and Abby was more honest with him that he suspected most kids were with big brothers.

At the end of the day, they were a team.

And they never, ever went to bed angry.

Devon hung her overloaded backpack by the door and went back to the kitchen.

A few minutes later, he knocked on Abby's door.

"What?" she called defensively from inside, her voice muffled by the door and her distress.

"I know you aren't five anymore."

He knew that entirely too well. Five-year-old Abby could be

distracted with candy and tickled. Twelve-year-old Abby was suddenly talking about her weight, and didn't want to be touched.

She was quiet, so Devon stumbled on. "But we have Pop-Tarts, and I already toasted one for you and they aren't as good when they're cold."

The door cracked open. "They taste like ass and cardboard when they're cold."

Devon dropped the hot Pop-Tart into her extended hand and she juggled it and took a cautious bite. "You aren't supposed to say ass," he reminded her.

"You're—"

"—not your dad," Devon finished for her. "But I'm your big brother and it'll make me look really bad if you're swearing like a soldier at school when I go in for conferences." He folded a Pop-Tart of his own into his mouth, wincing at the hot filling. "And I still gotta sign all your permission slips and crap."

Abby giggled. "You're not supposed to say crap," she retorted.

"You're not my mom," Devon mocked her.

Abby smiled around the last bite of her Pop-Tart. "Sorry," she said, not specifying what she was sorry for.

"It's okay," Devon said. He hung out at the door, not sure if he was going to get a hug and not wanting to ask for one, but he wasn't surprised when she shrugged and said, "I've got homework."

"Let me know if you need help," Devon offered.

"It's history," Abby scoffed.

"Nevermind," Devon chuckled. "I'm putting a pizza in the oven. Hawaiian or pepperoni?"

"Who lives in a pineapple, under the sea…"

"Hawaiian it is."

But he frowned as he went out to the kitchen. Where might Jamie fit in their team? Should he tell Abby about her? How did he *explain* her?

All he could see were roadblocks and confusion. He didn't want to fail his sister. He didn't want to fail his mate.

4

Jamie didn't want to admit how nervous she was, sitting alone at the table in the bakery waiting for Devon.

She didn't get nervous. She was a creature of impulse and action, a doer. She took risks, lived on adrenaline.

This was just a coffee date, she reminded herself, blowing on her hot latte. It wasn't like she was moving to Alaska, or accepting a marriage proposal.

She was good at handling people. She didn't care what they thought. She was tough and independent.

So why was her heart pounding in her throat?

She knew when he came in, before she even saw him, somehow, and when she did see him, she was struck all over again how handsome he was, how gracefully he moved, how deliberate every gesture was.

He looked around and found her at once, and Jamie remembered to raise her hand in greeting. He didn't pause to order his own coffee, only covered the distance between them with a few long strides and dropped into the chair opposite from her.

"My life is really complicated," he blurted, as if he'd been practicing what to say all night. "I'm sorry for that, and I don't want to pretend that I'm normal or like I can date like normal people, but I really *like* you and I'd like to make something work but I really have no idea how to do that."

"We could start with coffee," Jamie suggested gently, pretending like she wasn't feeling butterflies in her chest cavity. She ought to be terrified; this was way too intense for her tastes, far too fast. And she didn't like complicated things.

"Turner told me you're taking care of your sister," Jamie said, when he returned with a steaming cup of black coffee.

"Yeah," Devon said solemnly. "Our folks died when she was five. I was seventeen, just a couple of months from eighteen, and they let me have guardianship."

"How old is she now?"

"Twelve."

Jamie did the math in her head. He'd be twenty-four, just like she was. But instead of being able to hare off in any direction she felt like she had at seventeen, he'd been raising a *kid*.

"Twelve is a hard age," she said, speaking from her own experience.

"Yeah, especially..." Devon trailed off. "Yeah," he ended lamely.

Jamie felt a jolt of sympathy for him, essentially suddenly a single dad before he even got to be a kid himself.

Sympathy turned to admiration when he looked up and said firmly, "I won't say it hasn't been hard, but it's been worth it. She's a great kid." Unexpectedly, a smile quirked at the corners of his mouth. "You'd probably like her," he said. "She's got a habit of pulling pranks."

Jamie groaned. "Oh, lord, who's been telling you stories?"

"Andrea says you broke her record for suspensions in one year," Devon said.

Jamie realized that if he was devastating when he was being serious, or covering his embarrassment with scowls and glares, Devon with mischief dancing in his face could utterly undo her.

"It's Green Valley," she protested. "I was only suspended three times and people would make you think I was a hardened war criminal. God, I hate this town. I could not escape it fast enough, and I cannot wait to leave again."

That seemed to draw Devon up, and there was an awkward moment of silence. He couldn't be that serious already, could he? It confused Jamie that even the idea of it didn't send her running for the door.

"Were you born here?" Devon asked shyly.

"No. My mom moved here when I was about two," Jamie said, shrugging. "But I grew up here, spent every humid summer and crappy winter in this town."

"Are your folks still here?"

"My mom's dead," Jamie said briefly. "Dad...is long gone."

Devon made a noise of sympathy and Jamie was tempted for a moment to tell him more. Then he gave her a look so warm and understanding that she felt like her feet had been swept out from underneath her. "It's hard," he said simply.

Jamie hid her confusion by sipping her coffee.

"So, what's Alaska like?" Devon asked.

"Big," Jamie said seriously. "It's this great, huge, beautiful land with strange, loud, interesting people."

"I thought that was Texas," Devon observed.

"Bigger," Jamie said. "Arguably stranger. Far less peopled."

"What made you go?" Devon's gold-green eyes were full of what might-have-been.

"I hate Green Valley with a fiery passion?" Jamie scoffed. "And Alaska was really far away."

Devon chuckled, suspecting a joke.

Jamie went on, "I wanted to see more of the world than just Green Valley, and it seemed like Alaska was full of opportunity. They were looking for effers—emergency fire fighters—and it sounded...fun."

"Was it dangerous?"

"Less dangerous and more monotonous, honestly," Jamie said. "I mean, there are some days when you really hope the wind doesn't suddenly change directions, and you are reminded that nature is big and strong and uncaring. But there are also whole weeks that are just an awful lot of brushing and clearing and hard physical drudgery for really long days." She'd made enough during the summer that she didn't need to worry about working through the winter if she didn't want to.

"Will you…do it again?"

"Next summer, sure. It's a good gig. Hard on the body, though. It's not a settle-down career." Her instincts gave a shriek of warning. She wasn't ready to talk settle-down with this captivating man. She might actually want to do it.

"Speaking of, what gym do you go to?" she asked too quickly. "I've been meaning to get back into some kind of workout habit before I lose all my muscle tone."

Devon scowled and gazed into his long-empty coffee cup. "I don't really…ah...work out."

"Well, you don't get that kind of physique slinging plates of biscuits at Gran's," Jamie said, hoping she was hitting the right tone of tease and flattery. "What do you do, aside from waitressing?"

"I work at Dean's hardware shop on weekends," Devon said, looking like he wasn't at all sure about Jamie's tease-flatter ratio. Dean not only owned the local hardware shop, he was also the local volunteer firefighter that Jamie had come in to replace at Turner's request for the winter. Jamie wasn't sure yet how she felt about his new girlfriend, Shelley. She was pretty *city* for Green Valley.

But then, so was Devon.

"And I have a freelance business doing web programming on the side."

"Oh, an entrepreneur," Jamie said with admiration. "What's it called?"

Devon frowned. Jamie was beginning to realize he did that when he was feeling especially shy about something. "Broken Lynx," he said gruffly. "Lynx, like the cat. It's…kind of an inside joke, because I…fix broken links. It's stupid."

"It's not stupid," Jamie said, and she wanted to pound who or whatever had made him feel insecure about something he obviously had invested a lot of himself into. "Web programmers can make really decent money."

Devon winced. "I'm better at the programming than at the making money," he confessed.

"No shame in that, either," Jamie said fiercely. "Let me guess, you hate the invoicing part, and never feel comfortable charging what you're worth."

"Am I that obvious?" Devon asked.

Jamie opened her mouth, then closed it. She didn't think it would be, to just anyone. But there was something about Devon that telegraphed deeper than just his facial expressions and his body language…like she was actually feeling what he did.

That was absurd, of course.

But she couldn't shake the sensation that this was more than just coffee and attraction.

Or the unsettled feeling in her stomach that it caused.

5

The more they talked, the more Devon knew that his lynx was right. It wasn't just that Jamie was beautiful and he was in a dry spell of dating that he barely let himself acknowledge.

She was everything he'd ever imagined in one incredibly sexy package. She was clever, confident, sweet, and imaginative. Knowing about Abby hadn't frightened her off—he wasn't sure if anything could scare this fiery, bold beauty.

She is our mate, his lynx purred. Claim *her.*

He gazed at her hands, strong around her long-empty coffee cup.

Was she a shifter?

"I hear you bought Tawny's old house."

He was frowning again, Devon realized. He ought to be smiling, encouraging her, doing his part of this strange courtship dance. So far, he'd managed to insult her instead of flatter her, and point out every one of his own inadequacies. "Yes," he said briefly. "It's small, but close to the school and my jobs."

"I used to bike that neighborhood all the time," Jamie said, gazing out the window in that direction. "You should show me what's changed."

"We didn't change much," Devon said, not recognizing at first that he was scowling again. "The house was in good shape and there were just a few things that the inspector caught...oh." She had given him an excuse to invite her to his house and was watching him now with one eyebrow raised, her blue eyes dancing.

He swallowed. "Would you like to come see it? Compare it to what you remember?"

"There you go," she said with a sly grin as she stood.

Devon pushed back his chair so hard that it scraped on the floor and several other customers turned toward the noise. He scrambled to his feet and snatched his coat off the back of his chair. "I'll show you where it is. I mean, you already know."

To his delight and discomfort, Jamie put her coat on, pulled her hat over her head, and then came and threaded her arm into his. "You can show me anyway."

Devon spent the walk the few blocks to his new house—which would always be Tawny's old house in the eyes of the locals—in a dizzy blur of anticipation and despair. He was going to ruin this. He was going to make a fool of himself. It was a minor miracle he hadn't already. It was hard to think with her walking so close beside him, occasionally brushing a hip against his, her arm linked with his. He wished they weren't wearing winter coats; it felt like too much between them.

They didn't talk much, just inane observations about the weather (cold), the town (small), and the buildings (old).

Then, they were finally at the gate to the house and Devon was standing aside to let her go first.

"Sorry, I haven't shoveled yet," Devon said. There were a few inches of slushy snow accumulated on the walkway up to the covered porch. It would probably melt off in a day or two.

"Doesn't bother me," Jamie said.

Devon shut the gate and his breath was fast and didn't put enough oxygen in his lungs. Did his hands shake in anticipation as he unlocked the door, just a little?

"All we really had done was some roof work, but the decor is probably—" Devon started.

Then Jamie was up on her tiptoes, wrapping her arms up around his neck, and he was kicking the door shut hard behind them as he bent down to kiss her.

Fire flowed through him, head to toe, blooming from his mouth where he hungrily feasted on Jamie's eager lips. The coats really were too much then, and he struggled to keep himself from simply ripping them off, fumbling with the zipper at Jamie's throat with one hand.

"*Excuse* me?!"

He and Jamie froze, mouths and arms tangled, and after a moment, backed apart and faced the source of the interruption.

"Abby," Devon growled. "Aren't you supposed to be at school?"

Her voice was disgusted and defensive, a tone that Devon was getting more and more familiar with as she got older. "It was an early out, end of the quarter or something."

"This…is Jamie," he introduced awkwardly. "Jamie, this is my sister, Abby."

6

*A*bby looked very twelve, Jamie thought. Not quite 'young woman,' but definitely not 'little kid' anymore. She had a round, suspicious face with the same golden-green eyes that Devon had, and she was tall and lanky, with knobby elbows sticking out from her t-shirt. She had Devon's golden-brown mop of hair and his cultivated frown. Jamie would have picked her out as Devon's sister from a lineup in a red-hot minute.

"It's nice to meet you, Abby," Jamie said as casually as she could around her burning lips.

Abby mumbled something that had the cadence of a polite reply. "I'll be in my room," she added, sounding sulky, and then she was dashing out of the room, leaving an awkward tableau behind.

Jamie shoved her hands into her pockets. "I...should go," she said reluctantly. Their obvious plans had very definitely been shelved.

Poor Devon looked like he was being given a terrible choice. He raked a hand through his hair, face like a thunderstorm. "I warned you, my life is complicated. What if we have dinner? Tomorrow?"

"At Gran's?" Jamie suggested, half-dreading the audience.

Devon shook his head, obviously considering the same. "How about here? I can cook."

"He can't cook!" Abby's voice came from the obviously very poorly sound-proofed bedroom in the back.

"Then you can cook!" Devon retorted over his shoulder.

"Fine!"

Jamie smothered her laughter. "Um, that would be great."

Devon walked her out onto the porch. "I'm so sorry," he said. "I should have known. I would have…"

Jamie stopped his apology by dragging him down for a swift kiss, wishing with her whole body that the day had gone differently. She could see the desperation in his eyes, and feel a reflection of the same yearning she felt. He was so damn cute and earnest and she was more smitten with him than anyone she'd ever met in her life.

She thought that she'd had some epic crushes in her life, but they all paled to the way she felt faced with this man.

"Later," she promised, walking backwards down the stairs.

Hopefully not much later.

"Wait!" Devon called, and Jamie was alarmed by the way her heart leapt in her chest. This was ridiculous and utterly unlike her.

He ducked back into the house and emerged a moment later, before Jamie could decide whether or not to follow him. "Your phone," he explained, taking all the steps at once with no trouble to hold it gingerly out to her. "I had it in my coat pocket the whole time. I replaced the battery, and it works fine now. I...charged it for you."

Jamie took it, thinking that it wasn't the only thing he had charged. "Thanks," she said as casually as she could manage.

"I probably should have opened with that," Devon said, looking reluctant to leave her and go back into the house.

"Instead of 'My life is complicated?'" The phone felt warm in her hands and she was thinking too hard about how his hands must be much more nimble than their size implied to fix such a small item. "How much do I owe you?"

Devon blushed. "Nothing."

"You really *are* terrible at invoicing, aren't you," Jamie teased him.

Devon's slow, sheepish smile was like a crack through to sunlight. "What if you get coffee at Shaun's next time we go?"

"I shall also ply you with sweet pastries," Jamie promised, and she realized that she was smiling foolishly back at him. She didn't know how to make her face stop being stupid. "Anyway, I gotta go."

"Yeah."

They stood there another beat. Jamie finally said, "Bye," and turned on her heel to go.

She spent the entire block listening for his voice to call her back again, but he didn't.

The walk back to the fire station was lonely and cold compared to the walk to Tawny's house with Devon close beside her. Jamie pulled the collar of her coat up and jammed her hat down as far over her ears as it would go.

She wasn't sure if she was glad or sorry to find that the station wasn't empty.

Turner was sitting at the little table by the coffee maker, staring into his soul at the bottom of an empty cup. He looked up in surprise, clearly not expecting her.

"Want something in that?" Jamie asked, stomping her boots off at the mat.

"Too late for coffee," Turner said mournfully.

"What's it going to do, keep you up all night?" Jamie scoffed. "It's like three in the afternoon."

"Some day, you'll be old and young people will mock you," Turner told her sourly.

Jamie poured herself a cup of coffee; she could sleep through just about anything and her tolerance for caffeine was quite high at any hour.

"How was your date?" Turner asked.

"You're not my dad."

Jamie meant it flippantly, but it hung in the air between them with unexpected tension. She swallowed, not sure how to take it back. Turner didn't seem hurt, but there was a shuttered look over his face, one that always made Jamie realize what a jerk she could be without trying.

She did what she always did in these cases: she ran.

"I'm going to the grocery store for chips. Are we stocked on coffee?"

It was as close to a peace offering as he'd get, and Turner knew it.

"We're good," Turner said.

But Jamie had to wonder, as she turned and left.

7

"So, you're really into this girl," Abby guessed.

It didn't take any particular genius to come to that conclusion.

Devon was buttoning and unbuttoning the top button on his shirt, trying to balance between looking not-too-formal and not-too-casual. Maybe a collared shirt was too much altogether. It was the third shirt he'd tried on.

"At least this way, if dinner is a disaster, you can blame it on me," Abby pointed out.

"I wouldn't blame you." Devon stopped playing with the buttons and turned to face Abby with a scowl. "I would never blame you."

"Just saying you could," Abby said. "Unbuttoned is better."

Devon glared at his reflection and unbuttoned it.

"Very smooth, now all you need is some gold chains and some more chest hair…"

"Shouldn't you be burning something?" Devon asked in exasperation.

"It's in the oven. Salad is made and it only takes a few minutes to steam asparagus."

"Thanks for doing this," Devon said seriously.

"No prob," Abby said. They smiled fondly at each other for a moment, then she looked completely embarrassed and vanished back to the kitchen.

Just as Devon thought that he could not possibly get more nervous, the doorbell rang. He still hadn't decided what to do with his buttons, but it was too late now.

Abby got to the door first, by virtue of both being closer and pelting to beat him there.

"Hi," Abby said, and Devon was frozen speechless behind his sister.

He'd been sure that he had imagined how beautiful and perfect Jamie was. Surely it had been a false memory, exaggerated by his underlying feelings for her and his lynx's obsession.

Instead, she was even *more* gorgeous, with her freckled, tanned skin and her upturned nose. Her lips were redder than he remembered, and when she licked them, Devon had to fight down an urge to growl possessively.

"Hey," Jamie said casually, and when Abby stood aside, she swept into the room like she owned it.

"I'm making chicken," Abby said. "Like my brother."

It took Devon a moment to get the joke, but Jamie looked at him and laughed, and if he'd thought she was beautiful a moment ago, it was nothing compared to her face crinkled in joyous mirth.

"Smells great," Jamie said sincerely. "I'm looking forward to it."

"Can I take your coat?" Devon finally remembered to ask.

Jamie wriggled out of her blue and orange jacket, stuffing her hat and her mittens into a sleeve. "Thanks," she said, almost shyly.

Devon took it, stared at it for a few moments, then realized that he should hang it up. He hadn't planned on that, and all of the hangers in the closet were being used and the whole thing was stuffed tight. He managed to double up one of Abby's jackets with a raincoat and squeezed Jamie's coat into the space.

So smooth, he told himself sarcastically. *All I need is gold chains and more chest hair.*

While he was struggling with the contents of the closet, Abby more gracefully showed Jamie to the dining room.

"It looks a lot different than when Tawny lived here," she observed. "I'm used to seeing a piano over there."

"Do you play?" Devon blurted.

"Nope," Jamie said, shaking her head. "I took about a month of lessons before my mom realized it was just throwing money away."

The timer in the kitchen went off and Abby disappeared.

"This is nice," Jamie said neutrally, sitting in the chair that Devon indicated for her. "Festive."

He had agonized over adding candles when he set the table, finally decided that they were appropriate for a romantic dinner, but not a dinner chaperoned by his twelve-year-old sister. Instead, he'd found a Halloween centerpiece with a black wreath sporting sparkly bats.

"Well, it's not that far past Halloween," Devon said. He realized he was scowling in embarrassment and forced himself to smile.

"It looks great," Jamie said kindly.

"Do you need any help, Abby?" Devon called. *Please?* he didn't add.

"I've got it!" Abby sang back, more annoying than ever.

"She seems like a great kid," Jamie said, fiddling with her spoon.

"She's great," Devon echoed.

"I really am," Abby said, appearing with a platter of roasted chicken and potatoes.

She put them down on the hot pads waiting on the table and slipped into her chair. "Dig in!"

Dinner went much better than Devon had any right to expect. Abby kept her snarky observations to a minimum, and Jamie complimented her food sincerely. "When I was twelve, I was barely capable of making a box of mac and cheese," she confessed.

"Devon is an awful cook," Abby said loftily. "I learned to cook a few years ago out of self-defense."

"I'm not that bad," Devon protested. "Everything I served you was perfectly edible."

"Edible in the *won't actually kill you* meaning," Abby scoffed. "Not in the *starving isn't worse than this* way."

Jamie laughed. "After a summer of MREs and camp rations, I bet I'd have eaten it," she said.

That led to Abby asking about firefighting, and Alaska. Jamie told colorful stories, stopping some of them halfway through as she realized that the end wasn't appropriate. Devon caught himself staring at her repeatedly, watching her lips as she spoke, or licked food from her fork, and several times he dragged his gaze back to find Abby watching him suspiciously.

He focused on his food, and on not saying anything too stupid.

"I didn't make dessert," Abby apologized as they scraped their plates bare. "We have some cookies, I think."

Devon collected the plates and brought back a package of chocolate chip cookies to split.

"I should have picked up something from Shaun's," he said regretfully.

"This is just fine," Jamie assured him, and she smiled up at him like the sun.

If it hadn't been for Abby's presence, he would have tried kissing her again on the spot.

"Can I help with dishes?" Jamie asked, after she had crunched through a few of the commercial disks.

"I can…" Abby started.

"Cooks don't clean," Devon said firmly.

Abby looked pleased and Devon wondered if she'd neatly manipulated him again. He gathered up a few of the glasses and Jamie followed him into the kitchen with a pile of plates.

"I have homework to do!" Abby called after them. "In my room! With my music on! For a long time!"

"It's Friday night," Devon pointed out suspiciously, pausing in the door while Jamie went to fill the sink with soapy water.

"In which case, no one needs to go to bed early, and if you were to…I don't know…walk her home, no one would care when you came back," Abby said, her eyes huge and innocent.

"Abby," Devon groaned.

Abby gave him a pair of cheerful thumbs ups and disappeared into her room.

Devon turned back to find Jamie hastily looking back to the sink.

"I warned you," he told her. "My life is complicated."

"You're a good brother," Jamie said warmly.

A *brother* was not at all what Devon wanted to be at that moment, and he went to get the dish towel from the refrigerator door and start drying.

8

Jamie hadn't been sure what to expect from a dinner with Devon and his kid sister in Tawny's old house, but the whole thing went much more smoothly than she feared. Abby was sharp as a tack and had no illusions about the fact that she was camping in on what would otherwise have been a date.

Jamie had caught her appraising look several times, and found herself hoping that she'd made a favorable impression.

It was the first time she'd ever worried about what a twelve-year-old thought of her...or at least the first time since she *was* twelve.

When Abby vanished back to her room, a tense silence remained.

Jamie and Devon spoke inanely about the dishes to fill it, and about Tawny's house and how the kitchen had been different.

"They replaced the fridge. We had the option between paying more and getting a dishwasher, or accepting it the way it was," Devon said apologetically. "We were on a budget."

"The fire station barely has a kitchen sink," Jamie said, washing the last plate. "Having a dish rack is an unspeakable luxury. To say nothing of a full sized fridge. Is there anything else?"

"That's all the dishes," Devon said. He was looking all shy and geeky again, and if Jamie didn't already know how paper-thin the walls in this house were, she would have kissed him right then. Maybe he'd lift her up on the counter and... She let the stopper out and watched the water swirl down.

"I...I could walk you home," Devon offered softly.

"Yeah," Jamie said, and he literally threw his dish towel over the remaining dishes in the drainer.

"I'll get your coat."

He struggled with the tiny closet and emerged with her coat and his own. They both put them on in silence and Devon called, "We're going!"

"Don't hurry back!" Abby shouted back.

The evening outside was dark and bitterly cold, and Jamie zipped her coat up further and pulled her hood up over her hat.

Devon didn't seem bothered by the cold wind at all, but he didn't object in the slightest when she took his gloved hand and pressed up against him.

They walked close together, finding a synchronized step after only a few tries.

"That probably wasn't much of a dinner date," he said regretfully. "She's getting old enough that I could leave her alone long enough that we could grab a meal somewhere fancy in Madison or in Hamilton. She'd never forgive me if I tried to get her a sitter at this age, but she's...pretty responsible."

"It was a great dinner."

"I told you, my life is complicated."

"So you keep saying."

When they got to the fire station, Jamie drew him to a stop outside the door. "Devon," she said seriously. "I'm not sure what you're expecting..."

"I want...I..." He swallowed.

"I'm planning to go back to Alaska in the summer," Jamie said flatly. "I don't want to lead you on, or make you promises I don't intend to keep. You've got a sister and a house you just bought. I don't know how all those things go together long term."

"I don't either," Devon said intensely. "But I know that if I don't try to make something work, I will never forgive myself. I've never met anyone like you, and I know there's something here. Something real. Something...amazing."

Jamie stared at him. In any other guy in the world, she would have guessed that he was making wild statements to get her to invite him up.

"If you don't want to..." Devon said with effort. He was still holding her gloved hand in his and she could feel him flexing it, like he was making himself not clutch at her.

"I'm...willing to see where this goes," Jamie said slowly. "Take it slow, see what happens."

"Can I kiss you?" He asked it desperately, like he was afraid of her answer.

Jamie answered by stepping closer and lifting her face to his.

She had forgotten how delicious his kiss was. No, she hadn't forgotten, the pale memory just didn't compare to the actual touch of his mouth.

He kissed her deeply, pulling her close up against him, and Jamie felt her resolve slip. No one had ever set her on fire like this with a kiss. No one had ever kissed her like this, like he was losing himself in her. It was as if all the shyness and geekiness was burning away, leaving raw need and passion in its place. He was growling against her lips, kissing and biting and dragging his teeth along her jaw as he held her closer and kissed harder.

"Upstairs," Jamie gasped, when she could draw breath. She clawed at his shoulders, and hated his coat for keeping them as far apart as they were.

They staggered into the fire station and he kicked the door closed behind them so hard that it bounced open again. Jamie tackled him against it to close it again, wrapping her arms around his broad shoulders and kissing him hard.

He had his hands up under her coat, and they struggled together with her zipper as they shed gloves and hats, leaving them carelessly strewn behind them as Jamie led him to the stairs going up to her efficiency.

His coat was left halfway up the staircase, hers slightly after, and

Jamie was walking up backwards, undoing his buttons and pushing his shirt back off his shoulders when she ran into her door, hard enough to knock the breath out of her. Devon's hands were up around her face and he was kissing her again, even though her lips were already so bruised it felt like she was standing too close to flames.

"In," she said, but she didn't have her keys, they'd been left in her coat pocket on the stairs. She got free and skipped down to gather it up and dig into the pocket.

"You said you wanted to take it slow," Devon said, panting like she was. "I'm sorry…"

"That was before I got your shirt off," Jamie said honestly, fishing her keys out and raising them triumphantly. "Inside, now."

But Devon was suddenly shy again as they went into the tiny apartment. "I didn't mean to be so…"

Jamie threw her keys onto the desk and reached for him. "I did," she assured him.

He was frozen under her lips, and when Jamie backed away, she could see the doubt and fear in his eyes. "I don't…I've never…this is…"

Jamie blinked with a sudden suspicion. "Are you a virgin?"

Devon's blush was answer enough. "I told you, my life is…"

"…complicated," Jamie finished for him. She took him by the hands and drew him down to sit on the bed with her. "This *isn't*."

She put her hands on his shoulders, his broad, gorgeous shoulders, and traced the muscles down his arms. His shirt was outside the apartment door somewhere. He shuddered under her fingers and his breath came faster.

Jamie pulled off her own shirt and watched the hunger in his face sharpen like a knife. "You can touch me," she said, and to her own ears, it sounded like she was begging.

Maybe she was.

When his hands touched her skin, careful and clever, Jamie sucked in her breath like she hadn't ever tasted air. He traced the line from her neck, along each collarbone, and then down to cup her breasts reverently. He dipped his head to kiss her shoulder, and then the top of her closest breast, and when he leaned into her, Jamie fell willingly back onto the bed.

He explored her eagerly, struggling with her bra until she took pity on him and undid it herself. At every stage, he paused, assessing her enjoyment, and Jamie could barely keep herself from imploring for more.

He was huge inside his jeans, and when Jamie rubbed her hand over his straining cock, he growled like an animal and every muscle in his body tensed up. "Yes," she told him. "Yes…"

With his lips on her stomach, he unbuttoned her jeans, so slowly and carefully that Jamie caught herself pulsing herself at him and whining in need. As he slipped them down past her hips, the cool touch of air on her nethers made her squirm. "Yes, please...yes…"

"Jamie," he hissed, and he touched her so lightly that Jamie wanted to cry out, drawing one finger wonderingly along her swollen lips. She could feel how wet and ready she was, and he was still, frustratingly, wearing his jeans.

"Devon," she warned. "If you don't get out of your pants, we are going to have a problem."

She was not sure how he got out of them, but she spent the time getting her own jeans off her ankles, and then he was naked and urgent and beautiful above her, and she was spreading her legs in welcome.

"Wait, wait," he said suddenly, pausing with his freed cock just teasingly out of reach. "Condom. I brought one. It's in...my coat!"

"I'm on the pill," Jamie said swiftly, not sure how he'd been able to even remember what a condom was. She was so keyed up that her world seemed no bigger than the space between his arms.

"I...don't...I might...I can't…"

She could read the animal desperation in him. "You can," she told him. "You'd better…"

Then she was lifting her hips to meet him as he gave a raw noise of need and slipped, hard and huge, into her.

For a moment, he just held her there, and Jamie felt like she was wound to a fever pitch she'd never experienced before, poised on a wave of pleasure that she hadn't even realized was possible.

Then he was moving, slowly at first, then with increasing frenzy until he was crashing into her like a force of nature, faster and deeper, clutching her closer and closer until Jamie felt her last resistance falter and vanish and she was only pleasure and release and she was falling from a great height to a perfectly safe place.

At her cry of bliss, he found his own release, and she felt him tense and spill deep into her at last.

They coupled together a long moment afterwards, slowing and remembering how to breathe again.

"I'm sorry…I'm sorry…" he gasped. "I couldn't…"

"You…have got…to stop apologizing…" Jamie told him, willing her heartbeat to slow. "That was *perfect*."

"I should have…"

"Perfect," Jamie insisted, drawing his face back to hers for a kiss. "Absolutely perfect."

All the tension in his body slowly released as they lay together in her tiny, narrow bed. "Jamie…" he said, cradling her close. "My Jamie."

It should have terrified her, the possessiveness in his voice. She should remind him now that good sex was just making him feel delirious.

But she *felt* like his. She felt like she'd never been anyone else's, like she belonged here, in his arms the way she'd never belonged anywhere else in her entire life.

"My Devon," she whispered, too softly for him to hear. "My home."

9

They dozed together for a while, drifting in and out of contented comfort, until Devon started to feel cramped in Jamie's tiny bed. His feet were off the end, and he could feel the slope of the mattress falling off at the very edge of his back.

"I should get home," he said reluctantly.

"Want a shower in the utility room before you go?" Jamie offered practically.

That sounded marginally better than putting his sweaty, sticky body back into his clothing, and Devon had definitely not yet had enough of Jamie's silky skin yet. "Yes," he agreed. "If you join me."

"Deal." She spilled out of the bed and padded to the closet. "You're in luck and I've got *two* clean towels."

Wrapped in these towels, they went to the door and crept downstairs like burglars. Fortunately, there was no sign of Turner or Carter and they snuck into the shower where they leisurely soaped each other and stood in the blazing hot water exploring each other with care.

She was compact and strong, with perfectly proportioned limbs. Devon was enthralled with her collarbones, her hips, her breasts, the little dimples in the small of her back, the place her neck met her shoulder, her wrists...everything about her was simply fascinating and gorgeous.

Was she shifter strong? Devon wondered again, but he couldn't quite make himself ask. One world-shattering new thing at a time, he decided.

He wasn't sure how long they would have stayed in the steaming water...if the station alarm had not suddenly begun to shrill.

Jamie fell against the water controls, shutting off the heat abruptly, and began to towel off furiously as she fled for the stairs. "Turner will be here in just a minute!" she exclaimed, and Devon took the second towel and followed her, gathering their coats and hats and gloves and shirts as he went.

He had never dressed so quickly in his life, pulling reluctant clothing over damp limbs, but it wasn't quite fast enough. He raced after Jamie down the stairs still trying to button his shirt as she went for the turnout gear waiting in the station bay...and met Turner coming in from the outside.

He was keenly aware of his wet hair and the fact that he'd started his shirt buttons off-square, so he had three buttons left and two buttonholes.

"Er...hi," he said awkwardly. The radio in the truck was crackling with incomprehensible directions.

Turner gave him one raking look and was going for his own turnout gear as Jamie swung into the driver's seat of the fire truck and smashed the button to open the garage door. "First one ready gets to drive!" she called merrily. "Every second counts!"

Turner was still putting his arms into his coat as he pulled himself into the passenger seat. Jamie was pulling away before his door was even closed, and then Devon was alone, disheveled, in the cold, empty garage as the truck's siren faded away.

Not sure what else to do, he closed the garage door against the cold night air, fixed the buttons on his shirt, and let himself out the man door on the side of the garage.

He walked home slowly, wondering if he should worry for Jamie, if he should worry for *them*, if he'd been any good, what

Abby must think, how quickly rumor spread in Green Valley…his mind was a tumble of doubts and confusion.

Then he remembered Jamie's joyous face, and the feel of her in his arms and he knew that it was all going to be fine. His lynx was purring in his head, certain that everything was unfolding exactly as it should, and he knew that they were meant to be happy together.

She had texted him by the time he got home, assuring him that the call had been nothing more than an overheated car. "Poured some water in the radiator and watched Turner give them a fun lecture on car maintenance."

As Devon was still trying to figure out what to text back, she added: "See you tomorrow?" and his heart leapt in his chest.

"Shaun's at 10?" he proposed eagerly and a thumbs up emoticon had never looked so beautiful. He promptly called Dean and begged for the morning off.

They met for coffee the day after as well, and the following morning, Jamie showed up at his door in a jogging suit with a light jacket over it. "You're going to help me work off all of Shaun's rich desserts," she said, barely giving him time to change before she dragged him, with a brief hello at Abby, out the door to go running with him.

"Get to school on time!" he called back to his sister.

"I don't usually go jogging," Devon protested, as Jamie teased him and jogged in circles around him at the gate, looking at her watch. "Aren't you cold?"

"You have to actually start running to stay warm," Jamie said. "Try to keep up!"

Then she was off down the middle of the street, and Devon would have followed her anywhere. He sprinted to catch up, and she took it as a challenge, and then they were racing and laughing in the cold air.

The snow from the week before had all melted, so the roads were dry again, and Green Valley never had much traffic. Jamie led him down tiny alleys and through parks that Devon didn't even know about, and once they had slowed down a little, could tell him a little about some of the places they were passing.

"I caught Andrea in this park once, completely buck naked and with a sprained shoulder. She said she'd been sleepwalking, but I am *sure* there was a guy involved," Jamie said. They were barely jogging now, just above a fast walk, and the color was high in her cheeks.

"Shaun's wife?" Devon asked. He knew her a little; she was one of the other waitresses at Gran's. She was juggling a writing career and had a millionaire for a husband so he knew she was only doing it as a favor for Gran. She was also a terrible waitress, so he wasn't sure how much of a favor it really was.

Jamie was jogging backwards so she could talk to him. "Yeah. She and Patricia—do you know Patricia?—they were two years older than me in high school, and they were always really nice to me. When my mom died, they made sure I had like...a prom dress and heels and stuff."

"How old were you?" Devon asked.

"Eighteen," Jamie said, and they both gave up the pretense of jogging as she checked her watch and her heart rate.

Devon stared at the side of her face. Eighteen. Barely older than he'd been when his parents died and he'd taken custody of Abby.

"If it hadn't been for them, I probably wouldn't have finished school. They convinced me to do the last semester and graduate before I hared off to Alaska. I was old enough that I didn't have to go into foster care, and I had a lot of trouble seeing the point of...well, anything. But Andrea and Patricia...and Turner, they got me through."

"What happened to your dad?" Devon had to ask.

Jamie was quiet for so long that Devon wondered if he had said something wrong.

"My mom told me he was a war hero. Afghanistan or something. Died when I was a baby. Except that by the time I could do math and figure out dates, they didn't add up. Then it was Iran. Then it was just overseas, and the story of his service kept changing."

"He wasn't a war hero?"

"I don't know what he was," Jamie said, her voice completely neutral. "Was he a deadbeat? Were they ever married? She lied to me my whole life because she wanted me to have...I don't know...maybe a comforting fiction. But I never forgave her for keeping secrets from me. That's not what you do to people you love." The neutrality left her voice, replaced by bitterness. "I deserved the truth, and she was too cowardly to tell it until it was too late."

"You ever thought about looking him up?" Devon asked hesitantly.

"Lots of times," Jamie said, in that same blank voice. "I tried, after mom died. But I didn't really know where to start, or if I really wanted to know the truth. I mean, I do. Someday. I guess. If I even can. It was a long time ago, now."

"How'd...how'd your mom die?"

Jamie was quiet again, then flashed him an ironic smile. "House fire."

"Oh," Devon said. "*Oh.*"

"I'm surprised you hadn't heard already, thanks to the great Green Valley gossip line. Turner's never forgiven himself. He's the one who paid my plane ticket to Alaska, the first year."

"And you've been living there ever since?"

Jamie shook her head. "No. I travel a lot. Took some classes at a college in Calgary, spent a few years bumming around Hawaii. Footloose and fancy free."

Running, Devon thought. She'd spent so much time *running*.

"What made you come back?" Devon had to ask. Jamie was shivering, now that they weren't running anymore and he drew her into his arms and rubbed her shoulders.

"Turner," Jamie said. "I hate Green Valley, but he needed another pair of hands in the station...and like I said, he never had forgiven himself. He kept tabs on me the whole time. Sent me jail money once, so I kind of owed him."

"Jail money?" Devon sputtered.

"Trespassing and vandalism," Jamie said with a playful shrug. "No big." She hopped in place. "We should be running," she scolded him.

"Are you a felon?" Devon said in mock outrage.

Jamie made a rude noise with her lips. "Misdemeanor," she scoffed. "I got off with a slap on the wrist. C'mon, slowpoke. I got things to do."

They jogged without talking for a while and came back into town, with its tidy neighborhoods and little shops. Some of the neighbors were taking down Halloween decorations, and turkeys and ears of colored corn were being put up in windows. The grocery store had piles of pumpkins in the entryway marked down.

"What are you doing for Thanksgiving?" Devon asked. He plowed forward without pausing for her answer. "Abby wants to do a big turkey spread, but we'd never be able to eat it all ourselves. You could come. You should come. Will you come?"

"I don't usually plan that far ahead," Jamie said with a look of alarm followed by a carefully casual shrug. "Ask me later."

They took reckless advantage of Abby being gone at school, and afterwards, languidly lying on Devon's bed running lazy hands over each other, Jamie commented that she hoped that the neighbors had been out, too.

"It's not like they haven't guessed what we're doing," Devon said. "It's Green Valley. Everyone knows everything."

"You don't have to tell me," Jamie snorted. "Tiny, awful little town." She sat up and gazed down at him. "What are we doing here?"

Devon felt like he had a bird held caged in his hands. She wasn't struggling, exactly, but if he opened his fingers too far, she'd be gone forever.

"What do you want to be doing?" he asked carefully.

"I asked first."

Devon wanted to tell her everything. He wanted to explain that there was no one else for him, ever. She was all of his happiness. She was his perfect mate, and he would never be whole without her. But he knew that if he squeezed too tightly, he'd break her wings.

"I want this to...work out," he said cautiously, reaching up to touch the side of her face.

The conflict in her face was swiftly hidden with a laugh. "Well, *this* part certainly is," she said with an appreciative glance at his body. "Take me on a date this weekend." It sounded like a challenge.

"Harvey's?"

"I said a date, not a drink," Jamie scolded him. "Someplace fancy. Someplace *not* Green Valley."

"I'll make it happen," Devon promised.

10

J amie wondered if she'd made a terrible mistake.

She had half-hoped that taking Devon out in public would put him back in perspective. He'd be geeky and shy once she got him away from the safe, domestic backdrop of Green Valley and she'd remember that she went for alpha assholes and bad boys with tattoos.

And instead, he'd shown up at the station ridiculously early for dinner in a suit and coat that took her breath straight out of her chest, looking like someone from the secret service or a private bodyguard service.

"Where did you get *that*?"

He blushed then. "One of my father's last pieces of advice was that I should always make sure I have a working vehicle and a flattering suit. I bought it in Minneapolis for some work thing."

Jamie looked past him. "Well, it looks like you got half his advice right. And you probably spent more on the suit."

His car was...less impressive.

It was a beat-up Honda from two decades ago at least, with one off-color door and enough rusty dents that it went past 'having character' straight to 'having no resale value.'

"It has heated seats," Devon offered. "My lady?"

Jamie took his elbow and let him lead her to the questionable car and open the door for her. It stuck, and he had to wiggle the handle.

She was wearing heels, a long coat, and even lipstick. She had bought eyeshadow and liner, but after several asymmetrical applications, had given up on that and settled for just the Hot Cherry Bomb lipstick.

The seat was indeed heated, and the ride to Madison was better-sprung than Jamie had expected.

They argued good naturedly over the music selection, limited as they were to the radio and a collection of cassette tapes. "You have Depeche Mode?" Jamie had to laugh.

"The very best of," Devon said proudly.

They sang, badly, for part of the ride. Devon insisted the Britney Spears tape was his sister's, but still knew every word.

"Where are you taking me?" Jamie asked suspiciously, as the drive went on and on.

"You'll see," Devon said mysteriously. He cast her a sideways look and added, "I think you'll like it."

But they didn't stop in Madison. "I think you missed the exit," Jamie pointed out, wondering if he was going to be one of those terrible navigators who hated being corrected.

"We're not going to Madison," Devon told her.

"Are you taking me to *Milwaukee*?"

"You'll see," Devon repeated.

"What about your sister?" Jamie demanded.

"She's a very mature twelve, and she's babysitting the kid next door until late. Probably really late. I told her not to wait up."

Jamie had to smile at his smirking profile. "You're enjoying this, aren't you."

He looked over at her and grinned, sending her heart into involuntary flutters.

Over the next hour, he teased her mercilessly, and the traffic grew thicker. He cast worried glances at his watch and led Jamie through a navigation program on his phone. "We'll just make it," he decided.

"*Where?*" Jamie wailed.

He refused to tell her, guiding his dented car through the increasingly busy streets, straight downtown, until he pulled up in front of a tall building along the lake.

"You got reservations at *Bacchus?*" Jamie said in astonishment as a valet opened her door.

Devon looked triumphant. "Shelley had an in."

"They have probably never parked a car like this in the history of this restaurant," Jamie said as Devon gave the valet his keys.

The valet's face was professionally neutral as he opened the driver's side door with an inelegant creak and drove off with a grind of gears to leave them standing before the building.

"Are you surprised?" Devon asked, like a great, eager puppy.

"I'm surprised," Jamie confessed. "Wow."

"We can hit the club next door if you want to go dancing afterwards," Devon said.

"Have you ever been to a dance club?" Jamie asked him.

"No," Devon confessed.

"We'll see how we feel after dinner," Jamie said. She tucked her hand into his elbow and they went inside.

"Reservation for Maynard," Devon said at the hostess stand.

"I don't have a reservation under that name," she said in chilly tones, and her glance at Jamie was downright scornful.

Jamie was keenly aware of her aged coat and her sparse makeup.

For a moment, both Devon and Jamie were silent and she saw color creep up into his ears.

"Are you sure?" Devon asked diffidently.

"Quite sure," she said.

"I placed it two nights ago," Devon said.

Jamie's heart sank, and she regretted her earlier wish to see Devon out of his depth.

"It must have been lost," the hostess sniffed. "We aren't responsible for technical difficulties."

"Is it under Shelley's name?" Jamie suggested, but Devon surprised her by stepping around the podium to stand very close to the hostess and murmur to her quietly.

It was like he had changed completely in that moment, going from a soft, gentle guy who drove a rusty Honda and was single-handedly raising an almost-teenaged girl, to a man who *owned* the suit he was wearing, with an unexpected air of danger and strength. He was a whole different Devon: he knew exactly what he wanted, and he was going to *get* it.

The hostess shrank back, her eyes wide and alarmed by whatever it was that Devon was telling her, and she flipped through the pages of her reservation with determination. "We'll have a table for you in ten minutes," she promised. "Can I order you something from the bar?"

Instantly, Devon was smiling and Jamie could have sworn he was three inches shorter than he'd been just a moment before. "Do you want anything?" he asked her.

"Rum and coke," Jamie said, mystified.

"Make it two," Devon agreed.

"What did you tell her?" Jamie hissed at him, when she went to place their orders and they took a seat by the door.

"That I program the website for the restaurant critic Table For Tray and I'd make sure that they were removed from the directory. Because I *am* responsible for *technical difficulties*." Devon looked sheepish.

Jamie laughed out loud. "You are my very favorite geek in the whole world," she said in delight, and she sobered to hear her own words. She'd thought that Devon would be out of place once she got him out of the sleepy little Green Valley, and instead he'd proved himself tougher and even more versatile than she'd expected.

Then she got the last laugh after all, because the hostess offered to take her coat, and Jamie got to see Devon's face when she took it off.

amie's lipstick had been alluring enough to be terrifically disturbing on the drive over. Every time he'd glanced over, he was struck by how red her lips were, and how badly he wanted to kiss her, to see if she tasted like Kool-Aid. Only shifter reflexes had stopped him from rear-ending a car from the distraction at one point.

But the lipstick was nothing compared to the rest of what she was wearing.

The coat had been tantalizing on the drive over, and Devon guessed that Jamie was wearing something amazing under it. His efforts to turn the heat in the car up enough to make her take it off had been thwarted by the half-powered heater in the car.

And it wasn't really the dress, though it was in every way the perfect little black dress.

It was Jamie herself, her long, strong legs under the short skirt, her pale shoulders under the thin straps, the fascinating swell of her breasts over the low cut bodice. She wasn't wearing jewelry, or any makeup besides the scarlet lipstick, and she didn't need any of it.

She was a goddess.

She was a force of nature.

She was all the confidence that could be fit in that much skin, the way she walked to the table that was promptly prepared for them, the way her hips swayed and the curve of her sweet, perfect ass as Devon helplessly followed her.

The table that they were led to was tucked into a private corner; possibly pulled out of storage and set up deliberately for them.

Devon picked an item from the menu at random while Jamie studied it and smirked, undoubtedly knowing exactly what she was doing to him.

It was a long wait for the food, and Devon was perfectly content simply to watch Jamie make observations about the other people in the restaurant and sip from her water with her absurdly red lips.

He didn't taste a bite of the overpriced food once it came, too enthralled by the woman sitting opposite from him making his heart sing.

She was his mate.

He felt like they floated through the meal, and he paid the bill without even registering the week's worth of pay that he was signing away.

Standing on the city sidewalk afterwards, Jamie on his arm, everything felt surreal and strange.

"What do you want to do now?" he asked, looking down the brightly-lit city block.

"Let's get your car," Jamie said, smiling up at him with promise on her lips. She'd re-applied the lipstick, and it was brilliant red and utterly enticing.

Devon flagged the valet down and gave him the ticket. It was chilly, and there was a brisk, cold breeze making people tuck their coats closer. Jamie shivered, and he pulled her close.

"Jamie..." he started, but he didn't know where to go from there. Was it too early to ask her to marry him? They still hadn't resolved what they were going to do that summer when Jamie planned to return to Alaska, but at that moment, he would have followed her anywhere.

"I am glad your clunker has heated seats," Jamie said, as it appeared around the corner and the valet pulled it up for them.

Devon took the driver's seat silently, and Jamie slid in and shivered while he blasted the heater.

They talked casually on the way back, about the dinner, and about Abby, and gossip about the residents of Green Valley. Devon desperately wanted to broach the subject of the future, to finally ask if she was a shifter, and failed to find the courage about six times. Instead, they talked about food and politics and invoicing software, somehow.

"Turn here," Jamie said suddenly, pointing to a little road going off the highway shortly before the turnoff to Green Valley.

Devon turned obediently. "Where does this go?" he asked. It wound up into the low, forested hills.

"You'll see," Jamie said.

The trees opened onto a ridge where they had a view out over the wide valley, dark expanses and cheerfully lit houses as far as they could see. Jamie showed him a pullout by a rickety fence. "There!"

Devon pulled in and put the car in park. "Where are we?"

Jamie was unbuckling her seatbelt and pulling her coat off; the heater had finally put out enough energy to get that far at least. "This, my gorgeous, sweet, sheltered guy, is Make-Out Point."

Devon had figured that their date was nearly over and his heart rose at the idea that it might not be. "What are we doing here?"

Jamie grinned at him, her teeth bright in the darkness. "We're going to make out, silly."

She reached over between his legs and found the seat release, sending his chair back as far as it would go, then climbed over on top of him, jiggling in a fascinating way as she straddle him and began to loosen his tie.

"I'm okay with this," Devon said, strangled, as she started to unbutton his shirt and he struggled to unbuckle his seatbelt. "I'm definitely okay with this."

Her lipstick tasted strangely chalky, but the pressure of her mouth was perfect, and the body he'd been longing to touch all night was everything he'd been imagining. Her legs were smooth and silky as he pulled her dress up and she abandoned his shirt after a few buttons to fumble at his pants.

The seat went back with a CLUNK that made them both giggle and clutch at each other.

"Devon…" Jamie's teeth scraped his ear as they struggled in the tiny space to get aligned.

His cock sprang free from his pants and Devon got Jamie's underpants down around her knees. Knees knocked, and the steering wheel was a serious pinch point as they adjusted and then, finally, she was sinking down onto him, wet and slippery.

She moaned, and Devon realized that he was too, clutching at her ass under the crumpled dress. The windows were rapidly fogging.

He was suddenly, sinkingly aware of flashing red lights outside.

"Jamie, Jamie," he groaned. "We gotta stop."

Her fingernails sunk into the shoulder she had managed to uncover. His suit was definitely going to need to be steamed again.

"What…is…it?" she asked, not so much stopping as slowing to an unbearable pace.

"Someone's out there…cops…" Devon could just imagine the speed at which that story would swirl around Green Valley. Would they be cited for indecent exposure? Could he afford the fine after the dinner he'd just bought?

Jamie swore, rather creatively, and reluctantly stopped riding him, but didn't scramble to dismount.

They were both quiet, listening with hearts pounding, but the only sound was the dull rumbling of the running Honda. The windows, by now, were frosted.

"I saw lights," Devon promised.

"I was about to," Jamie said archly.

They remained still for a long moment.

"I don't think anyone is there," Jamie said, and she slowly began to rise and lower on him, faster, but still agonizingly slow. "Maybe…it…went…by…"

Devon shut his eyes, lost in the sensation of her, tight around him, soft above him, and was surprised when Jamie suddenly burst out laughing, clenching around him deliciously as she did.

His eyes flew open. "What? What?"

"Flashing red lights!" Jamie chortled. "It's from my foot on the brake pedal!" She demonstrated, and the red lights reflected off the ceiling of the car.

"Not cops," Devon said in relief.

"Better than cops," Jamie assured him, and she was speeding up again. "Much better," she gasped.

They were laughing together as they rose onto a peak of pleasure, and laughing afterwards, wrapped up with each other.

"Better than cops," Jamie giggled into his chest.

Devon might have willingly stayed there for an indefinite amount of time, curled uncomfortably in the driver's seat. Then the car gave a threatening cough. "Oh crap, I don't want to run out of gas…"

"It's a long walk to Green Valley from here," Jamie agreed.

They carefully untangled themselves from each other, cursing the steering wheel and knocking knobs akilter as they cleaned up and pulled their clothing back into place. The fan came on with a wail and the windshield wipers scratched across the front window.

"Jamie…" Devon started, adjusting his seat.

"*That's* what I call a good date," Jamie said, practically purring in satisfaction. She found the ice scraper and started to clear the front window. "How do you rate car sex?"

Devon couldn't help but grin. "Ten stars. No, nine. The steering wheel gets in the way."

"Next time, we'll do it in the passenger seat," Jamie suggested.

"No flashing red lights," Devon chuckled.

"I'm going to make you a checklist," Jamie declared.

"A checklist?"

"Geeks love checklists," Jamie said airily. "I'm going to make a list of the sex we're going have, all the stuff you missed because of your complicated life. We can check off car sex now. I'll add sex in the park, and sex on the beach, not the drink. There's a gravel pit about twenty minutes away that will count for that, though we should probably wait until spring. Sex at the library…"

"The library!"

"There's a conference room with a locking door. Just...check the schedule first. Don't ask me how I know that."

"I don't think I want to know."

"I didn't know that Tawny had a key!"

"I definitely don't want to know!" Devon protested, and he told himself that feeling jealous was counterproductive. Jamie was *his* now, and forever.

Some of it must have shown on his face anyway, because Jamie kissed him on the cheek. "Nothing to worry about, I promise. Youthful rebellion."

He might have worried further anyway, but the phone in his pocket gave a demanding buzz and he pulled it out to check the text.

He had to read it twice.

"What's that about?" Jamie asked.

"My sister," Devon started. He read the text a third time.

"Something wrong?"

"She says there's a flock of velociraptors in the yard."

12

*I*t was not, to everyone's mixed relief and disappointment, *actual* velociraptors in the yard that Jamie persisted in thinking of as Tawny's.

It was, however, a flock of furious wild turkeys, convinced of their own size and importance, and absolutely determined to keep anyone from the front door of the house.

It was already dark, and the creatures were menacing in the shadows cast from the dim porch light.

"Dean and Shelley came back about fifteen minutes ago," Abby reported. "I came home and...this." Like most pre-teens, she was not dressed for the cold, but it didn't seem to bother her. Jamie, on the other hand, was already feeling chilled, and wished she were wearing pants—for protection from the turkeys trapped in Tawny's yard, if nothing else.

The nearest and largest of them was strutting about on the far side of the gate from them, yelping and shaking its tail feathers. The others were agitating in the frozen remains of Tawny's garden, scratching and pecking and occasionally hissing.

"When I said I wanted to have a turkey dinner for Thanksgiving, I was thinking of something a little more...butchered," Abby said in disgust. "How do we get them out of there?"

"Are you sure they are turkeys?" Devon said, fascinated, and Jamie was reminded that he wasn't nearly the country boy he was trying to be.

"Turkeys. Insane giant chicken reptiles. I don't know!" Abby protested. "They're mean!"

"These are wild turkeys," Jamie assured them. "You just have to scare them out. They aren't as tough as they look!"

She put her hand at the gate latch and the nearest turkey launched itself at her, flapping wings and honking in outrage. Jamie flinched back and would have fallen if Devon hadn't caught her.

"Do they bite?" Abby asked in horror.

"They can peck," Jamie said, clinging to her dignity. She wasn't used to the shoes or the tight skirt. "It leaves a helluva bruise. Usually they aren't aggressive at this time of year, though, and they ought to be roosting right now."

"Maybe they've eaten coffee grounds out of Dean's compost or something," Abby suggested.

Two of them began fighting, in a brief flurry of feathers and raucous squawks. The others were making all manner of noises, and clearly trying to intimidate each other.

"How'd they get *into* the yard?" Devon wondered.

"They can fly," Jamie pointed out.

Abby gave a squeak of fear. "They fly?!"

"Why don't they just fly out?" Devon asked.

"Let's encourage them," Jamie suggested. She opened the gate firmly, stepping forward with a stomp and a yell as she went, and the birds exploded into a swarming mass of flapping, calf-high, yelping bird chaos.

There were beaks and beating wings and flying feathers everywhere as the flock swirled towards them. Their gobbling cries were ferocious and their eyes gleamed. Jamie had faced down raging forest fire and charging moose, but she had never been so sure she was going to die as she was staring into this maelstrom of angry turkeys.

Abby bolted for the porch of the house with a shriek and Devon swept Jamie into his arms like she weighed absolutely nothing and pelted after his sister.

Abby fumbled at the lock with her keys, finally got the door open, and they all fell inside and slammed the door behind them.

The turkeys gobbled, muffled, outside the door.

All three of them collapsed into hysterical laughter as Devon put Jamie easily back down on her feet. Perhaps the jolt of adrenaline had given him extra strength.

"Maybe a cat chased them over here or something," Jamie surmised, looking out of the narrow window by the door.

The creatures were milling at the base of the steps, looking far less terrifying than they had just moments ago as they pecked and fluffed their feathers. Some of them seemed to be drowsing in place.

She looked back to find Devon and Abby eyeing each other. Abby shrugged, though Devon didn't say anything.

"How long do you think they'll be out there?" Abby asked, coming to the window to look out with Jamie.

"This isn't normal turkey behavior," Jamie said. "I have no idea."

They looked sleepy and completely harmless, now, but she didn't really want to risk going out and finding out.

Abby apparently had the same thought. "Who wants to watch a movie?" she asked. "Maybe Hitchcock's *The Birds*?"

"You're hysterical," Devon told her sarcastically. "I'm not letting you watch that."

He tried to convince her to pick a Disney movie, she countered with a slasher. They finally settled on Ghostbusters, then argued over which version. Jamie cast the deciding vote for the original version.

She and Devon made popcorn in the kitchen, using an air popper so ancient it actually was 70s avocado green. Probably, it had been included in the purchase of Tawny's house.

Jamie was keenly aware of his hot gaze as they moved around in the tiny space. She was still wearing her little black dress and he was still wearing his gorgeous suit, but somehow this was a more comfortable place than the fancy restaurant had been, even dressed so inappropriately.

They came out of the kitchen to find that Abby had found every spare blanket and pillow in the house and set them each up a nest and queued the movie. She had claimed the easy chair, leaving the couch to Jamie and Devon to share.

Jamie self-consciously tucked her bare legs up under her, and nearly fell into Devon when he sat next to her and the poorly sprung couch sagged towards the middle. Abby completely ignored them once she had her popcorn, and they started the movie.

Jamie regretted her choice when they got to the gross parts, and Abby giggled through the sexy and violent bits...it had been years since Jamie saw the movie, and she had forgotten some of the more graphic scenes.

By the end of the movie, they were all sprawled comfortably, Jamie halfway into Devon's lap with the skirt of her dress hiked up underneath the blankets they were snuggled under.

"That was a terrible movie," Abby scoffed as the credits started to roll. "I can't believe they call it a classic."

"It was kind of awful," Jamie agreed.

"You're both crazy," Devon scoffed. "It's one of the best movies in history! Who you gonna call?"

Jamie sighed into Devon's arms, perfectly content for the moment and loathe to move from their comfortable den.

But something was bugging her, something she couldn't put her finger on, until Abby said in alarm, "Do you smell something?"

Smoke, Jamie realized, starting to struggle free of Devon and their blankets. She smelled *smoke.* Then she heard a familiar sound, a sound she'd been ignoring, because sometimes she imagined it when it wasn't there.

She heard flames, and the smoke detector began to scream.

13

*I*t took Devon a few seconds to identify the problem.

"Where's your fire extinguisher?" Jamie demanded, pulling away from him and throwing aside the blanket as she battled to her feet.

"Kitchen!" Devon said, after a blank-brained moment of worrying that they didn't have one. "In the pantry by the fridge!"

He could see the flicker of crackling light from the kitchen now, and terror made him clumsy as he staggered to his feet.

Jamie was already at the open door of the kitchen, coolly assessing the situation. "Turn off the circuit breaker," she said, perfectly calmly. "Abby, call 911." She had the wool blanket in her hands and before Devon could stop her, she was stepping into the kitchen.

Terror spiked in him and his lynx was a yowl of fear in his head. He wanted to rush after and stop her, he wanted to follow her, he wanted to protect her, he wanted everyone out of the house, and indecision rooted his feet to the floor.

Trust, he finally settled on. He had to trust her.

Abby was already dialing, and Devon bolted for the fuse box at the back of the house.

It took too long to fumble it open, and then he stared at the panel in consternation; everything was labeled in utterly ancient tiny scratching, and completely nonsensical.

In a few swift motions, he swept every switch to the off setting and the house went dark and silent, the movie credits very suddenly cutting out. He could hear the bang of the cabinet in the kitchen and a sudden, stunning *whoosh* of the fire extinguisher.

By the time he came back, everything was completely under control.

Abby was still on the phone, stammering their address to the dispatcher in the now-dark house, and Jamie was emptying the fire extinguisher blindly towards the kitchen counter, where the popcorn popper, no longer avocado green, was a half-melted plastic lump on a blackened, scorched counter. The cabinets above were streaked in black, and fine white powder was over everything. He could barely identify the items that had been on the counter next to the popper —a crisp bag that had been bread, some dirty dishes, melted tupperware, and several cereal boxes that were almost nothing.

The fire extinguisher gave a sputter and Jamie eased up on the trigger.

The whole room creaked and groaned in changing temperature and Jamie coughed. It was smoky, but not too thick.

"Do you have a flashlight?" she asked, as the last wisps of the extinguisher spray settled.

Devon realized that she must not have his lynx's night vision, and it struck him all over again that he needed to tell her about being a shifter. It was still possible she was one, just one without night sight…

But now was definitely not the right time.

"Yeah," he said, moving unerringly for the drawer on the far side of the sink. "Here."

Abby came in with her phone turned to light the area just as he turned the flashlight on.

Jamie flinched away from the sudden light. "Wow," she said. "That's a bit of a mess."

"They're sending the truck," Abby said.

On cue, Jamie's phone, hung in the closet with her coat, began to shrill.

Everyone jumped, then broke into hysterical laughter.

"That's the fastest I've ever turned out," Jamie said weakly, and Devon could no longer resist sweeping her into his arms, awkward fire extinguisher and all.

They all started talking at once.

"That could have been so much worse," Abby said, shaking her head.

"We're lucky you were here," Devon said to Jamie.

"The lesson here is not to leave avocado green appliances plugged in." Jamie squeezed one of Devon's arms. "You would have done the same thing," she said.

"Probably not as fast," Devon said. *Was* she a shifter? "You had the experience."

"This was the most excitement I've had since I moved back," Jamie laughed. "Every other call-out has been a total waste of time. The closest we've gotten to an actual fire was an invitation to a retiree party with too many candles."

For all of her bluster, Devon could feel an unexpected tremble to her. Abby was shaking more visibly.

Jamie's phone was still going off. "I should answer," she said, pulling out of Devon's arms.

There was a pounding on the door, followed abruptly by a crash, and Dean came barreling into the dark, smoky kitchen through the door he'd just pushed open. "Are you okay? Abby? Devon? Er… Jamie?"

He'd brought a flashlight with him, sensibly, and had an extinguisher in the other hand. Jamie, in the spotlight, scowled at him. "What are you doing here?"

"I'm still on call until after Christmas," Dean said.

A siren rose up down the street behind him, wailing about a block and stopping at the sidewalk outside the house.

Turner came pelting up to the porch. He was wearing his full suit, but took off his helmet as soon as he gazed into the broken door. "Where's your turnout gear, Dean?" he demanded. "Didn't you *just* get a reprimand for this?"

"I was right next door!" Dean protested. "Yell at Jamie, she's the one wearing an evening dress!"

"I was here already, you ingrates! And I saved you a lot of work, too!"

"You saved our *house*," Devon pointed out gently.

"You're welcome!" Jamie yelled, and Devon could tell that she was a bundle of nerves.

"Is it safe to turn the power back on?" he asked, fighting his impulse to try to pull Jamie back into his arms. Abby was looking equally shell-shocked, but when he put out an arm for her, she stubbornly ignored him.

Turner shook his head. "You should get a contractor out here to inspect it," he cautioned. "Wires behind the walls could have melted. Insurance bean-counters are going to want to see it first, too. You guys got a place to stay?"

"They can crash with us," Dean offered at once. "We've got a daybed in Shelley's office, and a couch in the living room."

"Grab what you need," Turner said dismissively. "And I swear to God, Dean, if I catch you at another fire without turnout gear..." He didn't actually sound angry.

Dean protested good-naturedly, and added, "Come on over when you're ready. We'll make hot chocolate."

"Are the turkeys still out there?" Abby asked suddenly.

Dean and Turner looked at her blankly, only more confused when Devon started to chuckle and Jamie burst into laughter.

"Nevermind," Abby said crossly. She vanished into her room as Dean and Turner shrugged at each other and left the house. Turner was muttering unhappily about incident reports, and Dean was chuckling.

The whole house reeked of nasty smoke, and Devon was glad not to stay. He gathered a change of clothes and his toothbrush, and found Jamie still frowning in the kitchen as she played the flashlight across the counter.

Her black dress was cloudy with the extinguisher dust, and her mane of hair was almost on end.

"I'm sorry our date didn't end that well," Devon said apologetically.

"Which part? The homicidal turkeys or the house fire? You know, I prefer to keep my work and romance separate," she quipped.

Devon recognized her humor for the attempt to deflect that it was. He might have said more, but Abby emerged from her room with a giant duffel bag just then.

"My clothes smell like smoke," she complained.

"Yeah," Jamie sympathized. "It's amazing how it gets in everything. I smell like a bacon smoker for a couple of weeks after every wildfire season. Doesn't matter how many times I shower."

"Our house wasn't even on fire that long!" Abby said, shaking her head.

They went to the door and all paused on the porch. Devon realized that Dean had broken the deadbolt out, and he wasn't going to be able to latch it, let alone lock it.

Shifter strength? And hadn't Jamie moved with shifter swiftness? Not *knowing* was so nerve-wracking.

But it was Green Valley and most people didn't even lock their houses, so he shrugged and went to the steps, where Abby and Jamie were both peering suspiciously out into the yard.

There was no sign of the turkeys except for the turf they had scratched up, and a few feathers in the brown grass.

Jamie went with them to the sidewalk in front of Dean's house next door and then hung back reluctantly, shivering in her coat.

Her legs were bare under her short skirt, and Devon stayed back with her, not sure what to do until Abby turned around and said, "If you want to walk her home, I can…"

"No," Jamie said swiftly. "I don't need that."

She started to pivot and walk away, but Devon caught her arm. "Wait," he said desperately, letting her go at once.

"Thanks for a very exciting date," Jamie said, too brightly. "The turkeys were a nice touch."

"Jamie…"

"Much better than cops," she joked, and in her high heels she barely needed to stand on tip-toe to put a swift, casual kiss on his cheek.

"Jamie…"

"Tomorrow at Shaun's before your shift at Dean's?"

Everything was too light, too off-hand.

"Jamie…"

"Good night, Devon. Your *sister* needs you." Firmly. No room for argument. And she knew the only thing she could say that would keep him from following her when she ran away.

"Good night," he said reluctantly, and then she was striding off and he followed Abby to Dean's door.

They were greeted by Aaron, dressed in pajamas.

"You smell like smoke!" the little boy observed eagerly. "Smoking causes cancer, you know. And besides, you stink."

"You want to take a shower first?" Shelley, Dean's perfect-looking girlfriend, was holding a pile of bedding. "The bed in the office is made up, and I've got some blankets for the couch. Aaron, you're supposed to be in bed."

"I heard the sirens," Aaron whined. "Daddy lets me stay up when he's called out."

"Daddy says you listen to Shelley," Dean reminded him. He was making room on the coat rack for Abby and Devon's jackets. "Nice suit. Big date tonight?"

Devon had forgotten he was wearing it. It was badly rumpled, between the car sex and the movie and the fire. "Yeah."

Dean grinned at him. "Did it go well?"

Devon couldn't help but grin back. "Yeah," he admitted. "Kind of a terrible ending, though."

"Funny how lighting a house on fire puts a damper on things," Dean joked with him.

Abby accepted Shelley's offer for a shower and Dean took a protesting Aaron back up to bed.

Which left Devon alone with Shelley.

Dean's girlfriend was terribly intimidating, with her chilly face and fashionable clothing. She looked like a mismatch for Green Valley most of the time, but Devon had seen how soft and vulnerable she could get with Dean and Aaron.

She didn't look soft and vulnerable right now. She looked cool and vaguely irritated.

It was nearly midnight, Devon realized as he took his suit jacket off and glanced at his watch. Aaron had apparently stubbed his toe and was wailing loudly from upstairs in that over-tired way he remembered from when Abby was younger.

"Thanks for putting us up," he said to Shelley, and then her face did thaw then.

"Of course," she said more warmly. "Help yourself to anything in the kitchen. If you need any help with the insurance or inspectors, just let me know."

Devon lay awake a long time into the night, after Shelley vanished upstairs and Abby had retreated to her office toweling her wet hair after assuring Devon that she was fine and exchanging a swift, tight hug with him. Aaron's wails were swiftly quieted, and after a while, the inevitable creaks and noises of people moving around in an upper floor going to bed went silent.

He wasn't thinking about the fire, or the insurance, though any of that might have kept him sleepless.

He was thinking of Jamie, of the distance she'd dropped between them after saving their house.

Her mother had *died* in a house fire, he remembered, and he wrestled with his lynx's desires to hunt her down and comfort her. *Your sister needs you,* she'd reminded him, and he didn't know how to reconcile his warring needs to protect the people he loved the most.

He fell asleep at last, and dreamed of angry wild turkeys that tried to tear him in two.

14

*J*amie was good at sleeping.

She had slept, without a tent or sleeping bag, on many mossy tussocks in the Alaskan wilderness, with the midnight sun trying to pry open her eyelids. She had slept on beaches in Hawaii. She had slept on uncomfortable cots, on awkwardly short couches, on airport and train station benches. She could make herself drowse off through sheer force of will, no matter how uncomfortable she was.

So she was surprised when she found no rest in a perfectly good bed in her perfectly good efficiency above the fire station.

She tossed and turned, bothered by every little sound and restless thought. She used every technique in her toolbox, and sleep eluded her.

Finally, eyes gritty from her terrible night, she got up at sunrise and staggered down the stairs to make coffee as strong as the industrial pot could manage.

She was still adding grounds when there was a knock on the door.

She ignored it, even though she knew who it was.

Devon, bless his ridiculously sweet soul, wasn't going to barge in on her.

He knocked again, louder, like he thought maybe she was upstairs with her door shut.

Jamie sighed. She wasn't going to be able to ignore him. "Come in!" she called.

To her surprise, Devon was dressed in sweatpants and a light sweater, and he was jogging in place.

"What are you doing here?" she asked, realizing that she sounded cross, when really she was just stupidly happy to see him.

"Taking you jogging," Devon said merrily.

"Uuuuuunnnnngggggghhhhhh…" Jamie replied. "I haven't had coffee yet."

"We'll reward ourselves with coffee at Shaun's afterwards," Devon said. "C'mon."

"It's cold out there," Jamie whined, but she was smiling despite herself.

"You have to start running to warm up," Devon teased her, throwing her hat and gloves at her.

"What's this really about?" Jamie wanted to know, as she shut the door behind her.

"I just want to talk," Devon said seriously.

"Talk?" Jamie laughed. "We could talk in my room, where it's warm. Maybe check a few new things off your list."

Devon cast her a sideways look, grinned, and broke into a ground-eating jog that Jamie had to scramble to catch up with.

He led the way, this time, winding past Gran's, and through the central park. He even swung across on the monkey bars, holding his feet up so they didn't drag in the gravel. Jamie followed, and was panting by the time they passed the library. "Where are we going?" she demanded. At least she wasn't cold now. She *was* getting hungry.

And watching Devon jog so gracefully, all easy strength and loping stride, made her hungry in all kinds of different ways.

Jame scowled at her feet, hitting the sidewalks in a steady pace.

He led her back, in a weird, meandering path through town,

past Shaun's tempting-smelling bakery, and finally out to the park at the edge of town where she'd caught Andrea after whatever kind of adventure left someone naked with a sprained shoulder.

They stopped at the head of the trail, and Jamie dropped into a stretch before she could cool down and cramp. They had a view back out over Green Valley, looking picturesque and cozy under the heavy veil of gray clouds that was threatening snow or rain.

The little houses had wisps of smoke from their chimneys, and Jamie could hear the sounds of the people getting up and starting their boring morning rituals. A dog was barking, somewhere, and there was a clatter of someone collecting bottles.

"You don't hate this town," Devon said at last.

"What?"

"This town," Devon repeated. "You don't hate it."

Jamie sputtered in protest, but Devon went on. "You love it. I can tell by the way that you show it to me, and the way you remember all the little details about everything. You like to say that you hate it, because that gives you a reason to run away from it."

Jamie found something very interesting to look at on her sneakers.

She didn't want to think about the truth in Devon's statement. She didn't want to think at all. "C'mon, slowpoke," she said, falsely bright. "You're not tired yet, are you?"

She led Devon up the trail to the clearing and he finally caught her arm and drew her to a stop.

"Tell me about your mom," he insisted. "Tell me why you're a firefighter."

"It's not like you think," Jamie said quietly. "We didn't have a big fight right before it happened or anything like that. I don't carry a huge weight of guilt over it like Turner does." She shrugged, feeling the emptiness of her protest. "It's an easy way to make money. The wildfire fighting, I mean. Not so much the volunteer work in a dinky town. And I...owed Turner. *That's* the only reason I'm here. To repay a debt."

She could taste the lie, and it surprised her.

She'd truly convinced herself that she detested the little town, that she hated how small and nosy it was, that she would never willingly live in such a place, that she'd only done it for Turner.

But coming back...meeting Devon.

Green Valley wasn't the enemy.

She didn't hate the little town or the people who lived there.

She didn't even hate her memories of it.

She only hated how vulnerable she felt here. Being vulnerable meant you could get hurt.

Except...being vulnerable also meant that other things could happen.

Better things.

It was starting to snow; big, fat flakes of white obscured the trees around them.

"Jamie," Devon started. He stopped, and then restarted, clearly nervous. "Jamie, I've got some things to tell you…" For a moment, Jamie was absolutely sure that he was going to propose to her on the spot and she was actually surprised when he didn't go down on one knee.

If Green Valley made her feel vulnerable, Devon, somehow, made her feel *safe*. It didn't make sense, and Jamie didn't trust things that didn't make sense.

"I don't plan ahead," she cautioned. "I don't commit. Everyone knows that I could hare off at any moment. I don't have roots. I don't *want* roots."

Except that she did.

Her warning seemed to draw Devon up, and some part of her wanted to take it all back and hurtle herself into his arms. "Look," she said desperately. "I like this. I like *you*. But I don't want to hurt you." She *desperately* didn't want to hurt him.

"You're not going to hurt me," Devon said, and Jamie was stunned by the faith in his voice.

"You don't know that."

"I *know* that."

Jamie squirmed, broken between her desire to admit that she was helplessly in love with this guy and her instinct to run and save him the later pain of realizing what a ridiculous loser she was behind the bold facade she'd built.

"I don't want you to ask me about the future," she said firmly. "I don't want to make plans. What we've got is good, but it's now, not forever." More lies, she realized, because she'd managed to nail her heart to him, and when she left, it was going to rip out of her and stay behind.

"I have to tell you…"

"Don't tell me," Jamie said. "I don't want to know. I only want this, just the way it is. That's *all* it is. Now come on, I'm getting cold and I can smell Shaun's cinnamon rolls from here."

"You can?" Devon said piercingly, as if there was any possible way that she could.

"Come *on*," she said, and she turned and broke into a run.

She told herself she wasn't *trying* to get away from him. And somehow, everything was right again when he caught up with her.

15

———————

A few days later, the bell at the door of Dean's hardware store gave a welcome jangle and Devon threw Jamie a look that was pure gratitude.

"Hi, Jamie!" he called too loudly.

"Hey," she replied, then with less enthusiasm. "Hi, Gillian."

Gillian stopped making eyes at Devon, to his great relief, and finished her purchase of three one-inch screw-hooks. She paid with a credit card.

Jamie looked suspiciously after her. "Was she hitting on you?" she asked as the door shut behind the older woman.

Did she sound jealous? Devon wondered. "I don't think she's *serious*," he said. "I hope not, anyway." He gave a dramatic shudder.

"Good," Jamie said firmly. "I don't share."

She sounded possessive, Devon thought, and he didn't dislike that at all.

"Quit grinning," Jamie warned him, and he did his best to smother his smile.

"Can I help you find something?" he asked professionally.

"The crew truck needs a new timing belt," Jamie said. "Dean said you've got some kind of ordering system set up?"

Devon woke up the computer by jiggling the mouse. "No problem. I wrote a subroutine that checks each of Dean's suppliers and sorts them by price and availability. How soon do you need it?"

Jamie leaned on the counter to look at the screen. "It's not an emergency."

"Whole rebuild kit, or just the belt?"

"The kit."

"Need any of the tools?"

"I've got all the tools I need," Jamie said, the edges of her mouth quirking up.

"You know, it's really hot that you know about tools," Devon told her. He didn't even try to stop grinning.

Jamie smirked at him. "It's even hotter that I know what to do with them."

Devon made a show of fanning himself and they both laughed.

"I had your job for a few years during high school," Jamie explained. "Of course, it wasn't Dean's then, but I learned my way around a hardware store. I wasn't a kiss-up like you, writing fancy new software for the computer, but I know my way around sorting some socket wrenches."

"Talk dirty to me," Devon said.

"I heard that Dean is going to be moving to Madison with Shelley so Dean can get a degree in engineering, and Shelley's doing some *fashion* thing," Jamie said, sobering. "What do you think will happen to the shop when they go?"

Devon shrugged. "I don't know. I guess it will close? It's sad that Green Valley won't have a hardware store, but I'm not too worried about myself. I'm getting enough programming work to cover the hours I'd lose."

"As long as your waitressing tips are good," Jamie teased him.

Devon laughed. "Maybe I should wear something more low-cut..." he suggested.

Jamie giggled and rifled through a display of flashlights on the counter and Devon watched her face, the sweep of her thick eyelashes, the sprinkle of her freckles. How could someone get under his skin so completely, so quickly? he wondered.

And was he under her skin the same way? Did she have an animal urging her towards him as well? She liked him, he was sure. Maybe more than *liked*. He tried to figure out a way to ask, opening his mouth to start, no matter how crazy it sounded, and then the door gave a less welcome alert.

"The timing belt will be here Tuesday," he said swiftly.

"Here's the station credit card," Jamie said, her expression briefly puzzled. She turned to look at the door. "Hey, Dean, Aaron."

"I'm hungry," Aaron whined.

"Go get a granola bar from behind the counter," Dean advised him, and Aaron scampered around and squeezed past Devon to reach into the box. "*One* granola bar," Dean added. "How's business?"

"Booming," Devon joked. "Just sold a timing belt kit and three screw-hooks."

Jamie signed her receipt and Devon logged out of the computer. "I'll close up," Dean told him absently, straightening a display. "See you at home!"

"Shaun's is open for ten more minutes," Jamie pointed out.

"Discount pastries, here I come," Devon said eagerly, and he pulled on his coat and followed her swiftly out.

"How's it going, staying with Dean?" Jamie asked, shivering and pulling the neck of her coat closed.

"Not bad," Devon said. "Abby's making dinner tonight."

"Time for a quick stop at the station after Shaun's?" Jamie suggested with a playful sideways glance.

Devon checked his watch. "Not quite," he said with regret. Privacy was a hard-won prize recently. Between work, living with Dean and his family, and Abby, it seemed like every precious moment with Jamie was better spent on things that weren't crazy-sounding confessions. Still… "Jamie, we really *should* talk."

She shot him a suspicious look. "Not if it means missing out on cheap cinnamon rolls."

Devon had to smile. "Priorities," he teased her. But he frowned thoughtfully as he opened the door to Shaun's bakery for her.

They raided the discount basket and Shaun locked the door behind them with a tolerant smile.

"We should talk..." Devon tried again, as they wandered down the sidewalk towards the residential neighborhood. For the moment, they were in a pocket of solitude, and he knew it wouldn't last.

Jamie looked nervous, and in terrible timing, the phone in her pocket went off. She pulled it out to glance at the screen, then gave Devon a swift kiss on the cheek. "Duty calls," she said regretfully, and she thrust her bag of pastries at Devon, turned and sprinted away.

His arms full of cinnamon rolls, Devon could only watch her go and remind his lynx that they had to be patient.

She wasn't running *away*, he told himself. And that was something.

16

"Where are we going?" Jamie asked, glancing between Devon and Abby. She looked rumpled from sleep, her mousy hair wild around her face. It had snowed the night before, so the streets were white again.

Devon thought that she sounded exasperated, but intrigued. "Ice skating," he said firmly, holding up the second-hand skates he'd found at Dean's hardware store. He wasn't sure why a hardware store carried ice skates, but the grocery store also carried shotguns, so maybe it was just a Green Valley thing. "The contractor my insurance company wanted to use had an opening today and I don't want to be underfoot while they worked on the kitchen. I asked around, and apparently the appropriate small-town November activity is to go ice skating. We can stop at Dean's and find you ice skates if you don't have any."

Abby, at his side, sullenly added, "He's making me come, too."

"You don't get enough exercise!" Devon said reproachfully.

"It's cold," she complained. "My skates pinch."

"Ten laps," Devon bargained. "Ten laps and we can go to Shaun's and have hot chocolate."

"I'm in for the hot chocolate," Jamie agreed. "And yeah, I'll go skating, too. I haven't been to Mueller's Pond since I was in high school, it'll be fun."

They all piled into Devon's awful car, Abby complaining bitterly about the lack of legroom in the back.

"You're lucky I'm not still making you use a booster seat, baby sister," Devon teased her back.

Abby kicked the back of his seat.

Dean had a pair of hockey skates in Jamie's size, and they set off for the frozen pond.

They weren't the only people from Green Valley to have the same idea; the ice was crowded with people. The pond had been cleared from end to end. Elderly couples were skating in sedate circles on one side, a wild and clearly free-for-all hockey game was being staged on the other. A handful of little kids were milling about in the middle. A golden-haired girl was bossing around a pair of boys, and Devon recognized one of them as Aaron, the other as Trevor, Shaun and Andrea's little boy. The girl was Clara, and her dad, Lee, was helping to repair a warm-up shelter at the shore.

Aaron recognized Abby and immediately pointed her out to his friends. "She's my babysitter! She's a…!" He clearly reconsidered what he was going to say and huddled with Trevor, to Clara's outrage.

"Hey! Hey!" she called after them, trying to make forward progress in skates that she was comically unsteady on. "I'm a princess! You're supposed to be my knights!"

"Which side are we skating on?" Jamie asked dubiously, as they pulled on their skates. "You any good at this?"

"I have no idea," Devon confessed cheerfully. "I've never been skating."

Abby, to Devon's approval, got her skates on and went to comfort Clara, who was clearly feeling left out by her friends. Abby swiftly coordinated a gentle chase-and-make-believe game that the much-younger children kept adding complicated rules to.

"I'm a dragon!" Aaron declared. "A *bear* dragon that breathes *plasma*!"

"Dragons aren't bears!" Trevor scoffed. "And you can't breathe plasma."

Abby declared that a bear dragon was a special exception, and that Clara could be the princess, and picked up Aaron when he fell on his face doing a dance of triumph.

Jamie pulled Devon out onto the ice with some words of advice. "Don't hesitate. You're never going to get in motion if you're mincing around with little baby steps, and skating relies on speed. It's like riding a bike, you can't go too slow."

Devon obediently followed her, and after a few false starts and a stumble or two, they were gliding circles around the sedately skating elders.

"You were totally lying!" Jamie told him, her cheeks bright and the hair from beneath her hat blowing wildly. "This *can't* be your first time skating!"

She had to be a shifter, Devon thought. She was strong and fast and her balance was amazing. He'd never seen anything so graceful or confident as Jamie.

They nearly collided with Marta, skating alone, and Devon caught her before the gray-haired woman could tumble. They clung to each other for a moment, and Devon was afraid that she would fall when he let go.

"Sorry, Marta," he said apologetically. Jamie had ricocheted off in the opposite direction, and when she saw that Devon had the woman well in hand, she darted off to do a circuit by herself, laughing.

"I'm fine," Marta said with a sniff, though she didn't let go of Devon. "I can see that the two of you don't have eyes for anyone else who might be skating here."

Devon blushed, and hoped Marta would think his color was just from the cold. She was the town's biggest gossip, and he wondered what she'd heard. "Sorry," he repeated.

Marta wasn't fooled. "She's a runner, isn't she," she observed.

"We do a lot of jogging," Devon said, confused. Marta knew everything that happened in town. She must have seen them doing circuits around the town.

"That's not what I meant," Marta said wryly.

Jamie was doing lazy loops around other skaters and the children, and Devon realized that Marta wasn't talking about skating or even jogging. He didn't know what kind of answer to give the nosy old woman.

Marta tucked his hand into her elbow and clearly expected him to skate with her, so Devon obediently did, finding, as Jamie had warned, that he had terrible balance at her slower speed.

"You're a good fit for Green Valley," Marta said approvingly, as they navigated around a flailing child.

"Er, thank you?" Devon said hesitantly. "I like it here."

"Your sister doesn't," Marta said flatly.

Devon winced, but Marta went on unsympathetically.

"Of course, at that age, she wouldn't like it anywhere."

There was a gaggle of older boys just arriving that Devon realized were about Abby's age, maybe even in high school. He looked anxiously around for his sister. She was helping Clara back to her feet and while he watched, she became aware of the newcomers.

Devon stumbled in his skating and nearly fell when he saw his sister's expression of longing and embarrassment, and when Clara scrambled after her friends, Abby looked lost. Devon nearly left Marta, but she was stronger than she looked, and led him around in a curving arc away from them.

Jamie swept up behind them at that moment. "Can I steal Devon back?" she asked Marta. "The hockey net is free and I want to see if he can score."

"I think he already has," Marta sniffed. "But we'll see if he can hold onto his points."

"What did that mean?" Jamie asked, as they cut across the ice. Devon could only shrug helplessly.

A pair of badly battered hockey sticks had been left in a snowbank. There was no hockey puck in sight, but Jamie found a chunk of ice that the last group had been playing with. "Let's see your moves, broken lynx boy."

Devon nearly face-planted; only the hockey stick saved his balance. "What do you mean?" Did she know he was a lynx?

"Like your business," Jamie reminded him. "Broken Lynx?"

"Right." Of course. That's all it was.

Jamie flipped the ice chunk back and forth in front of her. "Are you just going to let me win?" she taunted him. "Or are you going to try to get this away from me?"

They played hard, and Devon only landed on his ass once, but he pulled Jamie down with him, to her protest of "Foul! Illegal contact! Penalty box for you!"

He kissed her, because she was laughing and gorgeous and red-cheeked and everything to him, and he heard laughter that he thought was at their expense and didn't care.

Then he realized that it was the cluster of older kids that was laughing, and he let go of Jamie when he spotted Abby across the pond, sitting on the ice with Clara, Aaron and Trevor hovering over her. The older boys were approaching her and Devon felt his hackles rise as he surged to his feet, forgot he was wearing skates, and nearly fell into Jamie.

"Uh-oh," she said, observing the same thing. "Trouble in paradise?"

Devon kicked off on his skates. He wasn't fast enough to get to Abby before the pack of trouble-makers got there, though he might have been if he wasn't at least *trying* not to make a spectacle out of himself. He skidded to a stop in a spray of ice as the boys clustered around Abby. "Are you okay?" He glared around protectively, daring any of them to taunt his sister.

He heard Jamie come to a less dramatic stop at his heels, which is when he became aware that he'd completely misjudged the situation. The boys' laughter hadn't been cruel, and Abby was glaring daggers at *him* as they melted back from his forceful approach and went to take over the hockey ice.

"It wasn't my fault!" Aaron was whining. "Clara pushed me!"

Clara sputtered in protest. "I was falling! It was an accident!"

"She didn't push you!" Trevor came railing to Clara's defense. "You pushed Abby!"

They bickered over who had done what until Abby snapped, "Forget it," and got to her feet, refusing Devon's hand to help her up. "It doesn't matter! I hate this town!" She skated angrily away to the shore and sat down to pluck at her skate laces.

"Oops," Jamie said, at Devon's elbow.

"She's a runner," Devon said despondently. "When she doesn't know what to do, she runs away. I guess I'm glad, because it's better than fighting. But…" Devon closed his eyes. He'd already messed up by barging in where his sister didn't want him.

Abby had gotten her boots on and was sprinting back along the road. Was she running faster than she should? She knew that being a shifter was something they had to keep secret, and she and Devon had talked about how careful they had to be for years.

"Will she be okay?" Jamie asked.

"Yeah." Devon wanted to explain how he knew, but in front of a big chunk of Green Valley pretending not to watch was not that place. "It's not that far to town and she always comes back." He'd been watching her strength develop over the past few years, and knew she could protect herself from anything she found on the trip.

He wanted to hold tight and protect her, but he knew he couldn't.

Not Abby. And not Jamie. He had to let them be who they were, and that was the hardest thing he'd ever done.

17

*D*evon met Jamie with a groan, collapsing into the chair opposite from her at Shaun's bakery.

The bakery, Jamie had long since decided, was the very best part of the wave of billionaires in town. Shaun made excellent pastries and served decent coffee and didn't care if anyone nursed a cup for several hours. He sometimes brought them samples, if their timing was right.

"What's up, buttercup?" Jamie asked, pouring more sugar into her coffee.

"Abby," Devon said. "She says she has...*concerns*."

"About us?" Jamie asked, suddenly worried.

"No," Devon said, with a flicker of short-lived relief. "About...*growing up*."

"Oh," Jamie said, trying to remember herself at that age. "*Oh*. Haven't you had the talk?"

"We had the talk," Devon said, and then he was quiet while Shaun brought him a cup of black coffee without prompting.

"Well, sort of," he went on. "It was as awkward as you might imagine. I got her some books. Told her I'd answer any questions she had. But what do I know about girls? I can barely *talk* to girls. I mean, I'm not a girl. I'm not even close to girl-like. I had totally different problems at her age." His voice grew near-hysterical as he went on and he took a bracing sip of coffee that was far too hot and swallowed reflexively and then spent a moment gasping in pain.

"Wait," he said, looking up at Jamie. "*You're* a girl."

"Yeah," Jamie said cautiously, not liking the direction their conversation had suddenly taken. "You should know."

He blushed adorably, and plowed on. "Could you talk to her? Just, answer her questions about...you know...*periods* and stuff? Make sure that she's okay, that this is all *normal?* I don't want to be one of those oblivious dads—moms—brothers—whatevers—that brushes something off because it makes me uncomfortable, but..."

"But it's totally making you uncomfortable."

"It's *totally* making me uncomfortable."

Jamie stared at him. He stared back, with those beautiful golden-green eyes full of despair and hope.

"What makes you think I could help her?" Jamie asked.

"You've got a lot more experience being a girl than I do," Devon assured her. "And there are questions I just can't answer."

Which is how Jamie found herself knocking at the door of the house while Devon went to work at Gran's.

"Devon isn't here," Abby said sullenly. Her eyes looked red, and Jamie had a moment of pity for her.

Puberty was hell, and it had to be hard growing up with just a brother to go to with questions. They were new in town, Abby didn't have friends yet, and there were no female family members to reach out to. Jamie wondered what books Devon had found for her. His taste in literature ran dry and technical. Jamie wondered if she should have brought a selection of racy romance books with decent heroes.

Abby was starting to squirm before Jamie finally said, "He asked me to come talk to you. About, you know, *changing.*"

Abby's eyes got wide. "Are you...?"

"One of you," Jamie said jovially, hoping to lighten the situation. "And he thought that if you had questions about things, that I might be easier to ask. Can I come in?"

Abby stepped aside, looking understandably wary, and closed the door behind her.

"Can I get you something to drink?"

"Nah," Jamie said. "I had too much coffee at Shaun's as it is."

Abby got herself a can of pop from the fridge.

They sat gingerly at the kitchen table and stared across it at each other.

"I'm…"

"You're…"

"Go ahead," Jamie said, as gently as she could. "I don't bite."

Abby continued to be silent, staring at her untouched pop.

Jamie cast deep for a way to start the conversation. "I know it seems like a big secret, like something you shouldn't talk about. But it's all sort of natural, and it happens at about this time, and you can't go back to who you were, even if you sort of wish you could."

Abby's face flashed a hundred emotions, just like Devon's did when he forgot to cover it with a frown.

"But it helps to know that other people went through it, and it feels more normal after a while."

"It feels…normal?" Abby asked, so wistfully that Jamie's heart broke for her a little.

"I promise it does," Jamie said. "Eventually. The first little while, each one is just weird and unpredictable and believe me, I cried my eyes out more than once when it was new and crazy. But you sort of figure it out after a bit, and there are some tricks and tips. Like… don't wear white pants. Ever. And always have a change of clothes in your locker."

Abby giggled. "I figured that one out already," she said bashfully. "Last week."

"Let me give you my number," Jamie said impulsively. "And if you ever need me to pick you up or bring you something, you can text me. Any time."

A slow, shy smile was blooming over Abby's face. "Okay," she said gratefully. "Thanks." Then she added, "So, what are you?"

Jamie was puzzled by the question. "Your friend?" she offered.

Your brother's friend with benefits seemed inappropriate. She certainly wasn't ready to confess to more.

Abby looked pleased by that answer, but shook her head as she wiped the condensation off of her pop can. "I mean, what *are* you? A lynx, like me and Devon? Aaron, the little kid next door says he's going to be a bear like his dad, and his friend Trevor is already a lion shifter. I guess he started kind of early."

Jamie stared at her in confusion, feeling slow. "A lynx?" She was beginning to think they weren't talking about periods.

"Canadian lynx," Abby said proudly.

"Like...the lynx in Broken Lynx, the name of your brother's business?" Jamie guessed. *An inside joke,* Devon had said.

"Yeah, Devon thinks he's funny." Abby had all the scorn of a little sister.

As Abby popped her soda pop open with a hiss and a snap, all the clues and hints and crazy things Jamie had seen growing up in Green Valley fell into place with the sharp sound.

They were definitely *not* talking about periods.

18

"Can I get you anything else?" Devon asked, trying not to fret over the idea of Jamie and Abby talking about...*girl* things. He gazed past the windowsill where Gran's elderly cat was sleeping at the leafless trees and sleepy streets.

He shouldn't have asked her to do it. It was his job, as Abby's guardian, as her big brother. He should just suck it up and be uncomfortable, and make sure that his sister knew the things she needed to know, even if he had to spend an hour looking at unnerving diagrams on Google and reading forums.

He wasn't any good at this job. No better at this than anything else he did. But it wasn't a job he had the luxury of turning down. Abby deserved stability. Direction. A good example.

"Refills?" Andrea was saying, rattling her glass of ice cubes.

Devon turned to look at her blankly. "Right. You were drinking…"

"Iced tea," Andrea said, an amused smile at the corner of her mouth. "Patricia has a diet pop."

"Yeah, sorry," Devon said, picking up the glasses. Fortunately, they were the only customers at the time. Patricia's new baby, Victoria, was sleeping in a car seat on the bench next to her.

"You got girl problems?" Andrea asked, her voice teasing and low.

"No," Devon protested.

Patricia made a chiding noise, then looked over Andrea's shoulder to where the door alarm had just jangled.

Andrea turned at Patricia's expression of dismay, then choked on her laughter as she said slyly to Devon, "Well, you do now."

Jamie looked like a thunderstorm. Like the thunderstorm she'd once described rising off a wildfire, dark and furious and spawned from flames.

Devon stepped to meet her, at least in part to keep their conversation from Andrea's prying ears.

"Was it awful?" he had to ask quietly. "I shouldn't have asked you to—"

Jamie's voice was as quiet as his, an angry hiss. "I had a lovely conversation with your sister about periods," she said flatly. "And then I found out she wasn't talking about periods at all. She was talking about being a shapeshifter."

All the air went out of Devon. That was what Abby had been leading on about? He hadn't shifted until well into high school, he should have been braced for Abby to hit this point earlier, being a girl. Relief surged through him. He could talk about *that*.

Except, of course, to Jamie…

She was glaring at him with icy blue eyes. Her cheeks were bright spots of color.

"Let's go somewhere," Devon suggested, putting Andrea and Patricia's glasses down at an empty table and untying his apron.

"Let's not," Jamie said, loudly now. She glared beyond him at Andrea. "You! You're one of them, too, aren't you! This whole damn town is full of them and always has been. All the exotic animal sightings, the weird silences, the absurd number of not-so-closet nudists."

Andrea didn't try to deny it, nor the fact that she had overheard their hushed conversation from an improbable distance. "It's not the kind of thing you just…bring up," she said with an awkward shrug.

Patricia, peacefully, said, "It's a bit of a shock when you realize it, isn't it?"

"Are you one, too?" Jamie asked, looking betrayed. "Is *everyone* but me?"

"No, of course not," Patricia said. "I didn't know until I met Lee. You can see why it has to be a secret."

"And there are lots of normal people in Green Valley, too," Andrea said quickly. "But this place is great for shifters. Lots of wilderness nearby, a quiet community…not a lot of people who have embraced cell phones with cameras."

"We came here because of that," Devon said. "Growing up in a city was really hard, I wanted Abby to have something better. I was really hoping there would be other shifters here, given some of the news reports."

"You should have *told* me," Jamie cried generally. Then she glared at Devon. "*You* especially."

Old George had come to the window of the kitchen with a frown. "Order up," he called, glancing nervously at the door, where anyone could just walk in on their conversation about being shapeshifters.

Victoria chose that moment to wake up with an outraged wail, and the phone at the cashier's station started ringing.

Devon chose to ignore all of it except Jamie. "I'm sorry I didn't tell you," he said frankly. "I wanted to. I thought…you might even *be*…but it's…hard…" he didn't know how to end the sentence.

"Oh, was it *hard*? Was it *hard* to tell me the truth? Was it *hard* to be honest?" Jamie's voice went shrill and Devon couldn't look anywhere but at her outraged eyes.

Patricia had picked up Victoria and was trying to comfort her. Andrea, finally deciding to be useful, got up to answer the phone. It stopped ringing right before she could pick up the receiver.

The old cat who had been sleeping in the window rose to tired feet, stretched thoroughly, and then gathered herself to jump down —shifting seamlessly into an ancient, white-haired woman as she went.

"Gran?" Jamie squeaked.

The walnut-textured woman stretched again, clearly not both-ered by her own nudity, and reached for a folded garment that she'd been sleeping on. It proved to be a fleece dressing gown that she pulled around herself and belted with slow, careful fingers.

"Gracious, child," Gran grumbled crossly. "All an old woman wants to do is have a nice nap now and again. Are you really only now figuring all this out? Goodness, you've gotten tall."

"That's not fair," Devon said swiftly in Jamie's defense. "It's been a well-kept secret. Even I only knew there were *probably* shifters here, not for sure who they were."

Gran glared at him. "Who are you?" she demanded.

"Devon," he explained. "You hired me this spring."

"Hmm," Gran said, looking him up and down. "Yes, I remem-ber. You've got a feline look to you. Wildcat?"

"Lynx," Devon said shortly, feeling very awkward indeed about the openness.

"That'll do," Gran said. "You've been keeping secrets from your mate?"

"Apparently, you *all* have," Jamie said. Then she looked at Devon, eyes flinty. "What's a mate?"

Gran's laughter was like the crack of a whip. "What would you expect, child? It's not the kind of thing you talk about in polite company. I'll leave you to this, boy. Patricia, who is this squalling little angel?"

Patricia, bouncing her screaming daughter, angled the baby to view Gran. "This is Victoria," she said, wincing.

"Got a lot of complaints, doesn't she," Gran crooned. "I feel you, baby."

Then Gran was stalking back through the kitchen muttering something about tuna fish and gone.

"What's a mate?" Jamie hissed again, and Devon was keenly aware of everyone's attention returning to them.

19

Jamie wasn't as angry as she was pretending to be anymore; she was just numb and disappointed. Angry was just a familiar mask for *not sure what to do*.

It wasn't really like she didn't understand why Devon—why everyone!—had kept the secret. Being a shapeshifter, able to change into an animal at will, was the stuff of movies that didn't end well. A lot of people would undoubtedly assume they were monsters. They'd probably end up in laboratories.

She just felt…so stupid. Like she should have figured it out a long time ago. Like everyone was in on the secret but her. Like her whole life was a lie. Like thinking her dad was a dead war hero.

And Devon was still keeping something from her, his face full of conflict.

Well, she could make it really easy for him. "You know what, I don't care. I told you that the one thing I couldn't stand was secrets. You *blew* this one, *lynx* boy."

Everyone was watching them in horrified fascination and Jamie hated the pity more than the lies.

She turned away, running into a chair, and shoved it hard away from her as she fled the cafe filled with people she thought she knew.

"Don't follow me!" she shouted back, and she slammed the door behind her as hard as she could.

She broke into a run, just in case Devon chose to follow anyway, and she ran until she was out of breath and out of anger and out of care and her legs felt rubbery from shock and betrayal.

She was blocks away, in the park she'd taken Devon to, the park where she'd found Andrea, naked and with a sprained shoulder.

Which totally made sense for someone who could shift into an animal, but not take their clothes with them.

She fell to her knees in the frozen grass off the jogging path and rolled over onto her back, staring up through the leafless trees at the steel-gray November sky.

Shapeshifters.

Shifters.

Other memories came back to her.

The exotic animal sightings that she'd always dismissed as too much liquor or not enough sense; Stanley was not the most reliable of witnesses.

The unusual strength and quickness of people who had no right to be strong and quick.

Dean, caught talking about *shifters*. Jamie had thought he was referring to a group of manual-shift car enthusiasts and wondered why he'd gotten so cagey about it when she interrupted the conversation.

And she'd never once seen Gran at the same time as her cat.

It wasn't that she was angry about it, or didn't understand the steps everyone had to take to hide it.

It was that her chest felt exactly like it had when she found out that the father she had been bragging about was completely fictional.

And the very *worst* of it was that everyone else already knew.

The cold from the ground beneath her seemed to seep up through her coat and around all the little gaps. She pulled her hat down further over her ears and drew her arms around herself, but she knew that most of the chill was inside of her.

She lay there, thinking in circles, until her toes started to ache from the cold. Finally, she got up and walked slowly back to the fire station.

"Devon was by looking for you," Turner greeted her. He was sitting at the table, and he put down the book he'd been reading to give Jamie a long, appraising look. "He seemed worried."

"He doesn't need to worry about me," Jamie said defensively. "I can take care of myself."

Turner was quiet, and Jamie could feel the skepticism from him.

"Are you..." she couldn't quite bring herself to say it out loud. "One of them?"

Turner's brow crinkled in confusion. "One of who?"

"One of what, is more like it," Jamie said angrily.

Turner looked at her blankly.

Temper flared beyond retrieval, Jamie snapped, "Oh for...are you a shapeshifter, too?"

Turner's face softened in understanding. "Ah..." he said unhelpfully. "That explains it."

"*What* explains it?" Jamie demanded. "Explains *what*?"

Turner gave a half-shrug. "Devon should tell you."

"Yeah, he should!" Jamie shouted, despite telling herself she shouldn't. "But he didn't! Nobody does! I'm always the last one to know! I should *know* these things!" She hated the tears that sprang into her eyes.

They both knew she wasn't really talking about Devon.

"You want a cup of coffee?" Turner offered.

Jamie wanted to break something, or turn around and run again. Instead, she pulled off her coat and stuffed her hat into a sleeve. "Yeah," she said, feeling full of defeat.

Turner set up the pot and started the drip while she hung up her jacket and tried to surreptitiously wipe her face.

"It wasn't your fault," Turner said, when he set the cup down in front of her.

"I know," Jamie said, taking a sip. "I *know*."

But *knowing* was much different than *believing*.

Jamie wasn't sure if she was glad that Turner had never been much of a conversationalist, or not. He gave good speeches at school, when required to, but he was a lot better at just listening.

She didn't feel like talking.

They sat in silence through the entire cup of coffee, not quite looking at each other.

She wasn't sure how long they would have pretended to drink from empty cups if there hadn't been a knock at the door.

Devon.

Jamie told herself it was just logic that told her who it was, not a tingling certainty that it was him.

"Well, I'd best be getting home," Turner said swiftly, rising and dumping his coffee cup on the counter instead of washing it the way he normally would. He was pulling on his coat as he opened the door for Devon. "I'm just leaving."

Devon stepped in and Turner vanished behind him, much more swiftly than a man of his size ought to be able to.

It occurred to Jamie that Turner had never actually answered the question about whether or not he was a shifter.

Jamie remained in her chair, looking thoughtfully at Devon.

"I tried to call you," Devon said.

"I had my phone turned off," Jamie told him.

"Oh, good," Devon said inanely. "I mean, because I thought maybe the battery had died again, or...something."

"No, you fixed it," Jamie said. "It works fine now."

"Can we talk?" Devon asked nervously.

"Yeah," Jamie said. "You want some coffee?"

Devon shook his head and shrugged out of his coat. "I don't want coffee," he said firmly. "I want *you.*"

He had a piece of paper in his hand, and when he sat down opposite from her, he slid it across the table.

"What's this?" Jamie asked. It was too small to be a letter of apology or a poem.

"That's your dad's phone number."

20

Devon was watching Jamie's face when she took the paper slowly, like she couldn't help herself.

A hundred different emotions crossed her face in the space of a few heartbeats: surprise, grief, anger, gratitude, confusion, and pain.

"You...said you wanted to know."

She stared at the paper a moment, then glared at him. "You should have told me."

Devon guessed that he wasn't talking about her dad's number.

"I should have," he admitted. "I should have told you everything from the very beginning. Complicated didn't start to cover it, and I had to protect my sister as well as my secrets, but you're my mate and I should have trusted you."

"What's a...mate?" she whispered.

Devon had to laugh then, even in the face of her distress, because it all seemed so clear and easy at last.

"It's like destiny or fate, but more. A mate is the person who completes a shifter. The perfect match. The other half. The happy ever after and the love at first sight."

"This isn't a fairy tale," Jamie hissed. She was hunched over, her shoulders rolled forward defensively.

"It's more complicated than a fairy tale," Devon agreed. "But if you set me three impossible tasks, I'd do them for you."

Jamie almost smiled. "You really would, wouldn't you."

"In a heartbeat," Devon said honestly. "When I met you, I knew you were the one. My...lynx...recognized you and made it clear that I couldn't let you get away. Ever."

Her smile faded. "What am I supposed to do with this?" she asked, looking down at the slip of paper in her hands.

Devon thought she meant more than the phone number, but that was the easiest place to start.

"Whatever you want," he said promptly. "You don't have to call him, I just thought you should have it. If you want, we can invite him for Thanksgiving dinner. I know you don't like to plan that far ahead, but...you could. If you wanted."

"Did you hack into some government database to get this information? Devon Maynard, Private Investigator?"

Devon chuckled. "No hacking necessary; there's a lot of information in public records if you know where to look. Marta knew his name, I could figure it out from there. That's his work number. He's an accountant in Des Moines. He drives a better car than me."

"Well, if he was going to be a deadbeat, he could have at least passed on the genetic knack for math," Jamie joked stiffly. She folded the paper in her hands, then folded it again.

"You're pretty good at invoicing," Devon reminded her. "And you should at least let him tell you his side of the story."

"Why'd you do this?" she asked.

"You made me think a lot...about family. And I thought you'd want to know. And *I'd* want to know." Devon swallowed. "Jamie, I want you to be my family. Whatever you come with, however you are. You and me and Abby."

Jamie was still folding the paper, as tiny as it would go.

"I thought I'd start looking for a new house," Devon said, jumping off the deep end. "A place big enough for three of us."

The paper slipped from Jamie's fingers and unfolded.

"What are you suggesting, that we buy a house together?" She sounded outraged.

"We could get married," Devon said desperately, his lynx anxious in his head. He was making an utter hash of this. "I mean, I'd like to. Jamie, you're my *mate*. I love you like crazy, and I want to be with you forever."

"People say forever all the time," Jamie protested. "They never mean it."

"I mean it," Devon said fiercely. "I mean always, and I mean forever, and I mean you and me, and I will do whatever I have to do to make that happen."

Jamie stared at him until he felt uncomfortable.

"I can get a ring, if you want to do this right," he added more quietly. "It won't be a surprise, but we can go to the park, or Gran's, where we met, and I'll get down on one knee and stammer a lot." Should he do that now? he wondered. He certainly had the stammering part down.

She was still unhelpfully quiet.

"We could do a courthouse thing in Madison if you don't want a big deal," Devon suggested.

Still, she didn't say anything.

"Or we don't have to get married, if you think that's an antique requirement of the patriarchal establishment or whatever," Devon floundered. "I'd just...really like it."

"You want to live here?" Jamie asked at last.

"Green Valley, Alaska, it doesn't *matter* to me."

"What about Abby?"

Devon paused. "We're a team," he said cautiously.

"Don't look so stricken," Jamie said, with a hint of her usual spice. "I'm not going to ask you to choose between us. I was thinking I'd winter over in Green Valley anyway, though the wildfire season doesn't strictly follow the school year, you know. And we'd have to see what Abby wanted to do."

Relief flooded through him, and his lynx capered in his head. "I like the idea of Alaska," he said eagerly. "My lynx would love having real wilderness to get out in."

Jamie gave a dry laugh. "Your *lynx*. Is it like a different person inside of you? Does it *talk*?"

"Too much, sometimes," Devon said wryly.

"My boyfriend has voices in his head," Jamie said with a sigh.

Devon thought that it was an excellent sign if she was calling him her boyfriend, even if she hadn't answered the question about getting married. He smiled across the table hopefully and Jamie frowned.

"Show me," she challenged.

Devon had expected that, and he stood up and walked to the door and locked it before coming around to her side of the table. He started to pull his sweater off over his head.

"All the naked people," Jamie muttered, scooting her chair back so that she was facing him. "I didn't bring any dollar bills."

"You can tip me in other ways," Devon suggested with a slow smile.

"You *are* getting better at that invoicing thing," Jamie said with grudging approval.

Devon put his sweater on the table and started to slip out of his pants.

"Slower!" Jamie suggested. "I'm not over being mad at you, but you're still hot."

Obediently, Devon slowed, sliding his zipper down one link at a time. He had only the vaguest idea of how strip-teases worked, but he was willing to try.

21

Jamie felt like she'd gone through every emotion it was possible to feel. Devon had pissed her off, proposed to her, tracked down her deadbeat dad, promised to follow her to Alaska...and now he was giving her a blushing strip-tease to the best of his considerable abilities.

There was no soundtrack, but neither of them needed one. Devon was absolutely *gorgeous*, with his rippling muscles and big arms and those amazing planes leading down into the pants he was slowly removing.

"Boom chicka yeah..." he said, his ears charmingly pink.

The humor didn't dampen Jamie's ardor, and as his pants slipped past his cock, it was clear that it hadn't harmed his, either.

He was the whole package...he was funny, he was brave, and he was loyal.

And he was *hers*.

Jamie didn't know how much she believed in mates, but she knew that there was something amazing between them. Something special.

Something...*true*.

He was her *family* now, and that was as exciting as the idea of shifters was, now that she had gotten past her fury.

His pants were off now, with one little skip as he nearly lost his balance pulling them off his ankle, and Jamie rose to her feet.

She came up close to him, loving the hiss he gave as she closed her hand around his shaft.

"You...ah...wanted to see my l-lynx," he stuttered.

"That can wait," Jamie told him, using her other hand to trace down his chest. "I'm thinking that make-up sex may be in order first."

"Make-up sex?" Devon repeated with a groan.

"It was our first big fight," Jamie explained. "I'll let you check it off the list."

"It was on the list?"

"No, but I'll add it." She stood on her toes to nibble his earlobe and he groaned and the muscles under her hands strained. Though one of them wasn't *technically* a muscle.

Then Devon growled, and she wondered how she'd never noticed how *animal* his growl could be. He bent and picked her up, not bothering to hide how impossibly easy it was for him, and she let her arms slide up around his neck.

He went at once for the stairs.

"Keys!" Jamie reminded him breathlessly.

They paused at her coat to fish her keys from her pocket and then he was carrying her up the stairs like they were returning from a wedding, but considerably more awkward because she nearly fell out of his arms unlocking the door.

Then he was tossing her, laughing, onto the bed and shutting the door behind her and she was struggling out of her clothing as fast as she could because she didn't want anything between them, not one scrap of clothing, not one secret.

"I love you," he said, kissing her neck as he returned to hamper the removal of one last pant leg. "I love you."

Three little words. Words Jamie thought she'd never hear and that she'd certainly never believe.

They made her impossibly wet, and impossibly weak.

And she believed him, beyond the slightest shadow of a doubt.

She felt safe in his arms, safe and loved and sheltered.

He'd always been able to spark her desire, from the very first startled glance he'd given her. But now he set her on fire, and she wasn't *afraid* of his fire. He wasn't *wildfire* or *house fire*…he was *hearth fire*. He was *home*.

She wrapped her arms around his neck and drew him closer, wrapping her legs around him as he drove into her.

They coupled slowly, at first, savoring the closeness and kisses, then fell irresistibly into a whirlwind of need and desire, frantic for friction and touch. When she found her climax, he followed quickly, desperate and gentle.

"I love you," Jamie said, because it was true, and she didn't want secrets.

He gave a noise of delight and wrapped her tight in his arms. "I love you," he told her.

Jamie felt a rush of pleasure every bit as keen as the physical pleasure had been, and they lay, tangled together, until she fell asleep.

22

---

*J*amie woke up with a lynx.

He was purring, his plush sides rising and falling in a hypnotic rhythm.

She was curled around him, feeling blissfully comfortable. He was warmer and softer than anything she'd ever felt before. She squeezed, and was shocked by how much of him was *fur*.

He turned in her arms, rolling onto his back and lolling his head back to look at her.

"You're pretty fine looking this way, too," Jamie said admiringly. "Look at those murder mittens!"

His paws were the size of dinner plates, and when she stroked them, marveling at their softness, claws like curved box-cutters extended and caught her fingers.

Like all of Devon, they were gentle and strong, just holding her for a moment before retracting into the dense fur.

"Is it a trap if I try to pet your belly?" Jamie joked.

Devon wriggled invitingly, underestimated the width of the bed, and fell off the side of it with a miraculous twist that had him standing on all four feet.

Then he was human again, in a move like a sheet of silk blowing in a breeze, and crawling back up onto the bed to kiss her.

"My Jamie," he said possessively, and it thrilled her to her toes.

Then he backed away reluctantly. "I don't want to nag, and I won't ask again if you don't want me to…but I didn't get an answer."

Jamie knew what question he was referencing. "I'll…I'll marry you," she agreed, feeling excited and relieved and nervous all at once. It would be official. It would be *real*.

Devon took her face in both hands and kissed her soundly.

"Thank you," he said. "Do you hear something?"

Jamie didn't, but apparently, being a lynx shifter gave him super-hearing, because he followed the sound out the door and down the stairs to where his phone was vibrating in his abandoned pants.

He missed the call, but frowned at the clock. "I have to get home," he said reluctantly. "It's getting really late and Abby's wondering where I am."

He texted his sister, took the swiftest shower possible, did an equally sexy reverse strip-tease, and vanished with a sound kiss on Jamie's head.

Jamie took a much more leisurely shower and dressed slowly. She poured herself a cup of coffee and sat down at the station table, where her father's phone number was folded into the tiniest square that the paper could manage.

She was still folding and unfolding it when there was a knock at the door.

Jamie stood and called out, "Come on—"

Before she could finish, it was opened aggressively, and Abby stomped in and slammed it behind her.

"Look," Abby said firmly. "I'm here to talk about Devon."

"He just…"

"You have to fix this," she said almost hysterically. Jamie suddenly wondered why she'd never realized how kittenish Abby was. It wasn't just the half-grown puberty proportions, there was something about her golden-green eyes, and how she blinked, and the laser focus of her gaze.

That gaze was entirely on Jamie now, as she advanced across the garage.

"You have to take him back! It was my fault, he was trying to protect me, I'm the one who screwed up and told you instead of letting him do it, and—and *you* have to make it right because I *can't.*"

Jamie blinked at her vehemence.

"Devon has never been so happy," Abby said furiously. "And if I screwed that up and you go away, I will never forgive myself and this is all my fault I should never have said anything and I'm s-s-s-sorry!"

Jamie opened her arms and Abby staggered into them. "It's okay," she said, as comfortingly as she could. "It's okay. We...made up. I'm not going anywhere without you."

And she wasn't, Jamie realized, as Abby collapsed into tears in her arms, hugging furiously back. Jamie was done running away from things. She could no more leave them than she could leave her past.

Home was here in Green Valley, with both Devon and Abby.

She didn't consider herself good at comforting people, but she patted Abby and hugged her close and let the girl sob herself out, then took her to sit at the round table. "Devon would probably kill me if I gave you coffee at this hour, but we've got some hot chocolate powder."

Abby wiped her face on her long sleeves. "Yes, please."

Jamie dumped out the old coffee and the coffee grounds, and set a pot of just water to heat. She cleaned out Turner's mug and heaped it full of chocolate mix.

When she turned back to the table, Abby was picking up the folded paper and sweeping it towards the trash.

"Wait!" Jamie said in alarm.

Abby froze. "Sorry," she said. "I thought it was garbage."

"Maybe," Jamie said. "I mean, in a manner of speaking."

Abby looked confused.

Jamie set the chocolate in front of her and sighed. "That's my dad's phone number. Devon found it for me."

Abby blinked rapidly. "I guess I just figured you were an orphan. Like us."

"Nah," Jamie said casually. "I never knew my dad. He...left when I was a baby. I didn't know that for a long time, and I still don't know why."

"You going to call him?" Abby asked in a small voice. Her expression was complicated.

Jamie knew her own face probably betrayed as many emotions as Abby's did. "I don't know," she admitted. "I never knew him. He's not really my dad, you know."

Abby looked down into her mug of cocoa. "Yeah. I mean, I don't really remember my dad, and whenever someone says 'your dad,' I think of Devon. Even though he's my brother. I mean, I know that. But he was always the dad I *had*."

"I know exactly what you mean," Jamie said thoughtfully. "I have family now, too. Like you and Devon."

Abby's eyes were huge. "You sure?" she asked.

Jamie grinned at her. "Positive. Now, I have to ask you about some long-term things."

"Thanksgiving?" Abby said brightly. "Devon kept saying not to bug you about it."

"Longer than that," Jamie said bravely. "How would you feel about living together?"

"In our house?" the girl asked dubiously, doubtless thinking of their paper-thin walls and tiny footprint.

"Maybe not," Jamie agreed.

Abby scrambled to add, "I mean, not that I want you to think I wouldn't like living with you, just..."

"Someplace with your own space?"

"Yes, please," Abby said firmly.

"We could look at other towns, if you wanted. Devon might be up for going back to the city, and I'd do that. Or Alaska." Home wasn't a place, Jamie realized abruptly. It didn't matter where she lived, it mattered where her family was.

"I don't hate it here," Abby said too quickly. She turned scarlet, and took a hasty gulp of her hot chocolate.

"A boy?" Jamie guessed. She remembered how that felt. She *still* felt that, when she thought of Devon, whenever she thought about seeing him for the first time after any amount of being apart.

Abby didn't answer, finding something much more fascinating in the bottom of her mug.

"Green Valley, then," Jamie said with a smile, and it wasn't reluctant. She wasn't here just to repay a debt to Turner anymore.

Green Valley was...home. Over the space of a few weeks, she had forgotten why she even wanted to go anywhere else.

The door to the station suddenly burst open. "Have you seen...oh, Abby!" Devon looked ruffled and half-panicked. "Why didn't you text back?"

"You were the one who wouldn't answer me!" Abby protested. "I sent you like seven texts and tried to call!"

"And then I texted you back!" Devon insisted.

"No, you didn't!" Abby argued, pulling out her phone. "See...uh...oh. Never mind!"

Devon gave a sigh and shook his head. "Well, now that I've got you both here, let's talk about things. Future things. Jamie said..." he blushed absolutely scarlet. "She said she'd marry me."

Abby gave a little squeal, then cleared her throat as if she'd embarrassed herself. "It's about time," she said casually. "But there's one thing we should talk about first."

Jamie expected it to be where they would live, how they would work out a summer schedule, who would go where and do what.

But Abby's focus was much narrower. "I want to know if I get to make Thanksgiving dinner for everyone."

Jamie burst out laughing, because it was absolutely perfect.

All her life had felt like no. But now, at last, it felt like: "Yes."

Abby gave an airfist. "I am going to make the best turkey," she declared. "And yams. And pumpkin pie. And buttermilk biscuits. And green bean casserole with the crunchy onions on top. Oh my God, I'm starving. I forgot to eat dinner."

"There's pizza in the fridge at home," Devon suggested.

"Out of my way," Abby exclaimed, and she vanished out the door, leaving Jamie alone with Devon again.

"I like that she can come and go here," Devon said, with a fond look after her. "In the city, I worried if she went out. Here…"

"Green Valley has a few things going for it," Jamie agreed.

"You, for one," Devon told her.

"I don't hate it," Jamie said thoughtfully. "I don't hate it a lot."

"I don't hate you," Devon added. "I don't hate you a lot."

"I'm looking forward to not hating you for a really long time," Jamie said, smiling up at him.

Then he kissed her, and she really didn't hate that at all.

EPILOGUE

Turner had planned on a quiet Thanksgiving in his own house. Football games on the television, one of those rotisserie chickens from the grocery store. Maybe he'd open some olives and eat them all, sitting on the couch, straight from the can.

But Jamie invited him to dinner with Devon and Abby and when he tried to wriggle out of it, dropped the bomb that her estranged father would also be attending, and Turner didn't know how to turn *that* down.

The food was likely to be better, anyway.

Marta had been at Gran's when the invitation was brokered, and she had, in her usual forward way, invited herself as well.

Which is why Turner was at the door to Tawny's tiny old house with Marta's hand in his elbow while she complained about the snow and the ice on the sidewalk and the fact that one of her favorite television shows had been canceled ten years ago.

"Turner and Marta are here!" Devon called as he opened the door.

"I've already dibs-ed one of the drumsticks!" Jamie yelled in reply. She was setting the kitchen table, which had been pulled out into the living room so that chairs could be put around all four sides.

"It smells great," Turner said gruffly. He had to go sideways through the kitchen to get in past Abby, who was stirring something in a saucepan with a look of concentration.

Turner didn't tarry—Marta was hurrying him forward from behind. "I brought a pie," she said, putting it down on the counter next to Abby. "Apple with extra cinnamon." She cast a critical eye at Abby's work. "You'll skin the milk at that temperature."

"Only if I stop stirring," Abby retorted, not even bothering to glance at her. "And it's called lactoderm. We learned about it in biology."

"Kind of like life," Marta observed, and she walked into the living room with a sniff. "Just got to keep stirring."

"They taught you the word lactoderm in middle school bio?" Devon said, rifling through a cabinet to find another serving plate.

"This is Green Valley," Abby scoffed. "It's all cows, all the freaking time."

"I brought sparkling cider," Turner said gruffly, putting two bottles on the table. "Non-alcoholic."

"I didn't sign up for a Thanksgiving dinner without social lubricant," Marta said smartly. "I was expecting a bottle or two of your homebrew!"

Turner shrugged in embarrassment. He sometimes, very sheepishly, gave out bottles of his ales, but he hadn't been sure it was appropriate to bring to a dinner with a former and future high school student.

"We've got wine," Devon chuckled. "And some beer."

"I should hope so," Marta said.

"I'm on call," Turner said regretfully. "Just one glass for me." He might need something stronger than wine to get through this meal anyway.

"Who's going to have a fire on Thanksgiving in Green Valley?" Marta asked.

"It's not like people schedule them around holidays," Jamie laughed.

"If I'd known we'd get a kitchen this nice, I would have burned that awful popcorn popper months ago!" Abby sang from in front of the stove. "If I light my curling iron on fire, can we get the bathroom remodeled?"

"Insurance fraud is a felony!" Devon called back. "Can you at least wait until you're eighteen and not my responsibility before you plan your life of crime and arson?"

Turner winced and caught Jamie watching him. "Fire's not a joke," she said chidingly. It was surprising to catch her being the sensitive one in the group. But she'd grown up a lot since she was a gawky, rebellious student at Turner's high school. He could sense the nervousness prickling from her.

They'd all grown up. Even Marta looked a little older and seemed less blunt as she fussed with the table settings. Certainly, he had more silver hairs when he looked in the mirror these days, and the knee he'd hurt skiing twenty years ago was proving to be a reliable weather compass.

"I heard Dean is moving to Madison in the summer," Marta volunteered. "Getting a degree in engineering, and Shelley's working on some kind of fashion line for kids."

Turner watched Jamie and Devon exchange a significant look.

"Yeah," Devon said. "We're going to be moving into his house."

"You're buying it?" Marta always sounded sharp when someone scooped her on gossip.

"What about Alaska?" Turner asked.

Jamie shrugged with one shoulder. "We're looking into taking over Dean's hardware store. It's a more long-term career than fighting wildfire."

"And Dean's house has an office, so I'd have space other than the kitchen table to work on my programming business," Devon added.

"I'll do the invoicing for you," Jamie said, and they shared what was clearly an inside joke.

"That's a lot of advance planning for you," Marta observed skeptically.

"Yeah, yeah," Jamie said dismissively, clearly embarrassed now.

"Well, Turner keeps harping on how people have to be able to rely on each other."

"I'll be glad to have you on call for a while," Turner said gruffly.

Jamie gave him a brief, sheepish smile and hurried back into the kitchen for a load of plates.

"You look as proud as a *father*," Marta said with a smirk, pouring herself a glass of wine. It was clear she was only there because she wanted to see the anticipated reunion between Jamie and her real father, and her glance was appraising.

Turner shrugged. He was more nervous that he cared to admit to see Jamie meeting her father and it felt bittersweet being here, included in a family. Devon and Jamie were pretending not to make eyes at each other, Abby looked smug as a mother. Even Marta felt right here, the spinster aunt with an opinion about everything.

"It's perfect!" Abby called in triumph from the kitchen. "This is the best turkey ever baked in the history of the world."

"You need help getting it out of the oven?" Devon offered.

"Back off, big brother. This is my turkey."

"Dibs on a leg," Jamie reminded everyone.

Then everyone went absolutely silent at the sound of a hesitant knock on the door.

"I'll get it," Jamie said, squeezing behind Abby to answer it.

The man on the porch looked every bit as nervous as the people in the house when Jamie opened the door for him.

"You must be Jamie," he said, and for a moment no one moved or said anything.

Then Jamie, with uncharacteristic shyness, said, "Hi, Dad."

Abby was frozen with the oven half-open and Devon was wringing an oven mitt in his hands, looking like he might like to hit someone.

Just as Turner was considering whether he should sweep in and somehow save the situation, though he had no idea how, the stranger broke into a wild grin. "Well, *that* certainly is the damndest thing to hear!"

Jamie turned and gestured him into the house. "This is *Jim*," she introduced generally. "My fiancé, Devon, his sister, Abby, she made the dinner. This is Marta, and…" she paused as she reached Turner, still standing back at the entrance to the kitchen not sure what to do with his hands. "That's Turner."

Jim strode forward and extended his hand directly to Turner. "I understand I owe you a helluva debt," he said frankly.

Turner shot a look at Jamie, who was smiling foolishly with eyes full of happy, unshed tears, and slowly shook the man's hand. He realized that he was scowling and tried to smile instead.

It was Marta who said what none of the rest of them would, of course.

"So, where the hell have you been?" she sniffed.

"Beverly never told me," Jim explained at once, just as Jamie tried to say, strangled, "Marta…!"

"The turkey's ready!" Abby said brightly.

"I'll pour the wine," Devon offered.

"Lots of wine," Turner agreed.

They scattered back to the table, making small talk and chattering over each other.

The turkey was beautiful, golden-brown and covered in crisp skin. "Have a delicious, murderous mini-dinosaur," Abby said, putting it down carefully.

Turner chuckled; everyone in Green Valley knew about the flock of angry wild turkeys by now, and they'd left as swiftly as they'd appeared, but it required explanation for Jim, who tipped his head back and laughed in a way so like Jamie that there could be no remaining doubts about her paternity.

They all sat, said a brief grace, and dug in, praising Abby for the amazing spread. Even Marta agreed that it was an exceptional turkey, though she was unimpressed by the yams. Conversation was cautious at first, but by the end of the meal, they had gradually relaxed and were all chatting easily, and Turner decided he liked Jamie's father. Jim suggested that they go fishing some time—he had a friend with an ice shack further north—and Turner gladly accepted the offer.

Devon and Jamie talked about Dean's house and the hardware store, and Jim haltingly offered to help out with a down payment, if they needed it. "I've done alright for myself," he said sheepishly. "And you missed out on a few child support payments."

Marta then asked nosy questions about his financial situation until Devon firmly said that it was time for dessert and turned the topic to her pie.

Eventually, they all retired to couches, where they watched football and discretely unbuttoned their pants and groaned for a while and shared praises of the food.

"I'll go get started on the dishes," Jamie finally sighed.

"I'll help you," Jim offered at once, and the two vanished into the kitchen.

Everyone left in the living room pretended not to be listening to their hushed conversation except Marta, who scooted her chair closer to the door.

"We should be going," Turner said firmly, glaring at her. "I'll walk you home, Marta."

Marta pouted and dawdled as Turner got their coats from the overstuffed closet, and then managed to slip back into the living room under the pretense of getting a recipe from Abby while Turner made polite noises of farewell at the others.

He waited pointedly on the porch, but it was Jamie who stepped out after him and shut the door behind her.

"Thanks for coming," she said gruffly. "I...really wanted you to meet him."

She hadn't pulled on a coat, and she was shivering and fidgeting. Turner might have put an arm around her, but he couldn't figure out if she would want him to.

"He seems like a nice guy," Turner said, and he sounded almost sad to his own ears. "I'm glad you'll have a chance to get to know your dad."

Jamie shot him a sharp look. "He's my father," she said firmly. "But he's not really my *dad*."

Then she stepped into his arms and squeezed him tightly. "Thanks," she murmured. "For everything."

Turner hugged her close and let her go when the door squeaked behind them and Marta came out onto the porch, pulling her coat close around her and complaining about the cold. She had a tinfoil-wrapped casserole dish in one arm.

"Thanks for dinner," Turner said gruffly.

"It was surprisingly good," Marta agreed. "That Abby has a lot of potential."

"I'll tell her you said so," Jamie said, stifling a grin. "Thanks for coming." She slipped back inside, waving, and shut the door behind her.

Marta tucked her free arm into Turner's elbow and clung to him for balance as they walked down the icy path. "When are you going to find a woman of your own and raise a herd of your own young ones?" she asked pointedly. "You've clearly got a knack for it."

"I'm a little past planning for a family," Turner said regretfully. "And anyway, a family doesn't have to be your blood."

Marta looked pleased with herself. "No, it doesn't," she agreed, patting his arm. "But I'm still going to enjoy watching you find your own mate."

Turner gave her a suspicious glance, not sure how she meant the term. A skeptical grunt seemed like the appropriate response.

It started snowing again, as they meandered down the quiet street. "You ever regret not having a family of your own?" Turner asked her in return.

"I have a family," Marta scoffed, as they came up to the converted brick bank that she lived in. The gold lettering outside still proclaimed that it was the Habert Gutten bank and there was a historical plaque at one corner of the ostentatious building. "All of Green Valley is my family. I could have had my pick of Thanksgiving dinners tonight, but I'd heard that Abby was quite the young cook and wanted to see for myself."

"And you wanted to meet Jamie's father for yourself," Turner said wryly.

Marta laughed without shame. "So did you, fire chief." She unlocked her door—the small side door, not the huge front door. "And did you like what you found?" she asked pryingly.

Turner thought about Jim, his mannerisms surprisingly like his newfound daughter. "Yes," he said. But it was Jamie's warm hug that his thoughts returned to, and the kind, cheerful banter around the table. "Good night, Marta."

"Good night," she said, and then she was gone, and Turner was left to walk alone through the snow to his own quiet old farmhouse at the far side of the town.

It was dark inside, and only a can of olives was waiting for him on the kitchen counter, but he had family in his heart.

THE MORE THINGS CHANGE

Gran gazed out over the snow.

It was just after Thanksgiving, and a weather system that she felt in her bones had settled over Green Valley and dumped several feet of fluffy flakes on the town. Trees bowed heavy limbs over the street, and the sunlight that was breaking through the clouds turned everything to sparkling diamonds and long blue shadows.

The children were out, shouting and running in the empty streets. Residents were on their sidewalks, shoveling and trying to look as if they minded the labor, or the snow, or the shouts, hiding their smiles in their scarves.

It hadn't changed much, over the decades.

And in some ways, it had changed a great deal.

Some of the younger folks were taking photos on tiny pocket telephones, and a cellphone tower had gone in a year ago, but Stanley still came in to nurse coffee nearly every morning driving the same old truck and Marta usually read a book near the window if there wasn't much of a lunch rush. (And there was never much of a lunch rush.)

Old George was just getting started in the kitchen, emptying the dishwasher (noisy, new-fangled thing. Gran hated it with a passion.) and getting the grill hot. Devon was already there, pulling the chairs down from the tables easily with one hand and laying down placemats.

Ah, there was Devon's mate, Jamie, making the bell at the door ring. Gran remembered her as a child, always bucking authority. But she'd been gentle, for all of her defiance, never too busy to pause and pet a cat.

She stopped to do that now, automatically, only freezing her hand at the last moment when she remembered who Gran actually *was.*

Gran purred and arched into her hovering hand approvingly.

It had been a shock to the girl, finding out about the shifters who lived quiet lives all around the humans of Green Valley. But it helped that Devon was patient and persistent, and his little sister, a lynx shifter like he was, wanted them together so badly.

"Patricia got me to promise to building the set for the pageant this year," Jamie told Devon, dropping into one of the chairs he'd set upright. "Can Abby paint?"

"There's a Christmas pageant?" Devon said, putting a menu in front of her. He clearly found the idea quaint.

"Yeah. All the protestant churches get together, because none of them have enough kids to put on their own pageants, and a few years ago, Turner started hosting it in the school gymnasium and throwing a big potluck. The Cohens bring latkes, and Old George shows up with presents, and the Catholic choir does some songs and Marta brings seven pies and everyone eats too much and someone usually spikes the adult punch. It's kind of a Green Valley thing."

Gran remembered a time when such a thing would have been impossible; it was every church for itself, in a relentless competition that turned neighbors against each other. Turner had grown up in that time, and he'd almost single-handedly turned it around, reminding the little town that the holiday was more than a date on a calendar and an obligation for gifts.

Devon froze. "I have to get you a Christmas present," he said in horror. "I've got to get Abby something! Dammit, this holiday always creeps up on me. Sorry, Gran."

Was he apologizing for swearing? Gran had heard much worse, in her time. She groomed herself in Devon's direction and otherwise ignored him.

"What do you want?" Devon asked desperately.

"I was thinking about the chicken fried steak," Jamie said merrily. "Hash browns, extra crispy."

"For Christmas," Devon insisted. "What do you want for *Christmas?*"

"Turkey?" Jamie teased him. "Abby made a killer bird for Thanksgiving. And stuffing, and that green bean casserole. One of Marta's pies?"

"You're no help," Devon scolded her, but he was smiling, and he bent down to kiss her when he was done setting the last place. "I meant a *gift.*"

"Oh, I don't know," Jamie said breezily. "Maybe diamonds or ball gowns or…" her last suggestion was whispered into Devon's ear and he turned scarlet to the roots of his sandy blond hair.

"But maybe that will count as a *stocking stuffer*," she added innocently, and Devon nearly fell over a chair scrambling back to the kitchen with her order.

Gran chuckled, as only a cat can, and rotated twice on her folded bathrobe before she settled contentedly into place, looking outside over the snow once more.

In some ways, nothing had changed at all.

JOYOUS TIDINGS

The worst part of it all was the Clara knew she was overreacting.

"I don't WANT to be Mary!" she cried, stomping her foot. Being Mary was the tiniest part of the horrible feeling in her chest, but it was the only one she could talk about. "I want to be an ANGEL and have wings and bring JOYOUS TIDINGS."

Victoria was fussing, not quite crying, but definitely sensitive to the atmosphere, so Miss Mama Patricia was bouncing the little girl in her arms, trying to forestall a fit. "Mary is the most important role in the play," she said patiently. "We needed someone who was up to the part."

Clara recognized that she was being flattered, but she was too upset to feel good about it. "It's not FAIR!"

If Miss Mama's arms had not been full of squirming baby, Clara suspected that she would have gotten a big hug, and that might have made her feel better, but nothing was working out the way it was supposed to.

"Not everything is fair," Miss Mama reminded her warmly. "We just have to make the best of it and not let everyone down."

She was always having to not let people down and make the best of things, Clara thought sourly, but when Miss Mama offered a half a hug and suggested they go back to the rehearsal, she accepted it as better than nothing. Victoria crowed and tried to grab her hair. Babies were such a pain.

When Miss Mama sent her off with Trevor and Aaron to practice her lines, Clara still felt all prickly and unhappy inside. The boys were more ridiculous than ever. Aaron, who was Joseph, protested dramatically that he didn't want to marry Clara and Trevor teased him mercilessly.

"What's wrong, Clara?" Trevor finally asked, when they had gone twice through the script, Clara reading her parts in a whisper because she didn't want to sound like she was going to cry. "You know you don't actually have to marry Aaron."

"She's mad because she wanted to be an angel," Aaron said sagely.

But that wasn't it. That wasn't it at all.

They went through a rehearsal on the stage, Trevor reading as the narrator, Aaron acting as Clara's patient husband. Gabriel was played by a kid from a private school who looked like he wanted to be anyone and anywhere else. Clara didn't blame him.

Finally, Miss Mama released them to practice their lines behind the bleachers while the angels and shepherds, all the little kids from the preschool, practiced their ragged procession.

Aaron teased Clara for being too sensitive. "I'm too good to be Mary," he mimicked. "I'm an angel!"

"I bring joyous TIDINGS," Trevor mocked.

"Look at my wings!"

"Look at my sparkly halo!"

Clara knew they were trying, in their own cloddish way, to cheer her up, but she only felt sadder and more prickly than ever. She twisted the decoder ring on her finger and slumped down on the bleachers. Gabriel was sitting a little further away, memorizing his script by himself.

Trevor, who was wearing a matching ring, sat down beside her, dropping his angel act.

"Is this because we were teasing about getting married? Look,

I'll marry you if you want," Trevor said at her shoulder, slinging an arm around her.

"I'm Joseph," Aaron protested vehemently, plopping down on her other side. "I get to marry her!"

Twenty minutes earlier they'd been arguing about not wanting to marry her. Clara burst into tears and the boys started to fight about who had made her cry.

"It's not that," she sobbed. "It's not that at all! We're all going to move."

That silenced both of them.

"I'm only going to Madison," Aaron said quietly. "We're coming back some weekends and all summer. We'll still get to be friends."

"We're going to New York," Clara said in wild despair. "Miss Mama and Papa and Victoria and I are going really far away forever and we're never going to see each other again."

It was the worst news in the world that she could ever even imagine, and Clara had been holding it inside her chest like a horrible, heavy weight ever since she'd overheard her parents talking a few days earlier. She'd been carrying the secret around, snapping at everyone, desperate to tell someone and not sure how to. "I wanted to bring joyous tidings," she said miserably. Instead, she was ruining Christmas.

She loved Green Valley. She didn't really remember living anywhere else. All of her friends were here, Trevor and Aaron especially, and she didn't want to move away to a new house and try to make new friends.

She should have kept the news to herself and continued the terrible secret.

Trevor's arm tightened around her and Aaron flung himself against her from the other side, so that she was in a warm friend sandwich as she cried and they tried to comfort her.

"We'll keep in touch," Trevor promised.

"You have a phone," Aaron reminded her. A phone was a big privilege for a nine-year-old, Clara knew, because her Papa was very firm on the topic.

"We'll always be best friends," Trevor said firmly. "I know we will."

"I'll always wear my decoder ring," Aaron added. "We can mail each other secret messages."

"Every day," Trevor promised. "I'll ask for stamps for Christmas."

Clara cried herself out in their embrace until her misery finally eased. She still didn't want to move and dreaded everything about it, but it somehow helped that they knew now. She would come back to Green Valley someday and they would all be friends again.

"I'm sorry I'm such a ninny," Clara said in chagrin as she finally shook them off and wiped her face. She had read ninny in a book once and Miss Mama said it wasn't a bad word, even though it wasn't nice.

"You're not a ninny," Aaron was swift to tell her. He lowered his voice. "I cried when I found out we were moving to Madison."

"I'm going to miss you guys," Trevor said, sounding like he might cry, too.

From across the gym, Andrea called, "Trevor! Aaron! Shelley needs to see you in your costumes!"

Each of them gave her one last squeeze and ran to try on their robes.

Clara wiped her face before she followed them and tried to draw herself together again. She looked up to find Gabriel staring at her. He couldn't have helped but overhear everything, but where she expected to see pity or disgust, she caught envy.

"You're lucky," he said quietly.

Clara paused in smoothing her skirt. "Lucky?"

"You have really good friends," he pointed out. "People who care about you and want to make you feel better. I wish I had friends like that."

Clara blinked. "I have to move away," she reminded him.

Gabriel nodded sympathetically. "Yeah, that sucks. But at least you have them now." He shrugged and got to his feet, leaving her to examine her own confused feelings.

He wandered back across the gym, muttering, "I bring you joyous tidings. JOYous tidings. Joyous TIDINGS."

Maybe joyous tidings didn't have to be good news. Maybe joyous tidings could be reminding people of the wonderful things they already had, and remembering to appreciate them.

Clara stood up and smoothed her hair back. The last thing she wanted to do was make her final Christmas in Green Valley a horrible memory that lingered forever. It was going to be her last holiday here, and she didn't want her last months with Aaron and Trevor to be of her being crabby and self-centered.

No, she was going to make this a Christmas to remember, the happiest ever, and she was going to be the very best Mary that had ever been on that gym stage. This was going to be the most amazing multi-denominational Christmas pageant and winter festival holiday celebration *ever*.

A GREEN VALLEY
CHRISTMOOSE DISASTER

1

"*This is a disaster!*"

"More of a disaster than usual?" As the vice principal of a small-town high school, Turner was used to being greeted this way. He peered past Andrea into the gym, trying to gauge the exact nature of this one.

Every year, Green Valley High hosted a multi-denominational Christmas pageant that had swelled into a general winter holiday celebration. There were tables along the sides being decorated with social studies make-up projects presenting the holidays of Kwanzaa and Diwali. The Hanukkah table was already laid out, and it would have the addition of latkes and challah bread the following day.

Andrea was one of the two preschool teachers in charge of organizing the kids for the pageant, along with Patricia, whose baby was somehow sleeping through the chaos in a car seat by Patricia's feet as she handed out scripts and props.

The stage was being set with a nativity scene and several middle-school students were still painting the sets.

A doll in a straw-filled manger was being pushed around like a shopping cart by two young boys: Aaron and Trevor, Andrea's step-son. They were both yelling at the top of their lungs and someone's toddler was wobbling after them, punctuating the chaos with shrieks of joy.

Nothing appeared to be on fire, at least. As the chief of the tiny volunteer fire department, that was always Turner's first worry.

"It all looks situation normal to me," Turner said with a shrug.

"Clara is crying in the bathroom because she doesn't want to be Mary," Andrea explained. "She wants to be an angel because they are pretty. Aaron says he won't marry Mary, Trevor says he would marry Mary, and the three wise men have already lost all the gifts for baby Jesus. The shepherds want to bring real sheep for 'ethnicity,' though I think they mean 'authenticity,' and we can't get the power on the star working. Agnes is having a snit about the Catholic choir getting to do the songs that the Methodist choir wants to do, and the soloist for O Holy Night has a sore throat."

"Is that all?"

"No, it gets worse! I can't get ahold of Officer Stakes," Andrea continued. "I think he's ignoring my calls. Do you know what that means?"

"He's gone to spend Christmas with his folks in Omaha like he always does?"

"He said he would leave *after* the show," Andrea said. "What this means is that I don't have a Santa Claus."

Trevor and Aaron happened to be pushing the manger with baby Jesus past at that moment and both of them ground to a halt.

"There's no Santa Claus?" Aaron demanded.

Turner didn't usually have to deal with the "is Santa real" issue in high school. Andrea stepped in deftly. "The guy who was going to *help* Santa Claus is missing," she said cheerfully. "Santa is really busy at this time of year, you know?"

Aaron didn't look particularly appeased.

"Abby says Santa Claus isn't real," Trevor said direly.

The toddler who had been chasing after them caught up and crashed into the back of Aaron. "Sanna!" he hollered, falling backwards onto his diaper-padded butt. "Sanna Caws!"

From across the room, Patricia was clapping her hands for attention. "We're going to start the rehearsal for the pageant now, boys and girls!"

From the stage, Abby protested, "We're still painting!"

"Carry on," Patricia said. "We'll avoid touching any of the set. Can I get all the angels and shepherds over here, please? Agnes, do you mind if we move these chairs for now?"

Agnes said she didn't mind, but very much as if she did mind, and she took her chairs off the side of the stage in a huff while Patricia got everyone lined up.

Clara, looking very sulky indeed, stood with her arms crossed in the middle of the stage while Aaron and Trevor took their spots and Patricia gently herded everyone else into place.

"THIS IS THE STORY OF THE FIRST CHRISTMAS THE NIGHT JESUS CHRIST WAS BORN WE CELEBRATE THIS TO REMEMBER THE HOPE AND JOY THAT THIS TINY BABY BROUGHT INTO THE WORLD—" Trevor read from his script at the top of his lungs, speaking very fast and taking no breaths.

"Trevor—" Patricia tried to stop him.

"ONTHATEXTRAORDINARYNIGHT—"

Turner wasn't sure how the boy hadn't passed out yet.

"INBETHLEHAMTWOTHOUSANDYEARS—"

"Trevor!"

Trevor finally ran out of breath. "What?" he gasped.

"You have to slow down, honey! Remember that the periods are places we take breaths. Try it again?"

Trevor cleared his throat and shook his script. "This. Is the story. Of. The first. Christ. Mas. The night..."

Someone in the shepherds made a snoring sound.

"Well, it's nice to know that the Green Valley multi-denominational Christmas pageant and winter festival holiday celebration will always be an event of somber dignity," Andrea observed to Turner as Patricia got the shepherds hushed and Trevor reading his parts at a reasonable rate. "Now, Turner...or should I say Santa Claus?"

Turner shot her a look of horror. "You've got to be kidding me."

"You've already got plenty of silver in your hair. We'll get you a beard," Andrea promised. "You'll be great. You're definitely jolly."

Turner groaned. "I have enough trouble getting my kids to take me seriously without being called Santa Claus for the next six months."

"Who would even know it's you?" Andrea asked brightly. "You'll be in costume!"

"Green Valley is not that big," Turner pointed out. "I don't think anyone out of diapers will be fooled."

"Well, we don't have that many options who will fit the Santa suit," Andrea argued. "We might still have to take it in a little. It's hanging in the dressing room, go try it on. Shelley will be here any minute to fit costumes and she can alter it if we need. Oh, there's Marta, I need to talk to her about parking in front of the library. I'll be right back to check the fit."

Turner found the suit, sighed, and shrugged it on over his clothes. The legs were big enough that he could stuff his boots right through them. Andrea was nowhere to be seen when he emerged from the make-shift dressing room.

Patricia was on the stage, trying to convince Clara to put some emotion into her acceptance of Gabriel's great news. "You should be really happy, dear! These are joyous tidings! Show me how happy you are!"

The shepherds and little angels were starting to get rowdy in the wings. "Why don't you guys go with Gabriel and practice your lines over there. We're going to practice the procession to the manger now."

A few of the angels squealed in delight and Clara looked crabbier than ever as she led Trevor and Aaron and a bewildered-looking Gabriel off the stage.

The phone in Turner's pocket rang and he had to dig through layers of costume to find it.

"Go!" he said briskly, lifting it to his ear.

"Hey Turner," the dispatcher said with no urgency. "I've got a call about a dog in a car."

"A dog *in a car?*" he asked skeptically.

"A very large, terrifying dog, apparently. She sounded hysterical."

"Isn't that something for the police?" Turner asked, plucking at the extra folds of the giant Santa suit. He was as tall as Stakes, and as broad at the shoulder, but either Stakes had been stuffing his suit, or he had a lot more belly than Turner realized.

"Officer Stakes isn't picking up or responding to messages," the dispatcher said apologetically. "You were next on the list."

Turner frowned. That really was very unlike Stakes. Dodging Andrea was one thing. Ignoring the dispatcher was quite another. "Maybe something came up and he headed down to see his folks a day early?" It didn't quite add up.

"That could be it," the dispatcher said skeptically. The dispatch office was two towns over from Green Valley, but the county was small enough that everyone knew everyone in public service, at least a little. "It's probably not a missing persons case yet."

"I'll check in at his house," Turner promised. "Just as soon as I've saved some lady from a dog. What's the address?"

"Dean's place," she said. "Thanks, Turner."

"It's my pleasure," Turner said politely.

Across the gym, there was a crash.

"That paint is WET!" Abby hollered at the top of her lungs. "Don't touch it, you little munchkin!"

The toddler started wailing and the shepherds all broke out in fake farts.

Turner fled while he could.

2

*L*inda slowed the car at the curve and looked down over the little town for a moment. There was no traffic on the road to worry about; she'd only seen one truck since she left the highway, and Green Valley was a picturesque postcard beneath her, snow-covered and sparkling.

It was the perfect place to spend a few days of Christmas holiday before stealing her daughter Shelley and her new boyfriend away for a surprise vacation to Cancun.

"Are you sure you don't need anything?" she asked the phone in the center console as she continued the drive down into town.

"I promise that everything is going perfectly smoothly," Julie's voice promised. "I've been in touch with the caterer and the orchestra, and the planners say that everything is right on schedule. You should enjoy your vacation."

"Well, if you need me to lean on the mayor, or if Gladys in accounting gives you any trouble—"

Julie's laugh cut her off. "I don't need you to ride in the rescue," she promised. "The Christmas Charity Gala will do absolutely fine without you."

Linda chuckled sheepishly. "Alright, I'll trust you. You've got this, I don't need to babysit you." Did she sound a little wistful? She had single-handedly saved the Gala from obscurity ten years ago and turned it into Lincoln's greatest annual charity event. It was bittersweet that it didn't really need her anymore. She *liked* coming to the rescue.

"Pinch your grandson's cheeks for me," Julie said. "And say hello to your kids."

"I will." Linda hung up with a voice command and the GPS advised her to take the next turn, into a sleepy neighborhood strung with Christmas lights.

Three years ago, her stepson Shaun had come to Green Valley to take custody of his son, Trevor. To Linda's surprise, instead of bringing Trevor back to Milwaukee, he eloped with Trevor's preschool teacher and left his accounting business to start a bakery in the middle of nowhere.

Linda hadn't liked Shaun's ex-wife, Harriet, but she found Andrea delightful, and had vacationed with them twice in Florida.

Then, just this fall, Linda's daughter Shelley announced that she was also moving to Green Valley. She abandoned her successful law career to move in with a man she'd just met named Dean, who was from various accounts a mechanic, a firefighter, the owner of a hardware store, an aspiring engineer, but perhaps most unexpectedly, the father of a little boy that was Trevor's age. Shelley had always sworn off of children, but she was throwing herself whole-heartedly into the role of Aaron's mother and Linda was concerned that she didn't understand what she'd bitten off and might be looking for escape.

Linda knew a little about that. She'd been young and foolish when she married Shaun's father, Damien. Suddenly becoming the mother of an active boy mourning his mother had been a big challenge, and baby Shelley had come along not long after to complicate matters. Linda loved both of her children without reserve, but she also knew how hard it was to be in Shelley's shoes, abruptly a parent. Her own marriage hadn't survived it, though she had weathered it until Shelley was in high school.

Linda shook her head to banish the memories. Shaun and

Shelley weren't even the only ones from their broken family who had come to Green Valley; Shelley had let it slip that Damien had also chosen to settle down in the little town, buying a house in the nearby hills.

Clearly, something was up with this unassuming town, and Linda was here to spend a few days figuring out how it had ensnared both her offspring before she whisked Shelley and Dean off on the surprise trip to Cancun.

Shelley had already told her that his son would be with his mother's family for Christmas Day and the two weeks after. Linda couldn't imagine that anything in this tiny town that she'd spent hours driving through nowhere to get to could possibly have any appeal compared to a hot beach with cold drinks.

Shelly would be so surprised and delighted—two weeks in a luxury resort in Cancun!—and Linda could catch up with Shaun and Andrea and spend a few days socializing with him and her grandson Trevor before they left. It was a fun and impulsive plan, and they were all going to absolutely love it.

Linda pulled her car up to the sidewalk and double-checked the address on her phone.

It was a charming house, the lawn littered with toys and sleds. There was a blow-up Santa standing lopsided near the gate going up to the house and Linda exchanged a wry look of amusement with it as she passed.

Gleefully anticipating the look of relief and delight that would be on Shelley's face, Linda pressed the doorbell. Someone inside was laughing, and two voices were talking loudly. One of them was male, the other might have been Shelley. Linda could not quite make out what they were saying.

Linda didn't hear the bell from outside, and they didn't seem to be coming to the door. Maybe she should have called? She wrestled the rickety screen door open and knocked on the door. "Shelley? Honey?"

The door opened in an impolite burst and Linda let the screen door fall shut on her, nearly losing her balance in surprise. "Good heavens!" she exclaimed.

The man who had opened the door was young and handsome, and his face was lit up in laughter. "Sorry, can I help you?"

"You must be Dean?"

"We're going to be late! Where's my sweater?" Shelley came bounding from behind him in the house, and she skidded to an ungraceful stop when she spotted Linda. "Mom?!"

Linda had to stare.

Shelley's hair was down, loose and untidy around her shoulders, and her shirt was buttoned one-hole off from straight. More surprising than her mussed clothing and coif was the expression on her face. She had been laughing, her whole face easy and happy. Even the shock that had settled there couldn't hide the unmistakable joy and uncharacteristic softness behind her alarm.

Shelly wasn't soft.

Shelley wasn't joyful, and she certainly didn't bounce around like a child. She hadn't even done that when she *was* a child.

"Hi, honey," Linda said, less sure of her script than she had been. "I'm here to rescue you."

Shelley came to stand beside Dean in the narrow entry. "Rescue me from what?"

"I've got tickets for all of us to Cancun. You're invited, Dean! I got us a great little cottage on the beach, with a private pool. I've got a few days to catch up with Shaun, some presents for everyone…"

Shelley and Dean exchanged a look that Linda couldn't identify, a swift moment of silent communication that Linda was unexpectedly cut out of.

"We can't go to Cancun with you," Shelley said apologetically. "Mom, I told you we were going to Madison for Christmas."

"You said that Aaron was going to Madison to see his mother," Linda said, not sure why this wasn't working out the way she'd planned. Didn't they realize what she was doing for them?

"We're *all* going to Madison," Shelley said gently as if she was the grownup in the room and Linda was the child. "We're going to spend a few weeks over Christmas break with Juan and Deirdre to look at real estate in the area."

Linda felt dense. "You're staying with his *ex-wife?* For a few *weeks?*" How was it possible that Shelley *didn't* need to be rescued?

"Yes," Shelley assured her. "We're all very good friends."

"With his *ex-wife?*" The idea was just so absurd that Linda had to confirm it. "In her *house?* I mean, I know they call it ex-mas..."

"I'm sorry, Mom, we have to go to the school *right now.* I'm fitting costumes for the winter festival and Christmas pageant, and I told them I'd be there at the top of the hour. We have to pick Bingo up from the groomer on the way back and they close at three, so we've really got to go..."

"Hang on," Dean interrupted her, and he reached to fix the buttons on her blouse. They smiled at each other so intimately that Linda was almost embarrassed to be there.

"Well, we'll catch up over dinner then?" Linda offered. Who was Bingo? *What* was Bingo?

Shelley and Dean were shrugging into their coats and Shelley reached for her purse. "Oh, we're having a big early Christmas dinner tonight with everybody at Shaun's."

"You should come!" Dean invited. "We're meeting at six."

"I couldn't intrude," Linda said, feeling flustered.

"Oh, Tawny makes enough food for an army!" Shelley assured her. "There is *always* room for a few more people at the table."

"Bring a date!" Dean teased.

Who was *Tawny?* Linda wasn't sure if she liked Dean feeling comfortable enough with her to tease.

Shelley looked like she was having sudden reservations. "Dad will be there, of course," she cautioned, as if it had just occurred to her, but she didn't rescind the invitation.

"Damien and I can be perfectly civil with each other," Linda assured her. If Shelley could stay with her boyfriend's ex-wife for a week, Linda could make polite conversation with her ex-husband over some roasted turkey. "I didn't book a room because you said that you had a guest room and I was always welcome, but if it's an imposition, I could find a hotel..."

Dean and Shelley exchanged another one of those completely unspoken conversations. "No, no," Shelley said swiftly. "Of course you can stay here. The guest room is yours." She pointed back to an open door.

"Make yourself at home," Dean insisted. "Whatever you need."

"I'm sorry, Mom, we really have to go…" Shelley gave Linda one quick hug and a peck on the cheek, then they were rushing out the back door to where a car was parked in the alley, the door slamming shut behind them.

Linda stood in the empty house that they left behind them, looking around in confusion. It wasn't dirty, exactly, but it was a picture of chaos, like the front yard, with lived-in clutter. There was a dog dish on a mat near the door, but it seemed impossible that Shelley lived with a *dog.* She was a lion shifter, what kind of dog would be comfortable living with an apex predator?

But Shelley hadn't looked or felt like an apex predator. She'd looked…happy. Not just satisfied, but deeply content in a way that Linda had never seen…or felt.

Linda lifted her head. She was just going to have to make a new plan. Maybe Shaun would appreciate her surprise visit a little more. She'd stay here a night or two and go to Cancun by herself if she had to. She was a strong, independent woman who could travel alone and wasn't going to be jealous of her daughter's unexpected happiness. No, she wasn't jealous, that was *absurd.*

She peered into the guest room. There was a train set laid across the bed, and Shelley's sewing table was littered with costume parts, but it would do for a few days.

She left out the front door again, battling the screen door, to get her luggage and the Christmas gifts from the car, and she was thinking so fixedly about how much fun she would have traveling alone that she didn't notice the giant black form until it was barreling down on her.

It seemed to appear out of a snowbank, a huge, panting beast and Linda only saw its size and snarling mouth as it bore down on her. She was standing beside her car, with no time to get behind something or up in a tree somewhere safe and she fumbled with the handle and opened the door, hoping to somehow get inside before it was upon her even though it was coming at her with terrifying speed —and it squeezed right past her and jumped onto the seat.

Linda slammed the door shut right after it and stood there shaking in fear.

It went berserk, barking and bounding around in the backseat over her luggage, lunging at the door and licking the window.

Linda's heart was beating wildly in her chest. There was a violent, vicious dog the size of a small horse trapped in her car. It scrambled into the front seat, and then back, and Linda winced to think what it must be doing to her leather. She reached into her purse and found her phone, thumbing it on with shaking hands. She supposed she ought to be grateful she even had a signal here in the middle of absolutely nowhere.

This rescue was not going at all the way she thought it would.

3

When Turner pulled up behind the strange car, he had the lights on the fire truck flashing, but a "menacing dog" in someone's car didn't warrant the siren through the sleepy neighborhood. The woman pacing on the snowy sidewalk with the phone at her ear didn't turn and probably didn't notice the lights, between the daylight and the din of blinking Christmas lights.

Turner was struck by a sudden desire to startle her by honking.

He took his hand from the horn without pressing it and wondered at the impulse. Clearly, he'd been spending too much time with the pranksters at the high school; their high spirits and manic holiday mischief were starting to rub off on him.

Shaking his head, Turner swung from the cab and the woman turned from her conversation and put the phone away in a pocket of her fur-trimmed white wool coat as she swept to meet him.

The snow underneath Turner's boot seemed to turn into ice, or possibly his knees went to water. When her blue eyes met Turner's, he was suddenly, completely incapable of rational thought or grace.

Mate! his moose trumpeted in his head, and it was a little like being caught in the stampede at the end of a school day as all of his wits fled the scene.

With no conscious direction from his brain, his limbs all went their own directions and the sidewalk seemed to tip beneath him as his foot slipped in the slushy snow. Shifter instincts were all busy screeching in recognition, leaving him no reflexes to stop his downward progress, and before Turner could catch himself, he was on his ass in the snow.

The woman his moose had responded to was standing over him now, her eyes wide in alarm, her perfect scarlet mouth a little O of surprise.

"Are you here to rescue me?" she asked incredulously, staring down at him.

That was when Turner remembered that he was still wearing the Santa Claus suit. "Have you been naughty?"

He wasn't sure what had prompted him to say something that inappropriate, but he was grateful that her face split into the most beautiful smile he'd ever seen. She didn't quite laugh, and Turner realized that he had a new goal in his life. He was going to make her laugh—really laugh!—if it was the last thing he ever accomplished.

She offered her gloved hand and he nearly pulled her down with him, only remembering how to control his legs so that he could stand at the last moment. He didn't want to let go once he was on his own feet, and she didn't seem to want to either, continuing to smile tolerantly at him.

His *mate*.

She was the most gorgeous thing he'd ever seen, with pale honey hair curling around her face, blue eyes like a summer sky, and kissable red lips. She was dressed all in white like an angel, with an expensive-looking fitted wool coat, impractical wool gloves, and fur-trimmed, high-heeled boots. She must be close to his own age, late forties or early fifties, with an ageless elegance like a silver screen star.

"You have a...dog in your car?" Turner had to try really hard to look away from her, and he saw the problem at once. "Oh, that's the Dresden's new puppy."

"That's a puppy?" the woman exclaimed in horror, extracting her hand from his at last. "It's practically a horse!"

The big black hound was howling from the passenger seat, wiggling and licking the window as he scrambled big paws against the edge of the door.

"That's Beast," Turner said. He positioned himself between his mate and the car and opened the car door. "He's a Great Dane. Beast, get out of the lady's car."

The woman gave a little squeak of alarm and stepped closer to Turner, putting her hand on his arm as she peered carefully around him. Turner usually had a dim opinion of scaredy cats and fragile fainting flowers, but he found himself enjoying this role of protector.

Beast galloped from the car straight into the snowbank, where he buried his face and fell over sideways, rolling so that all four of his giant paws were kicking in the air.

The woman gave a shaky laugh. "I thought it might be a...hellhound or something."

"I don't think Green Valley has a hellhound problem," Turner assured her as she slowly let go of him. "But Beast is pretty big and can be exuberant. I'll get him back to the Dresdens and remind them to get their fence fixed up." He turned so he could look at her again, trying hard not to stare like one of his horny teenage students. She was so beautiful it made it hard to think.

"You're my hero, Mr. Claus. How can I repay you?"

"Turner!" he blurted.

"What?"

"I'm John," he added desperately. Never mind that no one ever called him that.

She put her gloved hand out and he shook it again. "I'm Linda, John. Thank you for saving me from the hellpuppy." Beast was still rolling around in the snowbank.

Her hand was warm through the light glove, and Turner wondered if he imagined her pulse through it. "Linda John," he echoed her.

She chuckled—it didn't quite count as a laugh. "I'm Linda," she said patiently. "Linda Powell."

"Turner," he said. "I mean, everyone calls me Turner." He was an *idiot*. His brain caught up with her name. "I didn't know Shaun had two sisters." Now that he was looking for it, she did look a little like Shelley; he had thought at first that the resemblance was only because they were both so perfectly made up. She was like a *doll*.

Linda's cheeks went pink, but she looked pleased. "Oh, I like you," she said in delight. "I'm Shelley's mother."

Turner realized that he was still holding onto her hand, which was probably pretty awkward by this point, and he let go of it so quickly that he probably only made it worse. "Everyone likes Santa Claus. Will you let me take you out to dinner, Linda?"

"In exchange for rescuing me from the giant black horse-dog?"

Because you're my mate, he wanted to say. *Because there has never been another woman for me like you.* He'd never even imagined a woman like her in his life but now he could imagine nothing else. "I would never ask for a date in return for doing my civic duty," he said gruffly. "But I would very much like to take you out if you are willing."

"I think your civic duty is getting away," Linda observed.

4

The giant black not-a-hellhound had gotten bored of romping in the snowbank and rolled back onto its feet. It looked marginally friendlier now, panting and covered in snow, but it was still a lot of dog and Linda was very glad to have Santa Claus —Turner—beside her in case it charged her again. When a car door slammed somewhere down the block, the dog's floppy ears pricked forward, and he took off into the street with a howl.

To his credit, Turner did not actually swear, he only said, "Dang it, Beast!" and sprang into motion with a lot more grace and speed than Linda was consciously expecting. Possibly because he was wearing a Santa suit that hung on him rather unflatteringly, and he'd fallen on his ass the moment they met. In fact, he appeared to be quite appealingly athletic, as well as startlingly handsome.

To Linda's surprise, his sprint was actually equal to the puppy's bolt, and he caught the dog by the collar at the far side of the road. "That's not the way home, you mutt," he said, hauling Beast back to Linda's side. He barely had to lean over to hold on, the dog was that tall. Beast tried to twist around to lick him, and Turner gave him a kind pat on the head but didn't offer to let go.

"I didn't get an answer about dinner," Turner reminded Linda.

Linda regarded him thoughtfully.

She was used to turning heads and fielding date requests. She wasn't used to feeling shy and girlish about it and Turner was clearly not just angling for her influence, since she had none here. He had a fresh, small-town honesty that was refreshing and an intriguing combination of self-confidence and fluster, like he was absolutely smitten with her, but not like he was embarrassed to be caught in a baggy Santa suit holding onto a squirming dog with one hand.

And he was *good*-looking. Not just wholesome, but he had strong, symmetrical features and a piercing dark gaze that wouldn't be out of place on a movie screen. He was just weathered enough to fall into the category of rugged, and probably only a few years older than Linda, who didn't like to admit that she was approaching fifty. Under the red velour, his shoulders were quite broad and he had strong hands on Beast's collar.

Linda was surprised to find that she was reacting quite insistently to his presence. Now that her fright over the dog had ebbed, she was actually not much less excited, it was just for a whole new set of reasons. She wanted to slip him out of that ugly coat and see what he had underneath it, and she thought that those hands would do a fine job of—

"Why don't you come with me to dinner at Shaun's tonight," she said impulsively.

Turner blinked at her skeptically. "Would it be an imposition?" he said skeptically. "Isn't that a family thing?"

A family thing that no one had thought to invite her to, Linda realized, though she reminded herself that there was no reason for them to know that she was going to be anywhere near the area. "Shelley assured me that there would be plenty of food," she said firmly. You didn't backpedal on an invitation. "Dean *literally* told me to bring a date."

"It's a date?"

If Turner was handsome before, the smile that bloomed on his face now was downright devastating. They really did grow them well out on the farm!

Linda realized that she was smiling back, and she schooled her expression. "I would appreciate your escort," she said formally. She started to give him her hand again, but Beast thought it was for him and lunged for her. She couldn't quite keep herself from giving a little squeak, even though Turner hauled him back before the lolling tongue could get close to her.

"Behave, Beast," he growled.

To Linda's surprise, the dog did quiet, casting a cautious look sideways at Turner.

A tiny warning bell went off in Linda's head. She'd seen animals who had reactions like that...to shifters. A terrible thought occurred to her. Damien was a shifter, a fact that he hadn't bothered to disclose to her until after they were already married and Shaun had started shifting. His secret had played no small role in their subsequent divorce.

Could Turner be a shifter?

He was certainly strong, and fast, and fit.

With Beast under control, Turner extended his own hand, and they shared another breathless handshake that Linda couldn't explain. She'd shaken plenty of hands, but she'd never wanted to cling to one quite like this.

"Dinner is at six," Linda said. "Will you pick me up here?" Even if he was a shifter, that wasn't a deal breaker as far as Linda was concerned. Though how he decided to tell her would certainly make a big difference in her charity towards him.

"I'd love to," Turner said. Linda believed him, too; he really would love to, and she was surprised how delighted that made her feel.

"I'll see you then. Thank you for the rescue."

Beast tried again to lunge forward and lick her, but Turner kept him back with ease as Linda went back to her car for the luggage she'd come out for.

She couldn't help but watch him go as he coaxed the big dog up into the fire truck and took off down the street.

A few hours later, she had settled into Shelley's spare room and hung a few things in the closet when there was a great commotion out back.

A dog—sure enough!—and a small boy who must be Aaron pelted in the back door together. The boy drew up in surprise, but the dog plowed headfirst into Linda's knees, barking and jumping.

"Bingo, down!" Shelley called, following behind with her arms full of costumes. "Mom, just put your knee up, he knows better."

Linda managed to deflect the loving leaps of a mangy little mutt who seemed an order of magnitude less alarming than the giant black dog that had startled her and said to the little boy, "Hello, Aaron."

"Are you my grandmother?" he wanted to know.

Linda looked at Shelley in alarm as she wiped the dog's spit from her hand. She knew that Shelley was surprisingly serious about this guy, but she hadn't thought much about her own role as extended new family to Dean's son. "I...uh...don't know, honey." She certainly didn't want to hurt Aaron's feelings. "I could be, if you want!"

Aaron looked unimpressed by that answer. "Trevor says you give him really awesome presents," he said.

Linda had disliked Harriet quite intensely, so she'd never spent much time with Trevor while he was in his mother's custody, but she always sent expensive gifts for birthdays and Christmas. Was she suddenly on the hook for another grandson, too? She hadn't brought anything specifically for Aaron, convinced that he would be with his mom for the actual holiday, but she had plenty of treats for Trevor in the car.

"We're opening presents tonight at dinner," Aaron continued doggedly. "Because Dad and Shelley and I are all going to Madison for Christmas after the show." He eyed Linda's luggage. "I like Legos and Iron Man and Minecraft and movies and books."

"Aaron, do you remember that you were going to have your room cleaned up before dinner so that Santa would know you were good?" Shelley's voice was firm, but warm.

Aaron was still staring at Linda. "Clara's grandmother sends her money and chocolates."

"Aaron," Shelley said warningly.

"Going!" Aaron said.

He went up the stairs one slow step at a time until Shelley added, "Santa's watching!" then scampered up the rest and began doing something noisy on the floor above that didn't exactly sound like cleaning a room.

"I think I've just been shaken down by a six-year-old," Linda said wryly.

"He's eight," Shelley said mildly.

"Well, he really is irresistible. I brought Trevor enough that I can divide it up," Linda said thoughtfully. "Do you have some gift tags?"

Shelley found her a large box of wrapping paper and bows, with a mix of gift tags and clear tape and Linda retreated to her spare room to do some hasty re-labeling. It certainly wouldn't be a hardship to have a second grandson to dote on.

She found herself thinking avidly about seeing Turner again, and wishing she had a gift for him.

She didn't believe in love at first sight—that was a thing of fairy tales and poorly written movies—but she definitely believed in chemistry at first sight and she could tell that she and Turner had that in spades. There was no reason she couldn't stay a night or two, spend time with her grandson—grandsons, apparently!—and indulge in some harmless flirtation with a hot fire firefighter who may or may not be a shifter.

5

Jamie was sitting with her fire boots up on the break table reading something on her phone when Turner arrived at the fire station. Jamie had left the tiny apartment upstairs in order to move in with her boyfriend Devon, but she still hung around in the break room from time to time for the free snacks and coffee.

"Does this look like a barn?" Turner asked her, kicking the snow off his boots as he came in past the battered firetruck. "Do you like to eat what you step in? Get yer feet off the table and at least pretend that someone taught you manners."

"Yes sir, Vice Principal Turner, sir!" Jamie said smartly, stomping her boots down onto the floor and saluting him. She had been one of his best and most frustrating students, and she had returned from fighting wildfire in Alaska to take Dean's place on the squad as he planned his escape to Madison to study engineering. At least for the winters.

"That's the kind of attitude that will get you far," Turner said.

Jamie stared at him. "That was not the suit I was expecting you to be wearing."

"You'll get to see Santa tomorrow like everyone else," Turner said off-handedly.

"Seriously, Turner, what's with the penguin suit? I thought you only wore that for graduations and proms."

"I have a date," Turner said, as serenely as he could manage.

He didn't want to admit that he was a little worried that he wasn't going to be up to snuff at the Powells' dinner table. They were all big city millionaires, and although they'd done a great job of trying to fit in with the humble, earthy Green Valley citizens, they couldn't hide all their polish with a plaid flannel shirt and a tractor magazine subscription.

Jamie stared at him even harder. "A date for...a funeral?"

"For dinner," Turner said frankly. "At Shaun's."

"With a *date?*"

Every time she said date, Turner's moose echoed, *Mate!* which made it rather challenging to think.

He grunted and went to rummage in the coffee bin for something that wasn't mocha or peppermint or hazelnut. The coffee selection had gone *girly* since Jamie had taken over Dean's role in the tiny fire department. At her insistence, they'd gotten one of those pod brewers that was horribly wasteful but made remarkably good coffee, even if they were sometimes scented like candy or perfume.

"So, who's your date?" Jamie demanded. "I honestly cannot imagine you stepping out with any of the Green Valley biddies."

"They don't call it stepping out anymore," Turner said as he found a plain coffee pod. "And you could be more respectful of your elders."

Jamie made a rude noise. "Yes sir, Vice Principal Turner, sir," she said mockingly. "You didn't answer the question."

"Linda," Turner said. The taste of the name in his mouth was like cream.

"Who's Linda?" Jamie prodded mercilessly. "Linda *who?*"

"Linda Powell," Turner confessed. "Shelley's mother."

"Oh. My. Lord," Jamie said. "You're dating a Powell? What on earth would possess you to do that?"

"She's my mate," Turner said warningly. "Careful!"

"Oh. My. *Lord!*" Jamie repeated, her eyes wider than ever.

Was it a terrible mistake? Turner's moose was absolutely convinced that she was the one, the only, and he couldn't deny Linda's sheer appeal. But there was a whole wide world of difference between him—high school vice principal and fire chief in a provincial little town—and Linda Powell, socialite, from big money and the big city. Where was their common ground? How could he ever make someone like that *happy?*

His fleeting doubts must have shown on his face, because Jamie said swiftly, "Don't worry, Turner, we will My Fair Lady you straight up into those circles, if that's what it takes."

"Didn't you sabotage the My Fair Lady performance your senior year?"

"Sabotage is a strong word," Jamie said defensively. "Anyway, I'm reformed. Have you practiced your compliments?"

"Done what, now?"

"Compliments," Jamie drawled slowly. "They are nice things you say to your lady friend in order to woo her. Is she pretty?"

Was she pretty? Turner had never seen anyone so pretty as Linda Powell in her snowy white coat and fur-trimmed boots. But pretty didn't even start to cover it. She was elegant and sophisticated. She was like a symphony.

And he was more like a banjo.

"Okay," Jamie guessed from either his silence or his undoubtedly sappy smile. "She's pretty. Is there something specific you can flatter? Her hair or her clothes?"

Turner frowned. "I prefer not to mention physical attributes," he said sensibly. As a high school principal, he had quickly learned to navigate girls with raging hormones and self-esteem issues by choosing praise with extreme care.

"Okay, that's probably smart. Let's talk talents. Remember to laugh at her jokes."

Laugh. Turner remembered her almost-laugh with longing. He didn't consider himself a comic, but he had never wanted to do anything as much as he wanted to make her laugh. Really laugh, not that company all-for-show chuckle. A belly laugh worthy of Santa Claus.

"Hmm," Jamie said, typing onto her phone. "I'll ask Abby for some tips. She babysits for both Trevor and Aaron, so she might have some good dirt on Shaun and Shelley's mom."

"I cannot believe that I am taking advice from you," Turner said with a chuckle. "Anyway, we have another problem that your investigative skills should be applied to."

"It cannot possibly be more exciting than this," Jamie protested, laughing.

"Officer Stakes is missing," Turner said firmly. "I swung by his house and found that it was empty. He hasn't picked up any calls today. There's no sign of him and his car isn't there."

"He always heads down to Nebraska to see his folks, doesn't he?"

"Yeah, but he didn't check in with Carter before he left and he told Andrea he'd stick around for the show to be Santa Claus."

Jamie sobered. "Well, that's not like him. Did you check with dispatch?"

"They're the ones who let me know," Turner said. "He isn't answering his phone."

"We have a mystery to solve!" Jamie said avidly. "A proper Christmas disappearance! What can I do?"

"I called the state troopers and they said they didn't think it was enough for a missing persons case yet, but I thought I'd go snoop around the office tonight after dinner if Stakes still wasn't back. Maybe you could ask around, see if anyone has seen him."

"Are you going to break into the police station?" Jamie said with relish. "I haven't committed a misdemeanor in *years* now."

"I thought you were reformed," Turner said quellingly.

"You take the fun out of everything," Jamie complained.

6

"When Dean said to bring a date, I didn't think you'd actually find one," Shelley said in astonishment from the bathroom door.

Linda finished applying her lipstick and did a test kiss towards the mirror. "Because I'm old and washed up?" she teased.

"Because this is Green Valley," Shelley said flatly. There was the humorless child she'd always been. "Who is it?"

"John Turner," Linda said warmly, remembering how his hand had felt in hers. "You didn't tell me that the men here were all so gorgeous! What else have you been hiding?" A nurturing personality, apparently. Linda was still amazed at how well Shelley handled Aaron and how patient and warm she was with everyone in this house. Even Bingo was treated with fondness and tolerance.

"John...? Wait, Turner? The vice principal of Green Valley High?"

"Is he? He drove up in a fire truck when he rescued me!"

"He rescued you?"

"It was just a loose dog, I guess, but Turner was very heroic."

Shelley sighed. "Did you call 9-1-1 for a stray dog?"

"Who else was I going to call?" Linda asked. "Triple A? It would have taken them hours to get there and extract that thing from my car."

"You can't abuse the emergency system!" Shelley said in outrage.

"I certainly didn't!" Linda protested. "I had an absolutely lovely chat with the dispatcher. She said she'd been bored to tears until I called, and of course I would have gotten right off if there *had* been an actual emergency. You really don't have a lot going on out here. I can't understand how you can possibly be thinking about moving back here after Dean has finished school in Madison."

"I like it here, Mom," Shelley said quietly. "I like the small town and I think it's a nice place to raise a kid."

Linda looked at her and shook her head. "You hate children," she said skeptically.

"I *don't* hate kids," Shelley said, looking behind her in alarm to where Aaron was playing something noisy that involved banging things together. Her voice softened. "Mom, don't even say that. Aaron is my favorite person in the world next to Dean."

"I see where I rank," Linda said. When Shelley frowned at her, she sighed. "Oh, don't be such a sourpuss, I'm only teasing. I think these two have been really good for you and I'm glad to see you so happy. Aaron is a joy, it's just a surprise that you get along so well. If you don't think I should bring Turner to dinner, I'll call and break his heart by canceling. What time is it? He might even be on the way over to pick me up now."

Why did even the *idea* of calling it off fill her with regret? She really wanted to see him again, and Linda was surprised to find that it wasn't that she needed to have someone on her arm to face her ex-husband at dinner. Turner was handsome and funny and she found herself smiling to remember how he'd looked at her. Like she'd swept him off his feet.

"No," Shelley said reluctantly. "Don't call him off. I think it will be okay. But…"

"Spit it out, Shelley. Hesitation doesn't flatter anyone."

"Turner's a nice guy, Mom, and this is a small town. If you do break his heart, everyone will know."

"You make me sound like a monster," Linda chided her.

"You're not a monster, Mom. But you can be a little cold, I should know."

Linda stared at her in astonishment. Shelley thought *she* was cold? Ice-queen Shelley, Shelley the Shark? Even as she started to protest, she paused and wondered if there was truth in the observation. She was always forward and warm on the surface, but she held her heart in careful reserve. Even, she realized as she looked at Shelley with regret, with her children. She had tried to encourage Shelley to protect herself from being hurt. Had it been obvious to a sensitive little girl that her mother was afraid of affection that ran too deep?

She loved her family, but what kind of heart did she have to offer to anyone? For a moment, she considered canceling with Turner in earnest, because she knew that Shelley's warning was true. Turner deserved someone who was exactly what she seemed, all the way down to her soul. But Linda was living a lie of confidence that no one else knew and she was deeply afraid that she was incapable of true love.

What kind of man was Turner that she was suddenly thinking about *true love?*

Shelley was still looking fixedly at her, her silvery eyes drilling into Linda.

Linda did as she always did, and gave a sparkling light company laugh. "Darling, you worry too much. I am sure that Turner and I will have a fine time at dinner, and that's all there is to it. We're both too old for broken hearts or silly crushes; it's nothing more than a holiday dinner with a cute new friend before I head south to Cancun." She could almost convince herself of it.

Shelley looked skeptical, but there was a sudden crash from the living room and Aaron hollered, "Nothing broke!!" so desperately that everyone in earshot knew that something probably had.

At that moment, the doorbell rang.

"I'll get it!" Aaron yelled, and Bingo went into a frenzy of barking.

Linda checked her reflection in the mirror one last time.

"It's Vice Principal Turner!" Aaron called from the front door a moment later.

Linda felt her heart squeeze as giddy excitement rose up from her stomach, and she wondered at her ridiculous reaction. This wasn't like her at *all*. She was never the nervous one.

Then she came more sedately to the door and saw Turner standing in the doorway. All of her unexpected nervousness turned to even more unexpected desire.

He had *shaved*. Linda wasn't sure if he looked better without the rough stubble he'd had, but she knew for sure that she wanted to put her hands on his jaws and feel his smooth skin under her fingers. She could smell just a hint of intoxicating aftershave from across the room.

"Mom?"

Shelley was eyeing her suspiciously and Linda realized that she had no idea how long she and Turner had been gazing at each other. She touched her hair self-consciously. "Mr. Claus," she greeted him. "This suit is an improvement."

"I got a call about a vicious dog," he teased, ruffling Bingo's ears.

"I am never going to live that down, am I?" she said merrily back.

"I assure you, it happens all the time," he said gallantly. "Roving packs of hellhounds, constantly harassing ordinary citizens in our sleepy little town."

"Let me get my coat before I die of mortification," Linda said with a chuckle. "We'll see you right over at Shaun's, darling?"

"Sure, Mom," Shelley said faintly.

Linda got her coat from the closet and pulled it on, then gathered her gifts. Turner held the door for her—first to the house and then to his fire truck, taking the presents as she climbed up into the cab and then handing them up to her.

"I'm afraid I didn't get you anything," she said, smiling down at him.

"We just met," he said with a grin and a shrug. "I don't have a gift for you, either."

But it didn't seem as though they'd just met, Linda thought, as they drove just a few blocks to park in front of a house with the same farmhouse aesthetic as Dean's. She felt easy with him, like he was an old friend she was just catching up with again, even though she knew next to nothing about him. A really gorgeous old friend that she was thinking about in exciting new ways, maybe, because her libido was apparently on overdrive. She felt like she was on a real date, wondering how it was going to end.

They chatted casually about Christmas traditions and snow, making observations about the house decorations that they passed.

There was already another vehicle in front of Shaun's house, and they could smell the food long before the door was opened for them.

"Mom!" Shaun greeted them. "Turner?"

"He's my plus one," Linda said quickly, handing Shaun her armful of gifts as she pressed inside and shook the snow off her boots. They weren't very practical boots, but they were cute. "Dean said you wouldn't mind."

"Of...course not," Shaun said, sounding strangled. "There's plenty of food. Tawny was really excited about cooking for everyone. We've got a folding table we can set up for the boys. They'll love having their own space to fence with the bread sticks."

"Hi Linda!" Shaun's wife Andrea was very short and full of energy as she greeted them from the kitchen door with a dishtowel over one arm like a waiter. Linda liked the young woman a great deal and had enjoyed their vacations together. "Um, hi, Turner?"

"Good to see you, Andrea," Turner said, sounding completely unruffled. "Thank you for having us."

"Plus one," Shaun said as he put the presents under a Christmas tree that was so thick with ornaments it rattled when he bumped it. "He's Linda's plus one."

Andrea took Turner's presence in stride. "Tawny and Shaun have been cooking up a storm, I'm glad to have some extra mouths! I don't think the leftovers will fit in the fridge as it is."

Who was *Tawny?*

Then the moment that Linda had been half-dreading came, as a large, familiar form came from the back hall.

Damien. He hadn't changed much in the years they'd been divorced, except that his beard was much, much shorter and perhaps more silver. Had he *shaved* it? To Linda's relief, she didn't have any lingering hints of resentment or attraction to him lurking below her calm facade. All of her feelings for him were safely in the past where they belonged.

He was also wearing the ugliest homemade sweater she'd ever seen, which was very unlike him indeed.

"Linda," he said courteously. "Turner?" They all shook hands very carefully indeed.

"I'm going to have to get used to the question mark after my name," Turner said wryly. "Merry Christmas, Damien."

If he felt awkward being at Linda's side during their careful reunion, Turner didn't give so much of a hint of it. "Have you folks been out to Mueller's pond yet this winter? It's frozen up early this year, and Lee's done a great job with the warm-up shed."

This led to a merry conversation about local customs, which appeared to include ice skating and hot chocolate and decorating a tree in a park downtown. Damien and Turner talked about ice fishing and local politics. Shelley, Dean, and Aaron arrived halfway through, and unloaded more wrapped presents under the tree. The boys ran off to the kitchen to get in the way and Andrea went with them, rolling her eyes as she explained again that dinner would be very, very soon and to *stop snacking*.

"You'll have to come to the Festival tomorrow, Mom," Shaun said. "Trevor is the narrator for the Christmas pageant."

"Aaron is Joseph," Shelley added. "But it won't be the caliber of show you're used to," she warned, as if Linda would be incapable of enjoying it.

"A pageant sounds like fun," Linda said warmly. "Is it Catholic?"

"Multi-denominational," Turner volunteered. "The churches each used to have their own pageants, but it was sort of a church versus church thing, all of them competing, until we started hosting one big one at the high school. Over the past few years we've made it a general winter festival and even added some Hanukkah and Diwali celebrations. There are some speeches about community and generosity and of course the kids are all there for Santa Claus at the end."

"Andrea says that you've taken on the role, since she can't get Officer Stakes to return her calls," Shaun said to Turner with a frown.

"It's a big suit to fill," Turner said.

"You do a fine job of it," Linda assured him, and they exchanged ridiculous grins as Linda remembered him looking up at her from the snow after he'd fallen, the hat askew over his face. She looked up to find Damien watching her curiously.

Did *he* have lingering feelings? Linda wondered if she'd made a mistake bringing Turner—or for coming at all. She certainly hadn't meant to stir up weird history.

"Dinner is being served!" Andrea called from the back.

Linda went with Turner back to a dining room, crowded with mis-matched chairs. The boys, as expected, were delighted to have their own table, and were already fencing with the breadsticks.

Tawny turned out to be a white-haired, no-nonsense woman with a sunny smile, probably a decade Linda's senior. "You must be Linda!" she said cheerfully, and Linda was aware that everyone was watching the two of them very carefully. "Turner?"

"Linda's plus one," Andrea and Shaun said in a chorus.

"It's lovely to meet you!" Linda said honestly, still not sure who this woman was. Andrea's mother, perhaps? "This all looks absolutely amazing."

"It looks great, Tawny," Turner said, pulling a chair out for Linda.

"I haven't made this much food in a long time," Tawny said cheerfully. "I forgot how much fun it is. Shaun, your kitchen is a dream!"

Shaun glanced at Linda like he felt guilty about it. "I had it remodeled this summer," he said.

Linda couldn't figure out why he seemed so twitchy about it. "It warms a mother's heart seeing her kids follow in her footsteps," Linda said. "I know Shelley had no interest in cooking, but I'm glad that you did."

"Let's eat!" Shelley suggested firmly.

Tawny was seated across from them next to Damien. Andrea took the crowded seat at the head of the table "Because I'm the shortest!" and Shaun sat next to her. Dean took the far end of the table, Shelley next to him looking cool and unruffled.

"You'll have to catch me up on everything," Linda said brightly as the conversation about food and seating gradually lulled and they heaped their plates. "Look at you two, all grown up and settling down. Small town life seems to suit you both."

"We're planning to move back after Dean finishes school in Madison," Shelley said.

"I don't know which of you surprises me the most," Linda laughed. "Shaun I could halfway see liking it here, but you? And your father? That was quite a shock. I nearly fell out of my chair when I got your text that he'd moved here. I can't imagine what would have coaxed him away from the city."

There was an unexpectedly uncomfortable silence that baffled Linda until she finally put all the little pieces together: how close Tawny was sitting to Damien, how Shelley and Shaun kept making little subtle secretive questions to each other with their eyebrows, how Damien was looking at Tawny.

The rings on both of their fingers.

7

Turner felt it the moment that Linda realized that Tawny was Damien's wife...and everyone else at the table recognized in dismay that she didn't already know that.

He wasn't sure if it was some supernatural sensitivity from his moose because she was his mate, or if he was just watching closely enough to see that clench of her jaw and the surprise in her eyes.

Was she hurt? Shocked? Offended that Damien had moved on? Did she have lingering feelings for him? Was she insulted that no one had bothered to warn her that Damien was bringing a wife?

For a brief moment, he wanted to stand up and bodily protect Linda from anything that resembled pain. But he couldn't exactly offer to box his hosts and everyone at the table looked painfully uncertain. Shaun and Shelley were shooting *I thought **you** told her* looks back and forth, with tiny shrugs and mortified expressions. Tawny looked like she wasn't sure what to do with her hands.

He cleared his throat. "I'd like to propose a toast."

Every single look that he got was grateful. "Yes, please!" Andrea said desperately.

Turner had a half-dozen speeches memorized for graduation and assemblies, and was good at variations on the fly. The topics covered responsibility, academic excellence, optimism, bright futures...not exactly subjects for a Christmas holiday toast.

But he could improvise.

"I'd like to thank you for inviting me to your table," he said solemnly. "Some of you I've known since you were kids at my school and some of you"—he glanced at Linda, who was looking back at him with warm blue eyes, her mouth crooking into a slight smile—"I met just this morning when I fell on my Santa ass in snow." That neatly deflected any embarrassment from Linda to his own comic clumsiness and there were a few chuckles.

At the kids' table, Aaron loudly whispered, "He said ass!" and the boys giggled, repeating the word until Andrea gave them a quelling look.

Turner swept his gaze back across the table. "I appreciate your generosity and your friendship. To families that aren't always blood."

Everyone toasted and the conversation slipped easily into food and how, exactly, Linda and Turner had met. The good food and sparkling wine were equal social lubricants and Turner ate until he wondered if he'd still fit in the Santa suit. Shelley surely wouldn't need to take it in, now.

The mood of the feast was light-hearted; everyone there was invested in a pleasant meal and a friendly atmosphere. They seemed, to a person, to want to make up for catching Linda off-guard. Linda even got to the point of asking Tawny how she'd met Damien and by the end of the meal, they were laughing over his impulsive purchase of a car for her.

"A car, can you imagine?" Tawny teased Damien easily, and he laughed and took it entirely in stride.

Shelley was excited to share information about the new business she was starting, a fashion line of kids costumes. "We should have the licensing straightened out by Easter," she said, smiling at Dean.

Dean was excited for his engineering classes and didn't have any regrets about selling his hardware store to Jamie and Devon, or closing his auto repair shop.

Shaun's bakery was doing very well. "We've actually got restaurants for a few counties in either direction with standing orders for some of our staples," he said proudly. "And Gran's Grits, of course. We're thinking about remodeling for a larger kitchen to serve even further out."

"I've got Patricia back from maternity leave at the preschool so I'm not going quite so crazy," Andrea reported. "Tawny, I may have to try taking piano lessons again, because it's like magic when she sits down and plays them back to calm."

They politely asked about Turner's plans for the new year. "Carter's wife wants him to retire," he said. "Going to have to find new blood for the fire crew."

The others proposed a few locals, but no one that Turner hadn't already considered; most of the young folks who would be interested had plans to leave soon for college and opportunities that Green Valley didn't offer.

"What about you, Mom?" Shaun asked.

Everyone's plates were empty by now and they had devoured dessert. The boys had been released from their table and were making noisy wound-up laps of the house in anticipation of presents.

Linda gave what Turner was recognizing as her company laugh —a gorgeous rich sound that was amused but completely under control. He still itched to make her burst out in a real laugh, but this sound was a close second.

"I'm not here long. I'd planned to leave for Cancun on Monday," she said lightly, not answering any long-term questions. "I had thought that Shelley and Dean might come with me, but apparently they have better plans for the holiday than cabana boys and cold drinks."

Turner felt like the rug had been swept under him, and half-expected to find himself on his ass in the snow like he'd just met Linda. Her blue eyes were on his and Turner suspected that he looked as pole-axed as he felt.

She was *leaving* in a few days.

As quickly as she'd waltzed into his life, she was going to waltz out. And what was he supposed to do? Beg her to stay? Ask her to *marry* him? He thought that maybe she liked him, but that was a far cry from 'stay here and marry me after I've saved you from a maybe-hellhound and you've survived a weird Christmas dinner with your ex.'

Shelley was reached over to pick up his plate and Turner remembered his manners. "Can I help clear up?" he asked her automatically, starting to stand.

"No, no," Shelley insisted, all but pushing him back down into his chair. "You're our guest. *Mom* and I will clear up and start the dishwasher." Linda made a little noise like she might protest, but Shelley handed her a stack of dishes and herded her directly out of the dining room.

"Tawny, let's take the kids out and get their presents ready," Andrea suggested.

Shaun made a joke about women's work and was rapped smartly on the shoulder by his laughing wife before she left him with a kiss that inspired the boys to make gagging noises all the way out.

Turner was still watching Linda go. She was his *mate*. And she was going to leave Green Valley.

His resolve hardened. If she was leaving in a few days, then he only had a few days to clinch his suit.

Turner realized that he was the object of all the attention in the room. Shaun, Dean, and Damien were all eyeing him thoughtfully.

"I'm grateful for dinner," he said mildly. "Beats the frozen dinner I'd been planning."

"You certainly got chummy with Linda quickly," Dean observed cautiously.

"Very friendly," Shaun agreed.

Damien didn't say anything, but he and Turner eyed each other in turn.

"Kind of like you were...mates, eh?" Dean's fake Australian accent didn't fool anyone at the table.

"Like there was some kind of animal attraction," Shaun suggested innocently.

Turner downed the rest of his sparkling wine. "You lot are about as subtle as students trying to pretend they don't know what alcohol is. 'Gosh, Mister Turner, is that a beer? I didn't know that!' Are you all shifters?"

The tension at the table eased.

"Lion," Damien offered with a growl.

"Tiger," Shaun said, and his sideways glance at Damien had a layer of complexity that Turner couldn't name.

"Bear," Dean said with a nod.

"Oh, my," Turner said, in his best Dorothy falsetto. "Are we off to see the Wizard?"

They all looked at him expectantly. "Moose," he finally told them, and he dared them to judge him for it. He might be in the deer family, but he was a *moose,* and even a big predator would think twice about tangling with a bull. "And Linda is my mate."

There was an unmistakable note of challenge in his voice, and Turner was keenly aware that he was talking about their ex-wife, step-mother, and mother-in-law, respectively. He was also aware of the fact that saying *mate* out loud again made it feel incredibly real. Linda was his mate and it didn't matter how she fit into anyone else's past as long as she was a part of his future.

"Congratulations," Dean said firmly.

Shaun echoed him, and Damien, after a thoughtful moment, added, "She deserves happiness."

Could Turner provide that happiness? Was there a note of skepticism in Damien's voice? He decided there was not, that the lion shifter's words were meant as a benediction.

Not that he was waiting around for anyone's approval. He and his moose were in perfect alignment. Linda was his, and he had just a day or two to convince her of that absolute truth.

8

"You really seem to like Turner," Shelley observed, in her best I-am-a-completely-impartial-lawyer voice. She opened the dishwasher and started loading it efficiently.

"He's lovely," Linda said warmly, handing her the dishes. And he was. The entire evening, Turner had been an absolute gentleman, attentive and funny, without once seeming sycophantic. Linda would have liked him even if he hadn't been so handsome and irresistibly sexy. The combination was absolutely devastating.

"I mean, you really hit it off right at once, didn't you?" Shelley prodded. "Was it kind of a lightning moment when you met? An...instant attraction?"

Linda sighed. "Honey, why are you being so weird? Would you get to the point? Is Turner a shifter?"

Shelley only hesitated a moment longer, then said frankly, "I'm going to guess so, because I bet that you're his mate."

Linda blinked at her. "His what?"

"His mate. A shifter has a soulmate, a perfect partner, that one person who completes them." Shelley's voice softened in that un-Shelley way that it did when she spoke about Dean or Aaron.

"When I met Dean, I knew without a single doubt that this was the man I was going to be with forever, no matter what."

"Not a single doubt?" Linda said skeptically. "Just from meeting him?" It sounded ridiculous.

Ridiculous and beautiful.

"Okay, I had doubts," Shelley said honestly. "But they were doubts about how I was going to suddenly be a mom and what I could possibly do in Green Valley, not doubts about Dean. He's the one, and my lion knew it. Everything else was just details to sort out."

"Is he a shifter, too?" Linda wanted to know.

"Yes. A bear."

Her daughter was living with a bear. Well, that seemed fitting, somehow.

Linda found herself feeling a little envious of Shelley. How amazing to know at once, with no reservations. She'd wondered what it would be like to be able to change into an animal since she learned it was possible, but she hadn't particularly *wanted* to.

But this was something else entirely, something...magical and just out of reach. To meet someone and know at once? Not to have to stumble along wondering what was attraction and loneliness? Not to have to settle for someone good enough, maybe right, maybe not...? Not to always wonder if there was a dealbreaker lurking in their future...

"Tawny is Damien's mate," she realized.

Shelley seemed to recognize that they were on dangerous ground. "Yes," she said quietly. "That doesn't mean that..."

"It's perfect," Linda said honestly. "I don't know why, but it's terribly comforting to know that there was a reason Damien and I couldn't make it work. Tawny is good for him and I'm glad that he's found her. I even understand why he never told me about mates, if I wasn't his."

"He didn't believe in mates," Shelley said frankly. "He used to say it was a ridiculous, romantic fairy tale meant for weak-willed people who needed fantasies to get them through life. I certainly thought it was fiction until it started happening to people I actually knew. But what about *Turner?*" Shelley could be relentless.

Was she his *mate?* Linda was surprised by the complexity of the desire that she felt. It wasn't just that she wanted to peel him out of that suit and satisfy urges that she'd spent entirely too long denying, and it wasn't just that he was funny and flattering.

She wanted to take off his vice principal and fire chief front and see who he was inside. She wanted to know his heart. She...wanted to give him *her* heart.

Would he want it?

She gave a sparkling, practiced laugh. "It would be much easier with an animal in my head saying yes or no. I honestly don't know, darling." There was no way she would ever know, because she hadn't been born a shifter.

"Can we do presents yet?" Aaron was standing in the doorway and from behind him, Andrea called, "I told you not to bug them yet!"

"I certainly think we should do presents," Linda agreed. "I know it's hard to be patient when you're little."

Aaron gave a whoop of joy and fell over backwards. There was an answering shriek of delight from Trevor somewhere back in the house.

Shelley gave Linda a hard look, but Linda shrugged carelessly at her and went back out to the living room, where her heart sank to find Turner putting on his coat. "You're leaving so soon?"

"Presents aren't really my part of this," he said sensibly. "I've got a six-pack of homebrew for Dean at the station, but his real gift was when I canned him from the force. I want to swing by the police station before it gets too late and see if Officer Stakes has turned up yet. The troopers said they'd be by tomorrow if he hadn't checked in."

Dean was being mobbed by the boys as he was cutting open a large shipping box from some distant relatives and he paused to laugh and say, "And I only got you socks!"

"IS IT OPEN YET CAN WE OPEN PRESENTS WHAT

DID THEY SEND US?" It was hard to tell what was Aaron and what was Trevor as they spoke over each other.

"Anyone need another drink to get through this?" Shaun offered. "Thanks for coming, Turner!"

"I appreciate the food!" he replied. Then he looked at Linda and added quietly, "And the company."

Dean had opened the box at this point and the boys' squeals as the presents and freezer bags of cookies began to emerge nearly drowned out Turner's words.

Linda didn't notice their din. She felt a little like the rest of the room went away as she stepped closer to Turner. "Thank you so much for coming," she said automatically. "I had a lovely time."

That was what you said to company, right? But Turner wasn't just company, and Linda suddenly knew that she couldn't let him walk out that door alone.

9

"I'll walk you out," Linda said, pausing at the closet for her coat and, to Turner's surprise, her boots. Over her shoulder, she called, "The boys can open gifts without me!"

The boys cheered, drowning out Shelley's half-hearted protest, and Linda closed the door behind her.

It was quiet outside on the covered porch, though they could still hear the Christmas cheer from inside. It was starting to snow, with big fat white flakes covering all the dirty old snow and bare branches. Everything looked very blue in the evening gloom, and holiday lights up and down the block sparkled against the fresh white.

"This was really unconventional," Linda said apologetically. "I dropped an impromptu Christmas dinner on you and my ex showed up with a wife I didn't know about and are you a shifter and am I your mate?"

Turner had to stare at her for a moment, because he had been expecting at least a little polite conversation to wade through and he'd been trying to decide if he should volunteer the information about being a shifter now or try to get a goodbye kiss before he dropped that bombshell on her.

He slowly smiled. He should have known that the perfect woman for him would be honest and forward and ask the questions on her mind. He loved that about her already.

There were moments in life worth taking risks, and this was one of them. Turner closed what little space was left between them and took her face into his hands to kiss her deeply.

Once he'd started, there was no stopping...mostly because she slipped her arms up around his neck and pulled him closer, kissing passionately back.

She tasted like pie spices and a little bite of rum from fruitcake, and Turner could not hold her close enough or kiss her hard enough and it was hard to believe that this beautiful, sophisticated woman might be his, but he knew in his soul that she was.

Was this what a Christmas miracle felt like? It was as if all the pieces of his life were falling together perfectly, despite all of the questions he had left.

"Wow," she said, when he finally released her. "Wow." She sounded shaky and uncertain, which was strange after all of her confidence. "I guess that's a yes?"

"Yes," Turner said, smiling foolishly at her. "You're my mate."

Saying it out loud with her family had been one thing. Saying it to Linda was like unlocking a box full of sunshine. She was his *mate.*

"Well," she said sensibly, straightening the hat on her head. "Then I guess we have a few things to talk about. Would you like to show me around town? You said you needed to go to the police station, we can start there."

"Right now?" Turner glanced at the house behind her. There were still muffled sounds of merriment from inside.

"I don't need to sit through the opening of presents," Linda said dismissively. "They weren't expecting me and it would only make them feel guilty that I have nothing to open. You and I, on the other hand, have a great deal of ground to cover and I would like to get started. Is it far? Can we walk?"

She tucked her arm into his elbow commandingly and steered him off down the snowy sidewalk.

"You'll have to tell what kind of animal you are," she ordered him. "I've known Shelley was a lion for almost as long as she has, and Damien is also, of course, because I'm certainly not. Dean is apparently a bear and——" she cut herself off. "How secret is all of this here? In the city it was completely unspoken. Do all the shifters in Green Valley know each other? Do you have a secret handshake?"

"There are a lot of shifters in this town," Turner explained patiently, leading her towards town. "It's a quiet place where development and technology aren't really encouraged, with plenty of forest and local wildlife. Most of us don't know each other for sure, just have a lot of suspicions. As the vice principal at the local high school, I run into more of them than usual."

"I imagine that new shifters are not great at keeping their heads down."

"There are a few normal reasons I might find a naked kid behind the gym," Turner explained. "Hazing. *Sex.* But here in Green Valley, it's usually that someone found out they weren't just from Kansas. It involves a lot of uncomfortable conversations and I've gotten good at figuring out who is who before it turns into a problem. Also, I make sure I have a good range of spare clothing in my office."

"You haven't said what you are," Linda pointed out.

"Moose," Turner said shortly, and he glanced sideways at Linda to see what her reaction would be. A moose wasn't a glamorous apex predator.

"Oh," she said with interest. "I understand those are quite...large."

Her coy look in return suggested that she was not disappointed.

"No one has ever *complained* about my size," Turner said just as slyly.

There was a promise of a laugh dancing at the corner of her scarlet lips. "I'll have to judge that for myself," she said, tossing her head. "Now, what else do I need to know about you? Do you have family that you will be dragging me to dinner with in return for tonight?"

"Only you," Turner said before he could stop himself.

Linda came to a stop and Turner halted with her. They were standing at an empty intersection, a single street light illuminating her like she was an angel.

"Where do you see us going?" she asked softly. "Do I live...here? Do you come to the city with me? You have a career, I have a social circle. Where do they overlap?"

"These are smart questions," Turner conceded. "And I don't have easy answers for them. I only know that when I look at you, I know that the place they collide is where I'll be, and I will never be happy without you."

"You aren't just a vice principal, you're a poet," Linda breathed.

Saying something that romantic clearly called for another long, breathless kiss, standing on that corner in a pool of magical holiday light.

They walked hand in hand after that, close together as they shyly spoke over a range of topics—she'd gone to private school, Turner grew up in Green Valley and attended the same school he now ruled over. They talked about favorite foods and hobbies—she liked to cook and he brewed beer.

"I am now picturing a mad scientist's basement with tubes and bubbling vessels," Linda said.

Turner laughed. "More like a few glass carboys in the corner of the pantry. It's not fancy," he said, feeling a little shy. Linda probably drank cask-aged bourbons and sparkling wines. "But it won't make you go blind like some moonshine."

"Is it legal?"

They were standing, appropriately, in front of the police station.

"I promise that it is entirely legal," Turner said. The front door of the police station was locked. "Let's go around by the alley. One of the windows in the back doesn't latch."

"You make legal homebrew, but know how to break into the police station," Linda said with her warm chuckle. "You are indeed a complicated man."

Fortunately, the back door was unlocked altogether, so Turner didn't have to climb into a window, which he suspected would be rather undignified.

"Hello?" he called. "Stakes?"

The police station was barely big enough for the name. There was an office, a holding cell, a break room even smaller than the one at the fire station, and a bathroom. The evidence locker was a literal locker. The building was empty, and there was no sign of a struggle or anything out of order. Stakes kept a tidy place.

"Can you hack a computer?" Linda asked, looking at the desktop.

"Probably not," Turner admitted. "But Officer Stakes doesn't really use it. He's an old-fashioned guy who uses old-fashioned methods. Ah-hah!"

There was a note by the phone:

Dec 22, 9 AM

Stanley -

ice shack @ Mueller's Pond

Animal spirits

Alien artifact??

"Who is Stanley?" Linda wanted to know, looking over his shoulder.

"Stanley is one of our more colorful Green Valley characters. Kind of a lonely guy, and he tends to ramble. He's constantly on about conspiracies and the latest government plots and will talk your ear off about discrepancies in history proving alien visitors and how smart phones are the new red scare wire tap something something. He makes a lot of unnecessary calls for emergency services. We've pulled his truck out of more mud holes than we've put out fires in the last year. Technically, he calls himself a farmer, but he mostly rents his fields and complains about taxes. He sometimes chases fads —at one point he tried raising emus, and he had alpacas for a while. It's even money on whether he'll fall for a scam and we've bailed him out more than once."

"A shifter?"

"I'd guess not," Turner said. "But there's no way to know. This note would have been just before Stakes disappeared, I wonder if Stanley knows something about where Stakes went." He checked his phone. "It's too late tonight, I'll swing by tomorrow before the festival and see if he's got any clues." He poked around at the other notes on the desk, but nothing else looked more recent.

"Detective Turner, on top of fire chief and vice principal," Linda teased. She sobered. "You're worried about him."

"It's not like Stakes to up and disappear like this," Turner said honestly. "He's a stand-up guy and this is really out of character."

"Where's his deputy?" Linda wanted to know. "Small towns have police chiefs and deputies, right?"

"Green Valley isn't big enough for more than Stakes. He doesn't even let us call him chief, says it seems too proud."

"Aren't there things you are supposed to have two cops for?"

"Stakes has a list of reserve officers. If he needs back-up, he calls or drives around until he finds one that can join him. I'm one of them."

"This...*is* a very small town," Linda observed. "And you wear a lot of hats."

Turner glanced at her. She was frowning seriously at the corkboard hanging by Stake's desk. There was a map hanging there, with some lost dog reports, along with a few complaints of nuisance.

"How many people are in your fire department?" Linda asked.

"Me, Carter, Jamie. I canned Dean, but I could count on him in a pinch if we needed help. Carter's wife is making noises about retiring him, and Jamie wants to do summers in Alaska, so it might be just me in the spring, depending."

"Can you recruit someone new?"

"Not a lot of draw in a small town like Green Valley. It's a volunteer position, and there's not a lot of work here."

Linda looked at him thoughtfully, probably thinking that there wasn't a lot of anything here.

"Our tour isn't over yet," he said lightly. "Wait until you see the picturesque downtown Green Valley. All two blocks of it!"

10

When Linda had said they had ground to cover, she hadn't really intended it literally, but she and Turner walked several miles through Christmas card neighborhoods and a charming little downtown with closed shops and a cafe named Gran's Grits. He showed her the high school, which was much larger than she expected (it apparently served many outlying farms and communities), and the fire station, which was much smaller. There were four quaint churches, a library, five bars, a playground, and two grocery stores (both closed).

"This time of night, you might have to drive out to the gas station on Wickersham if you need something. They have an all-hours convenience and liquor store by the highway." Turner pointed out a big brick building with a bank sign. "Marta lives there. She converted it into a house. Her closet is in the old vault."

"Where is the bank, then?" Linda wanted to know.

"There's a credit union on Jefferson," Turner said. "But mostly people can bank online now."

"I feel like I've stepped back in time," Linda said with a sigh. "I can see the appeal of this place."

"It's a good place to live," Turner said simply.

"Good for shifters," Linda agreed. But she wasn't a shifter.

She shivered, and Turner took his scarf off and wrapped it around her neck, tucking it carefully into her coat. Even through gloves, his hands were nimble and, despite the cold, Linda rather wished that he was taking clothing off of her instead of the other way around. It was fully dark now, the sky above them a deep shade of murky black.

There were no stars, and the streetlights made puddles of light in regular intervals as they walked. Most of the sidewalks downtown were shoveled, but the maintenance got spotty as they moved further out into the neighborhoods.

"Where is your house?" Linda wanted to know.

"A mile west past the fire station," Turner said. "It's small and bachelor. Like one of those fashionable tiny homes without a drop of fashion."

Linda laughed because he said it so drolly, but understood the implication at once: it wasn't a home for her. It wasn't as if she had expected him to have a surprise mansion with empty rooms and a staff waiting to spring into motion, but she was still a little disappointed.

"Will you come to Cancun with me?" Linda asked impulsively. "I know it doesn't answer the long questions, but there are a lot of things it would be nice to figure out on neutral ground." She couldn't help but imagine what it might be like traveling with Turner, walking on the beach with him, making love to him in a private courtyard.

Turner drew her to a stop. "I don't know," he said honestly. "I've got responsibilities here. We aren't going to solve every problem tonight."

Linda looked up in astonishment. "We're back at Shelley's!" She's gotten turned around somewhere, and hadn't realized that they'd made a loop.

"It's a pretty small town."

"Your fire truck is still at Shaun's."

"I'll walk from here," Turner said gruffly. "But your feet are killing you."

"Boots this cute are rarely comfortable," Linda confessed. "Can you tell because I'm your mate?"

"I can tell because you've been walking slower and slower as we go," Turner said with a chuckle. "It's not magic."

"Maybe I don't want this evening to end," Linda said. She could hear the invitation in her voice, even if she wasn't quite sure what she was inviting. Shelley and Dean and Aaron were probably already home and it wasn't like the guest room would offer that much privacy.

"I don't, either," Turner agreed, his voice low and gruff.

Linda wasn't sure if he failed to invite her to his house because he was embarrassed of it, or if he was just a gentleman who didn't think it was appropriate for a first date, but she wasn't going to force the issue if he wasn't going to make an offer. It felt like a real courtship, a slow burn, and Linda found herself savoring the anticipation. This was her mate and there was no need to rush to the finish line like teenagers.

"You'll be at the show tomorrow?" Turner asked.

"I wouldn't miss it for the world," Linda promised. "Apparently I have two grandchildren in it."

"It's not the theatre you're used to," Turner warned. He was drawing her into his arms now.

"I'm not sure it has to be." Linda was pretty sure that neither of them was really talking about the pageant as she tipped her head up to meet his kiss. "Maybe we could get a nightcap, afterwards," she suggested, when she had breath again. Then, feeling daring, "Maybe you should get a hotel room."

His arms tightened around her and he brushed her lips for a last, lingering kiss. "I'd like that," he said.

Linda had never looked forward to a second date so much.

11

Unfortunately, getting a hotel room turned out to be a lot more complicated than Turner hoped.

There were only two hotels near Green Valley—an eight-room, third-rate motel a few miles out of town on the highway, and a bed and breakfast east of downtown called Green Valley Courtyard. Turner called the latter the next morning and was dismayed to recognize the voice of Gillian, one of the small town's more notorious married man-hunters.

"Can I book a room for the night?" he asked, hoping that the bed and breakfast didn't have caller ID.

Either they did, or Gillian simply recognized his voice. "Turner? *You* need a room for tonight? Ahem, I mean, how many people in your party?"

"Two," Turner ground out.

She made a noise that might have been a muffled squeal, then dashed his hopes. "We're all booked up through New Year's, sorry. We even rented out the old carriage house to an aunt of Lee's. Can you believe her name is Mary? We've been joking about putting a manger out there."

"Ha ha," Turner said humorlessly. "Thanks anyway."

He hung up before Gillian could quiz him about who he was trying to rent a room with. It was a small town, and he knew that it was only a matter of moments before Gillian was on the phone with someone else—maybe Marta—with some of the best gossip of the month.

It took four calls before the motel picked up, only to give him the same news: everything was booked.

The closest thing he could find available on airbnb was a two hour drive. Everyone was full of Christmas visitors.

"Welcome to Green Valley, Linda," he said in despair as he hung up on the third not-very-nearby motel without making a reservation.

In the meantime, he had a mystery to solve, and Stanley hadn't answered his phone.

Mueller's Pond was actually a whole collection of ponds, leftover from a long-ago gravel pit and a time when the highway was much closer to Green Valley. In the summer, it was a gathering place for local teens, with a gravel beach and water deep and clear enough for swimming. In the winter, it froze over and was maintained as an ice skating rink. It had fish all year round, and was just big enough for a boat in the summer, and for ice fishing in the winter.

Stanley's ice shack was usually one of the first to go up, often when others were still discussing the thickness of the ice and the safety of going out on it.

Stanley opened the door a crack when Turner knocked on the door and glared out at him suspiciously. "I gotta license," he said defensively. He probably didn't; he was pretty vocal about the government having no need to know what he hunted or fished. His white hair was wilder than ever over his weathered face.

"Not here about the fish," Turner answered. "I'm looking for Officer Stakes."

Stanley looked a little less suspicious and a little more avid. "He was out here day before yesterday. He's missing? I knew this thing was trouble. They're probably looking for it right now. That's why I can't have it at my house, they'd look there."

Mostly, with Stanley, no one had to ask him many questions.

Prod him in the right direction and he just went on...and on...and on. Once he got started, the problem was that he never stopped.

Feeling trepidatious and wondering how long he was going to get stuck in a tiny ice shack with Stanley, Turner said hopefully, "I was just wondering if you know where Officer Stakes went after he came here. Did he say anything about where he was headed?"

"He knew that they were going to come looking for it. They've probably got him in for questioning now. He hasn't broken yet, or they'd be all over the place."

Turner didn't have to ask who. Stanley was convinced that there was a huge government coverup, complete with Men in Black who would disappear anyone who asked questions or talked about the wrong things. This didn't stop him from asking those questions or talking about those things to anyone who paused long enough for him to stick to them.

"I just wonder if you've an idea where he went after he left here," Turner said desperately.

Stanley stared at him through narrow eyes. "You're in danger now, too," he said, peering behind Turner at the fire truck. "You're too close to the truth." He looked up into the cloudy sky like he expected helicopters or drones to be attacking.

"What's the truth?" Turner asked with a sigh.

"I'll show you," Stanley said. He held open the door and pulled Turner into the ice shack.

Whatever other social flaws Stanley might have, he had a sturdy shack, with all the comforts of home...if all of the comforts of home included a bench over a hole in the ice and a bucket half full of fish. It wasn't heated, but the structure at least cut the bitter wind. There was a Coleman stove set up on a tidy kitchen counter, and the remains of a takeout lunch from Gran's Grits. There was even a bed at the far end, piled high with arctic sleeping bags.

The building didn't have a floor, but the icepack had been shoveled smooth and there were rugs in a few places.

In the center of the small shack, just away from the open fishing hole, was something covered in a towel.

Stanley slid a deadbolt home in the door behind him and

Turner tried not to flinch. The best method for handling Stanley was to let him run his course and hope to get something helpful out from around the edges.

"I bought it online," Stanley said, after he'd made a careful sweep of Turner with what had probably been sold to him as a bug detector in the back of a comic book. "It's really old. Like older than our world, old. It's supposed to unlock true forms. I got it in the mail last week. I've seen people following me since then, too. My phone's tapped, I gotta get a new one."

He pulled the towel off with a flourish.

Turner stared at what he revealed.

The artifact looked like something out of an Indiana Jones movie, with a bunch of different animals carved into it. It didn't look new, but it didn't look nearly as old as Stanley had implied, and there was some writing on it.

"It's not in English," Stanley whispered, and he glanced up at the roof of the shack like he expected aliens to come right down through it.

"It's Latin," Turner said. He recognized *animal,* and *ursus, cattus. Cambinare* rang a bell, but he didn't remember what it was.

Stanley looked vaguely disappointed, then brightened. "Well, the aliens probably gave us their language. It doesn't make sense any other way."

"I'm pretty sure that—" Turner stopped himself before he got into too much of a discussion of the roots of Latin. "Yes, it's very interesting. But really, I'm wondering if you knew where Officer Stakes went after he left here."

Stanley was kneeling beside the thing. "Doesn't this look like a person turning into a bird?" he suggested. "I was told that it was supposed to unlock an inner animal." He looked up at Turner with sharp eyes. "Did you know that there are people in Green Valley who can do that?"

Turner felt a twinge of alarm. "Turn into animals?" he asked, trying to sound skeptical.

"Aliens can look like anything they want," Stanley told him.

"Think about it. Someone saw a mammoth out on Jefferson street a few years back. And a tiger, last year."

"People drinking…" Turner said faintly.

"Agnes swears she saw Gran turn into her own cat at Thanksgiving."

Stanley's conspiracies had always been safely implausible; they'd never skirted so close to the truth. Would these ravings reach too far? "What did you say this thing was supposed to do?"

"Unlock the true form," Stanley said, lifting it up and handing it to Turner before he could wonder if he should take it.

He was jolted by an electric shock that rattled him to the soul and although it looked like wood, it was so heavy that he nearly dropped it.

Stanley didn't appear to feel anything and Turner tried to act casual, turning it briefly to look at the images on the far side. Besides the big animals forms, there were tiny relief carvings of hundreds of others: cats, deer, birds, even ants.

Turner put it back down, probably too fast, and it seemed to sizzle as he set it on the ice. The tingle remained in his bones.

"It's very mysterious," he told Stanley shortly. "But the mystery I'm trying to solve right now is the disappearance of Officer Stakes. Do you know which way he went when he drove off?"

Stanley shrugged, looking disappointed. "West, I think, around the pond." Had he expected Turner to shift? Did Stanley suspect that Turner had an animal form?

Turner's moose was loud in his head, but not really intelligible. Whatever that thing was, it had startled them both.

"You keep this hidden," Turner said firmly, and for the first time he wasn't really worried about feeding into Stanley's delusions. This was much different than his usual fantasies and frauds.

Stanley gleefully covered it again. "You can see why they're looking for it," he started. "It's clear that it's part of something much larger."

Turner was having trouble concentrating. He needed to find Officer Stakes and get out of this terrible little shack, which was feeling uncomfortably small and cramped.

Usually, he was too polite to escape Stanley, who was still talking about the suspicious person he'd seen at the hardware store and how cleverly he'd covered his trail. This time, Turner just cut Stanley off. "I'll see you later," he said gruffly and had a brief struggle with the deadbolt before he fell out of the ice shack and fled for the fire truck on the shore.

He felt better once he'd had that brisk walk and gotten back in his truck. He looked at his fingers. Had he imagined the jolt? What was the artifact? And what did *cambinare* mean?

12

Linda sat in the bleachers of the gym, watching in astonishment as her grown children expertly helped wrangle the cast of the tiny, active people for the pageant. Shelley had her sewing machine set up to one side and was patiently pinning and hemming and folding for last minute costume adjustments. Shaun was at some points absolutely covered in the smallest of the laughing children as he walked around the gym roaring like a monster.

It was absolute chaos, with shrieking children's voices echoing from the tall ceiling as they streaked around in happy anticipation.

The older kids, hanging decorations and putting out food, were all cheerful about their tasks, and the air was celebratory. Linda glanced again at her phone, wondering when it would be acceptable to text Turner. They had exchanged numbers, but she kept reminding herself that she was an independent, self-sufficient woman, not some kind of needy, clingy adolescent. They'd made a plan to connect here, at the show. And after that?

He was Santa Claus.

And he had every present she wanted in his red bag.

"Linda?"

Tawny climbed up into the bleachers and took a ginger seat next to her. "I wanted to apologize. I think everyone thought that someone else had told you about me and Damien and I'm sorry if it was an unpleasant surprise." She was twisting her wedding ring nervously, but held Linda's gaze bravely.

Linda stared back at her in astonishment. It would have been much easier for Tawny to say nothing, to continue to treat Linda as if she were a stranger. But that wasn't how Green Valley was. Green Valley was honest—except for the secret shifters!—and valued kindness. Was it only because the town was too small to avoid each other?

"I'm really glad to meet you," Linda said warmly. "Damien seems happy and I'm nothing but delighted for him. And for you!"

Tawny's face split into a relieved smile so genuine that Linda could not doubt her sincerity. "I think you'll fit in here just fine," she said confidently, as if Linda had just passed some kind of community vetting. "I run a book club on Wednesdays. You should join us! We're reading Twilight this week."

"Twilight, the vampire book?" Linda said dubiously.

"It was Damien's idea. We've all enjoyed it quite a lot. Not that there isn't a lot to be critical of, but everyone needs a guilty pleasure and broody sparkly vampire hunks."

Linda had to laugh. "I would love to attend that book club," she confessed. "I tried a book group in Milwaukee that I could not stand."

"Did they pass out an agenda?" Tawny wanted to know. "I think I know the one, or one like it."

"Tawny! Tawny! Can you play the accompaniment for the chorus practice?" Andrea stood at the bottom of the bleachers looking shorter than ever.

Tawny waved her agreement and stood.

Linda followed her down the bleachers, hoping to find some way to be helpful. She was used to being in charge of events like this, not idle in the sidelines, but everyone here already had something to do.

What would *she* do in a little town like Green Valley? It wasn't that she had to find a job, but Linda was used to having things occupy her. She liked a busy social schedule, and she was pretty sure that Tawny's once-a-week book club wouldn't keep her satisfied.

"You must be Linda."

The young woman who greeted her looked like a tomboy, with shoulder-length dusty hair and a cheeky grin. "I'm Jamie."

"The firefighter who summers in Alaska," Linda remembered.

Jamie gave a humble shrug. "That's me. I'm the smart one on the fire crew."

"Smart ass, you mean?" Linda remembered Turner's description of the young woman. It had matched Shelley's assessment.

Jamie grinned at Linda. "I like you!" she declared.

"Jamie! We need the banner for the bible study hung up and no one can figure out how to unfold the ladder!"

"Duty calls," Jamie said, and she gave Linda one last smile before she darted away in the crowd. Linda shook her head and her smile faded.

Shelley had filled her in that morning on the history that Turner and Jamie had. He'd failed to save her single mother from a fire and taken on a paternal role in her life. The discovery of her estranged father had been a big shake-up to the little town just a month ago.

"Mom, have you heard from Turner?"

Linda turned to find Shaun, hung with only two clinging children now, looking worried. "Shelley wanted to fit the Santa suit before the show and he was going to come by. He's not answering his phone."

Linda checked her phone hopefully and shook her head. "Sorry, no."

"We're down two Santa Clauses now," Shaun quipped, but the humor fell flat. "Hopefully, he'll show up soon."

But as the show grew closer, Linda checked her phone more often, and there was still no sign of him.

"This is really unlike Turner," Andrea said, when she'd called him a third time. "Someone should swing by his house and see what's up."

"Why don't I do that," Linda volunteered. "You kids clearly have your hands full here."

They all gazed at her for a moment and Linda smiled serenely back, trying not to admit how anxious she actually was.

She couldn't put her finger on what was bothering her. There was no reason to think that Turner was in any kind of danger, but Linda felt a tickle of concern and worry. If she'd been a shifter, she might have thought it was some kind of instinct.

But that was ridiculous...right?

13

Turner drove the long way around Mueller's Pond, stopping to head down a few long roads and driveways that looked like they'd been traveled since the last snow, searching for Officer Stakes' car.

A great big loose bull was wandering the latest road he'd turned on. Turner stopped when it swung out in front of him, and when it didn't move, honked the horn.

It stared him down. Just as Turner was considering turning on the siren, it lowered its head and snorted, shaking its horns in defeat and shuffling off into the field.

Turner might have tried to track down who's bull it was—they were close to the Anderson's farm, but the Andersons only kept dairy cows—but he glanced at his phone and realized that he was running out of time before the Winter Festival.

He drove home and stared around his house in dismay. He had about twenty minutes to turn his tiny bachelor pad into a place he could bring a woman like Linda, and it seemed like an impossible task even if he'd had days.

It wasn't that messy, really—though it desperately needed

tidying and there were dirty dishes in the sink. It was just small and well-worn and lacking any kind of aesthetic appeal.

Linda deserved a high rise with big windows and airy spaces, luxurious carpets and velvet curtains. All the rose petals in the world wouldn't hide the fact that Turner's bed sagged in the middle, and the dated wood paneling in every room was yellowed with age. The tiny kitchen only had a three-burner gas stove and one of the counters was actually a chest freezer. It was a perfectly serviceable house and it suited Turner just fine, but it lacked any hint of grace or glamor.

Turner's head was spinning, and at first he thought it was just a rush of despair. He didn't deserve someone like Linda. Could his moose be wrong about her being their mate?

His moose was certainly loud in his head right now, wordlessly snorting and pawing at metaphorical ground.

He bent to sort a pile of mail on the coffee table and a wave of dizziness swept over him. He nearly pitched into the couch, and when he caught himself and stood, he was suddenly standing very tall indeed, his antlers tangling in the ceiling fan.

Turner lifted each of his four feet in turn, surprised and chagrined. He hadn't shifted without intending to since he was a hot-headed teenager, and his house was not sized for a bull moose. Especially not a shifter-sized bull moose. He couldn't fully lift his head, he had one front leg on either side of the coffee table, and there was no room to turn. His clothing was in pieces around his hooves. He was lucky he hadn't come down on the table itself; as sturdy as it was, a seventeen hundred pound moose would punch right through it. His hooves were doing the floor no favors and it creaked beneath him.

He willed himself back to human form, and if he had been dismayed to suddenly be a moose, it was nothing compared to the sudden panic of not being able to be anything else.

He carefully lowered his head, hearing the fan blades scrape off of his antlers as he carefully tried to clear it and back away into the kitchen. There was a light at the bottom of the fan, he didn't want to—

Glass shattered as he misjudged the swing of his broad antlers and he froze, feeling shards scatter down over his back with a spit of sparks. Dammit, he couldn't see where he was going at all in the tiny dim-lit room with his moose's poor vision, unable to turn his head without endangering the fan further. He took a few ginger steps backwards and ran into a bookcase, rattling everything on it; he was longer than he realized, as well as taller.

If he couldn't shift back into a human, he had to get out of the house before he destroyed it, and Turner had no idea how to do that. He thought he might be able to squeeze his mass out of the door if he turned his head sideways so the antlers would pass through, but he had no idea how to manage a doorknob without hands. His mouth, maybe?

He managed to make a slow, seven-point turn, bumping off of the television and the bookcases, taking down one of the curtains with the prongs of his antlers. He was facing into the kitchen; the back door had the straightest access and there was no way he could fold himself through the porch outside the front door.

His phone went off twice while he was attempting to orient himself, and Turner tried nosing it on with absolutely no luck. His hooves would definitely not unlock it anyway. It skittered away under the couch as he tried mouthing it, hoping he could dial it with his tongue and he gave a groaning sigh as he saw Linda's number flash across the screen.

He wouldn't have been able to answer anyway.

He turned his attention back to trying to get out of the house. Maybe he could find someone who could help. Turner was sure this had something to do with the thing at Stanley's ice shack, the thing that had given him an electric shock and made his moose feel so supercharged. It had probably stuck Officer Stakes in his shifted form, too. Turner wouldn't have guessed that the police officer was a shifter, but it seemed like an obvious answer that he'd been the bull out by the Andersons'.

This didn't bode well for Turner being able to get back to his human form; Stakes had been missing for a few days now.

Turner had to fight down the impulse to simply lower his head and charge through the back door. He was easily strong enough to take out the entire door and jamb together, but his property value was not going to be improved by destroying his back door. Besides, he was still hoping that he'd be able to bring Linda back here, though that hope was becoming dimmer and dimmer as he continued to remain stubbornly in moose form.

The kitchen was narrow, and the doorknob was hard to reach from his towering moose height. Turner had to wedge himself against the stove to angle his mouth to it, and his antlers kept getting in his way. He mouthed at it uselessly, craning his neck in every possible way to manage to get his moose lips around the doorknob. Several times, he almost had it and slipped off, turning it only part way.

He was so tightly focused that didn't recognize the clicking sound until he smelled the gas. The sharp, garlic smell somehow changed through his moose's nose. He'd rubbed up against the controls on the stove and turned on all the burners. The snick-snick sound was the temperamental lighter mechanism he was leaning into; Turner usually used a lighter wand that he kept beside the stove.

He realized the danger too late, whipping his head around just in time to see a fireball whoosh up from the burners. He knocked the blender from the counter directly onto the flaming stove with the antlers that he'd forgotten about again, and when he staggered away from the stove, it was to run into the pantry cabinets on the opposite wall so hard he heard something crack.

The fireball was short-lived, but the curtain by the kitchen window caught fire and flames from the burner licked around the fallen blender.

Turner bellowed because he couldn't curse, and had to stuff his head directly over the flame in order to get his moose mouth around the knobs of the oven. He'd gotten close to figuring out the door-knob, but these were smaller and turned further. His giant head couldn't swivel enough to turn them off with his teeth, so he had to use his tongue, while his ears got hotter and hotter above the lit burners.

The smoke detector went off then and if his ears had hurt before, they were in agony now; a moose had sensitive hearing and the alarm was painfully shrill.

His terrible vision made the room seem even more smoky than it was, and between the heat and the wail of the alarm, Turner was fighting down panic.

He'd trained in burning buildings, of course, but he'd been wearing turnout gear, and he'd had working hands to use. Green Valley didn't have a lot of actual house fires; people here tended to be sensible and the population wasn't large. Turner was proactive about teaching fire safety and forward about making sure everyone had fire extinguishers. Every fall they did a big safety drive and he went door-to-door with reminders and checked people's alarms and exits for them. He'd put out a few contained oven fires, and gotten to houses where they were just finishing their own suppression. He had responded to fires in larger nearby communities, but usually the Green Valley team arrived with the truck in time to assist the outside crew, watering down the nearby houses and working containment.

There had only been one time he'd had to go into a burning building...and he'd been too late.

It all came rushing back now: the angry heat, the rushing noise, the black, disorienting smoke. The overwhelming helplessness as he found Jamie's mother and carried her out of the collapsing house...too late.

He'd never forgotten how Jamie looked, in her short, sooty nightgown standing on the neighbor's lawn. It was late morning, and they'd rushed Beverly to the nearest hospital. She'd died of smoke inhalation the following day.

Jamie hadn't held it against him, of course, but Turner couldn't help but blame himself. If he'd turned out just a few moments sooner... If he'd found her in the house just a little faster...

He was licking and gumming at the knobs on the front of the stove with his tongue, but he'd never mastered tying cherry stems, and his moose tongue wasn't nearly as dexterous as it needed to be for the task. His neck felt wrenched, pinched around in the tight space his tongue ached. The plastic blender began to melt and smolder merrily, blue flames dancing up around it.

Turner felt despair wash over him and he nearly bit off the knob in frustration.

He was going to die in a house fire, stuck as a moose, on the day after he'd met his mate.

Even just thinking about Linda brought a measure of peace to his soul, and he was somehow not surprised when there was a sudden sound of pounding on the door. He knew exactly who it was.

14

Linda found Turner's house with ease, despite the vague instructions Andrea had given her. It turned out that "really ugly blue house" and "giant broken tractor" were perfectly viable landmarks to follow. It was a small neighborhood between farms that looked like every other small neighborhood between farms in the valley, with tiny houses and snowy yards. His house numbers were large and easy to see and the fire truck was parked right out front.

As she pulled up and opened her car door, she recognized in dread that there was smoke leaking from several of the windows and there were fire alarms screaming a chorus inside.

Linda scrambled out of the car, leaving the door wide open as she pelted for the front door and fell upon it.

She only knocked a few frantic times before testing the knob. It was unlocked and she burst in, crying, "Turner? TURNER?"

The door opened into a small living room where it appeared there had been a struggle. Books and mail and broken glass were scattered across the worn plush carpet. It was thick with toxic-smelling smoke. Linda could see back to a kitchen where a gigantic shape was hulking between a pantry cabinet and a counter with a stove and sink. There was a lump of something burning on the stove, and one of the curtains was smoldering.

For a moment, she was alarmed. Was the creature a bear? Some kind of huge, horrible monster? Then it gave a snort and shuffled in place and she saw the rack like a great comic crown above it.

Turner. Of course, he was a *moose!*

Saying he was very large was one thing, but seeing his massive size crammed into a ridiculously small space was quite another and Linda might have been quite terrified if she had the time to digest it.

But the alarm was still shrieking and the stove was still on fire. Linda paused to cast around and find a fire extinguisher right next to the door where it ought to be. She picked it up, adrenaline making it lighter than it probably was, and yanked the pin from it, dashing to Turner's side.

"Turner, why are you a moose right now? You'd be a lot more useful with opposable thumbs!"

There was no room in the kitchen for both of them, so Linda aimed her extinguisher and shot it right past him at the stove. She knew that you were supposed to put out grease fires with a special kind of extinguisher, but she didn't have time to look for one, and this didn't look like a grease fire anyway. It looked...like a blender.

The fire sputtered and the curtains, with one short blast, went out entirely, but Linda could see that the controls for the stove were still set full-on. Putting out the flame would only risk filling the room with gas.

"I need to get in there, Turner!" she cried. Clearly, he was not able to shift to human or he would have long ago. Was it a stress response?

The moose—Turner!—gave a snort and started to back up into the living room with careful, shuffling steps. Linda squeezed past him and twisted all the knobs to off. The last flame sputtered and went out.

The blender—what was left of it—slowly slumped and groaned as it started to cool onto the surface of the stove.

For a moment, Linda only stood there, her legs shaking and the extinguisher, which was plenty heavy now, trembling in her hands.

Finally, she could turn and look at Turner.

He was a monstrous wall of mooseflesh and he had backed into a bookcase, knocking a picture off an upper shelf onto his broad back, where it was wobbling drolly in place.

Linda had been next to plenty of horses, but this was half again the size of the largest one she had ever ridden, with comparatively delicate legs that were nearly as tall as she was. He couldn't even fully lift his head in the house, and his huge, spreading rack must have been more than six feet across.

He also looked mortified, which was not an expression that Linda had expected to find on any deer.

"You've been burnt," she exclaimed as his ears flickered back and forth. His whole nose was blackened, but Linda wasn't sure what was soot and what was singed. She reached a hesitant hand to touch him and his nostrils flared as he gave a sigh and his head drooped.

To her surprise, his nose was velvety soft, and his breath was warm and gentle. "Are you stuck like this?" Linda wanted to know, then could have kicked herself for asking the obvious. He wouldn't be rattling around destroying his own house like an oversized pet if he could shift back. "What happened?"

Turner snorted, an alarming sound, and pawed the ground and shook his head like he was trying to mime something, but it was clearly far too complex for charades. Something had clearly gone wrong, but Linda didn't have the foggiest idea what.

"Are you sick?"

He cocked his head thoughtfully and then shook it.

"Did someone do this to you?" Linda wracked her mind to think how someone could.

Turner shrugged one giant shoulder and shook his head again, rattling the broken fan above him.

Linda took a deep breath that came out as a cough and shook her head. "Let's air this place out," she said practically. She put the fire extinguisher—which was now heavy enough to make her arm shake—down on the coffee table and went to open each of the windows in turn. It was cold and breezy outside and the smoke eased considerably. She flapped her hat at the smoke alarm and it finally silenced.

She returned to Turner, where he still stood in the center of the room, watching her but not offering to move around in the cramped space and risk more of his furniture.

"You have the most gorgeous eyelashes I've ever seen on an animal," Linda said with a shaky giggle.

Turner fluttered them at her like a teenage girl trying to catch a boy's attention and Linda's chuckle swelled and turned into a whole body laugh. She had to cling to Turner and gasp for air, she laughed so helplessly. It was probably partly shock, and partly joy that Turner, however he'd gotten stuck as a giant ungulate, was still in there.

Linda was not sure she had ever laughed as completely and when she could gather her wits again, she kissed Turner on his broad nose and said, "I love you, Turner. I'm not a shifter, and I don't have an animal who can tell me that you're my one, but I know that you do, and I trust your moose and know that you are a good man with a good heart and I'm already absolutely crazy for you. I don't know how we'll work things out, but I know that we will. I think I'd even love you if you were stuck this way forever."

15

*L*inda's words were like a salve over a sunburn. Making her laugh—*really* laugh!—had been a moment of triumph, but hearing her say that she loved him felt like a band across Turner's chest had been released.

She loved him.

Stuck as a moose or on his ass in the snow wearing a Santa Claus suit, it didn't matter to Linda because she loved him the same way that he loved her, like he was standing at the edge of a bluff knowing against logic that he could fly. This was the mate he'd been waiting for, and she'd been waiting for him.

"Linda," he said, and because he needed a human tongue to say it, he was suddenly human again, standing in the tossed chaos of his house in the center of the space that his moose had taken up. "Linda, my love!"

"Oh, thank heavens!" she exclaimed. "I really would love you as a moose, but I do vastly prefer you this way!"

Turner stepped forward to gather her up into his arms, only noticing at the last moment that he was completely naked.

That didn't seem like much of a problem for what they clearly each had in mind as she lifted her head to meet his kiss, but it wasn't long before she noticed that he was shivering in the icy wind blowing in through the open windows.

"You're cold," she scolded him, pulling back. Then she grinned. "Though, perhaps not *that* cold."

There was no hiding that he was hard as a rock for her, his cock more interested in claiming his mate than cowering for the warmth of his body. "There are blankets in the bedroom," he growled.

The door to the bedroom was shut, out of long fire safety habit, so it was both warmer in there and almost completely free of smoke.

Turner kicked the door shut behind him and carried Linda straight to his bed. He didn't care that it was small, or worn, or that he hadn't managed rose petals or music or candles, and he knew that Linda didn't care either. All that mattered was that they were here together, now, and would be forever.

"Turner," she said between kisses. "Turner, my love. My *dear.*"

Or maybe it was *deer?*

He undressed her with care, kissing down her neck as he exposed it, pushing her coat back off of her arms and holding her pinned a moment while she whimpered and begged and pressed herself against him.

He unbuttoned her shirt as she kissed his neck and the place where his jaw met his ear, which proved a powerful distraction; it took several tries to free the fragile garment without simply ripping off the remaining buttons.

It was a task worth the extra effort, and Linda made intoxicating noises of pleasure as he slipped her out of it and kissed down to the tops of her breasts. He lingered there, as delighted by her responses as the fascination of her soft, perfect flesh.

"Turner, please, *please,*" she begged. She shimmied out of her own pants and Turner lay her down on the bed, pausing to gaze at her in wonder as she spread her legs in welcome.

Both naked at last, raw with hunger, they met mouth to mouth, cock to hot, wet, ready lips. It was a slow, careful entrance, tiny adjustments for the most pleasure and deepest access, his hands at her hips, hers at his shoulders clawing him closer, further, harder.

When he was fully buried in her, his whole body on fire, focused on all of the places they were touching, Turner began to thrust, and he felt her body tense in answer as she pulled back her mouth gasping for breath.

"Turner," she panted. "Turner!"

When she cried out again at her crest of desire, Turner had to force himself to slow. He wanted to pound her desperately, but at the same time needed to prolong their joining. He wanted to make love to her in every position, find every spot that made her whimper and beg.

She was writhing beneath him and his world seemed to narrow to where they met, and how badly he needed release.

His name changed to something wordless and desperate in her mouth and she gave a cry of pleasure and arched beneath him. Turner lost his battle with himself at the sound of her climax and fell with her at last.

16

Linda lay in Turner's arms feeling completely full of bliss, and like she'd never been so comfortable in her life.

It wasn't just the toe-curling sex, and she didn't need an animal to tell her that this was exactly where she belonged, cradled in Turner's big, gentle arms. "You burnt your nose," she observed, because she was lying very close to him and could see that it was red. "Does it hurt?"

Turner shrugged. "It's not bad," he said, but he said it mournfully and held Linda closer. She could feel the tension all through him, in his shoulders and hands.

"What is it?" she asked quietly. "What's wrong?"

She didn't actually expect an answer, though something had clearly bothered him. She expected him to brush her off, to deny whatever it was that had occurred to him and pretend that he was fine.

Instead, Turner propped himself up on one elbow and gazed down at her in consternation.

"We'll make something work," Linda promised. "I don't need the city lights or theater to be happy with you."

"It's not that," Turner said quietly. "You probably heard the story by now. About Jamie's mom."

"You couldn't save her," Linda said, just as quietly. The fire had probably shaken all of those feelings loose. "Did you love her?"

"Nothing like that," Turner said. He tucked a lock of Linda's hair behind her ear in a gesture so intimate that Linda shivered. "But I didn't get there fast enough to save her, and I look at you and I have to wonder what would happen if I couldn't protect you."

Linda put a hand at his jaw. He hadn't shaved since the day before and there was a stubble of rough hair against her palm. "The problem with always being protected is that you never get to live," she reminded him. "I don't want you to keep me safe, I want you to be alive with me."

The poorly-sprung mattress creaked as Turner leaned over to kiss her deeply. "I have never felt so alive," he said, nibbling at her lip. "I have never felt this complete."

"I could be a firefighter," Linda said boldly.

Turner retreated to the length of his arms over her. "What?"

"Don't look at me like that," Linda scolded him. "You said yourself that you wanted someone else on the crew, that Carter wanted to retire, that you lost Dean and might not have Jamie for the summers. I may not be a spring chicken, but I'm not so old I can't learn new tricks, and I'm in good shape. I should be, I pay my personal trainer enough for this muscle tone. Are you afraid to be my boss?"

Turner wisely didn't answer that question, but his mouth gave a tell-tale quirk. "You've already rushed into one burning building without turnout gear," he observed skeptically.

"You'll have to teach me how to do it safely, then," Linda said matter-of-factly. "I have always wanted to rescue people."

He gazed at her appraisingly then burst out laughing. It was the kind of laugh that was infectious, not cruel but full of delight and surprise. He wrapped his arms around her and rolled her onto her side so that he wasn't crushing her, squeezing tight and shaking with amusement. "You really are my perfect woman," he said with a contented sigh, one leg wrapped around her. "How did I ever deserve you?"

"I am sure I have many irritating personal flaws that you will gradually discover," Linda said frankly. "But I hope I will always make you very happy, because that is very definitely a thing that you deserve."

He kissed her then, the way she had been hoping he would, and she was very aware of the long, hard length of him against all of her. She would not have been opposed to following that awareness to another satisfying romp but finally gave a sigh and pulled back. "They need Santa Claus at the pageant festival thing and still can't find Officer Stakes. I was sent to come get you because Shelley wanted to take the suit in before things got started."

Turner glanced up at a clock on the wall. "The suit is going to have to do as it is. We're already going to be late."

They had left all of the windows and the front door wide open and coming out of the bedroom was a cold shock. Most of the smoke had dispersed, at least. "Your poor house," Linda exclaimed, pausing to pick up a drift of magazines with a dinner-plate sized hoofprint through it.

"It wasn't much to look at before it was wrecked up by an out-of-control moose," Turner said sheepishly. He was dressed again, to Linda's mixed disappointment.

"We've figured out my career," Linda said thoughtfully, "but not where we'd live."

Turner grinned at her. "Rookies always bunk in the efficiency above the fire station," he said with relish.

Linda smiled back at him and chuckled. "We may have to negotiate something different than that," she said firmly.

"You going to try to get special privileges because you're sleeping with the fire chief?" Turner teased her.

"Maybe I'm trying to get special privileges *for* the fire chief," Linda said, standing on tiptoe to kiss him. "We'd better hurry."

Turner held Linda's coat for her to get her arms into. It smelled, like everything in his house now, faintly like toxic smoke, but Linda was keenly aware of how much worse it might have been.

She was frowning into the sooty kitchen as Turner got his own coat, unpacking his hat and gloves from one sleeve.

"I'm going to need a better cooking space," she told him, when he came to stand next to her.

"Better than a burnt-up three-burner stove with a blender permanently melted onto it?" Turner asked with comic skepticism.

"That's not negotiable," Linda said firmly. "I will move to this tiny little town if that's what it takes to have you for myself, but I am going to need a decent kitchen even if I have to learn how to build it myself. How much land do you own with the house?"

"Are you thinking of remodeling?" Turner asked in astonishment.

"I'm thinking about how to make this work," Linda said honestly. "How to make both of us happy. I love to cook, and I want a kitchen I can make magic in. Does the firefighting gig take a lot of time or is it mostly being on call?"

"You're really serious about this."

Linda had to smile at him, at the expression of awe on his face. "How could I not be?" she asked quietly. "You're my mate."

Turner made a small noise that Linda decided was very manly joy.

But all he said was, "We're going to have a long and serious talk about turnout gear."

The door to her car was still wide open and there was a dust of new snow all over her leather seats.

"Leave it here," Turner suggested, as she started to brush it out. "There won't be much parking space, and it doesn't look like a car that will handle a lot of snow if we have to park creatively."

Linda gave a sigh. "Am I going to have to get an SUV to live here?" she asked in mock dread. "Oh, tell me I won't need a pick-up. Surely not a tractor!"

17

They weren't as late to the Green Valley Christmas Pageant and Winter Festival as Turner feared they would be. The school parking lot was crowded, and there were cars and trucks parked at odd angles and on the sidewalks all along the road for three blocks in either direction, crowded in driveways and blocking store accesses. Turner couldn't quite bring himself to park the fire truck in front of a hydrant and finally found a space by the playground that was mostly snowbank and probably not entirely legal. Turner frowned to think that Officer Stakes was still missing and checked his phone for messages from the state troopers as he locked the truck and came around to help Linda out.

She was already shutting her own door, cheerfully uncomplaining about the snow she had to wade through in her impractical boots.

"I did not realize that there were this many people in all of Green Valley," she said in astonishment, tucking her hand into Turner's elbow. They had to walk in the empty street because of the people parked up on the sidewalk.

"We don't have a lot going on," Turner said with a chuckle. "Pretty much everyone turns out for what they can."

It was picturesque, as they hurried towards the warm, familiar school, with new snowflakes falling down on their shoulders. It was hard not to dally, to stop and kiss Linda. He had to resist the temptation to toss her into a snowbank, just to see what she would do, and Turner grinned sideways as they gradually walked faster and faster, until they were both running.

"I don't want to miss Trevor's big moment of fame!" she said, exchanging a laughing glance with him.

She was graceful as any deer, bounding at his side, and Turner thought that maybe she could hack it as a firefighter if it came to it. She'd seemed like a sheltered, big-city woman when he first saw her, but his moose had known from the moment their eyes met that she had a strong, flexible core of steel, and that no one in the world would ever complete him the way she did.

The snow leading to the back entrance to the gym was packed down hard—Turner thought grimly that it was going to take an ice chipper to get it up now and that it should have been shoveled before everyone showed up.

He'd been a little busy, though, turning into a moose and setting his house on fire.

"It sounds like the Methodist Choir is almost finished," he said, opening the outer door for Linda. There was a short hallway with bathrooms before the auditorium and the music and murmur of the large audience was warm and welcoming through the closed bank of doors.

She started to walk towards them and then realized that Turner wasn't following her. "What about you?"

"I left the Santa suit in my office," Turner explained. "Gotta go around the long way to put it on and be jolly. I'll make my big entrance at the end and you can pretend you don't know it's me. If you're lucky, I'll have a present for you."

"Mmm," Linda said in delight, and her gaze dropped suggestively to his pants. "I've been *very* good this year."

Turner could not resist drawing her back for a lingering kiss, holding the door open with his back. "Are you sure?"

She rubbed up against the length of him in a very naughty way indeed. "Check your list," she suggested.

The Methodist choir was belting out an enthusiastic holiday medley and there was a scatter of applause when they finished. "That's your chance," Turner said, letting go of her reluctantly. "The multi-denominational pageant is next."

"I have *two* grandkids in it, apparently," Linda said with a laugh. "I'd better not miss it."

It was hard to leave her, even knowing that he'd have her again soon enough, but Turner gave her one last kiss and went around to the back of the school, following the line of blinking Christmas lights.

To his surprise, not everyone from Green Valley was already inside the gym.

A dark figure was staggering towards the brightly lit building, panting and covered in snow.

At first, Turner suspected that someone was drunk, and he tried to decipher who it might be from their large frame. "Officer Stakes!" he exclaimed, partly relieved, but mostly alarmed. "Are you hurt?"

"Mother of angels," Stakes gasped, coming to a halt in front of him. "I'm human again!" He looked wild around the eyes. "I don't even know if I can explain it," he said, panting. "I think I was a bull. No, I am a bull. It is very strange in my head right now."

Turner knew new shifters when he saw them. "You *were* that bull out by the Anderson's farm," he said. Something didn't add up. "How are you still wearing clothing?"

Stakes stared back. "You don't seem as surprised as I thought you'd be." Then he laughed. "This explains so much. I thought it was just pranks and small town weirdness, but I can just circular file about half my caseload now."

"I'm a shifter, too," Turner said. "But I can't take my clothes with me."

Stakes looked down at his snowy, rumpled uniform. "That sounds inconvenient. And again, explains *so much.*"

"You have no idea," Turner murmured. "Now, take me through what happened after you saw Stanley."

"You saw that...thing he has?" Stakes said. "The probably-not-an-alien-artifact?"

"Yeah. Gave me an electric jolt. I think it trapped me as a moose...until Linda kissed me and I could change back."

"Was that about forty-five minutes ago?" Stakes wanted to know. "Because I was pretty suddenly human again then."

Turner nodded. "About that, yeah." True love's kiss broke spells in fairy tales, and nothing else made more sense. "Do you know Latin?"

Stakes shook his head. "Nothing but *carpe diem.*"

"You...don't have shifters in your family, do you?" Turner asked. "It's normal for this to follow genealogy."

"Not to my knowledge," Stakes said. "I suppose it's possible it just wasn't talked about."

Turner frowned. "We need to keep this from happening again," he said. "We gotta go get that thing and...put it somewhere safe. It didn't seem to affect Stanley, I wonder if you have to be a latent shifter for it to work. What are we going to tell him?"

Stakes frowned. "Nothing," he said. "I don't want to feed his delusions or jeopardize the secrets people clearly need to keep. I'll just...confiscate it as evidence and he can believe that the government is behind it or whatever he wants."

"You going to need a warrant for it?"

"Yeah, I'd better. I guess I need to head over to the office and get that going."

"It can wait until morning," Turner said. "Everyone's here for the big show now. Are you up for some jolly times? Your timing was pretty magnificent."

"Wait, tonight? What day *is* it? How long was I gone? I don't think time means as much to my bull."

"It's a little funny, yeah," Turner agreed. "Tomorrow is Christmas Eve."

Stakes rubbed his forehead. "Okay, then. This is definitely a thing. Everything makes a lot more sense now."

"C'mon, I've got the Santa suit in my office locked up with all the presents."

18

No one seemed to notice Linda's entrance when she snuck in and stood near the back of the gymnasium. The kids were all whispering and fidgeting in anticipation of their forthcoming moment of fame, gathered along the far wall with Patricia and Andrea trying in vain to hush them. A baby somewhere in the crowd was fussing and clearly on the brink of wails.

There were more people than Linda had expected, and more variety in their representation. The gym was well-packed and full of Christmas cheer.

As the choir shuffled off the stage and the middle school students started setting the scenery for the pageant, Linda slipped forward to find Shelley under cover of the chaos. There was a little space in the middle of that row where they were sitting on the bleachers and she had to walk up and squeeze past Damien and Tawny, Dean and Shelley, and Shaun, who looked like he was expecting nothing short of a disaster.

"Excuse me," she whispered as she passed them and sank into the empty space. She nodded at the stranger on her far side, who smiled back tolerantly.

"Where you have you *been?*" Shelley hissed at her. "You smell like burnt plastic."

Linda smirked at her. "You sure you want to know?"

"Not when you say it like that. Did you find Turner?"

"Yes, I found Santa Claus and saved the day," she assured her daughter. "He's just outside getting into character for his big entrance. He had to put out a fire before he came to the show. Of course, it was a fire that he set..."

Shelley looked like she wanted to demand more information, but Trevor stepped up to the podium then and cleared his throat impatiently.

The audience quieted.

Trevor took a deep breath and Linda found herself tense with anticipation. This was her *grandchild*, half grown-up and up and standing on the stage, which seemed both impossible and absolutely perfect.

"THIS IS THE STORY OF THE FIRST CHRISTMAS THE NIGHT JESUS CHRIST WAS BORN WE CELEBRATE THIS TO REMEMBERTHEHOPEANDJOY—"

Trevor completely ignored Patrician and Andrea waving at him to slow down and enunciate and rolled into a break-neck, non-stop, unintelligible reading of his script.

None of the other pageant actors could catch their cues in the unending chaos of his reading, so eventually they just started their parts at random intervals. Aaron and Clara stepped onto the stage to get the "glad" tidings of the angel, who looked like he would rather be anywhere or anyone else in the world.

Clara had elected to play Mary completely over the top, literally jumping with joy at the news of her role as Jesus' mother and hugging a surprised and dismayed Aaron. Later in the recitation, she seemed to decide that Mary was consumptive and feigned dizziness, staggering around with her hand at her forehead. It became obvious that the Jesus doll had been lost when she did a dramatic, unscripted swoon and the squash that had been wrapped in swaddling clothes fell out of her arms and rolled off the stage down the aisle of folding chairs that filled the gym.

Aaron ran after it, crying, "Come back, Baby Jesus!"

Someone had drawn a smiling face on the squash, which was obvious when he held it up in triumph.

The audience applauded and laughed and cheered, not entirely sure what was most appropriate, and Aaron scrambled back up onto the stage to return the bruised Baby Jesus squash to Clara, who wrapped it lovingly.

Some of the angels cried hysterically and the shepherds laughed so hard that one of them fell sideways and knocked the barn scenery over.

Trevor launched back into his narration even faster than before, if possible, and they ended with a ragged rendition of Joy to the World and took their bows. Clara blew kisses and Aaron got tangled in his beard trying to bow.

"At least there were no live sheep," Shaun said quietly, just past Shelley and Dean, as the kids were herded off the stage, some of them bolting out of place for their families.

"Sheep?" Linda had to ask. Was it a shifter joke?

"Trevor brought live goats to Lee and Patricia's wedding," Shelley explained under her breath.

Linda was beginning to think that Green Valley had a lot more going on than she realized.

The Catholic choir stepped in to take the stage and the children dispersed back to their families in the audience.

"I SANG!" one child screamed happily as she pelted down the side of the gym, and everyone laughed kindly.

"Good work," Linda lied kindly to Trevor and Aaron as they scrambled up the bleachers and sidled down the rows to sit with their family.

"When is Santa Claus?" Aaron wanted to know.

"At the end," Trevor told him confidently. "Otherwise no one would stay."

"Shh!" Shelley said, pointing at the stage. The choir was preparing to sing, the organist poised on the keyboard.

The boys continued to whisper, hushing whenever Shelley glared at them and then resuming almost at once.

Linda was surprised by an unexpected voice saying, "Excuse me, sorry, right, thank you!" and looked to see Turner squeezing into the row. She squished Aaron over and gave Turner room next to her. "Where's the Santa suit?" she asked quietly.

"Found the original Santa," Turner said back, voice low. "The pressure is off!"

"You must be so relieved!" Linda found his hand with hers, surprised by how natural it felt to sit in the echoing auditorium listening to what turned out to be an excellent choir, even if the acoustics were atrocious. Was this the Christmas spirit, sitting with her unexpectedly warm family in an unexpectedly welcoming town with an unexpected mate?

It felt like a miracle, like everything she'd never known to wish for was waiting for her under a tree.

"It's not exactly Broadway or the Met," Turner said near her ear. Did he sound apologetic?

"It's even better," Linda promised. And despite the uncomfortable bleachers and the terrible echoing acoustics and the ragged organization and the amateur enthusiasm—or perhaps *because* of all of that—she thought that it was true. It was a show full of community and love.

The last soloist was a girl who looked about sixteen. She was clearly very nervous, but when she opened her mouth to sing, even the children hushed in awe. The organ accompaniment was very simple, allowing her voice to carry the music.

Linda wasn't sure what could possibly follow that lovely act, and she applauded enthusiastically at the end.

To her surprise, everyone stood then, and joined a chorus of popular carols: "We Wish You a Merry Christmas," "Deck the Halls," "Jingle Bells" (Trevor and Aaron both hollered the words to Batman Smells but were drowned in the general swell of sound), and "Rudolph the Red-Nosed Reindeer."

Then Andrea raised her hand from the stage and said loudly, "Do I hear reindeer now?"

There was an unconvincing clomping sound that was more from the bathrooms than the roof, and then a huge, red-clad figure appeared at the door with a giant, bulging bag, just as the tree in the corner of the gym was plugged in and the star at the top lit up.

There was a squeal of delight and anticipation and the children that had been absorbed into the audience after the pageant all flowed out to gather at the tree and get gifts from a giant, grinning Santa Claus.

Trevor and Aaron clambered out over the bleachers, trailing half-hearted apologies to the people they wriggled past.

Everyone else gathered up their shed coats and purses and mittens and followed more sedately to where Santa was passing out presents, pausing to exchange hugs and holiday greetings with their neighbors.

"So where has Officer Stakes been all this time?" Shelley wanted to know.

"It's a long, long story," Turner replied.

19

*L*inda woke up on Christmas Eve feeling like she'd gotten everything she wished for. The sexiest Santa Claus she'd ever imagined was sprawled in the barely adequate bed next to her and she smiled down at his dear face in wonder and gratitude. There was gray at his temples, just like there was at hers if she didn't dye her hair, and the faint lines around his face betrayed the fact that he was almost always smiling.

She thought she wouldn't mind smiling her own way to more lines.

This was her mate, her perfect partner, and it didn't matter that his house was tiny and still smelled of melted blender and soot.

On the bedside table, his phone flashed on and began to complain.

Turner's eyes fluttered open and he stretched, nearly displacing her from the tiny bed.

"Good morning, gorgeous," he said appreciatively.

"Your phone is buzzing," Linda told him, but not until after she'd collected a good morning kiss.

Turner groaned. "I'm going to be reserve officer when Stakes heads over to get the artifact from Stanley." He had told her all about the sculpture, and the electric shock it had given him, and how her kiss seemed to break the spell.

"Do you have to go now?" Linda wanted to know. His hands were exactly as clever as she'd known they would be, and they were waking up with the rest of him now.

Turner kissed her reluctantly. "I don't want anyone else to get stuck shifted," he said regretfully. "Or suddenly turn into a shifter. We should take care of it sooner than later."

Linda didn't want to let him go. "Turner, do you think it would make me a shifter?"

This stilled his big hands. "Would you want to be?"

Linda had to pause. "Yes?" she said. "I mean it's kind of exciting, to be able to change into an animal. And to...know."

"That you're my mate?" Turner guessed. "For sure?"

Linda was silent, feeling foolish.

Turner's hands found her face. "I will spend the rest of my life convincing you, if that's what it takes," he promised. "You are the only one I will ever love like this, the one person who completes me. I would have loved you even without a moose in my head urging me on. I believe we were meant to be and things would have happened to put us together anyway because there is simply no part of me that believes in happiness without you. I just happen to have a noisy, bullish voice in my head that is telling me what I already know."

Linda tipped her mouth up to meet his kiss, wondering how she could ever have doubted.

It was much, much later that they met Officer Stakes out at Mueller's Pond, and Linda knew that there was no chance that she would find out if the artifact would make her a shifter, even if she had still wanted to.

"Whelp," Officer Stakes said, taking off his hat to rub his head. "I guess that takes care of that problem."

The ice shack had sunk into the ice and was nothing more than part of a tin roof and a little floating debris in a broken soup of ice chunks and dark water out near the center of the pond

Stanley was standing safely with them on the shore, along with a gaggle of people who had caught sight of the sinking building from the ice skating area of the pond.

He appeared to be unharmed, but he was clearly agitated. "I told you the government would be after it!" he hollered at Officer Stakes. "No reason for the ice to melt like that. Probably they did it with stolen alien tech. From space!"

"I'm going to need you to calm down," Stakes said firmly to him, but that only wound him up further and he turned on Turner.

"You told them where it was!" he accused. "You know what it can do! It can make people into animals!"

Several of the onlookers looked alarmed and all of them looked avidly curious.

Linda did what she always did, and waded right in. There was a fine line between encouraging a delusion and defusing it, and Linda knew exactly where that line was. "My goodness, you must be Stanley," she said, stepping forward to offer her hand. "I've heard so much about you!" She gave him a significant look and glanced around. "I'm so sorry about your ice house fishing thing. What a tragedy! I can tell that you're very upset, won't you tell me about it?"

By the time she was done with him, Stanley was more smug than dismayed. He seemed sure this was all proof that it had been a genuine alien artifact, but Linda had quietly convinced him that he didn't want anything too suspicious to be overheard and he couldn't be too careful about who he talked in front of.

He left in a beat-up pick-up, muttering about insurance and acts of God.

"Do we need to worry about it?" Turner asked Stakes in a quiet aside when Linda returned to his side. "Down there, I mean?"

"It was really heavy and the pond is pretty deep," Stakes said. "I don't imagine we'll see it again."

"People swim here in the summer," Turner said with a frown. "Kids especially."

Stakes shrugged. "Short of dredging for it in the spring, I don't know know what we'd do. Close the whole pond down as hazardous? What would I say to excuse using municipal money for hiring divers or a dredge for it? No one can touch it at the bottom of the pond, so it's probably not a danger from there."

"Yeah, probably," Turner agreed.

The little crowd of Green Valley citizens started to slowly disperse, realizing that the shack was gone and the brief entertainment was done. Linda helped Turner and Stakes set out hazard cones so that no one would accidentally go out on the broken ice.

"I'm sorry we didn't get more answers," Linda said as they headed back up to where the fire truck was parked. "What do you remember about what the sculpture looked like? I have archaeologist friends who might be able to tell us more about it."

"It was covered in Latin writing," Turner remembered. "I knew some of the words. *Animal, cattus, ursus.* And *cambinare.*"

"Animal, cat, bear, and...what is *cambinare?*"

Turner shrugged and Linda verified the spelling that he remembered and looked it up on her phone. "Match or pair," she said thoughtfully. Then she looked up at Turner. "Mate," she guessed.

"True love's kiss broke the spell," Turner said as they got to the truck, but he made no move to open the door for her. "Sorry you won't get a chance to test it."

"I'm not," she said warmly. "I know and you know, and by now, all of Green Valley knows. I'm utterly yours."

Turner made his very manly noise of joy again and bent to kiss her warmly. "I'm yours," he promised.

"Are you coming to Cancun with me, or should I start looking for a contractor right now?" Linda asked.

"You're not going to find a contractor on Christmas Eve," Turner scoffed. "Not in Green Valley."

"You underestimate my powers of persuasion," Linda said mildly. "Like right now, I'm planning to persuade you to take even just a week off and come to Cancun with me. School doesn't start again until January, Dean can rejoin the force temporarily, and I have a really *tiny* bikini that I could not possibly wear here."

She slid herself up his long hard body to claim a kiss and knew that she'd won by his sigh of defeat.

"I was going to talk to you about Lee and Patricia's house,"

Turner said when she released his lips. "It's out of a vice principal's budget, but it's much more your style than my burnt-up house. It's got a great kitchen. No melted blenders or anything."

"Lee and Patricia?" Linda remembered them from the festival. "Oh, Patricia was in charge of the pageant. Their daughter was the very dramatic Mary who couldn't keep ahold of Baby Squash Jesus."

"They're moving to a town in New York state where Clara can be closer to a good dance school. A little shifter-friendly town called Virtue with a bunch of remodeling work for Lee."

"Let me know who their realtor is," Linda said. "We can go out and look at it together. If you think we're at the point of buying a house together. Because I honestly do."

"I'm going to need some proof," Turner said.

"Proof of income?" Linda wanted to know. "Proof that I'm serious?"

"Will you marry me?"

Linda froze in his arms and drew back. "Marry you?" she managed.

"We could call Cancun an early honeymoon," he suggested, making it sound completely practical. "Stop at Vegas on the way and make it official, even."

Linda laughed, not because it was funny, but because she couldn't keep the joy inside of her from bubbling out.

Turner grinned in triumph. "I have wanted to make you laugh since I met you," he said, leaning to kiss her.

"I didn't say yes," she teased him.

"You laughed," Turner said, sounding perfectly content. "*Really* laughed. That's good enough for me."

EPILOGUE

FIFTEEN YEARS LATER

"Stop the car here," Patricia said and Clara put on her blinker and moved over onto the shoulder of the road. They got out of the car and looked down over the little town in the valley. There was no traffic to worry about, though Clara could hear the distant sound of a far-away highway.

She'd left Green Valley fifteen years ago, when she was eight, and she didn't remember the view very well, but she thought that it hadn't changed much. Downtown was still tiny, surrounded by tidy little neighborhoods fenced in by patchwork farms. There were a few church steeples, and Clara remembered where Green Valley High was, with its football field. Did it have a new running track beside it? The park where she'd played with Trevor and Aaron still had a shining silver slide that was visible from here, and the library would be the building next to it.

Clara looked up to find Patricia smiling sadly down on it and she put an arm around her. She was as tall as her stepmother now, and it felt weird to be in a position of comfort. "Are you sorry we didn't come back to visit sooner?"

"I just wish it was for happier circumstances," Patricia said, slipping an arm around Clara's waist. "It shouldn't take a funeral to come home."

"It doesn't feel like home anymore," Clara said thoughtfully, but she wasn't entirely convinced, especially as they got back in the car and drove down into the town itself.

It was like stepping back into time, and driving down the quiet little streets brought back a rush of memories. There was Dean's house, where she and Trevor and Aaron played in a pile of leaves like a fortress, the day that their dog Bingo had bit her. There was the downtown park, with the same monstrous metal slide. The swings looked new.

They passed the preschool where Patricia had taught, and then the elementary school that Clara remembered more keenly. She could almost smell the whiteboard markers and feel the warm papers that were passed out in class right off the copy machine. In third grade, the teacher would put four students at a cluster of tables, and she and Trevor and Aaron always jostled to sit together. Being separated in class was a dire punishment.

They spent recesses together, inventing games of imagination and adventure over the jungle gym and into the forest that pressed up against the playground. Games that involved being lions and bears. In some ways, the worlds they'd invented were as fresh in her memory as the town itself.

It was her eighth birthday when Trevor finally told her about being a lion shifter, and two birthdays later after they had moved to Virtue when she realized that her father was a bear shifter.

"Will I be a bear?" she had asked wistfully. "Was mother a shifter?"

Patricia wasn't, but her birth mother had died when she was a baby. She'd been a dancer, a bright, beautiful star who stole everyone's hearts, and everyone said that Clara was *just* like her.

"If she had been, she'd have been a swan shifter," Papa laughed.

Clara wouldn't have minded being a swan shifter. She wouldn't have minded being a bear shifter like Papa.

She desperately wanted to be any kind of shifter.

As a dedicated dancer, she was already stronger and more graceful than most people, but she waited breathlessly through puberty and only grew breasts, which were generally useless, not fur or claws like she really wanted.

"Tell me again about meeting Miss Mama," she begged when she was a child.

"Every shifter has a mate," Papa told her. "There is one perfect person for us, that will make us happier than we've ever imagined. And our animal knows them when we meet. When I met Miss Patricia, I recognized her, like a bolt of lightning. I knew she would be my happiness."

"Why did you marry my mother, then?"

It was a tricky question, and one that only got trickier as Clara got older.

"I loved her," Papa said firmly. "And I will never, ever regret her because of *you*, because it all happened exactly as it had to for me to meet Patricia."

"Will I have a mate?" Clara wanted to know. "Even if I'm not a shifter?"

"The world isn't fickle enough to deny you that happiness," Papa told her. "Have faith that there is purpose we can't see. I know you will find the person that will make you complete."

Clara looked around now as she pulled into the parking lot in front of Green Valley High, wondering if her happiness waited for her here...and if she'd recognize it if she found it, without an animal to show her what—who—it was.

"It looks just the same as when I graduated!" Patricia exclaimed as they got out of the car. "I swear, they must have special ordered the paint in that shade."

Clara found a parking space between a shiny BMW and a truck so beat up that she was surprised it still drove—or that it was street legal if it did. The window was down and the door latch was missing on the outside.

Another car pulled in as they were getting out, and another after that.

Clara and Patricia walked to the door holding hands, both of them looking around for familiar faces.

The gym looked more like it was set up for a wedding than a funeral. The people gathered were wearing dark clothing, but there were bright, cheerful flowers everywhere. A placard inside the double doors affirmed that they were at the right place: Welcome to the memorial for Margaret "Gran" Sheldon.

Rows of folding chairs faced a little stage. Although the bleachers were pulled out, it was not crowded enough for the audience to fill them.

It wasn't long before someone recognized Patricia, and she was soon enfolded in welcoming hugs. Everyone was very kind and warm and Clara found herself smiling and nodding at a lot of faces that blurred together in a haze of barely familiar as everyone exclaimed about how much she'd grown up and how surely it hadn't been that long since she was just *this* tall and did she still wear sparkly shoes and ruffled skirts (she did not!)?

"I hear you are a famous dancer now!" Andrea said warmly.

Clara blushed and shrugged. She was second in a company, and her tutors talked about following in her mother's dance shoes to the top, but she didn't want to admit that, as much as she loved dancing, she wasn't sure she had gone the right direction with her life.

She wanted to ask Andrea if Aaron was there, but her courage failed her and she was glad when a large figure took the stage and cleared his throat, preventing further discussion. She recognized him as the fire chief, Turner, from the memorable demonstrations he'd given at their school about fire safety. Was he still the fire chief?

She and Patricia found seats together in the back and Clara caught herself peering through the milling people as they sat. Were Trevor and Aaron here? What would it be like to see them again after so long? Maybe they had nothing in common anymore. She wasn't the same girl she'd been at age eight. Probably they had changed, too.

"Gran was greatly loved here in Green Valley, and she will be dearly missed," Turner said gravely. Clara remembered how jealous she'd been when she realized that Gran was her own cat, and how kind and yet terrifying the old woman was, the few times that she'd been human around Clara.

Patricia's hand in hers squeezed.

"Gran had very specific requests for her final rites. She didn't want us to mourn her passage, but to celebrate her life and honor her wishes for Green Valley to be a place of joy and sanctuary." He cleared his throat and smiled. "She directly asked that we not tell a lot of boring moral stories about her life that make her sound better than she was, but that you all mingle and remember her fondly. She did not want anyone to waste a day sobbing and wearing black outside in August."

Turner gestured towards tables set up to one side of the gym. "We have food today, a breakfast bar with her special recipe of biscuits and gravy, and the local band, The Tantalists."

The Tantalists proved to be a quartet of gray-haired men playing a banjo, an accordion, a flute, and a tuba who launched into music so cheerful that no one could help but smile, even the ones who were crying. Everyone stood and lined up for the breakfast bar, and if there were a fair number of tears, there were definitely no boring moral stories.

They did praise Gran, talking about how she'd been a single mom at a time when being a single mom was Not a Thing, starting her own business and running her small family with a gloved iron fist. There were many stories about her riding to the rescue and taking in strays. Even Marta said kind things and wiped her eyes.

Clara stuck to Patricia's side, smiling and nodding every time someone exclaimed over how *tall* she was, and how grown up. They each took a plate of biscuits piled high with creamy gravy dense with sausage and went to find a place to sit and eat it, balancing a paper cup of orange juice in their other hand.

The sea of folding chairs flowed into little conversational swirls and Clara drank her orange juice first so she didn't have to find a place to perch her cup.

A few classmates she didn't remember more than vaguely said hello, then almost everyone was sitting and Clara could eat her food, listening to Patricia catch up on fifteen years of local gossip with

Andrea and Jamie. There were kids running around everywhere, shrieking and laughing, absolutely oblivious to any sense of decorum or somber dignity.

Of course, it was hard to be serious with the band belting out a ridiculous up-tempo version of "What Goes Up."

"Three of those are mine," Jamie pointed out. "John didn't want to come, and at thirteen, I wasn't going to make him." She lowered her voice. "They're all shifters, even the twins at age four. It's been a nightmare managing childcare."

"And they're only four!" Patricia exclaimed in a whisper. "That's so young!"

"It's happening more and more," Andrea said just as quietly. "And at the other end of the spectrum, too—adults who don't even know about shifting have spontaneously been able to. It's getting hard to keep it a secret."

"Something in the water?"

"Maybe literally."

"Clara?"

Clara took too big a bite and nearly choked on it.

She had imagined meeting Trevor and Aaron again so many times that it didn't feel real when she finally did. She scrambled to her feet, her plate in her hand and her mouth full of biscuit, and the three of them stared at each other in wonder.

The story continues in Loan Wolf!

A THANK YOU FROM ELVA

Thank you for reading my books! I had so much fun writing all of the misadventures (or mooseadventures!) in Green Valley.

I always love to know what you thought—you can leave a review at Amazon or Goodreads or Bookbub, or email me at elvaherself@elvabirch.com.

If you'd like to be emailed when I release my next book, visit my webpage to join my mailing list! I also have a full reading list there. Find me on Facebook and join my Reader's Retreat, where I show off new covers first, and you can get sneak previews and ask questions.

Readers like you are why I can write, and I am so grateful for your support.

~Elva (aka Zoe Chant)

A Day Care for Shifters: A feel-good series about adorable shifter kids and their struggling single parents in a town full of mystery and surprise. Start the series with Wolf's Instinct, when Addison comes to Nickel City to take a job at a very special day care and finds a family to belong to. A gentle ice-cream-straight-from-the-container escape. Sweet and sizzling!

The Royal Dragons of Alaska: A fascinating alternate world where Alaska is ruled by secret dragon shifters. Adventure, romance, and humor! Reluctant royalty, relentless enemies…dogs, camping, and magic! Start with The Dragon Prince of Alaska.

~

Suddenly Shifters: A hilarious series of novellas, serials, and shorts set in the small town of Anders Canyon, where something (in the water?) is making ordinary citizens turn into shifters. Start with Something in the Water!

~

Lawn Ornament Shifters: The series that was only supposed to be a joke, this is a collection of short, ridiculous romances featuring unusual shifters, myths, and magic. Cross-your-legs funny and full of heart! Start with The Flamingo's Fated Mate!

~

Birch Hearts: An enchanting collection of short stories and novellas. Unconstrained by theme or setting, each short read has romance, magic, and heart, with a satisfying conclusion. And always, the impossible and irresistible. Start with a sampler plate in Prompted 2 for fourteen pieces of sweet-to-sizzling flash fiction, or dive in with the novella, Better Half - which you can get free for joining my mailing list at elvabirch.com!

WRITING AS ZOE CHANT

Shifting Sands Resort: A complete ten-book series - plus two collections of shorts. This is a thrilling shifter romance set at a tropical island resort. Each book stands alone but connects into a great mystery with a thrilling conclusion. Start with Tropical Tiger Spy or dive in to the Omnibus edition, with all of the novels, short stories, and novellas in my preferred reading order! This series crosses over with *Fire and Rescue Shifters* and *Shifter Kingdom!*

~

Fae Shifter Knights: A complete four-book fantasy portal romp, with cute pets and swoon-worthy knights stuck in a world of wonders like refrigerators and ham sandwiches. Start with Dragon of Glass!

~

Green Valley Shifters: A sweet, small town series with single dads, secret shifters, sweet kids, and spinsters. Low-peril and steamy!

Standalone books where you can revisit your favorite characters - this series is also complete with six books! Start with Dancing Bearfoot! This series crosses over with **Virtue Shifters**, which starts with Timber Wolf.

BEHIND THE SCENES

What is Patreon?

Patreon is a site where readers and fans can support creators with monthly subscriptions.

At my Patreon, I have tiers with early rough drafts of my books, flash fiction, coloring pages, signed and sketched paperbacks, exclusive swag, original artwork, photographs…and so much more! Every month is a little different, and there is a price for every budget. Patreon allows me to do projects that aren't very commercial and makes my income stream a little less unpredictable. It also gives me a place to connect with my fans!

Come find out what's going on behind the scenes and keep me creating at Patreon! patreon.com/ellenmillion

SNEAK PREVIEW OF WOLF'S INSTINCT

Don't swear in front of the kids, don't swear in front of the kids, don't swear... Roderick wrenched his shoulder nearly out of the socket trying to reach through the tiny hole under the sink to get to the fitting. Inside his head was a far less censored litany.

"Uck!"

Had he said it out loud after all?

"Uck! Uck!"

Roderick craned his head around and saw a little girl with a blond halo of fuzzy hair standing in the door. She looked about the age of his own daughter, Gabby, but was standing confidently on both feet, a spit-soggy stuffed animal in one hand.

A spry middle-aged woman with salt-and-pepper and electric-blue pigtails swooped in behind her and lifted the child out of the way of the spreading puddle of dirty water leaking from beneath the sink.

"How did you get past the table?" Cherry demanded cheerfully of the child. Her wild-colored hair was at odds with her conservative country plaid shirt and plain jeans. Her feet were in socks, and she was careful to stay clear of the mess.

"Uck!" the toddler replied merrily.

Roderick looked sheepishly at Cherry.

"Yuck," Cherry agreed. "Yuck is right!"

Oh, yuck. Yuck was okay, even if it wasn't at all what Roderick had been thinking.

"What's the news?" Cherry asked, lowering her voice.

"Not good," Roderick said, shaking his head. He'd finally gotten his fingers around the fitting and could unscrew it and draw it out of the tiny access panel in the wet wall. "Whoever plumbed this building ought to be…" he glanced at the little girl chortling in Cherry's arm. "Yuck," he said. "Let's just go with yuck."

He wriggled out from under the sink and inspected the fitting. "I really should take a look at the rest of them, too. If they put these everywhere, you could have a big problem on your hands."

Cherry peered at the fitting. "What's wrong with it?"

"Besides the fact that this is a totally inappropriate fitting for this spot, it's the wrong material. Not to code for potable water."

"Is it toxic?" Cherry asked in horror, exchanging a look with the child in her arms.

"Uck!" the little girl added, trying to squirm free and play in the water on the floor.

"It's relatively harmless," Roderick promised. "But it should all be replaced if this isn't the only one. This stuff tends to wear out faster, especially if it goes through a lot of temperature changes. It also looks like maybe the system was frozen with water in it." He pointed out a crack in the fitting. "There may be other cracks."

"The place was empty last winter," Cherry said, looking around in despair. "Maybe it wasn't winterized first?"

"I hope you're not having second thoughts about expanding your day care business," Roderick said.

"No," Cherry said firmly, and she gave him a genuine smile. "I'm excited about it. I just dread explaining to Veronica that she's going to have to spend money on the place."

"It's a great place," Roderick agreed.

Cherry's scowl spread effortlessly to an excited grin. "I love it already," she said frankly.

Cherry had been babysitting for Roderick and other shifters in

Nickel City for decades, and he'd watched the demand for her services outgrow her house and her ability to watch them all on her own. She'd decided to make the leap to opening a day care downtown and hire a helper or two.

Roderick had been the one to find the place, despite his reservations about the landlord, and was sorry that her opening day had been met with a bathroom flood; he wished that he had better news for her.

The girl in her arms fussed and then seamlessly shifted into a fuzzy little owl chick, beating downy wings in protest of her captivity as she wiggled from her clothes.

"Whoops," Cherry said, easily tossing her in place as she gathered up the clothing. "Clever little Amy, but you still can't play in this mess, even as an owl! I gotta go check on the other kids. My new hire should be here in just a few minutes."

Roderick was surprised by a jangle at the fringes of his wolf's senses. Why would his shifter instinct be excited by *that* news? Sometimes he felt like instinct was a game of hot-and-cold with a kid who had forgotten where they'd hid something, with no hint of logic or direction. He'd learned to treat it with a degree of reserve—since a simple *that way* could lead him right off the edge of a cliff—but never to ignore it.

"Who did you get?" he asked, grabbing the mop to clean up the mess.

"Wendy—you know Wendy from the DMV? Her cousin from Buffalo was looking for work. I haven't even met her yet," Cherry confessed, "but her resume was impressive. She has a certificate in early education, and she worked as a nanny for a shifter family who gave her a glowing recommendation. Wendy said she'd suit me and, well, it's not like I have a lot of choices."

Hiring reliable help for a day care was hard enough. Hiring help for a day care for shifters? That could get complicated. Not only did they have to be part of a secret community, but they still had to meet all the usual human-world qualifications and pass background checks. Maybe his instinct was just confirming that Cherry had picked a good candidate. After all, whoever she was, his daughter would be spending time in her care, so she definitely mattered to his little family of two.

"I'm going to get my ladder and check out the other fittings in the ceiling," Roderick told Cherry. "I'll let you know what I find."

Why would his instinct insist that he was about to find happiness?

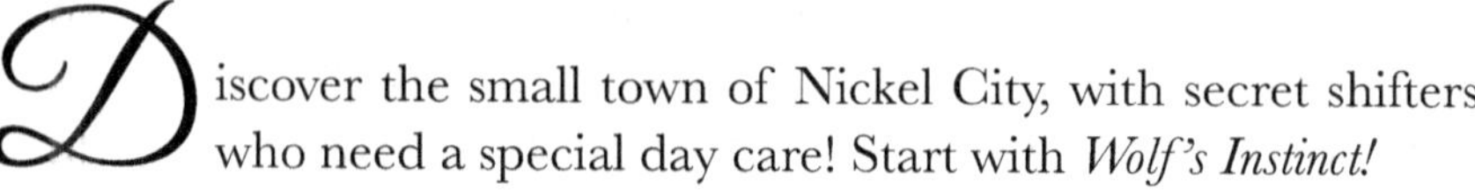

*D*iscover the small town of Nickel City, with secret shifters who need a special day care! Start with *Wolf's Instinct!*